SONG OF MADELEINE

SONG OF MADELEINE

A Crusader's Chronicle

With Eleanor of Aquitaine on the Second Crusade

To EZRA & Beulah
Cherished Healers on the Journey

Mary Bolton

Mary Bolton
9-10-02

Writer's Showcase
San Jose New York Lincoln Shanghai

Song of Madeleine
A Crusader's Chronicle

Writer's Showcase
an imprint of iUniverse, Inc.

For information address:
iUniverse, Inc.
5220 S. 16th St., Suite 200
Lincoln, NE 68512
www.iuniverse.com

As a work of historical fiction, some of the events in this book are based on fact; however the major work of the book is the invention of the author and bears no resemblance to actual persons, living or dead.

ISBN: 0-595-21648-X

Printed in the United States of America

I dedicate this book to my daughters, intrepid travelers all: Catherine, Bridget, Mollie, and Madalain.

Contents

Chapter 1   Bethany (Anno Domini 1149) 1

Chapter 2   Vezelay 7

Chapter 3   Ile de Paris......................................15

Chapter 4   A Visit From Bernard............................21

Chapter 5   Ile de Paris......................................25

Chapter 6   Via Crucis 33

Chapter 7   On Route to Metz................................41

Chapter 8   At the Moselle River.............................51

Chapter 9   On the Danube...................................61

Chapter 10   Nearing Hungary 69

Chapter 11   Sofia...79

Chapter 12   Sofia...91

Chapter 13   Constantinople..................................97

Chapter 14   Constantinople.................................105

Chapter 15   Constantinople.................................111

Chapter 16   Constantinople.................................117

Chapter 17   Lake Ascania, Asia Minor 125

Chapter 18   Lake Ascania 135

Chapter 19   Ephesus 145

Chapter 20   The Meander River 155

Chapter 21   Cadmos Pass....................................163

Chapter 22   Through Cadmos Pass..........................171

Chapter 23   Cadmos Plain 179

Chapter 24   Trial on Cadmos Plain. 187

Chapter 25   Wandering 197

Chapter 26   Sattalia. 209

Chapter 27   Antioch 219

Chapter 28   Antioch 233

Chapter 29   Antioch 245

Chapter 30   Antioch 255

Chapter 31   On Route to Hammim 265

Chapter 32   Hammim. 277

Chapter 33   Heading for Acre 287

Chapter 34   Acre 295

Chapter 35   Jerusalem. 307

Chapter 36   Bethany Abbey 315

Chapter 37   Bethany 323

Chapter 38   Bethany 333

Epilogue 341

Acknowledgements

I want to acknowledge my first, patient editor, Nora Lehman; the Every Other Thursday Writing Group of Sacramento; my women's group; the numerous other friends who have read this manuscript and given me thoughtful feedback; and especially Marj Stuart for pulling this fish out of the fire.

CHAPTER 1

Bethany (Anno Domini 1149)

Saint Mary Magdalene's feast day it is, and at the splendid Abbey, named in honor of our Magdalene and Martha, her sister, celebration spills from the walls. But before I join the others, I must complete the telling of my adventures and how I arrived back here in Bethany. My tall desk in the scriptorium stands beneath the high narrow window overlooking a grove of olive trees, leaves silvertipped in the gentle breeze. They still grace the eastern slope of the Mount of Olives. Jerusalem's saffroned walls glow in the distance. With this sight as inspiration, I hasten to complete my chronicle.

The task falls to me because of the negligence of the holy monks, among them the king's deputy, Templar Galeran. The smoothskinned eunuch is gifted with sums and figures. His brooding eyes are quick to dart about in search of some feminine fault. He pronounced (sourly, you may be sure) that it was a waste of time and parchment, indeed, an exercise in vanity, to name the women who joined Eleanor of Aquitaine on the Second Crusade.

But who will know of us, of our trials and our courage? Over the past two years, I have scribbled entries here and there; on the backs of gourds, on belts, on scarves, whatever was at hand. Sometimes, I wrote in blood. I put these notes together now, to detail, perhaps not in the purest rhetoric employed by the fathers, but more embellished (Augustine to the contrary), the events of our journey, led by my daring cousin, Eleanor, Queen of France.

I take my quill in hand, dip it into smuggled ink from India to write upon contraband parchment from Cairo. As you will discover, I have learned to speak in boldness.

Our venture began that March Sunday when we gathered in Vezelay to hear the famous Bernard of Clairvaux read Pope Eugenius' "Call to the Crusade." First, we attended Easter Mass at the magnificent Cathedral of the Magdalene. Vernal sunlight poured color through the brilliant new windows. The crowded septum was noisy as people rustled and prayed. I strained to hear the words of a young cleric. He was singing the part of the angel who asked the women at Our Lord's tomb that first Easter Morning, "Quem Quaeritis?" (Whom do you seek?)

The words, sounding soft as a coo in a dovecot, were near lost among the shuffling movements of the packed congregation, yet they haunted me. Incense—surely the fragrance was spikinard—curled heavenward in the shafts of light. It mesmerized me. Suddenly, Queen Eleanor, eyes glittering with excitement, jarred me from the strange trance-like spell.

"Cousin, are you dazed? You look faint. And no wonder; come now, it's time to break our fast." The queen, a golden circlet on her head, dark honey-colored hair plaited to one side, fastened the emerald clasp on her jade-green cape, a wondrous match to her eyes.

I fought my trembling knees. That fragrance, at once so familiar, yet strange.

"Hurry along, dear Madeleine, the multitudes are gathering rapidly. The old rabbit, Abbot Bernard, has arrived and the king is anxious for him to issue the call of the faithful. Cardinal Lisieux has requested us to join him for breakfast. Louis won't refuse, so let's be off. Besides," Eleanor flashed her most mischievous smile, "we have our own plans to complete."

I had been in Queen Eleanor's court for almost a year and had come to love that impish smile. My cousin has many qualities I admire, especially her generosity. In her kindness, she sent for me after my husband had been slain in a border skirmish. Our lands were sacked and burned by mercenaries. In the smoky aftermath, two brigands, one of them a knight (I glimpsed a corner of his shield), had brutally murdered my field hands. My old serving woman, Thecla, and I had plunged beneath a thicket. We remained there until dusk and so escaped to an abandoned hunting shed in the Gascony woods. It was there that Eleanor finally traced me and placed me under her protection. But I digress, and must continue to chronicle our journey.

Later that same Easter afternoon, I climbed the sloping Burgundian hillsides just beyond the cathedral. Swirls of people jostled me as I tried to reach the section that had been cordoned off for the royal court. The countryside resembled a tapestry. Women's bright capes the color of emeralds and rubies weaved together with the coarse umber woolens worn by peasants. Cardinal red highlighted the first rows. Black-robed Benedictine monks set out the borders here and there.

Many prayed aloud. Other folk, singing or weeping, hurried toward the festooned platform set up high in the wide, grassy meadow. Thousands streaming from all over the Frank provinces elbowed their way past me to catch a glimpse of King Louis and Queen Eleanor and to hear the famed Bernard of Clairvaux. His words are esteemed as salve for the soul, but not necessarily Eleanor's, as you will learn.

Finally, I reached my place. Beyond the platform to the east, the Cathedral of the Magdalene pushed its rosy, rounded tower high above the soft, curved land. The words of the morning ritual hummed softly in my mind. "Whom do you seek?" There was little time to puzzle for a rush of activity erupted near the platform, and I craned my neck to see.

A group of husky students hoisted a gaunt Cistercian monk onto the crude dais. Templars and well-frocked priests bunched together with the Cistercian novitiates stationed directly in front. They set off cheers and the rest of the crowd followed. The noise was thunderous.

"So there is Bernard." Eleanor had spoken of him often, rarely in the terms of adulation that burst forth from the hordes around me.

The holy man brought his arms out from under deep folds of his cloak. He raised them, thin and white as the robes he wore, high over his head to signal silence. His eyes, amber and quick as a kite's, gleamed with passion. Bernard of Clairvaux spoke in a strong voice that carried above the last shuffling latecomers.

"Let there be silence, my dear children."

Stillness settled on the gullies and meadows. I leaned forward so not to miss a phrase.

"His Holiness Pope Eugenius has instructed that I bring his urgent message to your king and to you, his loyal subjects. The Holy City of Jerusalem lies in great danger from the Infidels. It is for you, the Faithful of this land, to answer the pope's plea for help!"

His eyes rolled heavenward. "To Jerusalem! Hearken now, for I set my lips to the apostolic trumpet in a call to pilgrimage and a call to arms!"

Another outburst rang from the packed masses. Bernard's voice blared from his cadaverous chest belying his apparent frailty. So stirred was I, I leapt to my feet.

"A Plenary Indulgence awaits you!" His message resounded from the frothy silver mustache sparkling at his lips. Zeal laced his words. "Take the cross, and save your souls from the damning fires of hell for all eternity! On to the Holy Land!" He shuddered with passion, his voice a wail.

Bernard paused to gather strength, his small chest heaving, "Come forward on this day to take the cross. Led by your holy monarch, pledge yourselves to rid the Infidel and to seek God in the Eternal City."

Promises, including mine, reverberated down every hillside in response to the firebrand on the dais. From my vantage point, I noticed devotion flush King Louis' cheeks and brighten his eyes as he answered Bernard's call. Climbing the steps to the platform, he prostrated his slight frame before the holy man. As a boy, Louis had been educated for the priesthood and was known for his piety. Now his shoulders shook visibly. He lifted his pale blue eyes upward as though transfixed, then rose slowly from his prone position and knelt to receive the first cross. The multitudes cheered, but the din seemed lost on Louis. His body again lay limp, overcome with devotion. Minutes passed before he rose and took his place on the reviewing stand.

Queen Eleanor followed her husband Louis to the dais. She appeared to weep as she received the small cross from the old abbot's hands. Her face, framed by a halo of golden hair, held a serene beauty, a pious expression rarely observed. The impression was short lived. Soon after receiving her cross, Eleanor turned toward me and waved irreverently. She then joined Louis where she stood proudly at attention.

On a signal from the royal guard, half a hundred trumpets blared and echoed off the hillsides sending a thrill through me, making my skin prickle. The sight that followed brought tears to my eyes. Led by pennants of every color raised high, with heraldic banners flowing, hundreds of nobles and knights in full battle dress marched before our rulers, paying tribute to them and the crusade they were to lead.

Wave after wave of the queen's own men passed first; nobles from all the reaches of Aquitaine marched forward to receive the cross, pledging their wealth and loyal arms to the pope's cause. To tabor and drum, the armor-clad lords of Aquitaine, Poitou, and Gascony marched by. Their light chain mail clanked a rhythmic chorus in measure to their footsteps.

Close by the queen's countless vassals, the king's barons and nobles marched by, followed by the Knights Templar, red crosses blazoned on their shields. The Order of St. John, the Hospitallers, closed ranks behind.

When the parade had cleared, I rushed with the others to receive my miniature cross. Pledged to march with King Louis on this crusade, I had become part of the Holy Expedition. My heart filled with pride and devotion. Trying to avoid the crowd, I edged closer to the high stage. What I overhead disturbed me. Was it an harbinger of things to come? I can tell you now, it was.

The irascible Cardinal Lisieux's voice carried over the commotion. "That Lady Madeleine bears a false title. A widowed cousin of the queen's, she comes from obscurity." He elbowed Abbot Suger, "Look how the queen has convinced these royal women to join her. There goes Countess Sybelle and the young Florine of Toulouse. Women on a crusade, bah! I hope the pope forbids it. Pray to Jerome that we hear no more of them. May God be merciful."

Turning his head this way and that, dewlap of a chin rubbing against his ermine collar, the cardinal carped his disapproval, "It seems the queen is already bored. By Saint Martin's eyes! Once her nobles passed by and the rabble appeared, she departed the ceremonies."

It was true. Eleanor had left the dais and I knew why.

CHAPTER 2

Vezelay

The path to my pavilion felt spongy beneath my feet. A lavendered overcast had frosted the wide, newly thawed meadow. I cut a wide arc past the merchants, artisans, troubadours, shopkeepers, shepherds and peasants milling about. Their breath, rising like prayers, steamed upward in spirals. Darkness fell softly on that Easter Sunday and the last aspirations floated heavenward to the silence of the stars.

Beyond the throngs in the high meadows, servants stirred aromatic pots and tended roasts that spat juices into crackling flames. A pair of cook boys, rowdy from too much wine, tussled over a piece of mutton that had fallen into the ashes. Tempting fragrances made my nose twitch, and I realized how hungry I was.

No time for that now, for I must meet the queen. Once inside my tent I foraged for a hunk of cheese, broke off a bit, and stuffed it into my mouth. Then I hastened to a large chest from which I removed the special attire that had been under close guard. Extinguishing all but one faint candle, I changed quickly in the semi-darkness, donning my boots last. I grasped at their fresh stitched sides, luxuriating in their sharp, new smell, and pulled on soft leather boots of deepest red. A perfect fit and the sturdy soles felt strong under my feet.

My voice sounded hoarse calling to Eleanor's squire, waiting in the field outside the tent. "Psst! Germer, it's time. Bring my horse." I had chosen the spirited gelding with the soft pink nuzzle.

Germer handed me the bridle. My smile answered his sly grin. We both knew it wasn't my horse at all. The night air quickened my spirits, and I spurred the glorious mount onward, skirting the outer edges of the encampment. I picked my way along the back trail toward the cathedral leaving the smell of smoke and rosemary behind me.

"Madeleine, over here, quickly." Eleanor's voice cut through the cold.

Nudging the creamy palfrey in the direction of the call, I rounded a cluster of high brush. Everyone was there as planned.

"Madeleine, you took so long. We were afraid you weren't coming." It was Sybelle speaking; she has become a worrywart ever since her marriage to Count Phillip of Flanders. She seemed as carefree as the rest of us when we were all together as girls at Eleanor's summer palace. Sybelle is from Anjou, and the noble family of Anjou does not worry about anything. But Sybelle's husband, the stern Flemish Count Phillip, does. A steely man twenty years her senior, he insists that she take her wifely duties very seriously, expecting her to run his vast holdings as smoothly as if he were there, which he isn't very often. If Louis' passion is praying, then Phillip's passion is warring, and he spends most of his time fighting to expand his territory. He has been to the Holy Land most often, perhaps three times.

Sybelle's brows were still tightened as I greeted both her and Lady Fluorine of Toulouse, the youngest of us. They, too, were mounted on great white geldings usurped, as was my own, from the king's royal stables by his queen.

Eleanor had insisted that we all dress alike. The styled garments, including the gilded buskins, fashioned with secrecy in the queen's chambers, fitted close to thigh and hip. Over them, we wore white tunics, reaching just above the knees. Bold red crosses emblazoned the fronts. Eleanor had taken great pains to bring gleaming leather from Cordova, and our calf-length cherry-red boots completed the uniform.

"Here, take this plumed hat," urged Sybelle. "Did you remember your banner?" More worry.

"Yes!" I held it high. "I had it furled tightly so no one would see me leaving the pavilion with it."

My horse was restive, and I stroked his muscled neck here, gave a gentle tugging of the reins there, before Eleanor turned to us, her face radiant, her eyes, almost indigo in the dusk.

"Make fast your pennants. We don't want to stumble on them. Stay on the trail." Firm of voice, she continued the orders. "I shall ride out in the lead, and then you, Fluorine, follow close by. Next, you, Madeleine, and Sybelle, you last. Remember, as we practiced, ride fast around the encampment once, back up the hill among the stragglers, then down once again through the nobles' pavilions. Then take the turn to the royal tent where Germer will groom and stable the horses for the night."

Eleanor gripped the sides of her gelding with her knees and bolted toward the encampment below, calling out, "Now, onward, sisters of the cross! Via Cruces!"

With reins in one hand, I hoisted my banner high. As one, we spurred our horses down the hill close behind the queen. Our shouts filled the night.

"On to Jerusalem!"

"Via Cruces!"

Red-heeled boots dug into horses' flanks as we cantered toward the massive crowds that pocked the hillsides. Our calls rang above the solemn conversations and quiet prayers. Riding a twisted trail through the encampment, we sped past merchants and startled monks. The king's nobles appeared to be plotting strategy and looked askance at our jovial parade.

The rancorous Cardinal Lisieux was completing his evening toilet when our shouts urged him, in his fragranced state, to "Take the Cross!" and "Save Jerusalem!" His quietude thus intruded upon, his excellency blanched while his chubby fingers clutched at the fur-trimmed robe pulling it tight around him as if to shield himself from some sudden defilement.

"What is this outrage? The work of the devil? Debasing such a noble purpose! Brother Norman," he shouted, "take a message to the king!" He peered into the blackness after us. I suppose he hoped to identify just who was atop the white whirl of horses galloping into the night. He spun around, eyes popping, to bellow at the startled brother, "Good God and Sweet Jesus' wounds," The words faded, "their leader is the queen herself!"

Next, as we had rehearsed, our horses pounded up the rise beyond the Aquitainian encampments, where my young brother, Charles, had removed his hauberk and stretched his slight frame before the fire, his feet resting on the chestnut log that fed the blaze. His was a pensive look as we clattered upon him. Was he reviewing the Hospitaller oath, so recently administered by Abbot Bernard?

"The faith, enforced by knights, shall be aided in great degree by those who care for the men wounded in the defense of their most Christian faith."

When our spirited cavalcade raced by, he recognized me at once for I shouted to him, "Via Cruces! On to Jerusalem, Charles, my brave brother!"

The evening wind whipped my face and exhilarated me before we slowed to approach the numerous pavilions of the Aquitainian lords. Rush lights guttered and thick candles sizzled atop the oak slabs that served as tables. Remnants of roast goat and head cheeses lay strewn by the trenchers.

Cantering close, we shouted our slogans. One man stood out as he pulled his burgundy cape around his broad shoulders. He turned to face us. The handsome noble caught my eye. He smiled broadly at the raucous distraction galloping his way.

"Ho, Rancon! How goes it, Sir Geoffrey?" Eleanor addressed him directly in their native Langue d'oc dialect. "Hail, my lords!" she greeted the others while she reined and wheeled her horse in a show of equestrian excellence. We women circled with her, then, following her lead, guided the glistening white palfreys back into the darkness.

I slowed enough to observe that the knight called Sir Geoffrey had raised his goblet to his fellow barons. The firelight accentuated his strong profile, and when he seemed to turn, deliberately looking my way, I felt a flurry of excitement. Wheeling the palfrey toward the others, I was surprised by the feelings stirred in me.

We cantered to a stop in front of the queen's airy pavilion. I dismounted, noting how near we were to the reddish stone monastery where King Louis had chosen to spend the night. I caught sight of him, standing by the small cell window, hands folded in prayer. The king was taking the urgent directive from the pope most seriously, and I think it had to do with Eleanor in some way. I had the feeling that Louis worried about her "worldliness." And why wouldn't he? His closest advisors, especially the pompous bishops, always had some remark about her behavior. They thought she was irreverent, too vain and bold; yes, I'd heard the word "bold" spoken many times behind their jeweled hands. It was because she exuded so much self-confidence, and why not? She was a beautiful and bright woman, a woman of education; she wrote as well as any scribe. And at the summer palace in Bordeaux, hadn't we all spent our mornings reading Latin, from Augustine to Virgil? Eleanor translated faster than any of us, and when her father died, she became the holder of more lands than the Capatian kings—and now she was queen. What else would it take for a woman to be confident, and somewhat vain?

Our exuberant arrival surprised Germer, asleep by the hissing fire. Though startled, he took to his work in a steady fashion, helping us dismount. He called to Thecla to ready the basins of hammered copper for baths.

"Rub down the horses well, Germer." They were lathered from their hard ride. When I joined the others in the pavilion, they were reviewing the success of our venture.

"I do believe that we have stirred up loyalty and faith tonight." Sybelle removed her cross-emblazoned tunic.

"Save that cross for the pilgrimage," Eleanor called from behind a screen. "We will be wearing these garments from time to time to keep up the spirits of those who would let them flag. Our brothers from Provence hailed us well, did they not?"

I agreed, and as I began laying out the tunics, grey Flemish wool, my thoughts flitted to Sir Geoffrey's hearty smile. That surprised me, but I gave it little thought, and busied myself finding the black girdles, richly embroidered with deep blue fleurs-de-lis which I placed beside each tunic.

"Yes, they cheered us loudly," Florine chimed. "But," she let out a high-pitched giggle, "did you see the cardinal peer after us into the night? His eyes looked like old grapes, so large and green." Florine's usually pale cheeks were splotched with color.

Laughing, we banished the horse-smell by splashing each other with water fragranced with sage and mint. Sybelle and Eleanor, the fairest of us, applied some of Thecla's camphor-braced ointments to their chapped legs where the buskins had rubbed.

"What about Louis, Eleanor? Do you think he heard us? Do you think he saw us from the monastery window?" Mine was more household concern than curiosity.

"Would that he had! Straddling that horse has given rise to my desire." Eleanor flashed a smile. "And I would ride Louis a while!"

"Eleanor!" Sybelle placed toweling over her mouth with a squeal of disapproval.

"It's all right, Sybelle. Lent is over now, and spring comes once again." I gave Eleanor an approving pat on the cheek.

"Yes," Eleanor nodded, a wistful look to her eyes, "Spring does come again. But with Louis and this crusade, we are in for an eternity of Lents. He has taken an undue interest in, of all things, my soul. Yesterday he whispered a prayer of thanksgiving aloud. Said he believed he would save our souls, especially mine, his beloved queen's. 'I will lead them, O Lord,' his words exactly, his eyes tearful, 'to the Holy City and everlasting redemption. That is Your Holy Will.' It's a burden, really, to have someone else hovering over the good of your soul besides my chaplain and that solicitous old Cistercian, Bernard."

Eleanor flushed with annoyance before signaling Hulga to fetch the wine flagon. "Louis sings of God, the barons sing of war, and we, we shall sing of them all…and love. Yes, we shall sing of love. Hurry now, we'll have sweetmeats and wine, the best from Bordeaux. When our jongleurs arrive, they will sing of love and spring and nightingales."

Toweled, freshened, and dressed in our soft, new woolens, we heralds-of-faith relaxed on the cushions and furs in front of the raised braziers. Florine, the chubbiest, sat with legs tucked under her, her knees rounded like small pillows under her tunic. Her dark hair had frizzled with the bathing.

Sybelle, taking up her small flute a bec, played melodious notes, worry banished by her artistry. My companions sang along with her, while I watched for the jongleurs. So mirthful was this gathering that I wondered if the approaching entertainers questioned whether they would be needed at all. After I greeted them, I remained outside under the star-sprinkled sky.

The turmoil of the day had faded, and on the hillside, the abbey stood watchful and silent, staunch guardian of souls. Its inhabitants may have been disturbed by the gay sounds of the flute's warble and women's voices floating through the slit window. And as the king gave way to his repose, had he been lulled by the strains of laughter and bits of rondelay that sounded like a nightingale's variations on the Te Deum?

CHAPTER 3

Ile de Paris

$\mathcal{R}$ emembering rondelays sung and promises made at Vezelay, we spent an unseasonably hot summer on a dusty tour of Eleanor's domains, enlisting men and money for the great expedition to the Holy Land. We were always welcomed by Eleanor's subjects, greeted with cooled wines, offered herbal baths and the best rooms the airy, southern castles had to offer.

"My liege men have been most generous," remarked Eleanor as we crossed the old bridge to return to the cooler, autumnal climes of Paris. The city had taken on a frantic pace. Messengers swarmed to the royal palace scattering copper leaves in their traces. From Germany, Bohemia, Sicily and from the Holy Land itself, they came, scurrying to the newly formed councils convened by King Louis to plot the course of the crusade.

However, the activities of Bernard of Clairvaux began to disturb Eleanor. "That driven Cistercian has traveled to numberless countries sounding his apostolic trumpet, Madeleine, coaxing all of the other powers to join the French in the grand campaign for Jerusalem's protection." Her mouth took on a sardonic twist. "Now, as a crowning star in his oratorical diadem, he has persuaded Emperor Conrad of Germany to join the cause. So we must endure the arrogant Teuton and his overbearing emissaries." Eleanor donned a magenta cape trimmed in vair and left for the council hall, calling over her shoulder as she left, "Heaven only knows when I'll return. These Germans are a ponderous lot."

My afternoon errands took me past the great hall, where I was near stampeded by a crush of Teutonic pride. Emperor Conrad's ambassadors swelled, four abreast, marching to Louis' council. I dodged into the stairwell to avoid being trampled underfoot. From my vantage point I surveyed the noble liegemen, cleansed from their traveling and adorned in colorful leather costumes.

Cloaked in the darkness of the stairwell, surrounded by the rhythms of many languages, the fevered pitch sweeping the palace touched me as well, yet I felt uneasy. I sensed an ill will. It seemed to me that Eleanor's requests for increasing baggage wagons and her relentless participations in the discussions of provisioning and logistics provoked differences between the king's vassals, the factious northern barons, and her own noblemen, the Aquitainians of the south. The more I tried to pinpoint the cause, the more confused and troubled I became, yet the sense of foreboding would not ease.

Cardinal Lisieux padded down the hallway hissing his opinions to a handful of men. I darted into the stairwell to avoid him. His words stung my ears as I remained concealed, pressed to the damp wall behind a tapestry.

"It is unwomanly—unqueenly—unnatural, to have such female intrusion into these matters," Lisieux harrumphed, nearly brushing me with his wide skirt. My heart pounded so wildly I had to strain to hear his next words.

"I said from the beginning that she and her wanton court women should remain at home. Each day she adds another baggage cart." Lisieux rolled his eyes. "With the wiles of Eve, she overly influences our unsuspecting king. First, His Majesty succumbed to her going, and now it is only a step to his giving special grants and privileges to her and her Aquitainian lords. They outnumber the king's followers, poor warriors that they are."

"Yes, your eminence," agreed a man whose voice made me freeze. Through a wedge of space, I caught a glimpse of the speaker. The slack jaws, the black, untidy hair; ah, God, there was no mistake. It was the same mastiff-jowled knight who had so viciously murdered my serfs! I clutched the tapestry for fear of falling down the stairs.

"And the queen's dandy men already have relatives holding rich provinces in the Holy Land, isn't that so?" he persisted, his tone sinister.

"True enough," Lisieux nodded, "at the northern frontier of the territory, the queen's uncle, the debauched Raymond of Poitiers, aggrandizes himself with power and wealth as Prince of Antioch. Her avaricious nobles champ at the bit to garner more than their share. It is good to have devoted knights such as yourself to fight for the holy cause, Sir Mortimer."

Sir Mortimer! My stomach churned at the sound of his wretched name.

The villain stifled a grin as he bowed low before continuing. "And the queen's deputy general, that Geoffrey of Rancon, strains to curry the king's favor, does he not?"

I winced to hear Rancon so maligned by this perfidious murderer. Was this wretch one of the cardinal's followers? The men passed beyond the stairwell, leaving me free to scamper up to Eleanor's apartment, where I tried to calm myself, to shake the feeling of ill-will that had engulfed me.

The long, narrow, room rather bare for royal quarters, had the desired effect, and I began to breathe more easily in the peaceful surroundings. Eleanor's bed frame was of a deep hazel wood, carved with intricate floral figures. Upon the thick mattress lay a coverlet of dense emerald wool. An Oriental tapestry covered the west wall. Deep blues and reds were background to complex designs woven in threads the color of goldenrod. The wall-piece, a gift from the Holy

Land, had arrived the summer before from Eleanor's uncle, Prince Raymond of Antioch.

Eleanor returned in an irritable mood, complaining of a headache. I impulsively spilled out the story of Mortimer. "The man who murdered my field hands appeared in the company of the cardinal. His name is Mortimer, I knew not from whence he comes."

"Ah, Mortimer de Mur." She rubbed at her temples. "That rogue has the misfortune of being a third son, willing to do anything for lands and title. If he, acting as a mercenary, were in the service of the rebel Lusignans at the time, then anything in his way was fair game."

"Should he go unpunished for murder?" My voice shook with anger.

"He acted as a hired warrior, a mercenary. There are many knights who have done the same for their pillaging lords. In Mortimer's case, it was pure cowardice, and cowards are treacherous, because they are unpredictable. He is dangerous and bears watching. But for you to reveal yourself as an eyewitness to his deeds might be far riskier, especially since it appears that he is in the cardinal's good graces. You're certain he didn't get a look at you on the day of your escape?"

"Oh, I prayed God that he didn't. Surely, I would have been murdered—or worse."

With my insides churning, I reported how Prince Raymond had been described by Lisieux. Eleanor snapped, "You see, dear cousin, that's what they're really jealous of. Raymond's prestige in Antioch." Gesturing toward the wall piece, she shrugged off my information with a toss of her head, curls flippant. "Let them carp. The churchmen have always thought I took too much a part in ruling with Louis. Let them have their vitriol, their endless wrangling. They don't own the way to the Holy Land. That's why there's need of an expedition—and my forces!"

Eleanor was nettled and I was reluctant to bring up the remarks about her being unwomanly and the rest of us referred to as wanton baggage. I began to repeat the conversation when she interrupted.

"Say no more! Lisieux is worse than Reynard the fox with all his posturings. Let him do what he will." Posing in front of the rich tapestry, hands on her hips, her eyes bright, jaw thrust upward, she pledged, "I am going on this journey, and I am going my way!"

Barely pausing for a breath, she veered to another subject. "Meanwhile, I will travel south to Poitiers one more time to collect the last revenues from some of my recalcitrant subjects."

She was making lists in her head, I could tell. Eleanor had a penchant for planning and her energies were quite high when she so engaged herself, pacing the floor in long strides.

"There are supplies that I need to see to. I'll nudge a few more hesitant vassals into the fold as well. If they, themselves, won't join this venture, by Saint Benedict's boots, they'll help finance mine."

One thing I had learned and learned well in my year as Mistress of the Royal Household: pursuing the cardinal's complaints about the baggage with Eleanor was a waste of time. When she became headstrong, curtly dismissing the subject, it was wise to drop it.

However, the subject was not dropped by the queen's critics. The churchmen and disgruntled barons did what they would and sent the most holy man in all Christendom to call on the queen. Abbot Bernard hastened through the keen winter air to request an audience.

Eleanor and I were seated at the writing table, working with inventory figures when her page announced, "Your Majesty, the Abbot Bernard is here and wishes to see you."

"Saint Benedict's beads!" Eleanor erupted, "Why would he come now? He must know I'm busy with these preparations." Eleanor shoved aside the list she'd been studying. "Well," she shrugged, "we'll soon know. Tell Abbot Bernard that I will receive him here in my chambers. Better yet, Madeleine, you so advise him."

When I respectfully advised Bernard, the monk recoiled. His stature was shorter than I had remembered. He had looked so grand high above us at Vezelay. Now as he stood before me, fretting to himself, his left hand twitched uncontrollably. I recalled that he had forbidden his own visiting sister to enter his monastery walls! I imagined he wanted no part of queen's chambers.

His body tensed as he blessed himself. Whatever the inner dialogue, he recovered quickly enough. "Pray tell the queen that I dare not intrude there. Perhaps," he hesitated, an expression of disdain curling the lines of his mouth, his dry lips struggling to form the words. "perhaps her Highness, yes, her Highness, will see me in the library where we have often had our times of instruction." I turned to go. "Times of petty argument would be more like it," he amended when he thought I was beyond earshot. With my back to him, I smiled. Eleanor, influenced by the brilliant Abelard, had probably deemed herself capable of using logic and syllogism to debate with Bernard over matters of faith.

Though ruffled by the old man's refusal to accommodate her, Eleanor took my arm. "Oh, come, let's humor him. Bernard's set in his ways, but I best not ignore him; he's such a favorite with Louis and those damn Burgundians. Do join me in this exercise; whatever it is, I suspect it won't be pleasant, so let's be done with it."

Falling in step together, we marched down the narrow stairs toward the library.

CHAPTER 4

A Visit From Bernard

"**M**ajesty, your Highness," Abbot Bernard greeted the queen.

He graced me with a grim nod. Dispensing with other formalities, the wizened monk launched into his mission. "It saddens us, your Highness"—here a dolorous shake of his head—"that we must speak once again to your Majesty. It is in regard to your meddling in the councils regarding the proposed holy journey to Jerusalem."

"Nay, Father Bernard, not meddling, involvement." Eleanor, her body tense, was miraculously ready for him. "And it is with a certain humility that I must remind you, I am Louis' wife and thereby, as queen, I must be involved in this most important of our royal charges!"

While Eleanor had been quick to respond, her nervous manner did not escape me. Her color was too high, her reply quick and too clipped, not delivered with her usual ease and style.

Eleanor hurried to present her case. "Dear Abbot, I desire to go on this journey myself, with many of my women. Numbers of my noble vassals will travel with me. There are many things to be done in preparation. It is crucial that I know the plans—make arrangements for the provisioning, the equipage—since we are to be in entourage together, yet, except for the presence of the royal guard, we will be traveling entirely separated from most of my vassals and lords."

From her recovered composure and the set to her shoulders, I sensed that she was preparing to fire a salvo.

"You do recall the Papal Bull that directed separate travel, that specified that the women must not travel with the marching men? That directive makes me even more responsible for the people in my charge." She glanced over inviting me into the debate.

I gulped for air, then launched into the conversation. "Yes, Abbot Bernard, there is much provisioning to see to, as well as gathering the needed workers to come with us, repairmen and cooks, armorers and wheel masters. The preparations are endless, but not," I forced a smile, "overwhelming." I was glad for the strength in my voice, and I hoped my smile had masked the discomfort I felt in my bold confrontation with a man of God. Eleanor may have been practiced at this; I certainly was not. It didn't matter, for Bernard ignored me.

He thrust up his hand. "Your Highness, perhaps I have not made my words clear. I represent many of the lords who speak against you. The northern barons and very high-placed churchmen demand that you not attend the councils at all. It is their desire that you not meddle in their affairs further. It is not for your sex to do so, Majesty. What do women know of logistics, and so forth?"

"I would remind you, reverend Abbot, that a queen must know a great deal, particularly one who staffs and visits numberless castles from here to the Pyrennes. Logistics and supplies are not mysteries to us."

His profile set like chiseled stone. Bernard's pale eyes held both contempt and threat as he spat out, "Remember, dear lady, that silence is a woman's glory."

Eleanor showed a strange mixture of fear and fury. There was something frightening in this man from Clairvaux. The fire in his eyes, the set to his lips, seemed to make her uneasy. She grasped the edge of a nearby table for balance.

"Very well, Abbot, since you appear to be acting as the spokesman for the king's barons, I shall speak for my own. The Aquitainian and Poitavian lords who have rallied to your apostolic trumpet come from my domains."

Hearing Eleanor's voice, clear and unwavering, made me want to cheer aloud. It appeared that a new strength suffused her, dissolving the tightness in her throat.

"Perhaps I have not made myself clear," she went on, "I have suffered the innuendoes and carps from those stuffy lords, and from Cardinal Lisieux as well when I'm at the planning sessions. Hereafter, I will, in my stead, send my representatives to the council; Geoffrey of Rancon, as deputy general, and the Duke of Toulouse as counsel. Have no fear that I'll remain uninformed, for they will report to me after every session."

Eleanor glanced at me as though to gather more strength before continuing. Her words were deliberate. "The lords of the north need to be reminded again that I am their queen."

She took a few steps toward the door before she spun around. "However, it makes no difference. My men will attend the grand councils, then meet with me. We will be kept informed and hold councils of our own. And I will meet with my husband whenever I choose. I know that his Majesty would want that. And hold no hope that I will remain in Paris, captive to fools. I will go on the expedition, leading my forces!"

Bernard, white-faced, froze like a rabbit on the fox trail, when confronted by such willful disobedience. His spine stiffened, for he now had indisputable testimony to what he had always suspected; the trusting, pious King Louis had been married into a family of Satans. And here before him, willful and rebellious, yet beguiling and beckoning, was one who could do the devil's bidding, a daughter of Eve—no, worse—of Belial, indeed.

"You do not understand, daughter," he whispered, eyes smoldering with righteousness, "you endanger the whole expedition with your presence."

His glance barely passed over me, but I felt the sting of his condemnation. My cheeks turned hot and the accusation made me feel guilty. As though he had sensed my spiritual confusion, Bernard added, "I pray for you and your women, your Majesty. I will tell the barons of your reply. It is good for them to know how their king must forbear."

That last remark riled Eleanor. "I doubt that we endanger the whole expedition with our presence, Abbot. Surely you recall that Saint Jerome himself has written proudly of Saint Paula's pilgrimage to places deep in the desert, as far away as Mount Sinai." Turning, she prompted, "We all studied it together one summer in Bordeaux, remember?"

"Oh yes, it was an instructive account," I chimed, hoping that Eleanor would dare to go on.

"According to the wise Father Jerome, this holy woman, Paula, trudged all the way up to the Hill of the Foreskins in Galgala, near Jericho. Imagine that, to the Hill of the Foreskins." Eleanor, unblinking, faced Bernard with a sweet smile. "Let me refresh your memory. Jerome admired Paula's zeal, saying that it was wonderful, and her courage, scarcely credible in a woman."

Bernard seemed paralyzed with loathing, and I knew Eleanor had made her point. She drove home one more.

"We are ever exhorted by you, Abbot Bernard, to imitate the ways of the saints. Now here is a real opportunity, why is there so much objection?"

Words failed Bernard. He bolted from the room and out the door to spring onto his waiting mule. Scowling, he pulled his heavy black hood close against the brisk winds. With his back straight as a church pew, he escaped across the bridge to his happy, celibate brothers at the abbey.

CHAPTER 5

Ile de Paris

*R*etributive threat had bristled from saintly Bernard as he had fled from us that afternoon. Neither Eleanor nor I were prepared for how quickly he would act. But when the Templar monk, Thierry of Galeran, first swished into court, we realized that Bernard and the bishops had scored a grim victory. They had prevailed upon Louis to appoint the gaunt monk as King's Deputy. In this capacity, Thierry of Galeran would watchdog the royal treasury, and as it turned out, us.

Galeran was a man of forty years whose long, narrow face, was topped by a wide forehead lined with black forbidding brows. His hair was closely tonsured, his skin smooth as a eunuch's, chin whiskerless. Dark eyes, quick to dart about at debate, were flat, joyless. Yet Galeran gloried in his call to serve the fair-haired Louis, smiling tenderly at him in unguarded moments.

We learned that Thierry of Galeran was a eunuch, castrated as a boy to preserve his dulcet singing voice, though it was hard to imagine this saturnine man had ever wanted to sing. He brought to the court his ability to do figures and sums lightning fast. Considered by the prelates to be strong and unyielding, he was a rare man, free from the taint of the flesh, sent by God through dear Abbot Bernard to safeguard the royal resources. The factions opposed to the queen and her women could be heard singing, "Glory be to God!" The Templar would be the king's shield against ill-advisors and syco-phants, but most of all, they rejoiced, he would guard against the wiles of Queen Eleanor and those senseless baggages of frippery tag-ging along with her. Would that we had paid them more heed, for with Galeran at the helm, their judgments knew no bounds.

Candlemas found the muddy streets of Paris crusted with sleet, icing the stairs that lead into the stronghold of the Capetian kings. Slippery and mean as they were, I took them two at a time, just back from the blacksmith where I had seen to the completion of our chain-mail vests. Hoping not to be late for my meeting with Eleanor, I burst into her chambers only to collide with her deputy, Count Geoffrey of Rancon. My parcels flew across the fresh rushes scatter-ing upon the floor.

"Aye, lady, you are in quite a rush." He stepped forward to help me with my packages, a doll and a new linen tunic for little Princess Marie. His eyes, deep hazel, shone above a friendly smile. Handsome in a dove-gray mantle of fine Flemish wool, he stood tall. His face was still tan, in spite of the winter's constant overcast.

"Oh, Sir Geoffrey, how—how pleasant." I dipped a curtsy, trying to give the impression of one composed, which dissipated altogether when his hand brushed mine as he helped me remove my cape. I hoped the throbbing in my temples didn't give away the unsettling flutter in my heart.

"Saint Benedict's boots!" Eleanor salvaged my awkwardness, Geoffrey has reported on our plague, Galeran. The new deputy out-does himself. He speaks on matters completely out of his realm. "Oh, this monk is going to be a problem, a nasty problem."

Perhaps Geoffrey had already heard these lines, for he interrupted, "With your leave, Majesty, I'm expected at a meeting with Lord Hugh." He bowed, his mouth tilting in a wide smile. "A pleasure to see you again, Lady Madeleine." He was gone.

I had barely time to sort my thoughts for Eleanor continued to rant about Galeran. "Ah, yes, devoted Bernard rides off into the night and the next thing we know this devious Templar monk arrives in our court."

"Devious?" I reluctantly let go of the image of Rancon's smile and replied, "How do you know he's devious? He's here to watch Louis' treasury."

"A ploy, dear cousin, a ploy. He's here to get in my way. And I'll tell you how devious he is. It seems he has dug up some teachings of the early church fathers on whether or not women have souls! He wonders since we have them not, what our need is for salvation in the Holy Land."

"How insulting! How is it they know so much about our souls? Better to look to their own. Did Rancon say how Louis responded?"

The question disarmed Eleanor. She moved closer to the fire, her immediate anger purged, her features softening. "No, not specifically, but, Louis surprises me. He now deflects all the arguments by saying, 'Our queen and royal wife must come on the Holy Expedition, and, as she desires, her ladies with her. It is God's will"

A sharp wind rattled the shuttered windows. Rubbing her hands together vigorously before the fire, Eleanor went on. "I've heard him say it almost as though intoning a prayer. He has that vapid expression more and more, and," Eleanor spoke as a wife of nearly ten years, "rarely looks at me, directly at me, as though he's really seeing me. It's a worry."

The fleeting change in her face did not escape me. It was as one altered by an artist's stroke whose single line can change the portrait's mood. A look of disappointment, perhaps sadness, appeared, then was quickly erased with a smile.

But Eleanor wasn't through with Galeran. Her expression darkened in the firelight shadows. Pinching her brows and tossing her head in the way of Galeran, she put her hand on her hip and outrageously mimed the eunuch Templar.

"I can't stand the idea of that frivolous queen going on this march." Eleanor threw herself down on the cushions. "Galeran and I were destined to clash from the onset, weren't we? And why not? Now, he has the ear of the king at all times; and in spite of Louis' insistence on our going with him, he seems dangerously swayed by this new deputy."

"Yes, he reminds me of a viper, slithering here and there," I agreed, glad that Eleanor's wrath had ebbed. And hearing of Galeran's latest contemptibility, I was beginning to comprehend his menacing ways.

I have to admit, however, that prior to his arrival at the court, Eleanor had begun to behave as though the enterprise to the Holy Land was in some way exclusively hers, tending to innumerable details, some of them obviously out of her domain. While Bernard had effectively acted to curb her influence in the royal councils, and that had angered her, now her response to the Templar was extreme for he had dared to curb her plans for her own separate entourage, and that was going too far!

Eleanor pushed up from her cushion and crossed to the table where her lists were. "I've been working on this expedition from the very beginning. He's not to dictate how I'm to take part in this wonderful adventure, and Madeleine, that's what it is, a really grand adventure, with the possibility for salvation included in the bargain."

"I think, Eleanor," I plunged ahead choosing my words carefully, "that's what you've made it, a grand adventure. The pope's intention from the start was to free the Holy Land, and in the doing, save our souls." I knew I was on thin ice, confronting her, so recently in an explosive mood. I added gently, "Perhaps, were we to follow only that quest we wouldn't need so many baggage carts."

"Perhaps I have made it a little more than a pilgrimage, but why not?" As my mind went back to the day when we first heard of this expedition. I had been kneeling in the small chapel, when she came bursting in upon my prayers, her cheeks flushed with excitement. "Madeleine, come quickly! Pope Eugenius has just sent messengers to the king. He wants Louis to head an expedition to the Holy Land, to lead a holy war against the Infidels. Oh, isn't it wonderful? We can go to the Holy City. How I've always wanted to travel there." She had paused for a moment, perhaps sensing her thoughtless interruption. "For my soul, Madeleine, I have always wanted to go there to pray for my soul—in Jerusalem."

As I recovered from the shocking news, I studied Eleanor. Since childhood I had known her as rather irreligious. She claimed not to believe in the devil. And her thoughts about Eve were outright heresy. She had expressed them only recently. "I am sick of the stories of Eve. They must be lies. Why in every village and town, there would be a stake waiting for us with faggots ready to leap into flames, if any of us ran to our bishops with reports of a talking snake. I tell you it is a story of fancy and we get all the blame."

It was not to expiate the sins of Eve that Eleanor was making the trip. Nor was it the promise of a Plenary Indulgence, that erasure of all sin, that passage straight to heaven promised by the pope. For Eleanor it was an adventure, and most of my efforts at restraint were cast aside, to our great jeopardy, as you will learn. So it was in this instance, for Eleanor had deftly sidestepped the baggage issue. "You've been with me for over a year. You can see how easily life in Paris could become dull." She lowered her voice, "In fact, life as Louis' wife has become tedious. He sees less and less to his conjugal duties."

Her remark did not surprise me. From my first meeting with Louis, I sensed a vast difference in their personalities. The king was as reserved as Eleanor was vivacious, modest as she was flagrant. In some circles, such a pairing might have been called a mismatch.

When I encountered the mild-mannered king on dark afternoons as he paced back and forth in the chill courtyard reading his psalter, I could have mistaken him for a monk. One eventide he looked up, his pale blue eyes gazing at the dusk, and whispered "Contemptus Mundi." Mindful of my intrusion, I hoped to slip away, but Louis detained me, "What think you of worldliness, Lady Madeleine?" He swept his hair, the color of summer straw, from his troubled brow.

The question found me dumbstruck. How peculiar, coming from a man who was married to one of the most beautiful and wealthy women in the world. Mumbling some excuse, I left him. He seemed to be ruminating still on the motto of the monasteries where he had prepared for the priesthood, where he had spent over ten years practicing contempt for things worldly.

"Too many years, dear cousin," Eleanor had complained, "too many years was he at his devotions, praying not to be of this world. Who would not want to be of this world, especially if we make it to our own liking, which is what royalty can do." She had stood regal in a burgundy silk gown trimmed in ermine at the cuffs, a golden goblet in her hand. "Worldliness means aliveness, present in this glorious world as opposed to the unknown one of the next."

Her revelations about Louis' conjugal attentions only confirmed my earlier suspicions about their sexual intimacy. As Mistress of the Household, I often spent the night in the small alcove adjacent to the queen's chambers. There were few visits from Louis, and when there were, they seemed restrained and passionless, missing the soft laughter and intimate conversations between husband and wife that follow lovemaking. When Eleanor had visited Louis, she seldom returned in high spirits, eyes brimming with pleasured satisfaction. Tonight was the first time Eleanor had expressed the truth aloud. How painful for anyone as beautiful and passionate as she and as prideful.

Before I could respond, she went on, "A good adventure never hurt anyone. By the breath of all the angels, I'm seeing to the details myself and paying for it as well! Now if this mincing monk thinks he's going to thwart me!" She hit at the cushion. "Oh, how he galls me! And that look on his face." Eleanor mimed him perfectly again, dilating her nostrils and tightening her lips. "Must he eternally look like a shift in the wind has brought up the stink from the castle latrines?"

In spite of my concern, the baggage discussion had been diverted once again and Eleanor had managed to make me laugh. "I know our friends enjoy your jests and barbs regarding this newcomer, as do I. They dislike him, too, but I wonder how wise it is to incur his wrath this early in the game? He has the backing of so many powerful nobles, including Cardinal Lisieux. You're daring in your ways with Galeran, Eleanor. I would be careful. He frightens me; I'm not sure why."

"Oh, indeed, he's bilious, testy, and dangerous. And, yes, he's gathering minions around him like flies to bad meat," Eleanor agreed. "It may promise a thorny path to the Holy Land, but I'm not going to have another churchman telling me what to do."

"Now Lent is upon us, and there's much to finish up," she turned to the maid, "Hulga, fetch the parchment and crayon. We have more lists to make."

"Will we be ready to leave when warm weather arrives."

"I believe so. Louis promises his forces will be ready by St. Denis' Feast Day, in mid-June."

"Good. With God's help, we'll outdo the king and his barons, and have our people ready by the end of May!" I hoped Sir Geoffrey of the winsome smile would march in the vanguard with us.

CHAPTER 6

Via Crucis

With the aid of many saints and our own diligence, we were finally ready. The Lenten season helped, with songs and tambourines muted those forty days. Throughout the kingdom, prayerful petitions for the success of our mission were recited thrice daily. Eleanor and I had labored from first bells till vespers seeing to the preparations.

On Easter Sunday, exactly a year after Bernard's call to arms in Vezelay, King Louis summoned his followers. "Gather in Paris on St. Denis' Feast Day, June 11th. His Holiness, Pope Eugenius, will be present to give the farewell blessing." The long months of planning, compiling lists, securing supplies, garnering shifting loyalties, had come to an end. Or so I thought.

"Ride out to meet Sybelle, dear cousin. Invite her to join me at the ceremony so all will be ready for our leave-taking." Eleanor was seeing to the smallest details, and though it seemed unnecessary, I was content to be early on the road for I love the feel of a soft summer morn, with leafy trees o'er arching and bird songs above me. Though the streets were crowded with hoards of faithful on their way to St. Denis Cathedral, I happily made my way to greet one of the Lady Knights, Countess Sybelle of Flanders.

Sybelle, astride a handsome bay gelding, was pleased to see me. The soft June air colored her cheeks, and a slight perspiration framed the curve of her lips, now parted in a smile. Her dark blue eyes had lost some of their customary worry. Count Philip, her husband, guided his stocky mount, a breed of Arabian and Flemish mix, to her side. His receding gray-flecked hairline framed a flushed, long, Nordic face. Phillip sat rigid as a pillar upon his silver-trimmed saddle; his eyes, darting with anticipation, were as gray and cold as the steel vest he wore.

A trace of arrogance played at the edges of his mouth. His nod was perfunctory, and why not? Phillip of Flanders, proud to be a proven veteran, was one of the king's most trusted allies, and as such, eager to return to the Holy Land. He had received many honors for his bravery against the hated Saracens, and now, rumor had it, he was on a search for more riches for the infant sons Sybelle had given him.

Predatory energy seemed to surge through him as his leg grazed Sybelle's. I hung back as the couple rode in step, noting the look of desire and conquest on Phillip's face. Sybelle had faced it many times for their life together as husband and wife had spanned ten years.

I recalled that hot and sticky summer in Poitiers. Eleanor, Sybelle and I had hung over the high parapet as Geoffrey Plantagenet, Sybelle's brother, accompanied her groom-to-be, the Count of Flanders, through the narrow streets to the courtyard at Poitiers. Closer than Bordeaux to Anjou, it had been chosen as the site for Sybelle's marriage.

Pennant bearers, their red and gold flags slack in the breezeless day, led the entourage followed by twenty or so knights. Colorful banners, flashing symbols of their respective allegiances, half to Anjou, half to Flanders, flapped with the motion of the horses.

"Well, Sybelle, what think you?" Eleanor studied her friend. The blond crisp curls of a few seasons ago had been tamed to stay under the emerald-shaded caplet on her head.

"I think he is quite passable for his age," she had paused for a moment as if to gather some inner courage, "and I hope that he will love me and treat me well."

Her shoulders rose in a little shrug. Sybelle tried to be enthusiastic, yet I sensed her feeling of disappointment, but we, and certainly she, knew it was her role as a young noblewoman to be offered as prize in negotiating a kinship alliance. No woman had any say in who led her to the marriage bed.

Immediately after the wedding ceremony, Count Phillip, bristling with vitality, and brusque in the manner of the Flemish, had whisked his new bride to the lowlands of Flanders, with its perpetual fogs and floods. Sybelle's farewell smile could not mask the sadness in her eyes.

Now as I rode beside them, Phillip described Outremer to us in explosive streams of speech. "There will be new alliances to watch for." He grinned through clenched jaws. "Melisende, Sybelle's stepmother, is Queen of Jerusalem." He oozed a distasteful confidence. "As such, she will be pleased to offer me special favors, in the name of kinship." His eyes glowed with the possibility of gain. "There will be possessions for our second son, and future sons we may have."

He took Sybelle's wrist forcefully. "Isn't that so, my wife?"

Without replying, Sybelle looked at her husband with a puzzled expression, her eyes dark as cornflowers. Phillip seemed to want some specific response, and when it was not forthcoming, he uttered an oath under his breath, and wheeling his horse, spurred the animal so forcefully, bystanders leapt off the road as he raced to the rear of his brigade.

Sybelle shook her head, "Phillip's lusts are all the same, Madeleine. For war or for women, they must suit his needs at the time. I hope by joining him on this march, I will better understand the hardships he has recounted so often on his return from his campaigns."

Her brow cramped with worry, Sybelle went on. "He often expresses resentment toward me as if I were at fault for not having been subject to the same trials as he. It puzzles me for I do not choose to be a warrior. But, with Eleanor's encouragement, I am glad to take the cross. I pledged to join the pilgrimage to be a part of Phillip's adventure."

I wish now I had kept track of all the reasons people were going on this crusade. Phillip for riches, Sybelle to better understand her husband, Louis for his soul and the souls of all his subjects, Galeran to guard the king's soul from the likes of the queen, and Eleanor for a lark. And I—I seemed not to know what I was seeking; mayhap some part of myself. We were passing underneath the verdant umbrella of broad-leafed chestnut trees that line the roads to Paris, when the image of the Magdalene Cathedral flashed before me and the words from the Easter ritual—"Whom do you seek?"—came to mind. My thoughts vanished as Count Phillip galloped past, again forcing people to jump out of the way of flying hooves. It concerned me to see the hard set of his jaw, its muscles taut when there was no danger or threat. He charged forth to take the lead as we drew nearer St. Denis.

All year at the councils, Phillip, as the powerful count of Flanders, had been part of the northern faction arguing with turbulent outbursts over the number of noblewomen invited along by the queen. A stoic northerner, Phillip was as opposed to women going as were the bishops. While Sybelle was a friend of the queen's, Phillip was a staunch supporter of the king, adding one more division to the many already existing among the various expedition forces. Those divisions appeared to run deep as any fissures in the Pyrenees. My brow began to cramp as tightly as Sybelle's.

In the hot forenoon of a close day, I took my place among the royal hundreds who crowded into the Cathedral of St. Denis. Colors swirled: cardinal scarlet, royal purple, shimmering armor, and pilgrims' gray merged into shades of consecrate devotion. Sir Geoffrey of Rancon stood straight and elegant before his men. His deputy's chain shone like a talisman around his neck. Our eyes met briefly before the trumpets announced the arrival of the Vicar of Rome, Pope Eugenius, and following a few steps behind, the King and Queen of France.

With much ceremony, Pope Eugenius presented the sacred oriflame to King Louis. The same vermilion banner carried thusly on a golden lance had been borne by our magnificent Charlemagne. My heart surged with pride to be part of such a valorous tradition.

After a long ritual, Louis grasped the banner and fell to his knees to receive Eugenius' papal benediction. Over the muffled coughs and sobs echoing to the high walls of the cathedral, the Pontiff invoked the Knight's Blessing:

"Bless, oh Lord, your servants, who bend their heads before you. Pour on them your 'stablishing grace. In warfare in which they are to be tested, preserve them in health and good fortune. Wherever and whyever they ask for thy help, be especially present."

The Pope, overcome by the fevered congestion of his throat, forced himself to speak louder as he looked out at the weeping throngs. Hot tears flowed freely down my cheeks.

"Protect," he cried out, "protect and defend them!"

King Louis prostrated himself before the altar, then rising, he raised the standard of St. Denis aloft and facing us, began the procession that would lead to the very gates of Jerusalem.

I tried to join the choir in the anthem which accompanied Louis down the cool limestone aisle, but my voice closed with emotion. The Easter morning service in Vezelay intruded again, an inner presence whispering, "Whom do you seek?" Though the cathedral walls shuddered with blessings, the answer wasn't here.

Finding my voice, I chanted with the throng, "He who goes forth with Louis, what has he to fear from hell? For surely his soul will dwell in Paradise with the angels of the Lord."

My spirits had calmed somewhat by the time Louis stepped out through the high cathedral doors into the daylight. His face was drawn and pale, eyes blinking uncontrollably till he pinched them at his nose; Galeran sprang to his side, but the king seemed quickly revived by the jubilant townsfolk blessing themselves and him.

Eleanor signaled for me to join her, her face filled with a rare spiritual bliss. She let out a deep sigh as she stepped proudly from the cathedral's incensed cavern out into the open. Her hands shook slightly as she blessed herself.

"Surely, Madeleine," she whispered loudly, "I have done the Redeemer's work in my own way."

Her words were drowned out by the cheering crowds. They erupted from every corner; from the gabled rooftops, from shop stoops, from windows draped with multicolored scarves and long red cloths.

"For my soul, too, Majesty!"

"Via Crucis!"

"For St. Magdalene and France, our queen!"

Eleanor basked in the glory of the moment, waving joyously in return. "How pleased they are with me," she confided, her face upturned to the applause and blessings showering down from every side.

"And why not, Madeleine? From the promise of Vezelay to this moment, I have struggled almost daily, battling for a say in the councils, shaking monies loose from Galeran's tight fist, raising enormous funds from my own vassals for this expedition, defying the clergy and Eugenius himself to be allowed to go on this crusade. I have done it all and I have won!"

Though Eleanor's remarks I found a bit o'erweening, I said nothing for her exuberance was contagious as we mounted the white geldings waiting for us. "Much that parades from here is my doing," she reveled, "mine and yours, cousin. We've done it as well as any noble or, for that matter, any king!" Her smile was as radiant as the day.

Sybelle and Florine joined us. Astride our white horses, we paraded slowly through the jammed Parisian streets. Behind us traipsed our entourage, gaudy as a serpentine column mumming on Shrove Tuesday.

We wore the same soft cordovan boots and white tunics that we had worn at Vezelay. Today, the long red crosses blazed in the June sun, rousing ardent cheers. Queen Eleanor's Lady Knights were on their way, and I was one of them!

CHAPTER 7

On Route to Metz

Once out of the city, Eleanor dared me to race her to the wooded promontory overlooking the main road. There we could see her glorious cavalcade before the thick forest swallowed it up, wagon by wagon.

"Good it is to observe the order of travel before we get into the woods," I called, reining my horse to a halt at the hilltop. "We may want to change it at Metz. The carts lugging the skins for ground cover and the sleeping mats are near the front, I see. Good."

Headed by the queen's point guard, with its flowing colors of Aquitaine, France, Flanders and Toulouse flashing to the country-side, the cavalcade, a magnificent sight, stretched like sparkling gem-stones on a necklace. Excessive or not, it was magnificent, and I, as Mistress of the Household, had argued with Eleanor more than once about its size.

"We really have to watch how much we're hauling, Eleanor," I had advised.

"Why"

"Because the churchmen rail so much against it. You know where churchmen lead, others follow. I don't know." My doubts had begun to feel like disloyalty. "It makes us more visible, more vulnerable to the criticism and hard feelings already aroused by our going."

"Vulnerable? Madeleine, I am the queen, and queens as wealthy as I are not vulnerable. Vulnerable is not a word I like. Power, property and armed protection, those are words I like. You'll notice that neither propriety nor piety is among them!"

It had been an unpleasant exchange, and now with the pageant and plenty progressing before me, wagons flaunting tricolor pennants and hiding rainbow silks in exquisitely woven hampers, it disturbed me that I had remembered it at all. Yet my unease lingered.

"There, the kitchen wagon comes next." My spirits lightened at the sounds of a high cart, pots and kettles jangling. Cooks and scullery servants rode donkeys while the chore boys and girls walked beside them, chattering gaily. A few wayward rascals fell out of step to torment a load of witless chickens stacked in cane cages.

Eleanor scanned past them. "Ah, there they are, and just where I want them to be, ahead of us so that we know their whereabouts at all times."

A victory grin spread across her face and widened with every passing wagon. A series of festooned wains, covered in heavy canvas, concealed the forbidden finery. Table settings of silver and gold; fine silk tunics, wimples of whitest linen, belts and necklaces; shawls and scarves, multicolored as the fields speckled with summer bloom; all had found their way into scores of wardrobes and baskets procured by us during the long year's preparations.

"Seventeen wagons in all. It isn't so many. All that fussing over a few extra wagons. But where is Thecla's cart?"

"There it is. It follows so close to our litter, it's hard to distinguish." Thecla, my serving woman, well versed in the healing arts, in her usual obdurate way had insisted that she travel near the royal party.

"And so that there be no mistake about my services," she had warned, "my cart should be painted exactly like Her Majesty's." She had faced Eleanor, wearing a scowl, her arms folded like two guards under her heaving bosom. I feared that she had overstepped her boundaries this time, but to my surprise, Eleanor had agreed.

"I want you to assist with the supplying, Madeleine. It is a long trek, and Thecla's right. We'll need the medicine cart filled with curatives to be close at hand."

Now, following the queen's litter, and painted the same lustrous red, the medicine wagon tagged along, crammed to its top. Thecla, had assembled an array of remedies that Galen himself would have envied: herbs for the treatment of dysentery and agues; salves, made of equal parts of pressed violet juice, olive oil and goat fat, to heal rashes or abscesses; ointments of plantain to treat insect bites or sunburns; poultices to soothe muscles aching from a long day's ride; crocks of linseed for treatment of burns; vervain for wound abscesses; fennel, licorice or civit for nausea or poisonings. For general well-being and to keep the humours in balance, bags of dried hyssop and almonds perched in the corners.

High stacks of whitened flax and linen cut for bandages served as ballast for innumerable flagons of wine. When questioned about the wine, Thecla had a quick reply "The wines have many uses. The first," her eyes danced, "we know is for gaiety and celebration, but I will use it for cleansing and cauterization, too. And as you well know, m' lady, it works like a spell to bring sleep to the restless, and tears to those who cannot cry."

Jacques and Eliaze, Eleanor's favorite royal troubadours, followed directly behind Thecla's wagon. Eliaze's pack mule swayed with the weight of the troubadours' trade. Spread first upon the creature's sagging back were heavy blue and red tapestries to cushion the falls and tumbles of the acrobats.

A basket filled with Jacque's richly carved dumbbells and balls of every color and size perched against a woven chest harboring costumes, and grease paints brought all the way from India. Wrapped in soft flaxen towels rested Eliaze's true treasure, her stringed lute, its long fretted neck and pear-shaped body made of delicate woods.

The remaining gems traveled in the person of the troubadour herself, in a voice of sweetest pitch. Eliaze sang as she walked beside Jacques untouched by the storm of protest that had erupted when the queen defied Pope Eugenius' proclamations forbidding any entertainers on the expedition.

Eleanor had eloquently defended her decision to bring them. "As for no jongleurs or troubadours, that is utterly beyond reason! Life without singing, dancing and verses is like no life at all! We are not criminals on this march, though, Madeleine, Eugenius, himself, has charged Bernard to recruit all kinds of ne'er-do-wells to come along." She shook her finger, pretending to be in the presence of his Holiness.

"I would say to the holy father—I would say it respectfully, mind you—I would say, 'It seems utterly unfair to deprive Jacques and Eliaze of a plenary indulgence when every mean cut-purse in the land will be trudging along at Bernard's invitation.'"

I awaited Eleanor's logic.

"Bernard has boasted to Abbot Suger that a remarkable Providence has furnished the hope of rescuing Jerusalem while at the same time ridding the kingdom of the burden of its paupers and criminals. Therefore, Bernard has promised murderers and ravishers hope for redemption!"

Her hands held in a posture of benign justice, Eleanor continued her charade, "'Your Holiness,' I would say, 'surely I would be expected to do the same for my subjects and my dear jongleurs! Of course, they will come with us, and so will the falcons! It can be no other way.' And wouldn't the pope have to agree?"

Eleanor's study of syllogism had not been wasted. Her logic was quite persuasive, but still, I wasn't so sure. The falcons had raised another sore point, but only after I had gone to great lengths to prepare them for the trip.

"Since it has been decreed that we must travel separately in a contingent of our own, then we should see to our own hawking as well." Eleanor prepared another argument. "It is good for us to have some sport and exercise along the way."

She had me purchase rounded wicker baskets lined with hessian for the birds' transport, and I sent Germer to gather the swivels, leashes, tyretts and the varvels. I was present when a perturbed Louis had learned that we intended to bring the royal falcons on his Holy March.

He objected to the queen, "Dear wife, Pope Eugenius has banned them on the pilgrimage. He preaches that they are things of luxury and sport, and not fitting for our purpose." Louis' eyes drooped with fatigue. The plans for his enterprise had been so overwhelming, he had little energy to stand firm against his wife's retorts.

"Pope Eugenius simply cannot be dictating what to bring on a long journey," Eleanor had argued. "We have both seen the documents which chart our course. We'll be going a great distance and I for one, dedicated as I am to this most holy cause," her voice sounded impatient, "just cannot pray for all that way."

She had tossed her hair, loose on this summer afternoon, copper highlights glinting amid long auburn tresses. "No hawking when we go to the land that originated the sport? Come, dear Louis, don't be unreasonable."

So, counter to papal desires and Cistercian pronouncements, both the falcon mews and the merry troubadour cart clipped along secure in their places in the kaleidoscope line of conveyances that had started into the woods.

The queen was pleased with the convoy, and with a nod, we raced again to catch up with the others already on board the litter.

Sun-dappled through the tree patterns, the litter's deep red sides gleamed highlighting the elegance of its gilded illuminations. Admiring the small emblem on its door, the roadside crowds had recognized their Saint Magdalene, though few could read the Latin motto surrounding her, "Quem Quaeritis?"

As we paced along, I welcomed the cool depths of the forest. Liturgical incense and the miasma of my earlier spiritual feelings gave way to fragrances more subtle of pines, elm and ash crowding each other for sight of the sun. Their towering majesty dwarfed me.

"We're off at last!" Sybelle's face glowed with excitement as she settled back onto the velvet-cushioned seat. "I have always wanted to go on pilgrimage with Phillip. I had hoped at least to get to Compostella and never did." Her mouth drooped momentarily in disappointment.

"On this trip, I hope to walk the blessed streets of Jerusalem, to pray atop the Mount of Olives, to stay in Bethany, and to visit the convent Queen Melisende has built on the site of Martha and Mary Magdalene's home. Melisende will welcome us and the huge army we bring." Sybelle paused for a moment, then proceeded slowly. "Phillip reports that there are many riches in those lands for those brave enough to seize them."

"Uncle Raymond agrees. He has sent messages and rich gifts to Louis and me; I wonder what he's like after all these years. His messenger spoke of opportunities and lands to be conquered, yet he warned of the mounting dangers to the occupying Franks. Don't you think the women brave who rule there?"

"Are we not also brave to go?" Sybelle countered, arranging the folds of her tunic, her brows knitted together. "But we are surely to be protected. Phillip believes we are bringing the largest army that anyone ever remembers."

"True enough," Eleanor interjected, "but my nobles think it may be too large and unwieldy. Still, they are full of high hopes. And think of the courts where we'll be welcomed as royal visitors. The Byzantine Queen Irene has sent runners to assure our stay in Constantinople. We'll pretend that we are not looking at the fashions so our intentions do not seem frivolous." Eleanor laughed, alluding to another of the pope's strict measures of deportment.

Merriment filled the wain, but Florine seemed withdrawn from the fun. The wife of a favorite of Eleanor's, Lord Hugh of Toulouse, she is the youngest of us, not yet nineteen. She isn't the sort of person I would have chosen to go along on an extended trip, but Eleanor had wanted to honor Hugh for his longstanding loyalty and did so by including Florine in her immediate circle.

Today, the young woman's dark eyes were luminous, made more so by the heavy shadows framing them. Her puffy cheeks seemed especially pale, in contrast to their usual splotchy rose circles.

"You are quiet, Florine. Are you well?" inquired Sybelle. "Have some sweetmeats and wine. Perhaps you are hungry."

Florine forced a weak smile, blanching at the sight of the pastries that bounced in a basket on the cushioned bench of the litter.

"I am not hungry—I—I don't feel well. It is the excitement. I will be fine, I'm sure, though I do find the ride unsettling. It makes me feel queasy. Tomorrow, I'll ride my horse."

"Oh, so shall we all!" Eleanor, noticing Florine's pallid face, nodded her head in affirmation. "It is far too lovely to be in here all the time. We will use this when the weather is cold or wet, or in Outremer when the desert sun becomes too hot. I wanted us to be here, together, at the start just as we will be at the end, in procession to Jerusalem, we brave women of the Franks."

Eleanor leaned back against the soft seat, lost in her own thoughts, as though debating the course of her conversation. Her mood seemed to have shifted, jaw set as she spoke with a caustic edge.

"And pure women, too," she continued with a ring of sarcasm. "Louis has pledged total abstinence as a way of preparing us both for the blessing of our plenary indulgence."

Beneath the sarcasm, I recognized the look of hurt flitting across her face. Louis' sexual abstentions seemed increasingly like rejections to her. His chaste ways had Eleanor baffled. They hurt, too.

"I believe it will be so for all of us. Phillip has said that he will ride with the king as a member of the rear guard." Sybelle continued with a sigh, "Knowing Phillip as I do, I'll wager that he will not keep any pledge of purity. With or without me, I might add. He, the dukes of Burgundy, as well as the Norman lords with other forces will be the guard at the rear, to see to the stragglers, the poor pilgrims on foot. By sweet Magdalene, there are thousands of them. The rear guard will make sure that they keep up. I hope they don't trade their arms for food along the way. The guards will be watchful and vigilant against thievery and whoring, too."

"I know," Florine added while she fanned herself, "Hugh says that our archbishop complained of the women on the crusade because it will lead to lechery and whoring aplenty, enough to soil the very intention of the holy march."

"How farfetched!" Eleanor flared. "Do they think there will be no females in any of the villages and towns along the way? No whores or harlots to be had? Is there to be an end of rape when Christian soldiers swarm through a village? Not likely."

"Eleanor, you sound so angry. What bothers you?" Hoping to comfort her, I placed my hand on her arm, surprised at the tension there.

"Yes, on this point I am angry. It puts a damper on the trip and I am made irritable by it. By Saint Benedict's boots, why is it that every time some bishop gets a stirring in his loins, it results in lengthy diatribe concerning the temptations of women?" Eleanor tapped her foot nervously. "I learned only this morning that Louis will have his pavilion arranged so that both Odo of Duilio, his scribe, and that miserable Thierry Galeran sleep with him. It's as though they needed to protect him from some sinful lure. I am his wife!" She poured herself a goblet of wine gulping half of it.

"It's hard to believe," she sputtered, "that with knights from throughout the kingdom at his side that Louis' life is in any danger. No," she carried on, "it's a bold measure aimed to keep me from his side, day or night. I am married to him! It was the same strategy that Bernard used to keep me from having any part in the important matters of state. And that angers me!"

Making a sour face, she handed the wine to Sybelle. "And I know it gets my bile all in a flux. Thecla says it's bad for my liver. I try not to be so furious. But no one can get past the king's watch dogs. My nobles complain bitterly."

She drew the intricately embroidered curtain aside to allow for more air. Pungent moisture from the loamy forest floor wafted in.

"Thank the Holy Magdalene that my own army will march with me in the vanguard under the command of Sir Geoffrey." Turning to me she inquired, "Did I tell you he will join our company permanently, since he also acts as my deputy and must be the liaison between our contingent and the king's?"

Suddenly, my face felt hot, for the mention of Geoffrey Rancon's name sent a tingle of excitement racing along my spine. We had come to an easy acquaintance since the day of our collision, but I had not realized until this moment how much the promise of his frequent presence excited me. The image of Geoffrey's easy smile came to my mind, and the sound of his voice, deep yet well spoken, made my heart race. Thank Saint Agatha, the litter had come to a halt. "We seem to be stopping. Have we arrived at the river already? Quick, let me see."

I crouched my way to the curtained door, springing lightly from its step to the soft forest ground. Happy for an excuse to leave the stifling confines of the carriage, I welcomed the escape for fear my emotions might betray me. My pulses were throbbing. I was quite taken aback by my reaction. The possibility of seeing Sir Geoffrey's handsome face every day added a tantalizing flair to the venture.

CHAPTER 8

At the Moselle River

By late afternoon, the queen's wagons took leave of the old Roman road that tunneled its way through the umbral forest. The caravan stopped on a cleared slope surrounded by a cuff of soft sage green stretching some two or three miles to the banks of the Moselle River, the boundary line demarcating where the Frankish Kingdom ends and the Holy Roman Empire, ruled by Emperor Conrad, begins.

Brush on either side of the wide slopes was thicketed in feathery shrubs. Small clumps of sapling willow and ash stirred with the faint breeze that came off the flowing river. It had been a dry summer with early heat so the river was down from its usual depth, leaving bits of wood and trash exposed on the rocks baking on the arid mud banks. However, water flowed vigorously at its center, majestic with swirling, deep green pools.

In the parched meadow area covered with short wide-leafed sedge, we set up encampment. Florine seemed grateful to be out of the tumbled experience of the litter and walked slowly toward the river. I joined her as she brushed her dark hair back from her wide forehead. She pointed to her head apologetically. "My head aches, and I feel unsettled. I pray God for good weather. I cannot stand the confines of that litter. I'm afraid I'll suffocate."

Drops of perspiration dotted her upper lip, as she pushed the loose sleeves of her tunic past her elbows and stooped to dip her handkerchief into the waters.

"Here, Florine, let me help you." I daubed her cheeks and temples with the cloth. She welcomed its cool droplets.

"Ah, that is better. Now the landscape around me has stopped swirling."

She rested listlessly on the bank. Behind her, in a tangle of poles and ropes, tent-keepers launched the business of setting up camp for the coming night.

Looking past Florine, I caught sight of Eleanor stretching while she surveyed her surroundings. The long year's work and preparation had left her tired and thinner. The continual frustrations with the plans had taken an edge from her verve. However, she had insisted on having the last word where her own vassals were concerned, and in this she had prevailed, and few would dispute that her leadership and preparations had stemmed from an astuteness rarely observed.

Now, as we made our first stop, Eleanor's buoyant spirits surfaced once again. "The marchers will string out behind us for miles, Madeleine. How jolly it is to realize that several armies and thousands of pilgrims stand between me and the king's watchdogs. It frees me to be queen and pilgrim in precisely the ways I wish."

Eleanor twirled in a small circle, her hands upheld to the sky. "I feel like celebrating with some sport. Let's exercise our birds. Call Germer to fetch them while we wait for the others to arrive. It's several hours till dark." Her earlier irritability dissipated, Eleanor loosened her hair from its tight coils.

Heading toward the falcon cart, I found that I was secretly longing to see Sir Geoffrey of Rancon leading the vanguard. To help Germer provided a useful distraction. Besides, I wanted to see how the birds had fared thus far. Pulling on my glove, I joined Germer in the portable mews.

"I see you have done your work diligently, Germer; these pigskin jesses have been renewed and well oiled." Removing my sparrow hawk from its perch, I put it to glove with care. A new glove it was, made of stiff leather and strange to my bird. She probed with restless claws.

"Can you carry Sybelle's hawk on your fist and Eleanor's in the basket? I'll tote Florine's. It is such a small bird." Germer made his way toward the baskets while balancing Sybelle's peregrine on his steady fist.

Germer grinned broadly, proud of his mastery. "Her majesty has a good thought here. The meadow offers fine hunting and exercises the birds. I've had no time to work them in recent days because I was so busy getting the horses ready and helping with the pack animals."

We stepped from the mews and started down the slope to search out the others. "Let's have the sparrow hawk start with rook birds, but the peregrine would do well over by that far swall to the east."

Germer agreed, motioning with his head toward the sun, lower in the sky, casting golden hues on the shadowed swall. "There will be hare over there or squirrel, I'll wager."

"Good. Let's beat the fox to them."

At Germer's instruction, the servants spread a thick rug on the sedge at the top of the high slope near the fringe of the woods.

"Excellent, Germer! You have chosen the most workable site." I trudged up the slight incline, holding my bird steady and straight. The hawk's sharp talons searching for a familiar hold dug fitfully into the new glove. "Yes, all is strange now," I whispered, "there will be much strangeness from now on. We best get used to adventure."

The bird bated vigorously in frustration. jangling the small bells tied to her legs, just above the jesses. Delicate oriental bells, one a semitone above the other, rang so happily that, I felt like singing out in joy.

As a girl, I had sensed a wonderful magic when first I had worked the hawks. What a feeling of freedom to watch my bird soar on the winds, a surveyor of fields and hedges, rocky climes and castles. Those days on the bluffs of Gascony returned to me, watching my first small sparrow hawk ride the wind currents as they blew in off the sea. What would it be like, I had wondered, to be so free? I had wanted to spread my arms and run with the hawk, over the fields speckled red with poppies and aloft, trace the line of chalky rim that stretched along the azure coast! But I had learned that a good hawker remains still with a ready fist to let the bird roam free, while its mistress stays fixed to take the prey from her returning bird, so only in my imagination did I sail above the meadows.

Now, with the long-shadowed afternoon dappling the banks of the Moselle, I held my rising excitement in check and spoke calmly to my hawk, still fretting on my arm. But beyond the newness of the surroundings, beyond the sense of adventure that had begun to ripple through me, I had to admit that much of my excitement hinged on the growing realization that, due to papal declaration, Sir Geoffrey Rancon would be in my company daily!

"Remain calm," I advised. Slowing down, I maintained an even pace, but it was not a true measure of the joy and anticipation I felt on this eve.

"We can see the slope's wide sweep here, Germer, and the wind is right. Should one of these critters choose to stay with her prey down in that thicketed swall, we can hear her bells. Feel the breeze. It has picked up and will carry the bell sound to us. Look how it ruffles their plumes."

The queen's bird sported a plume of dark purple feathers tied with pieces of spun gold that glittered now in the slant of sunlight. All but the working hawk remained in its jeweled hood and each waited her turn on separate ring perches, which Germer had wrestled into the dry ground.

Eleanor's hawk hunted first, soaring high, then swooping toward the sun. It dipped quickly to strike its prey, then returned to Eleanor's ready fist where she landed like a heavy blow. In the bird's talons, a plump hare with its neck broken, hung lifeless, blood dripping from its mouth.

"You offer me your quarry, good creature!" Eleanor shouted gleefully holding the bird aloft. "Such a fine bird! Here Germer, share the head with her, save us the rest for supper. Take it to cook to dress."

Sybelle's sparrow hawk lifted off with a great surge, to pursue a rook in mid-air. We cheered loudly, and Sybelle allowed her bird to devour the whole catch undisturbed.

"You next, Madeleine. Whoops, now let her be off."

I lifted the hood by its plume. My bird, still nervous, bated vigorously once again. When I released her, she shot far into the open blue sky.

"She is going so high, Madeleine! Will she come back?" Eleanor ran to my side. "We have worked her long days. Surely she is trained well enough."

"Oh, I am not worried. She is fidgety in this strange place. She'll return with a fine squirrel, I'm sure." I knew how I had worked her long hours, often until dusk, coming back to the courtyard with cold, cramped hands. Now, in these golden shades, my elated spirits would not let me fret.

Soon, sailing low over the hilly contour, the hawk came into view. It was not a squirrel she was carrying but another small hare. She dropped it as she hit forcefully on my extended fist.

"Gather it up, Germer, we'll have a good stew." Placing it beside the others, the lad waited for the next bird to fly.

"And you are next, Florine." Eleanor clapped her hands together to hurry the girl who had reluctantly joined us.

In a half-hearted manner, Florine pulled on her glove and removed her bird's hood. The dark merlin hawk flew from her fist immediately. She anxiously followed the bird, her dark-circled eyes tracking while the hunter flew sharply upward toward a white cloud floating overhead. Finally, its tilted wings stayed still as the bird floated in a slow circle, riding the upper wind current toward the river. A sharp dive, and then, amid cheers, she was on her return.

I watched Florine's technique. We had not hawked together before. She blanched as she held out her fist and closed her eyes.

"No," she cried, "Oh no! I can't." With the insistent whirr of wings coming toward her, she began to retch, her face held a terrified expression.

"Pray, St. Catherine," she called aloud, "do not cover my face. No!" she called hoarsely, "you will suffocate me!" Loathing seemed to engulf her as the hawk wings came closer. She put her free hand over her face, throwing her gloved hand across her breasts.

I raced to her side, supporting her arm from beneath to hold her gloved fist extended. Blood dripped from the dove clutched in the merlin hawk's talons. Florine began to sink to the ground, her face a contorted, fearful mask. I lowered her carefully to the sedge.

"What is it Florine?" I knelt at her side trying to comfort her.

"I—I don't know what is the matter. Nothing, really; I need to rest. I feel so tired."

"I think that you must see Thecla." I helped her to her feet, nodding to Sybelle.

Sybelle led the distraught girl toward the medicine wain. I had no inkling what would help Florine, but perhaps Thecla would have some remedy.

I gathered up her glove and carried her bird back to the mews. Florine had not seemed herself. Yes, she had changed since we were all together in Vezelay. Something seemed amiss. It isn't as if she had left her husband behind, for good-natured Hugh was one of the queen's most reliable advisors and would travel with us. Perhaps, though it seemed farfetched to me, she just may hate the sport, as some women did.

"We had not sensed it." I spoke aloud.

"Sensed what?" Eleanor looked puzzled.

"Florine must detest the sport. Why else would she act that way?"

"It seems o'er squeamish to me," Eleanor paused, "but I remember that Florine was always an easily frightened child. I had assumed she had outgrown it." Her tone held an edge of impatience.

"Perhaps she'll feel better with some rest."

When I found Florine alone, I attempted to delve further into the cause of her strange behavior. She was quite short with me, saying she just needed some respite. Feeling somewhat put off, I left her in Thecla's care for the evening.

"We will celebrate this first night of our journey, Germer," Eleanor ordered. "Send word to the others to join me for songs and entertainment." Soon, guests began to arrive, other ladies not in the royal company, and knights who were members of the advanced guard, seating themselves on the many carpets Germer had set out for them. Wines and cakes graced a small table, while a maidservant kept a vigilant eye out for the lacewings and moths hoping to settle on the sweets.

Midsummer dusk washed the lilac-colored sky long after the first star appeared. Around our tent, humid June air rang with the sounds of crickets and cicadas, background to the songs of Jacques and Eliaze. The last shore birds called over the river's swirl.

Above the lively conversation, the sound of men felling trees cracked through the woods nearby. They were busy constructing rafts for the crossing to take place soon after the arrival of the king. My heart raced. The arrival of the king meant the arrival of Rancon!

Jacques and Eliaze had just finished a tuneful roundeley and were bowing to the applause when I thought I heard sounds coming from beyond the woods.

"Hold a moment, will you? I hear other music not from here. Shh. Listen."

A long silence followed. Wimpled heads turned toward the forest to listen. By the night-dusk, the women's faces, framed like frescoes on a chapel wall, glowed in the firelight.

From out of the shadowed forest came the clear sounds of a horn. Like the ancient trumpet calls of old, ringing from steeps and meadows, from antiquity's forests and mountains, these haunting notes heralded the measured step of marching men.

Eleanor jumped to her feet, swiftly dispatching a messenger to her royal guard to light torches at the edge of the forest. At the same time, a runner sent from King Louis burst into the clearing to announce the arrival of the king, his army and the pilgrim hordes.

The rustle of jeweled bridles and clip-clop of horses' hooves rose from the depths of the forest paths. Wagons clattered above the murmurs of hundreds of human voices and rumbled above the calls of children. Swept along, carried on the wave of pilgrims' chanting, thousands of voices soared beyond the leafy heights.

Behind the singing devout trudged merchants, engineers, wagon masters, and wainwrights. Leather masters, tent makers, groomsmen, blacksmiths, armorers, and steel smiths preceded the companies of foot soldiers, leather shields at their backs in marching position, bows at their sides and daggers at their belts.

Louis' standard, held aloft, cleared the way for the ganflons of the lords of Aquitaine and Bordeaux. How valiantly Count Geoffrey rode at the head of Eleanor's proud knights! His sword hilt studded in rubies and diamonds captured the torchlight's gleam. Did I only imagine that he smiled at me?

The shield bearers followed in turn, leading carts that rattled with armor and lances. Behind them, came the foot soldiers and bowmen, not so straight and proud as the knights, but an orderly group. A break in the military ranks left a void at the forest entrance. Soon countless pilgrims poured forth in full chant, their eyes glowing deep with faith. Clothed in their plain gray garb, they carried little with them other than their pilgrims' purses—and their souls.

The lords of Champagne, the dukes of Normandy and Langres followed the counts of Main and Flanders, each with their own contingent of squires and shield bearers.

In the darkness, the black-clad Knights Templar seemed invisible, until the torchlight caught the bright red cross covering the fronts of their tunics. New recruits swelled their ranks, close-tonsured, muscles hardened by drill. They looked neither to right nor left.

I spied my brother, Charles, in the crowd of a large force of the Hospitaller knights as they marched out from the forest. Their white crosses with the split horizontal arms shown new as did the fresh, sweet faces of holy youth who had left farm and field to aid the ill and faltering on the holy march. Charles' shy wave could not hide the pride that marked his bearing.

Cardinal Lisieux and the Bishop of Langre formed the apex of the royal guard. Galeran, eyes sunken and brooding, rode atop an elaborately cushioned saddle. At his side, Odo of Duilio, the second watchdog monk, sat atop a gray pony, his looks, sharp and dark as a shrew's, darting here and there.

Following close behind, his pilgrim's staff held high in one hand, the bannered oriflamme in the other, King Louis stepped into the torches' arc. He wore no crown. His silver pilgrim's cross glittering on his shoulder was the only emblem that distinguished him from the droves. Above a beatific smile, his eyes shone with tears and he seemed swept along on the waves of chanted promise. The surging melody floated back and forth among the trees,

"He who goes forth with Louis, surely his soul will dwell in Paradise."

When he sighted Eleanor in the crowd, her golden circlet crown gleaming in the firelight, love, faith and purpose filled his soul. Lips moving in prayer, Louis rode close to our area, fixing his eyes on Eleanor. "Ah, yes, my queen, you are with me this day in Paradise. I will see to your soul."

Though Eleanor was at my side, if she heard Louis, she didn't show it. She was already planning ahead.

"Tomorrow we leave the boundaries of France and set out on our grand adventure. I will lead my forces across the river into the Holy Roman Empire," Her eyes blazed triumphantly. Torchlight flickered across the angular shadows of her face.

Anticipation pulsed through me. I slept fitfully that night, wide awake at sunrise. The sky glowed Mars red.

CHAPTER 9

On the Danube

"How glorious to be free from Louis' confining nobles and grim-faced clergy." Eleanor, her eyes dancing with pleasure, looked resplendent in a deep blue tunic. She sipped plum wine as she sat on a pile of green Turkish cushions, sheltered from the sun by a wide awning, its golden tassels swaying with the motion of the boat. We were sailing for Beograd by way of the pulsing Danube River aboard a craft that was a step-masted vessel with the long mast lashed larboard along with the canvas sheets and halyards. We were seated on cushioned benches along the side, and at our backs, the steersman worked the tiller directing the oarsmen, six on each side. Personal chattel, tent poles and carpets rode yarboard to serve as ballast, while the colorful banners of Aquitaine, France, Toulouse and Flanders snapped both fore and aft as the boat's full wake splashed brilliant gems to the sunlight.

Eleanor stretched luxuriously. "I've always known I was meant to travel far beyond the boundaries of Louis' kingdom. What a fortunate decision to come by water. I wouldn't have missed this festive journey. And now, Sybelle, since runners were dispatched through the Benedictine chain of monasteries, we're given the opportunity to visit your cousin, the Abbess Gertrude, along the way toward Linz."

"Yes, we should soon be there," Sybelle replied. "However, as I recall the stormy meeting in Metz, I think Galeran went too far when he convinced the king's council that separate parties, taking separate routes, would aid the purposes of the crusade." Sybelle fretted with her flute. "I shall never recover from my amazement at Phillip's response; that a man of such military experience would consent to such a delightful diversion."

"As I recall his position," I added, trying to keep the sarcasm from my voice, "he said it would aid the army's travel to be free of all the cumbersome chattel that women bring with them. 'A true army,' he declared, 'marching by land travels light. Let the queen and her companions go by boat, an excellent tactic. We'll be well rid of them and can meet up at Beograd.'"

Sybelle winced at the memory. "Phillip seemed happy enough to be done with us." Her voice had a momentary wistful tone, her customary frown deepening. She toyed nervously with her small flute.

"And we of them!" Eleanor chimed, ignoring Sybelle's concern.

"Yes, Louis' aides were very surprised when you agreed so rapidly, Eleanor." I stifled a giggle.

"And how pleasant a time it has been, avoiding the heat and dust these summer days—and the snarling dispositions of the king's watchdogs, dreadful Galeran and obdurate Odo, protecting Louis' chastity, stationing themselves at his tent, day and night. I've had quite enough of them."

"I know what's been decreed is offensive to you, and Louis offered no resistance at all. I don't blame you for feeling insulted, for resenting Louis' so-called watchdogs. But, Eleanor, we're back to the same disagreement, the real purpose of the journey. For Louis, it is a deeply religious event. For you, admittedly, it's a marvelous adventure."

"And what is it for you, dear cousin?" Eleanor parried knowingly, mirth dancing at the edges of her lips.

"Oho, touché." I felt the blood seeping into my cheeks, for in truth, I had begun to glory in the sinful condition of accidia…and Sir Geoffrey's presence. Hour after indolent hour of river journey lay behind us. Days spent exchanging smiles with him as Jacques and Eliaze sang the jolly songs of Provence, meeting his eyes as Eleanor and Sybelle recited poetry while our boat slid by the waysides of the Danube past slopes fragrant with pine and beech.

Yesterday afternoon, thunderstorms had sent us scrambling under the canvas awning to escape the large, cool drops. Turbulence churned the waters. Fed by the storm, the swift current swirled dangerously close to great rock outcroppings. The river seemed a blue-black vortex. The helmsman, heavy by his tiller, called orders thick-voiced, while his men, hard at their oars, struggled against the current, attempting to stay the craft in a torrent of foam and splash.

I clutched the bench's edge so hard my fingers numbed; clenched teeth held back dread and I closed my eyes as though to shield myself magically from disaster. Suddenly, Sir Geoffrey was close by. He secured me tightly to his side, his muscled arm high under my breasts. I felt safe, and more for a fleeting moment. I desired him, wanting him to remain close, taking pleasure in the feel of him.

When momentum slackened and oar blades gleamed once more in a serene arc over calmer waters, Geoffrey left me without speaking, as though there had been only casual contact between us, yet his glance held mine for a long moment assuring me that all was well. His look, far from casual, rushed color to my cheeks. I guess my expression had not escaped Eleanor's notice (little does). Perhaps her innuendoes were not off the mark. I resolved to be more devoted to the high purpose of the journey, and the abbey at Linz would offer an excellent opportunity. I was readying a retort to Eleanor's jibe when the boatmaster's orders cut through the idyllic time.

"Take 'er close into the shore. Careful to steer for the sandbar! Watch the mud now!"

"We must be near the abbey, Sybelle." I hurried to boatside where boathands, thick-boned and strong, set themselves and grasped their poles, pushing the long boats from mid-river closer to the embankment. The men, sweating freely, forced the boat toward the shore, while others on the foredeck struggled hard at their poles holding the craft back against the forward surge of the great Danube. The workers, whose faces bore the look of dark leather, were a filthy lot, their soiled red sashes wound around stained, worn leggings. They grunted and urged one another at the labor.

"Throw out the lines!" The steersman barked to hands standing yarboard.

"Lower now the door!" the master called. With each man holding his station, a creaking chain and wheel apparatus lowered a section of the side planking. Like the rest of the ship, it was clinker built, daubed with a heavy pitch. When it was thrust out slowly, the siding reached to the shore and formed an unstable gangplank for us to disembark.

"We're going ashore!" Eleanor stood next to me, wayward wisps of her golden hair dancing at the nape of her neck. "Sybelle, are we approaching your cousin's abbey?"

"Yes, it must be so! Look there, the message got through!" She pointed beyond the grassy slopes to a red-roofed abbey settled against rising hills covered with vines. The sun spread the feathered clouds and splashed ochre on the high abbey walls where a floating Angivan banner welcomed us.

Through a wrought-iron gate, a line of black-robed nuns made their way toward the large makeshift table that had been hastily set up under a white awning. Donning my white linen wimple, I hurried across the damp, weedy basin halfway up from the river's shore and headed toward the awning to join the queen and Sybelle. The three of us approached Sister Gertrude, Sybelle's kin, who greeted us.

Gertrude had deep blue eyes. Strands of reddish hair had slipped from underneath her wimple. "We will pray with you at holy mass.

May our souls be remembered at the Holy Sepulcher. And may our prayers to the Holy Virgin protect you as you go."

She motioned to the standing line of nuns. "Some of our members have made this grueling pilgrimage when the Franks had secured the roadways, made the way safe. Now it is more dangerous. Many adventures await you." Gertrude seemed lost in thought before she turned to me, addressing me directly. "Certainly, for you. You must know whom you seek."

Mystified by the singling out, and recalling my recent resolution, I could only murmur, "I pray it is so, Sister Abbess." Still it was an unsettling exchange. Anxious to change the subject, I inquired of Sybelle,"Where is Florine?"

"She says she does not feel well again today."

"We will send Thecla to tend her after mass."

"Thecla is with her now."

The frail priestly tenor at the altar silenced us. Outlined against the clovered slopes, the black-robed sisters' responses sailed past the heads of the faithful and flowed with the waters of the great river.

"Kyrie eleison."

"Lord have mercy on us."

"Christe eleison.

"Christ have mercy on us."

I bent my head in prayer, but only after I had noticed Geoffrey's gaze intense upon me. I lowered my eyes, ignoring the flush creeping up to meet them. Desire stole my attentiveness at the offertory prayer.

"Agnus Dei qui tollis peccata mundi."

"Lamb of God, who takes away the sins of the world, have mercy on us."

It is not my intention to falter on my soul's pilgrimage toward salvation, I scolded myself, but even when Geoffrey is not in sight, his presence persists. The image of his eyes twinkling deep beneath his dark brows nudged through the veil of my prayers. I closed my eyes tightly to shut out all distraction save the sweet chanted responses floating from the Benedictine choir.

After mass, Rancon, handsome in a claret-colored jacket, joined us for a festive meal consisting of fruits from the convent orchards nearby, and from the river, the morning's fresh catch, fleshy river trout, cooked over coals along the sedge bank.

Sister Gertrude expressed her concern over the Teuton marauders marching through their lands, stealing food and supplies as they went, all in the name of Christ.

"It is a problem, and one which the Emperor Conrad should see to," acknowledged Eleanor. "I hope our people will not commit such evil deeds, but it is hard to say, since many were already criminals, long before any holy march."

"And," Geoffrey added, "there are always the brigands who will sell a loaf of bread for a lump of gold. That's where most trouble erupts, trouble and bloodshed. I don't envy King Louis and his men the task of maintaining order when the marching line is so long and unwieldy. I have by far the lighter load, here with the vanguard." He looked at us, wearing a wry smile, "Here we have almost no misbehaving."

He rose from the table and winked at me. Feelings again flared unexpectedly through me. I must pray the harder.

The Abbess said her farewells and we prepared to leave. The master waved his arm and Sir Geoffrey boarded with the royal guard as did the forward complement of knights in the pilot boat. Lances and shields rattled aboard. Each man placed his shield on one of several pegs studding the gunnels.

We boarded the next vessel. There was room for Florine, but still feeling poorly, she chose to travel with Thecla in the vessel following, perhaps not a wise choice for at the shore's edge behind us, a scene of confusion and curses erupted where the flat barges carrying two-and four-horse carts had yet to load. In a voice that carried strong above the men's whistles and invectives, Thecla, arms flailing, stood on the shore.

"Take care, you laggards, that you don't spill my unguents and remedies." Holding the skirt of her russet tunic high, she followed the men into the water to rail at them the more.

Sisters lined the shore. Their black habits reflected in rippling blue water like pieces of jet in a colorful mosaic. Twenty white handkerchiefs fluttered like doves' wings as they chanted a traditional farewell, "Dominus Vobiscum. God be with you."

The queen's boat put off slowly from the cove and onto the river's deep vibrant byway. The last ship in the convoy bore the royal travel wain, glistening deep red in the August sun. The emblem words, "Quem Quaeretis," shown bold and clear, and remembering the abbesses' remarks, "You must know whom you seek," I felt a prickly confusion as I pondered what their import was to me.

CHAPTER 10

Nearing Hungary

Side by side, Geoffrey and I gazed at the towering eeyries above the river where rugged castles stood bold as Valquerie sentinels. Past them, on precipitous ledges, monasteries guarded hillside vineyards carpeting their way to the forest's edge. Hooded monks strolled in meditative paces at the wall's rim and observed our indolent convoy gliding past. The worldly joys of lute and laughter floated upward toward their towers, luring them from prayers.

"How much longer on the water, Geoffrey?" Eleanor inquired after Eliaze had put aside her lute.

"Not long, Majesty. We disembark past Beograd, at the river's confluence. It is beyond there that the Danube turns sharply toward warring Wallachia. We have no wish to go there. We'll await the king's massive contingent at Beograd, where he will cross to meet us."

When he spoke, I found myself fascinated by Geoffrey's mouth and the way his upper lip had a tightness to it when he wished to make a serious point. Yet the twinkle rarely left the deep hazel green of his eyes.

"I've sent messengers ahead, and with God's help, they will begin the work of getting supplies. I'm to purchase more boats for the king and his army. The crossing could take some time because of our numbers. From there it's still many a good days' march to Constantinople."

Eleanor sank to the cushions and reached for a goblet of wine. "Ahh, I can smell the orient!"

Geoffrey turned to me and whispered, "Yes, M'lady, new uncharted lands." His arm reached around me. My response was much too worldly.

We were but two days away from Beograd. Throughout the day I had been mesmerized by the endless wheat fields stretching like giant oriental fans open to the sunlight, blue corn flowers and bright red poppies dotting each curved ridge. Suddenly, the watchman on the pilot ship split the placid mood, "Yo Ho! Count Rancon! Look to the bluff. A rider! He carries the warning flag!"

We craned our necks upward. There a horseman waved a banner back and forth from his position above the river. The pennant, a red axe on a black background, originated from the king's land forces and signaled danger. The muscles in my stomach tensed.

Geoffrey strained to see the messenger who drove his horse at a hard pace over difficult terrain to keep up. Catching sight of the emblematic signal, Rancon's jaw tightened.

"Haul to, and anchor at the first inlet, captain." The oarsman pulled hard and our vanguard boat angled into an estuary. The following vessels berthed close by, out of the mainstream. Anchors hurled into the shallows startled flocks of small white egrets that shot up from the dark green water lily pads dressing the water's edge.

We had come to a halt in a wide marshy cove at the outer reaches of the vast Hungarian plain. I wondered what urgent news caused us to put in so abruptly.

Tall reeds stood guard at the shore like hostile sentinels, foreign and threatening. Reaching as high as twelve feet, they overshadowed my view and obscured the king's messenger from sight. At intervals, his small deer horn signaled his location guiding the searchers to a wooded rise where he awaited them. Geoffrey put the bowmen on alert. His knights, moving swiftly, fastened on their scabbards, still warm from the sun.

"Disembark all vessels, with the Lord's protection! Follow the vanguard ashore."

Rancon's captain peered upriver, cupped his hands to order, "Let the last boat answer."

From a distance beyond the curve came the bowman's response, "Disembark all vessels, we will sir, for the love of God, sir."

Quick to respond, I doubled my tunic and tied it high around my waist with a cord. I took Geoffrey's offered hand, felt him release it without a look.

"See to the women, Germer." He barked his command and was over the side and gone. I lurched my way down the improvised gangplank into the gray, oozing marsh mud that swept for several hundred feet inland. Reeds towered above my head. Earlier thunderstorms, now clearing, had left a damp chill to the air.

"Where to, Germer?" The slight tremor in my voice annoyed me. I couldn't see any way through the reeds, and felt panic when I sunk up to my knees in the quagmire. Why this sudden landing? I had searched Rancon's face for answers, but he was intent on his command, barking orders, checking arms, and seeing to supplies. My body still rocked with boat motion when Germer reached to steady me.

"Look off to the right," he gestured with his staff. "You can see where Raoul has hacked a narrow path through the reeds. There on the rise."

"Oh, yes." Dwarfed among the reeds and their rattling sharp-smelling spindles, I turned to beckon Eleanor and Sybelle in my direction. "Over here! There is a narrow path."

They had taken up their tunics to the waist and tied their wimples around their heads in the way of village women; fastened around the back at the nape of their necks, protecting them from the vengeful mosquitos swarming to protest their disruption from secret ponds.

"Can you see where Raoul is? We'll put up there." They slogged on to join us.

"God willing it is drier than this. We must make a fire quickly to discourage these pests." Eleanor swung her hand around her head. "I hate to be bitten by these devils!"

Sybelle turned, looking back toward the other boats. "Dear me, I wonder if Florine is alright. Oh, thanks be given, I see that she is with Thecla. Florine does not look well."

"You are right, Sybelle." Eleanor pulled her foot from the ooze, shook it, then took another step, shuddering slightly. "And she eats little, yet remains nauseated. I wonder if she's with child, don't you? She has said nothing to me. Has she spoken of it to either of you?"

I swept a mosquito from my face and took another step in the forbidding goo. As though to dispel my own fear of danger, I embarked upon a lengthy discussion of Florine.

"No, she has said only that she is sorry that she is not better company. I asked her if anything was wrong, but she just shook her head, and put me off. I'm mystified."

"Wait for me," Sybelle called out, "I can't keep my balance in this treacherous stuff."

She took her small dagger from its sheath at her waist and cut through the tall reed to make herself a staff. Germer, quick to seize the idea, soon had staffs for us all. Still, the mud pulled at our legs, making progress slow. Germer forged ahead toward Raoul. A small water snake slithered out of his way toward us.

Sybelle beat the water with her staff. "No more of those creatures, wicked tempters of Eve!" With each step, she continued to snap the water ahead of her with her light staff.

"I am puzzled, too, Madeleine," Sybelle agreed, "but maybe Eleanor is right. She might be pregnant," she gasped, slapping at the snakes. "I have tried to help her, but she shuns my approaches and wants to stay only in Thecla's company. I hope I haven't said something to offend her. Can't any of us give her some comfort? She isn't herself, so withdrawn"

"Well, I don't know if she is herself or not." Eleanor took a long step up to the shore, finally free from the pull of the mud. "I have always found her to be quiet. I thought to be away from the court and with us might bring her joy. I'm afraid I misjudged."

"I'll try to approach her. I'll talk to Thecla first, though I feel a stirring of guilt. I've tried several times to engage Florine myself. She cloaks herself in veil of silence, not that she is ill-mannered but just absent."

At the top of the rise, I turned to pull Sybelle up the slippery bank. The wind had picked up, blowing from the east where the massive range of mountains hovering in the distance provided barrier to the press of Barbarian hoards. Their granite peaks wore a pale purple at dusk. A chill shuddered down my back, and the pinch of the slate-colored mud caking my calves felt like stiff cold leggings.

Free of the marshland, we were now among the sallows, their green, feathery brush resembling dwarfed willows. A clearing, an often-used site, would do well for the pavilions to be set up. From the rise, I watched the servants hauling up the gear.

Geoffrey, his hand on his sword, and followed by his aides, made for the gray-green alders where the messenger waited in the shadows. After a lengthy conversation with the king's man, he approached the crude site where we had gathered around a copper tub set upon the fire. We had washed away the river mud and put on fresh tunics.

"Geoffrey, what is amiss? What's the news?" Eleanor looked toward the thicket where the men had met.

"There's danger, your Majesty. While we have had a peaceful voyage on the waterways, such is not the case for the land forces. It seems that Abbess Gertrude was right, Emperor Conrad and his men have caused havoc. They don't just forage the countryside but pillage as well, murdering the native folk at will. The Bulgarians are up in arms and filled with revenge. They have brutally attacked many of Conrad's forces. There is every sign that they will do the same to us, waiting for us at different points along the shore." He lowered his voice. "Now there exists peril of ambush at each supply station on land as well as on the waterways. There are Bulgarian pirates who would kill us without conscience. From now on, we will put in at unknown places on the route and reconnoiter before we set up camp on land, just as we have done tonight. And, we must watch for pirates as well."

"Then we must take great care." Turning to us, Eleanor directed, "Keep your daggers in your girdles at all times. We'll fetch the chain vests, too."

As Eleanor spoke, bowmen and knights of the royal cadre quietly surrounded the encampment, their backs to the tents, their eyes riveted past the slope toward the rise thick with a scramble of hawthorn and hazel bushes.

"I hadn't anticipated danger before the Holy Land. The king and Galeran were always busy with treaty negotiations. We hadn't anticipated that Emperor Conrad would proceed without Louis." Eleanor paused for a moment, observing the movement of the guard, then inquired of Rancon, "And what news of the king?"

"The king's army has been assured safe conduct through Hungary with markets serving all the needs. Even our poor continue, by God's goodness, to eat."

Geoffrey moved to my side. "But I've been ordered to go without delay into Beograd to negotiate our safe passage into Bulgaria. From there to Sofia, and then to Adrianopolis at the borders of the Emperor Manuel's domain. We're promised good treatment from him. The messenger informed me that Louis and other holy men have held several meetings with the Greeks and have arrived at a friendly concord. Now I must check the patrols."

When Rancon returned to give his report, the moon, wide as the river, had risen from over the plains to the east. A thousand geese appeared and silvered the horizon with moonlit wings. Calling to one another like prophetic swan, they set the sky aswirl and floated earthward, one by endless one, to feed among the marshy reeds.

I ached at the thought of Geoffrey's leaving us, however briefly, but my question hid my true feelings.

"Should we be ready to set out at dawn then?"

"As soon as the mist is off the river." Geoffrey replied in clipped tones. There was no twinkle to his glance.

"We should have not unpacked at all. We will begin now to repack." Eleanor called a terse order to Germer to begin repacking before asking, "How much do the others know?"

"The men are all informed."

"Good. Send heralds to all the tents. By the grace of God we have been forewarned. We'll be ready to leave at dawn."

A supper of sturgeon and wine briefly dissolved the sense of impending danger. We listened to the quiet, careful planning between Geoffrey and his captains. But now, with clouds covering the moon and Geoffrey so engrossed with the details of his mission, my shoulders felt tense and tight as a thickening ground fog began to obscure our surroundings.

As though reading my thoughts, Eleanor rose quickly and spoke to Rancon.

"We will be ready at your earliest signal. Good night, gentlemen."

After I lit a torch from the fire, we carefully picked our way over tent stakes and fog-shrouded baggage.

Huddled on our sleeping mats, we were shielded by the stacked baggage and rolled carpets which Germain had packed against the sides of the tent.

Once settled in, Sybelle lead the Compline devotions, a practice that had become neglected in the holiday mood which had so prevailed on the water journey.

Dear Mother of the Prince of Peace

Protect us from the evil foe

And bliss at death on us bestow.

Amen.

I slept fitfully, waking when the night guards walked their rounds. At the guards' change, I thought it was Geoffrey's voice I heard through my sleep. Perhaps it was the owl who had called to the reedy sentinels on her night watch. Or was it Florine who sobbed quietly to the dark?

Suddenly, a sharp breeze stirred through the tent. Next a hand covered my mouth. Terror-stricken, I turned in the blackness to face Rancon lying beside me. He kissed me tenderly on the cheek, then put his finger to my lips, quieting my words, but not my pounding heart.

"Lie still, sweet Lady Madeleine. We will be up in a few moments. The fog has lifted and we will break camp early and slide down river in this moonlight. The scout has returned to tell us of pirates in the next cove. We will glide right by them. But first," he held his lips to my ear and whispered, his breath hot and close, "I had to lie beside you, to feel your warmth. Forgive me, Lady." His lips moved to my neck, then to my mouth, warm and searching.

I began to tremble. There was no thought of turning him away. I wanted to push aside the cover and urge him closer.

"I must take my leave now." He kissed my cheek again and sprang lightly to his feet. He was gone as he had appeared, silently. With a soft step, he reached Eleanor's mat.

"Up, your Majesty, and quickly. We are using the moonlight. Watch your step. The pavilions will be struck at once and then we are on our way. There is no time to lose. Lady Madeleine will tell you the rest."

We stole aboard in the last moonlight, and laid flat on the decks, bunched under a thick covering of skins. Our convoy slipped by the glowing fires of the cursing, carousing pirates. Silent as a fleet of crocodiles, we floated past the danger.

Miles past the pirates' cove, we berthed again, and stayed off the river for a full day and a night. The second morning, the mists and geese had lifted skyward in slow gray swirls. Wrapped against the chill in long vair vests, we stood at the ship's prow. While the frenzied activity that usually accompanied every loading followed its routine, this morning, was different. Guards stood at each gangplank, while silent men loaded and prodded the animals, urging them to be still. The ship passenger assignments had changed. Squires boarded with their knights. Weapons were carefully accounted for; lines and halyards neatly stowed, oarsmen at the ready.

Geoffrey climbed aboard every ship to check the bowmen posted astern each craft. He spoke with each helmsman, reminding them that they were in enemy territory, never taking his eyes off the thick woods beyond the marshes. Finally, he dropped to the deck of our boat, reporting to Eleanor that all was in readiness. He closed his heavy vest against a stiff wind. It began to drizzle.

"Helmsman," he called, "give the order to weigh anchor, by the Grace of God!"

"Weigh anchor! By the grace of God." The call traveled to each ship at metered intervals.

In a roil of water, the royal vessel pulled away from the inlet. A flock of purple herons glided down to disappear among the rippling tall reeds. With our arms around each other, we huddled on the foredeck by the brazier's sputtering fire.

So occupied was Rancon that he behaved as though his rash, romantic incident with me had never occurred. Or had it? Shivering, I felt sadness settle like a mantle of mist around me. Now we were bound for Beograd to join the land forces. Our glorious Danube summer had slipped away. I realized how much I had savored the close company of Sir Geoffrey. Would that vanish as well?

CHAPTER 11

Sofia

The crossing at Beograd had its hazards. A few horses were drowned due to careless handling, some cargo floated away, but considering the numbers, it went fairly well. Once all were accounted for, we headed for Sofia where we would meet up with the Frankish land forces. It was there I hoped to catch up with my brother, Charles.

Near dusk, the smoking fires and colorful pavilions of Louis' sprawling contingent came into view. After our own tents were set up, I braved the carnival atmosphere in search of Charles. Soon, I was lost in a crush of foot soldiers, bowmen and knights, all breaking ranks to seek family or friends. Though the ban on intermingling had been read at daily Mass, I observed that many a maidservant and bowman were most amorous in their greetings, exchanging kisses not to be interpreted as the kiss of peace.

I thought of the brief moment when Rancon lay at my side to tell us of the threatening dangers on the river. The longing I felt surprised me. I had seen little of him since that night, for he had remained occupied and aloof on the remainder of our journey, often taking a watch on other vessels in the convoy. I hoped that now we were reunited with the land forces, perhaps I might soon see him, to speak to him, to welcome his arms, his lips.

However, my attention was given to finding my brother. Though the turmoil was great, I knew that Charles should have no trouble seeing me in the white tunic with the dark red cross at its front. Eleanor had thought it would be fitting to be so attired once the grand pilgrimage was reunited again.

"Madeleine!" The call came from the charter wagons. I wheeled around and there stood Charles. No wonder I had not spotted him sooner. He had grown through the summer, his tunic sleeves were much too short for the long, muscled arms they covered. He swept me up in a crushing embrace.

"Greetings, my sister. To see you once again! How well you look. God has graced you with good health."

"Oh yes, my brother. And he has graced you with more height than I would have thought possible in so short a time. Come, let's get away from this confusion. I've been jostled long enough." I beckoned toward the row of tents set up a few hundred yards up the slope.

We found shelter under one of the dining canvases set up by the Hospitallers. Rough-hewn logs served as benches. A group of young men ate plain bread and some gruel made of green peas and smoked pork. They viewed me with suspicion.

"May I present my sister, Lady Madeleine, with the queen's entourage."

The men nodded and continued to eat in silence, all the while attempting a surveillance of me in a knight's tunic bearing a red cross on its front.

We found a bench away from the others where we could talk. I began to tell of our wondrous river journey when Charles interrupted me.

"I would not say too much of your idle journey, sister," Charles teased as he revealed more. It seemed that now the forces were merged and readying to move on to Constantinople, Galeran had become more rancorous with every mile. According to Charles, Galeran was heard to say how he resented the Aquitanians the more, especially those who took the river route, while so many other Franks endured the harder days' fast march.

"It must nettle Galeran to think of our entourage dallying its way aboard boats filled with luxurious pillows and padding, sweets and wines, while he and the other men had bounced astride their horses all that time."

"It is said that his castration wound bothers him." Bless Charles, ever the sympathetic. "You know about that?"

"Indeed I do. Some surgeon monk got o'er steamed in their own fine ale, maimed him badly while performing the castration operation. Now he detests his hours spent in the saddle."

"Sister, more than that. I heard it first hand. I was tending an ailing bishop in Louis' tent, when Galeran flew into a rage and ranted at Louis, at the king. 'Yes, Majesty, the Aquitainians dally with the queen, her endless carts of baggage and her gaggle of servants, particularly her wanton maidservants. Their disgusting actions, showing of breasts, raising their tunics, will bring us all to hell.'"

Charles's gray eyes widened. "Galeran does so loathe the carnal behaviors he had to recite, 'Yes,' he spat out the words, 'they incite lustful sin and debauchery among the troops and even our own knights.'" Having put away a trencher of porridge, Charles was about to embark on another report when a page rushed up to us.

"Charles, sir, you are needed in the infirmary."

We said our farewells, planning to see each other next day. I sat quietly with Charles' information. I had hoped that once we were on the road and working as a competent unit on our own, we would have done with the Templar's rantings. But no, for the sins of Eve are ever present. I was still debating whether to tell Eleanor of this latest outburst when she stormed into the dining tent, throwing her riding crop to the ground.

"How that wretched monk infuriates me," she exploded, "he is guilty of alchemy, having transformed Louis into a—a—puppet! That man allowed me only a few minutes with my own husband." Though her eyes blazed, there were remnants of tears on her cheeks. "Oh, Madeleine, I had wanted to visit Louis, to show him some affection." Her face held a rare shyness. She spoke in the hushed tones of the confessional, "I wanted him to hold me. We haven't been together for weeks." She struggled to mask her tears. "Yet, Louis pulled his hand from mine the minute Galeran stepped into the tent. He backed away and appeared to be praying before he whispered, 'I am pledged to chastity for love of you and of Our Lord, Jesus Christ.'"

She gently wiped away the tearful residue. "By Saint Benedict's boots, I swear he has adopted that same expression of feigned spiritual concern, that inane smile of priest-like condescension, I so despise."

She bit her lip before saying, "I asked myself why I had come to him. Had I deceived myself into thinking that Louis would have welcomed me after our weeks of separation?" Her pace slowed before she continued, her voice resigned, "I can see now that he has become totally monkified. Galeran, the eunuch, and the pompous bishops have done their work well."

I wanted to comfort her, to hold her myself, but only managed to ask, "Will you have any chance to talk to Louis?"

"Yes, I will see to that. I reminded Galeran that I am the queen, and I will visit my husband whenever I like. Not as wife perhaps," she said bitterly, "but certainly as his queen. I told Louis I would see him in the next few days. We have the business of supplies, and the numerous royal events in Constantinople to plan for."

Eleanor appeared more composed, but as we set out for our campsite, the hot tears splashed from her thick lashes. I reached for her hand. When we drew near to our pavilion, she called for Germer. I was surprised at the calm in her voice.

Germer came from tending the horses. "You called, Majesty?"

"Send Eliaze and Jacque to my pavilion in a short while, Germer. I need to have some gaiety, Holy March or not!"

A crisp, copper sunset tinted the heavy canvas door that was closed against the late September cold. Through it we heard a man's voice, familiar but not immediately identifiable. I pushed the fold aside to see pallid Florine in deep conversation with her husband, Lord Hugh, a sizable, good-natured man with hair the color of sorrel. His wide face wore a happy smile as he bowed to Eleanor.

"Ah, Your Highness, and Lady Madeleine! I'm pleased that you join us. Have you heard the wonderful news? Florine carries my heir to be born in the Holy City in the spring, the Blessed Mother willing." He looked at Florine affectionately, clasping her to him. She hung, arms gangly, an awkward drape at his side.

Hugh and Florine had been betrothed in their early years, she only ten, he twelve, an arranged marriage that had blossomed to form close and loving ties. Married now seven years, it was no secret that Lord Hugh had vexed himself over the lack of an heir for his extensive holdings in the rich valleys of Toulouse. His uncle and guardian, Duke Berthold, had advised putting the childless Florine away for another wife, but Hugh had steadfastly refused. Florine's news had made him ecstatic.

"I know now why I have come on the Holy Journey," he beamed. "It is to see my son born in the city of Our Saviour. 'Let him who goes forth with Louis…,'" he sang in an outburst of joy, holding Florine at her widening waist. Florine's color improved, eyes very bright, yet around her mouth a gray outline shaded her lips, and her smile seemed forced. Hugh didn't notice, and reluctantly released his wife.

"Well, noble ladies, I have been here far too long. I must return to my men. We are stationing watches for the night. There are…some dan…." He stopped himself from further conversation and kissed Florine on her splotchy cheek instead.

"Beloved, I will see you tomorrow. I will arrange for us to receive the Holy Sacrament together to honor my son and heir. Good night, my dear one."

Another deep bow to us, and Hugh left, disappearing into the confusion of the massive encampment.

"How pleased he is, Florine." Eleanor, still awash in her own feelings, appeared annoyed at Florine's downcast look. "How is it that you mope about so? Are you feeling so poorly? Thecla works hard to comfort you with her potions and all the sweetmeats she can stuff into her apron. Yet, you remain distressed. Are you worried about delivery? Remember Blessed Mother had the sweet Infant Jesus in a strange town, among strangers, and in a stable at that. You'll have the finest quarters, and you will have all of us and Thecla. It will go well, Florine. Surely it will." Eleanor searched for some signs that she had raised Florine's spirits, but she saw agony cross Florine's face.

The queen's own rawness rushed to the surface. Patience eluded her. "For God's sake, Florine, say something. I cannot bear your sullen suffering any longer. What is it?"

Silence, thick as cobwebs, hung in the air. From deep within a darkened corner of the tent, Thecla, never far from Florine these days, scooted forward to sit beside her charge. Ashen-faced, Florine huddled next to the fire, chills trembling through her hunched frame. She held herself across her stomach and began to rock. An unrecognizable voice came from her throat in a groan; she continued her rocking.

"It is not his. It is not his. Ah, God, it is not his." The words were agonized bursts.

Eleanor sank to the cushion; I moved toward Florine. She was like one possessed. Thecla wrapped her heavy shawl around Florine's shoulders and held her, rocking with her in unison. Only the sound of fire biting at beechwood snapped the silence. The heavy pall made my throat ache.

Florine, face taut, her lips drawn, began to talk in a monotone as one in a moribund state.

"It had been going on a long time. Since I was five or even a little before. Remember when I was sent to my uncle Ranulf for fosterage? To learn the ways of a lady, my mother had said. It was shortly after the marital terms had been worked out for the betrothal of Hugh and me." Her expression changed slightly while the reflecting fire painted macabre copper lights onto her clay-like face. "Hugh and I had already been introduced. He and his father had come to Angiers to have the contract witnessed. We were still just children and had such fun that day running up and down the great hall while the others celebrated the final agreement."

The brief and mild animation drained from her. "Then, the leave-taking. I waved goodbye to my mother; she had begun to cry. So had I. Uncle Ranulf rushed to lift me up, hold me to the window. 'Don't cry, little Florine. We'll get along very well,' he promised." Thecla ran a cloth over Florine's brow, so damp with sweat it was.

"He was very kind, sitting me on his lap as he told me stories. And then, then it began. His hand would find its way under my tunic." Her voice raised now, like a badgered child. "No matter how I would sit, his hand would be there. I told nurse Beatrice. She said to be silent. I told Aunt Margaret. She slapped me and shook her head." Florine began to sob. "I went to the Monsignor. He said to pray for pure thoughts. I did. When my menses began, I begged nurse to speak of marriage for me right away. When Hugh sent letters of courtship, I returned them by first messenger."

Florine took a breath, a sigh of relief. "When Uncle learned that the wedding was imminent, he urged my silence. 'You would not want Hugh disinherited and you off to a convent, now would you, my pet lamb? Besides, you do rightfully belong to another, now that you are nubile. More's the loss, fair Florine.' He had stroked my hair one last time."

The younger woman withdrew a bit from the fire. Her forehead glistened with crystals of sweat. Thecla loosened the shawl about her shoulders and daubed again at Florine's brow, then moved to one side.

Florine shuddered, her mouth down in a gesture of hopelessness. She appeared drained, finished. Eleanor attempted to speak. Thecla shook her head, amber eyes glowering, and put her finger to her lips. "Shhh. She must go on."

"Hugh and I were married. You remember, Eleanor, you were there." Eleanor nodded, relieved to see Florine more herself.

She continued. "We moved to Torquery, so far from my uncle's dreadful place, I could avoid him easily after that. He and I were never alone together again, I saw to that. I have never spoken of it to Hugh. I cannot. And now…," she began to moan and rock again.

"When Uncle learned that we were going on the Holy March, he sent word that he was coming to say goodbye, and that he wanted me to pray for his soul since I was going on Pilgrimage. It happened that Hugh was called away early to assemble with his company for the ceremony at Saint Denis. I had him send a messenger to Uncle not to come." Florine took a long deep breath and released it in a deadly sigh of despair. She continued to speak, her voice flat.

"Later that week, during a farewell hunt and festival, I was return-ing to my chambers when Uncle appeared as from nowhere, seated there by my window, He, the fox, had been watching for my return from the hunt. My lady in waiting had stayed in the woods to gather herbs. He had told the maidservants to leave. My other ladies were in the great hall celebrating the kill with the rest of the hunt party. I will never forget the song." She clapped her hands over her ears, shook her head to banish the sound from her inner memory.

Eleanor looked stricken, and my mouth was dry, as we listened to the unfolding horror. Florine went on. "I sensed danger," she recalled, looking with haunted eyes past the fire into some stark vision.

"I lunged for the door. He grabbed me, forced me to my bed, his hand over my mouth. He threw his cape over my face. I tried to call out, but he pressed the cape into my mouth. He pulled at my legs, entered me cruelly. I screamed. Finally, he lifted the cape from off my face. I wish he hadn't. I will always see him leering." Florine began to retch. "And now I bear his child." She stood up and screamed, "Now, oh Jesus, I bear his child!" She raised her fist in a gesture of defiance to the heavens. Tears streaked her cheeks. Thecla urged her to lie down, crooning softly to her.

"The rest doesn't matter," her muffled voice trailed off. "I prayed every morning at Mass that I would die. I confessed to the Monsignor. He said both my soul and Uncle's would be purified in Jerusalem; that I must journey there to pray for forgiveness for both of us." Her face contorted as she shook her head. "For both of us! Hear you that? For both of us?"

Exhausted, Florine fell asleep whimpering, "for both of us," her head shaking like one palsied.

Eleanor rose from her place to lie by her side. She cursed to the night, filled with her own and Florine's outrage. I was suffocating, my chest felt tight, and I sped for the outdoors. The night was too close; I had hoped for a breath of fresh air, but the encampment had now reached such great numbers, stretching for miles, only foul odors reached my nose. Horses, humans, goats and dogs contributed to a heavy smell of excrement, which hung like a dung cloud over the landscape. It cleared only when a sharp breeze blew off the canyons of the mountains at the west. When venison fat dripped into the fire or when dove slipped from the spit onto the red coals, we had some relief, for then the odor of charcoaled poultry was acrid and prevailing, and the smoke drove the waves of flies from the campsite if only briefly.

I hurried to the garderobe, so nauseated was I. Recent rains had turned the newly worn roadways of mud and offal into byways of stenched slime, treacherous but for the stripling pine, lashed together and laid down by camp fellows along the network of paths weaving among the nobles' tents. It was at a crossroads that I saw Sybelle and Phillip standing together under a torchlight held unsteadily by him. He was kissing her roughly, almost jarring her off the narrow, makeshift walk. I couldn't help overhearing the exchange.

"Phillip!"

"Yes, dear wife, did I startle you? Make you fear for danger?"

Phillip's face was flushed with drink, perhaps from an excess of the dark Bulgarian ale our men were consuming with such gusto.

"It is wonderous to see you, husband. I had expected you later, at Compline hour." Sybelle's voice sounded edgy, apologetic, as though she were guilty of some trespass. "You have traveled well?" Her voice faltered.

Phillip cocked his head to one side, a crooked grin twisted his darkened face. "And you also, Countess?" His voice had a cut to it. "Your pleasant journey afloat the river seems to have done you much good. No hardships for the ladies, none at all. And were the knights of Aquitaine as entertaining as ever with their dances and roundelays?" His eyes glinted meanness. I hoped Sybelle would humor him. In the torchlight, I could see his ire, the red of Mars coloring his cheeks.

"Phillip. I…I don't understand."

"What would you understand of warriors? We are sent forth to quell that pagan dog. What know you of bloodshed, of bravery? We have lessons taught a plenty, by Saint George!" Swaying noticeably, he seemed lost in his thoughts. "The king orders hands and feet cut off the cut-purses and thieves. I found a wretched lad needing a sterner lesson. Trying to rob the nobles of Flanders, he was. An extra bezant for his barrel of ale? Extort from a Christian on his way to wage a Holy War? I taught the little bastard a lesson." He raised his voice, clenched his fist wielding the torch in a gesture of running the lad through.

Shaken by her husband's reckless motions, Sybelle shrank from him, "Please, Phillip," Her voice had an imploring edge, "It is cold here. Come into our tent." She gestured in the direction of our pavilion.

I sneaked behind the garderobe, feeling like a spy, but had no other choice. I didn't want to embarrass Sybelle, and I certainly didn't want to meet the Count of Flanders in this mood.

The torch began to sway, and Phillip dogged his wife's steps, raising his voice. "If you had made the march by land, dear countess, you would see that all is not merry on this crusade." Following her, he persisted, "And so would Sir Geoffrey Rancon and the others. The Germans marching before us have provoked much hatred with their wanton plundering. We have traveled roadways with bloated corpses and staked heads used as road markers pointing the way to Constantinople."

Sybelle shuddered as Phillip laughed at his own macabre remarks.

"You will see, now that you travel the roads, Sybelle, you'll learn the life of a warrior." They had reached the approach to the pavilion.

"Come on, Phillip. We'll have some broth before retiring. I'll tell you of our journey. There was much to see and we braved some dangers as well."

"No, dearest Countess Sybelle," he mocked her, "a noble commander belongs with his men. We plan for your safety on this journey, now that we all go by land." He seized her wrist, held it fast. "The gallant Sir Geoffrey may not be able to buy our safe passage clear to the gates of Constantinople. It will be to the soldiers of God to do that. I'm expected at a strategy meeting in the event that the queen's dandy fails in his mission. I must join the military monks and our Deputy General, Galeran." With a leer, he announced, "Warriors of the king will take over where the dandies of the queen left off."

His free hand cupped her breast in a vulgar gesture. "Good night, Countess." He bowed with a stumble and wove his way toward the royal headquarters.

Across the encampment, fires were burning low except at the watch stations around the outskirts of the huge enclave. There, the sentries' flames shot high into the blackened, star-shot canopy. Tracing Sybelle's lonely movements toward our pavilion, I was concerned for her safety in the darkness. Her troubles coming on the heels of Florine's revelations made me want to flee far into the night, but instead I ran to join her, and arm in arm, we returned in silence to the queen's quarters.

CHAPTER 12

Sofia

T oward dawn two days later, I was prodded from a troubled sleep. "Geoffrey?" I muttered, still dreaming. But it was Charles who urged, "Madeleine, quick, come and bring Thecla's ointments! There's been an attack near the river's edge where the pilgrims camp. Men are wounded."

Thecla, already awake, grumbled that she should go. The fact that not she, but her remedies, had been called for, had escaped her. I gestured toward Florine. Thecla took note of the sleeping woman's sallow countenance and turned with a sulk to remain by her side.

I dressed hastily, not wanting to disturb the others, then, with my heart pounding, hurried to the medicine wagon where I grabbed a satchel of healing supplies.

"Psst. This way to the horses." Charles guided me.

We picked our way down the slimy road. Linnert, an untrained assistant, followed us through the maze of tent lines, fires, braziers and kitchen wagons. We passed the royal pavilions where Louis' shadow formed an ethereal silhouette against the canvas as his tent glowed like a luminous mushroom.

"The king often rises at Matins, the midnight hour, frequently staying awake till dawn," Charles explained, "a habit he had learned in his early training in the monastery."

"It appears this practice has been reinstated under the tutelage of the celibates who hover around him now." My acerbic tone puzzled Charles, but the memory of Eleanor's report of her encounter with her husband still lingered. At Vespers last evening, I had observed Louis closely. His appearance had become ragged, his eyes bloodshot and his gray pilgrim's tunic clung to his slim figure. His lack of sleep concerned me, because I believed it would interfere with his abilities as commander, and that set me to wondering where Geoffrey was and when he might return safely from his assignment. He should have returned by now.

We trotted past scores of maintenance stations. They bustled with activity. In the early light, grooms tended to horse's hooves, examined harness and saddle. Wagoners wrestled wheels off axles, checking felloes, or larding the hubs with fat. Beyond the maintenance camps by two or three miles, and quite separate, the pilgrim poor, many clothed in threadbare short tunics, shared their sparse victuals while they huddled together, their worn packs at their sides. I was appalled at their condition. Some had boots or simple shoes. Many were barefoot, their feet swollen with scabs and lacerations. Yet, chanted prayers and psalms could everywhere be heard over the drone of countless flies buzzing over mounds of excrement.

At the north end of the miles-long encampment, we came upon the victims, six men sprawled just off the road. They lay in the field close by the stream where they had been ambushed. Charles was the first to reach them. He put his head to their chests, each one, to listen for heartbeats. He shook his head. "They are beyond help Linnert."

As Linnert moved the first man, a groan escaped his ashen lips. He struggled to tell us what had happened. He and several others leaving the camp in search of grain had been set upon and stabbed. Brigands had ripped their pilgrims' purses from their shoulders and emptied them of their meager contents, then had trampled them viciously.

Linnert and I lifted the thin victim up by the shoulders, careful not to let his head roll to one side for fear his gaping cut would scrape the dirt. Swiftly, Charles set to work washing the wounds. He took some long leaves of dried comfrey and laid them along the split in the man's scalp.

I knelt down on the blood-soaked field beside Charles to assist him, and hastily reached for the unguents and herbs from Thecla's bounty. Charles's Hospitaller's apron soon carried a long red stain across it, as did my own tunic.

"Bring the unguent here, and run it along this line. I have staunched the bleeding."

Charles daubed at the stitches crisscrossing the wound. His youthful face, framed by a cowl of thick hair falling almost to his shoulders, held the kindness of Our Savior himself, so gentle was his expression. He wound the dressing adroitly round the head of the injured man. I proffered more bandages. A snapping twig in high underbrush stopped me cold. With a wrench to my stomach, my memory slipped back in time to the road from San Sevier, the sky a smoky yellow, the smell of blood heavy in the air as Thecla and I buried my two serving men. Mortimer's wicked face loomed before me, and I began to shiver.

"Sister, are you all right?" Charles shook me gently.

"Yes, yes, quite all right. I—I thought I heard something." I recovered my bearings. "We need to get this man to his people. I am relieved that he will survive." There had been no survivors on the road from San Sevier; only Thecla and I, hidden in the woods for days.

We delivered the man to his group, a contingent from Brabacon, warning them to stay within the camp's confines. Then we made our way through the labyrinth of sodden trails leading back to the our quarters at the south end. Low clouds, the color of pewter, threatened rain. We spoke softly, wondering at the faith of the wounded poor, while to myself I worried anew over the whereabouts of Geoffrey. The dense smell of blood stayed with me, and I wanted to get to our tent, to rinse in warm water, then to fall on the piles of skins. The sentries' cook fires served as guideposts to my pavilion.

A towering blaze at the path's junction was a welcome sight. Three horses, still saddled, stood tethered to the saplings at the edge of camp. There, his chain-mail vest reflecting deep bronze from the firelight, stood Sir Geoffrey, deep in conversation with the watchmen. My heart raced and I shut my eyes tight, vexed at the sensations that filled them with tears.

Wheeling away from the circle, his hand to his sword, the guard called, "Who will pass here in the name of Our Lord?"

"It is Charles, the Hospitaller." Charles held his hand up in the salute of peace used by his order. "I escort my sister to the queen's pavilions."

Geoffrey turned, his brows raised in quizzical disbelief. "Well done, Hospitaller." He saluted Charles. "I'm going in direction of the queen's quarters where most of my men are bivouacked. With your sister's permission, I will see to her safety. By your leave, M'lady?" He moved quickly to my side, grasping my horse's bridle. The wrinkles of fatigue at his eyes could not diminish their glow. Suddenly conscious of the bloodstain that had traced its way across my front, I closed my cape.

"I would be honored, Count Geoffrey." My calm belied my excitement, yet I was amused that the formality between us was for the benefit of the onlookers and young Charles. Geoffrey's men remained a discreet distance to the rear, leaving us to make our way to the next watch fire, which burned at the outskirts of Eleanor's settlement. But Geoffrey did not go directly to the station. Instead, he guided my horse to a small enclosure, away from the path, shadowed with sporadic rushes of mist that sprang skyward whenever the wind rustled the beechwood trees.

His profile, hair tumbled, beard uncombed, held me. He gazed out toward the incoming thunderheads. His cold hand reached for mine, much warmer from being within the folds of my tunic. He moved his mount closer so his leg touched mine firing excitement through me.

"Lady Madeleine, I know that you honor this pilgrimage, as do I. But I must say what's in my heart. You are with me always." His voice, tightened with emotion, hoarse. "I think of you all the hours of my watch, on the hunt, on the king's business." He shook his head. "My father has arranged a wife who waits for me." He laughed, a bitter hollow sound. "And wait she must, since she will be eight years old by Saint Agatha's day." His voice trailed off, like a vapor in the misty air.

In spite of the cold, he had begun to sweat at the brow and at the edges of his moustache. I could smell the days' ride, a scent that pleased me. Warmth spread to my heart, made my cheeks hot. I could not hold my tears; there had been so much in so short a time. Both fatigue and emotion held me fast. And now, to hear Geoffrey's sweet words.

He took my hand, putting it gently to his lips. How warm they were! As warm as if he had just quaffed hot wine. I could not speak, but nodded, smiling. Wanting his lips to find mine, I leaned toward him. His mouth held the promised heat. It pulsed through me; his warmth, his scent, his strength flowed to me. Deep female power surged from the depths of my being, sent desire coursing through me. The horses fretted one another, forcing us to pull apart. My lips burned and I had no wish to stop.

Geoffrey took a deep breathe, reached over, tracing the curve of my mouth with his finger.

"We have safe passage through all the strongholds to the very edge of Constantinople itself, where the Emperor Manuel Comnenus will honor King Louis. But the Emperor's Byzantine troops are needed to fight against the Turks, and cannot stay in these lands for long." He spoke quickly. "And there is uncertainty—it is reported that German Emperor Conrad presses on into Cappadocia. He has not waited for us, as agreed, so we must march today for Constantinople," he announced softly. "There may be dangers."

I nodded, smelling the pilgrim's blood that had seeped onto my tunic, but said nothing.

"I have sought safe passage from the Emperor Manuel, and I have gotten promise from his emissaries, but I'm still not sure. There is something that I feel uneasy about, my lady-love. I don't trust the Greek Emperor."

The lines at his mouth tightened. Shifting in his saddle, jaws set, his weary eyes scanning the surroundings, he had become a warrior again "I'll inform the queen. We must ride out for Constantinople at first light. There is no time to lose."

Taking my hand once more, he caressed it, placing a kiss on my palm. That brought more heated flush to my cheeks. Great drops of rain began to fall, and somewhere up the road wild wolves yipped in the new day.

I grasped his hand in both of mine, holding him fast with my eyes as well. "Geoffrey, I can't speak my heart right now. I feel a struggle between my heart's desires. I have taken vows to make the pilgrimage in solitary chastity in exchange for redemption at Our Lord's beckoning. I would be as my namesake, Saint Magdalene, and approach His tomb, as she did, in purity, dedicated only to Our Savior. And, yet, my love.…"

My eyes widened in shock at that slip. I covered my mouth. How had those words tumbled out? Confused, I fought to regain my poise. Facing him, I suggested, "We best join the queen, Sir Geoffrey." Not daring to look back, afraid of so many feelings, first among them, deep desire, I urged my horse toward camp.

CHAPTER 13

Constantinople

*I*n a week's time, we had arrived in Constantinople. The airy upper chambers of a grand Byzantine palace had been set aside for us by Empress Irene. There, I enjoyed the luxury of lolling in a raised marble tub situated by the window. Gold-studded steeples, painted domes and the bustling bazaars of the city were mine to behold. While warm, perfumed water lapped at my breasts, Nubian slave girls poured more hot water into the bath. The Empress, in a gesture of welcome, had provided her well-trained servant girls and eunuchs for our comfort during our stay in Byzantium's greatest center.

"How pleased I am to wash away the dust of all the worn roads from Beograd to Adrianopolis," Eleanor remarked from the tub next to mine, repeatedly scrubbing arms and elbows. She seemed to have a pressing need to cleanse something more. Her last meeting with Louis on the eve of the march to Constantinople, she told me, had left her feeling empty and derided.

"Perhaps I had been too forward with Louis, considering the vows he'd taken, but, cousin, his rejection had sting to it. He said that he could not 'sully' himself on the pilgrimage."

That remark had wrapped itself into Eleanor's mind like a worm curled in the leaf it devours. Whenever she recalled the interlude, which was often, she said it made her feel bilious and dizzy.

"And, Madeleine, he has never expressed any sense of desire, no feeling of loss at the many months of abstinence from conjugal love ordered by Pope Eugenius."

The regrettable episode seemed to have opened the door to a part of Eleanor's mind long closed, and as though it had become an obsession, she began to number all the times that her husband, inventing some flimsy excuse, had not come to her bed, or when there, had not sought her open arms. It was, according to her reports, always the Vigil of something, or within the Octave of Saint Someone else, or Lent or Advent.

"I have tried to overlook his other faults with forbearance; after all, he is the King of France. It didn't matter if he was slow to get the point of most of my discussions, and, eventually, I grew accustomed to the way he pouts like a child when some event has disappointed him. And, I will have to say, Louis has always shown me kindness."

"Surely, he has," I agreed, but I was also bothered by the reality that Louis had an aspect of good-natured inefficiency about his reign. It was a worry and Eleanor had tried to correct these short-comings through her own skilled efforts and intelligence, though such efforts were often regarded as "unwomanly" and "overbearing" by the king's advisors.

"But," she harped on, "given the constraints imposed by this expedition, I have no access to him at all, save to accompany him to a litany in some obscure monastery here and there. I must admit a chilling thought; I feel quite unwanted."

Calling for more hot water, Eleanor sighed while her eyes traveled the length of her well-formed limbs shaped firm by months of riding, walking and an absence of sweets along the way. The infusion of hot water had spread a rosy flush from her thighs to her breasts, the same blushed-rose hue that colored the marble floors of our bath chambers. Lost in her own ruminations, she remained still for some time, letting the attendant massage her shoulders.

With the rhythmic soft splashes, fantasies overtook me. I imagined what it would be like to have Geoffrey so touching me. Suddenly, Eleanor sat up. Perfumed suds spilt everywhere. "Sully indeed, Louis! I shall not tempt you further. Go your holy, celibate way!" She smacked at the water, startled me completely from my imaginings and scattered the attendants, who quaked behind the large mosaic urns.

There seemed little I could say to comfort her, so I coaxed the hesitant servants to fetch some of the exotic perfumes which Empress Irene had supplied for us. From a large, exquisitely designed ewer, an Arabian girl hastened to pour perfumed water into our tubs. Inlaid with precious stones, the ewer gave off an iridescence that tossed dancing bits of color throughout the room, lightening our spirits.

"Ah," Eleanor's mood soon changed, "luxury, how I welcome you." Out of the bath, wrapped in fine Turkish toweling, Eleanor looked from the window toward the sparkling azure strait that separated the mainland from the beckoning shores of the Orient. In a clear voice, she began to sing to a verse we had learned many years ago in the sunlit Bordeaux spring.

A lady commits a great and mortal sin
Who does not love a loyal knight
But if she loves a monk or clerk
Her mind cannot be right!

Remembering the verse as one of her Grandpere William's, I laughed and sang it with her before requesting our clothes to be brought. Her improved spirits pleased me, but at the same time, I felt sorry for Louis. He was simply too removed from reality, especially the needs of his wife. And I worried for the queen's future happiness. She was still subject to the king, which meant she would have to make the best of it...or so I thought.

The servants brought in our clothes, reminding us it was time to join Empress Irene at the royal palace.

Germer assisted me into our waiting litter. It had withstood the trip well, its deep red sides gleaming in the late afternoon sun. Sybelle, free of frown, eyes shining with excitement, greeted us. "Eleanor, if ever I thought you wise for packing so many trunks, it is today. To see the riches of this place! I have caught only glimpses of these royal women, and we would have looked shabby indeed if we had not brought our finest gowns and capes. I do hope we are dressed well enough."

"Well as can be expected after traveling all those miles," Eleanor said, teasing a stray lock back under her golden crown, "and yet I worry whether we are as formal or grand as they. Their laces and decorated costumes! I know Empress Irene must have a province's worth of jewels sewn into her royal robe."

Through the curtain, the long avenue of columned buildings, each with a glorious fountain spewing rainbows in the afternoon light enchanted us.

"Columns of marble, like those in our guest chambers, are everywhere." I looked down at the roadway, wondering at the smoothness of the ride. "We must be nearing the palace. This entire street is marble. Quite different from the rutted lanes leading to Paris."

"It's all quite different," Sybelle agreed. "Do you think that it will be so stiff and formal tonight?"

"Emperor Manuel stands like his robe is made of armor. An armor of emeralds and diamonds. He can hardly move in it." Sybelle began to laugh. "And when his court men have to help lower his vassals to their position of total prostration at his feet—." She broke off in a fit of giggles.

"I dared not look at you, Sybelle. I knew you were ready to burst."

"I hid my face in my handkerchief," Eleanor admitted, smiling and shaking her head. "But then, by contrast, there arrives Louis, King of France, strolling in with his spun wool pilgrim's tunic. I should be grateful that he wore his crown. He did look ill at ease with so exaggerated an obeisance."

The smile left Eleanor's face. "The journey teaches me much. I am learning that Louis is more pilgrim than king and," she so lowered her voice, barely audible above a wave of bells pealing throughout the city, "far more monk than husband."

Crowds lining the wide approach to the royal palace cheered wildly at the sight of our horse-borne litter. Held in strict check by numberless guards, they called out to their royal visitors. Their voices carried above a chorus of echoing bells.

While Sybelle and I were pleased at the reception, Eleanor basked in its effusiveness. She bowed and smiled, turning to each side of the promenade so that all could see her beauty and receive her radiant smile and hearty waves. I hoped that the pain of her relationship with Louis might recede amid the grandeur and welcome of Byzantium.

When we arrived at the Empress' chambers, the Byzantine aristocrat greeted us cordially. She attempted to speak in French at first. Were we comfortable? Were our accommodations suitable? However it soon became clear that using a Teutonic variation of the language of the Franks would not suffice for when Eleanor began to answer in French, Empress Irene, smiling all the while, responded in unrelated sentences.

"What is she saying?" I nudged Sybelle.

"She says she is happy to be perhapsing us today."

Eleanor requested the aid of an interpreter and began to speak in Latin enabling the two women to hold a lively conversation.

Irene, a short, sturdy young woman, bustled with energy. Her fair complexion, pale brows and light lashes spoke her German heritage in spite of a clever application of face paint giving the empress a pair of cheeks the color of strawberries. She talked about the tourneys, doing so with a great deal of enthusiasm and knowledge.

"The tourneys in Constantinople are colorful, a scene of great pageantry, but," her nose wrinkled between her strawberry cheeks, "the tourneys in Sulzbach are much better. The knights are very strong and their horsemanship is excellent. There is none better with a mace than a Teuton warrior."

Did her royal guests like to hunt, the empress inquired. "Do you know the sport of falconry?"

When we replied in unison, "Indeed," and "Oh yes, we have brought ours with us," Irene clapped her chubby hands together, pleased that we had found a mutual ground.

"Good! We will go out tomorrow to hunt and feast." The Empress' light blue eyes glowed with the evening's promised excitement. Seemingly, not wishing to stumble aloud over so delicate a subject, Irene moved nearer her interpreter.

"Ask the Lady Madeleine where is her husband? Did he not come to Constantinople?"

I tried to explain my widowed state as gracefully as possible, but Irene queried me further, "And you are not remarried since the loss of your young husband? Oh, that is much too long to be an attractive lady in waiting, especially in the queen's court."

Put off by such personal inquiry, a weak smile was my best reply. Irene's pale eyes lingered on me in a way that I found unsettling.

Satisfied for the moment, she moved on to more pressing business.

"Now, we will have the gifts." Empress Irene presented each of us with a small image of the Blessed Virgin carved in creamy stealite, a kind of soapstone. Every detail—the veil, the folds, the face, the downcast eyes—a minute perfection.

The smoothness of my small icon with its circular width fit perfectly in the palm of my hand. Turning it over, I read the words Via

Cruces engraved on the back. I took it to my heart, a sacred talisman for the rest of the journey.

"These are for your protection." Irene became somber in the midst of the festive exchange. "It is a dangerous place that you go. I pray that Our Lord and his Mother will protect you so that we may visit again one day." Her eyes, meeting mine, bore a calculating look. "Or perhaps she may be delayed, not go at all," she muttered in Latin to the interpreter, then silenced him with a shake of her head.

"Come, now we can't be late for the Emperor; we will go to the cathedral at once." As we followed Empress Irene into the waiting chariot, I puzzled over her remark, "May not go at all."

Go where?

CHAPTER 14

Constantinople

We boarded the royal chariot with sun, far to the west, shining like a golden orange, its rays lighting up the gilt insignia on the coach's front. Sleek, ivory-colored Arabian horses hurried us down the roadway weaving in and out of the shadows created by thick limestone walls. They towered above me, reaching for the amber sky.

Constantinople, encircled by this imposing vigilance, boasted walls stretching endlessly around its city, guarded by a hundred towers. They formed insurmountable barriers against encroaching tides, and thwarted unwelcome armies. As the royal chariot sped over the marbled roads toward the Hagia Sophia for vesper services, Empress Irene rattled off an endless array of facts.

"We have here one hundred and fifty-three baths, eight public ones. We have twelve palaces, and another being built at the far end of the city, by the forest there in the foothills. You will see it tomorrow when we hunt. Over there toward the harbor, stands one of the many granaries; we have five." She held her hand up to show five stubby fingers, heavy with the weight of seven jeweled rings, pearl, emerald and ruby.

"You are enjoying your chambers and your baths?" she inquired. "We have eight aqueducts, running from all over." She shrugged as though overwhelmed with the facts of the exact pathways of the water system. "So many people here; so many more than in—Bavaria."

Reverberating bell sounds halted Irene's travelogue. We had arrived at Hagia Sophia. In the vespered dusk, its great swelling domes, rising one upon the other, beckoned me mysteriously.

Several small trumpets blared a greeting. They were held aloft by rows of black-clad eunuchs. The young clerks wore square, black head-coverings. At some signal, the beardless youths dropped the instruments to their sides, rotating their smooth faces toward the end of the long promenade where Emperor Manuel Comnenus' valets scurried here and there, fussing with his apparel.

Clothed more elaborately than the previous evening, the emperor wore an outer vestment whose entire front panel reached across his chest and hung the length of his frame. Dazzling in its design, a series of jeweled squares filled with lapis lazuli and emeralds contained within each square gold cubits, all stitched into place. Enclosing the several squares were rows of pearls and circles of rubies.

Manuel was a young man, and I wondered if he moved slowly because of the weight of his regalia or to balance his crown, made of heavy gold, inset with large pearls and fronted by a massive emerald set in gold. Topping his crown was a cross inlaid with ivory or pearl. From the bottom, hung a perpendulia of pearls, reaching to his shoulders. Eleanor and I exchanged glances. Even Eleanor the extravagant, had never dreamed such opulence.

The row of young monks fell to their knees as Emperor Manuel, followed by the Orthodox patriarch and surrounded by various clergy, proceeded down the carpeted walk. There followed bishops and priests, all superbly garbed in the style of the emperor, but without the multiplicity of jewels. They made their way toward Hagia's heavy silver doors.

Louis and his bishops followed. The king looked beatific in his simple pilgrim's gray tunic and short cape. The golden circlet of majesty was his only show of wealth, yet many of his Latin bishops displayed their jeweled miters. Ruby-studded croziers appeared from nowhere. Capes of ermine and vair had somehow found their way over the Hungarian plains as had Cardinal Lisieux's glittering, gold-embossed shoes.

"I see we are not the only ones so finely turned out," Eleanor hissed. "were those trappings smuggled in the baggage carts so bitterly complained about?"

Manuel's court moved along the promenade; Many of the members were on the edge of adolescence, dwarfed by their long flowing gowns. Their awkward limbs, lost under the wide, trailing sleeves, remained veiled from scrutiny. One lad, wearing a golden chain around his neck, fixed his wide eyes upon me with a rapt glance. To smile warmly at his youthful friendliness seemed innocent enough—a mistaken notion.

Irene whispered, "That's the emperor's favorite nephew. He will one day be very wealthy. Isn't he a handsome young man? You will see him later at the feast. But come now, we must go in."

Led by the Empress, we entered the long vestibule that ran across the full width of the church. From the inner narthex I peered curiously into the hushed interior. At once, my gaze was drawn to the stunning central dome; its feeling of suspension infused me with a sense of floating. Color, texture, and the light of a thousand tapers flooded the area, holding me captive.

Half-seen spaces, obscured as they were by rich silk tapestries suspended between vast columns of exquisitely patterned marble held mosaic figures who pulsed brilliance, and stared directly at me. Halos of gold cubits caught the reflected lamplight and shimmered grace around saints, women and men, reliving the days of Christ's life, robed in vivid color; deep red, radiant yellow and emerald green tesserae.

Caught up in the fragrance of unseen mysteries, I quavered at the holy grandeur that lay under Hagia Sophia's great dome. Here, swirling round the marble pilasters, concealed among the tapestries, seeping from the relics, lurked the cloying, unfathomable desires of my Creator. I could sense them, but couldn't guess what they might be.

Golden censers, chains clanking, broke the silence. Smoke from aromatic pine resins filled the air. My knees trembled as I clutched Irene's gift, the creamy soapstone Virgin. Every wall held a scene I wished to enter, to touch the fine mosaics, to trace with my finger tips the slight raised texture which made each world whole.

My wandering eye discovered the Holy Tomb scene at the same time that deep bass voices, two hundred strong, thundered like the desert patriarchs of old. Their ancient supplications, "Kyrie eleison."—"Lord have mercy"—filled the Hagia. From the other side of the nave, dulcet castrato tones floated like the incense, heavenward, to the gold-encrusted dome, "Christe eleison"—"Christ have mercy." It was easy to pray.

Hours later, the chariot glided along darkened streets returning us to our chambers. Weary from the late-hour entertainment, her voice languid from Greek wine, Eleanor shared two observations with us. "Galeran must be in paradise since there seem to be three eunuchs for every man in Constantinople, and, Madeleine dear, the emperor's nephew seems to have been most taken with you."

Despite the late hours, Eleanor managed a devilish twinkle in her eye. I nodded in chagrined agreement. Several times I had felt someone's gaze upon me and desiring Geoffrey, turned discretely to see if my wishes were answered. But, to my disappointment, I had encountered only the fawning eyes of the overdraped adolescent hard upon me, with an ever-ready nod and a smile.

Whenever I had found Geoffrey, he had given me faint recognition by way of the slightest nod. What so occupied him now, that there could be no time for a greeting? I wanted to be annoyed, but in truth, I was hurt by his manner. In what should have been celebration, he seemed overly preoccupied as did Florine's husband, Lord Hugh. Bunched together in their ermine-trimmed dress tunics, the Aquitainians engaged in serious conversations, often turning their backs to the entertainment. Geoffrey conferred repeatedly with the king's brother, Robert, Count of Dreux, while malevolent Mortimer du Mur, between brazen stares at me, wound his way in among the Greeks, then meandered back to the heated exchanges among Louis' advisors, Galeran among them.

Sybelle nursed a silent frown, her spirits flagging because Phillip had been far more engrossed with the dancing girls and libations than with anything else. Well, no matter. We were all to be off together on the hunt tomorrow. I hoped she would see Phillip then to assuage the nagging discomfort of her heart. I looked forward to some festivity as well, for I was certain Geoffrey would attend the hunt.

When we retired for the night, I welcomed the soft silk sheets. My head ached from the heavy wine, and I felt uneasy, confused. There had been no moment alone with Geoffrey, no touch or smile. Still, there would be the hunting party tomorrow. I hadn't worked our falcons for much too long. Then, I thought, I would like to revisit the Hagia Sophia when it is empty and silent. I went to sleep quickly. It was toward dawn that I experienced my first Jerusalem dream, an experience as unsettling as it was mystifying.

In the dream, I see myself at the hillside near the Tomb of Our Lord. It is daybreak, and I rejoice at the fresh golden sun. Remaining hidden in the shadows, I see three women approach the Holy Tomb. Like flute sounds, a voice floats from a dim apparition within the tomb. "Quem Quaeritis?"

I want to cry out to the other women for I know they are the three Marys.

They respond, "Jesum Nazarenum, crucifixum."

My hand flies to my lips, for I realize the words have come from me; I am one of them. I, standing with the women, chrism oil spilled upon my shaking hand, am Mary Magdalene.

"Non est hic"—"He is not here."

The apparition fades from within; the rest of the words cannot be heard.

Startled awake, I sat bolt upright, rubbing my trembling hand. An unfamiliar fragrance—was it nard—lingered in the air. Filled with profound sadness, I pulled the dampened bedclothes around me like a silken cocoon, surrendering to sleep, for though frightened by the vision, and for reasons I could not explain, I ached to return to the world of that dream.

CHAPTER 15

Constantinople

The next morning, with the dream still haunting me, I set about the day's activities and began to dress. Reaching for my sheepskin hunting jacket, I noticed a slight burn on my hand. My shoulders twitched involuntarily. Coincidence, I argued. I could have gotten it from any number of places. Summarily, I banished the dream. Soon, I would see Geoffrey at the hunt. The thought excited me.

Eleanor and Sybelle waited in the lush, perfumed garden. Eleanor scrutinized me curiously, scrutinizing the shadows beneath my eyes.

"Madeleine, you don't look rested. Are you well?"

"It—it's nothing, really." How difficult it was to keep anything from Eleanor, but the dream now seemed so elusive, I couldn't put words to it. "I had an unusual dream, that's all."

Eleanor's reply was cut off by a cross-looking palace official, his horse snorting steam in the cool air. "Please, your majesty, follow me. I am to escort you to the hunt."

Mounting the horses, we followed him along an avenue lined with large trees, their long branches heavy with persimmons bulging under their sleek orange skins. Beyond them stretched a hillside boasting manor houses surrounded by lines of vineyards and olive groves.

"We will join the rest of the royal party. It is not a long ride," our escort explained. "This is but one of many reserves, a wide-ranging meadow surrounded by thickly wooded lands. Good for the falcons."

My enthusiasm picked up considerably. Under cobalt-blue skies, the walls of Constantinople stood bold against the amber fields, and gloried in the morning light. Heat waves shimmered from the towered parapets. Like scattered crystals, sunlit flecks of mica dazzled the surfaces. Gulls circled overhead. The saffron vineyards reminded me of my first October in Bordeaux almost two years ago. I urged my horse to catch up with Eleanor.

"It is the season for turning. Today reminds me of our first weeks together, Eleanor. It feels like harvest time back home."

Eleanor kept her palfrey close, gave me a fond smile. "That seems a long time ago, doesn't it, my cousin? And now, imagine it, we are hunting in the royal preserves of the Emperor Manuel!" Her head tilted coyly, as though she, rather than Empress Irene, had made all the festive arrangements for the day's diversions.

"Come now, we're delaying." Sybelle, brows crooked to her hairline, pointed toward the glowering escort who had wheeled about in our direction. We flicked our horses, chiding the guide with Frankish words.

The rest of the hunting party emerged from another city gate just as we arrived. The emperor and king were not among them, but Empress Irene, grandly dressed in deep green leather, rode with her falcon atop her saddle. Her entourage consisted of three ladies-in-waiting and two of the emperor's nephews.

Eleanor swung around to wink at me, for the adolescent nephew of the bows and smiles was present. While he appeared to be more comfortable in his hunting regalia, the jeweled, blue wool tunic still hung on his raw-boned shoulders. He cantered to my side wearing the same fixed grin, addressing me in words I didn't understand. But the intent was clear; he was to be my ardent hunting partner for the day's outing.

Protocol required that I respond with courtesy, but it was hard to hide my disappointment. Was Empress Irene behind this? Avoiding his fawning brown eyes, I pretended to scan the countryside. Shielding my eyes against the sun, I surveyed the hunting party. Where was Geoffrey? Where was Phillip? I suspected the king was at his devotions, but I felt uneasy without the other two.

In spite of their absence, the hunting was good, and we enjoyed our sport. The sun was high overhead, and the aroma of roasting lamb had set my stomach to growling, when another hunting party cantered our way from the direction of the palace. In addition to members of the emperor's court, a cadre of Louis' knights, mostly Burgundians, joined the larger group, with the exception of Florine's husband, Lord Hugh, who rode casually toward Eleanor. His blue eyes flashed and his cheeks matched his bushy, roan-colored hair. Perhaps he had joined us for the noon meal. Perhaps, Geoffrey, too, might be along soon.

"Good day, ladies," he said loudly, "I'm sure you'll find good sport today." Reining his horse closer to Eleanor, Hugh lowered his voice out of my hearing.

Both he and Eleanor appeared to be indulging in light banter, nodding and smiling at other members of the hunting party. But I knew Eleanor well, and reading the inclination of her head and the intensity with which she listened, it was obvious that Hugh had brought troubling news.

My thoughts became suspicious. What was amiss that gave Hugh such concern? Was it Florine? Where were our men, Geoffrey and Phillip? Was it my imagination? I turned to question Sybelle, but my hunting partner's gaping, hot-breathed smile was in the way. When I looked ahead, I noted that Hugh, not waiting for the feast, was now making his way slowly back toward the city. He had left Eleanor's side as quickly as he had come. He walked his gelding toward the

Golden Gate with such lassitude that the Greek knights, dismounting near the festive tables, paid him little heed.

I had hoped for a private word with Eleanor, but my suitor followed on my heels. By the time I reached her, it became clear that whatever the news had been, she had not liked it. Addressing her in Langue d'oc, rude but a sure way to talk with some privacy, I asked, "Eleanor, what has happened? Is Florine all right?"

Between her clenched teeth, she announced, "No need to worry about Florine. Plans for this evening have been changed somewhat, that's all."

Eleanor's cryptic message escaped me, though the acerbic glance at the emperor's nephew did not. The day spent birding with the Greek lad breathing his garlic breath at my side came to its tedious end, with never a sight of Sir Geoffrey. Back at my palace quarters, I had just removed my hunting vest when Eleanor, her face pinched, swept into my room. She looked to right and left as though followed by some evil.

"You are in danger, Madeleine. Listen carefully. Germer will bring you clothing. You must bind up your breasts, dress as a squire, and prepare to leave here at nightfall. Ask no questions, feign illness, stay in your room till your disguise arrives, then follow Germer."

"My disguise? Whatever are you—Eleanor, what is this about?" I sank to the bed.

"It's about your freedom! Now do as I say and lay abed till Germer arrives. I must go on to the celebration with Sybelle. We can't arouse any suspicions."

"But I won't stay here in ignorance. Jesu, what is the danger?"

"It seems that "safe-conduct" negotiations with Emperor Manuel have broken down. Because Manuel's nephew is wife-hunting, and the request was made, Galeran pressured Louis to offer you as hostage in exchange for our safe passage through Turkey. The next step would be marriage, I'm sure. I won't allow that, Madeleine. You are part of my court, not Louis', and certainly not Galeran's property to be used as a bargaining jewel. Geoffrey won't stand for it either. Now eat something and be ready to flee."

Eating something was the last thing I wanted to do. My stomach churned, my mouth was bark dry. I tried to swallow and when I licked my lips, I tasted salt and fear. My mind was numbed as I watched Eleanor reach for her silk gown, "I must dress and not tarry. I pray everything will go as planned. I'll find you after we cross the straits. Here, take this." It was her small gold dagger, its crest shining in the slanting light. "I hope you won't need it, but you must take it."

Before I could object, Eleanor, gown in hand, embraced me and was gone to the dressing closet, calling out, "God bless you. May Saint George ride with you tonight, dear cousin."

The thought of being indentured to the stiff eastern court horrified me and for a time I sat hunched as though shackled, unable to move or think. Finally, I began to pray, and as I did so, I was reminded of the queen's words, "Sir Geoffrey won't allow it." I trusted them both. It seemed forever until Germer showed up with a packet of clothes and more instructions.

At nightfall, Germer and I waited in the shadows of the eucalyptus trees marking the avenue to the wide marbled steps of the Philopation. Germer stood by his horse, and looked to be an ordinary page; I, mounted, hoped to appear a young knight clad in a long-sleeved tunic covered by a chain-mail vest of finely wrought iron. Boots of deep cordovan leather gripped the sides of my horse.

My head stung with a host of prickly questions. Why had I been singled out as a bride? I had no property, no family, and was much older than the emperor's nephew. Yet, Galeran had dared to use me as hostage. I struggled to curb my anger, to remain as calm as possible. The moon, three-quarters full, hid behind a puff of billowy cloud. I peered into the dark. Night creatures skittered in the underbrush as an owl skimmed along the road searching for a kill.

What will happen if this plan fails? If we are apprehended, would Emperor Manuel "forgive" me by forcing the marriage, or will we all be made prisoners? Or worse, might we be clamped into chains, shipped to the forced labor camps that keep Constantinople in these strong limestone walls. The answers made me shudder. Bile rose to the back of my throat. "I'd best just pray. Sweet Magdalene protect me. Deliver me to the Holy City, so that I may linger in the sacred places and walk the paths you walked."

Galloping hooves echoed out of the darkness. Closer, closer. The pace slowed. My heart would not stop its pounding. What if we had been betrayed? Could these be Palace Guards approaching? Suddenly, I was scooped aloft from my mount and placed in front of the dark-clad rider. The quiet command to Germer, "Follow on the abandoned steed, and return it to the stables," was a voice I recognized, firm and clear.

Muscular arms encircled me, pulling my buttocks close. Knowing whose strong thighs held me to the horse, I sank into his grasp. With pulses hammering, released momentarily from fear, I allowed myself the luxury of sudden rapture.

CHAPTER 16

Constantinople

*A*fter a hazardous ride through Constantinople's crooked and unfamiliar byways, we jerked to a stop near the old harbor wall. My pounding heart began to calm; the throbbing in my ears stilled.

"Good, we were not pursued. They aren't on to us yet." Rancon dismounted and I waited for him to help me down. He signaled me to jump off.

"Squires don't get lifted off their mounts, young lad." His serious frown had left for a time at least. I laughed; it felt good to laugh. I leaped from the saddle with a bounce, right into his arms. We held each other, and Geoffrey's expression changed from concern to tenderness. Drawn to him, my lips met his in an urgent kiss more passionate than I could have imagined. I held his face in my hands, searching for more, but his concerned expression returned.

With his lips warming my ear, voice hoarse, he explained, "I've arranged a meeting with the same boat captain who piloted us down the Danube. There is no time to lose. We meet him at The Jolly Oarsmen. You'll see it is well named. This plan was made earlier in the day, when Queen Eleanor took action. Raoul made the contact and the Bavarian captain will sell us safe passage across the Bosphorus to the shores of Anatolia."

"When do we cross?" His nearness had been distracting. I was aware that my breasts were too tightly bound, How could I feel desire and discomfort as well as fear? My feelings made no sense.

"Won't we be pursued as fugitives?" My anxiety returned.

Rancon's terse reply confirmed my fears. "At any moment. We'll cross as soon as it can be safely arranged. And once on those shores, dear Lady Madeleine, Turks hunker in Cappadocian caves, waiting for our vaunted Christian march. Here, in Constantinople, Emperor Manuel is poised to seize you as a pledge of safe passage for the Franks. By helping you escape, we'll surely be arrested for treason. But," he took my hand in his, "by all the honor of Charlemagne, I won't let that happen."

He brushed my cheek with a kiss. "I am not going to let you out of my sight. It's the queen's command," he whispered, "and the desire of my heart as well, lady love. Come, I need to find my men."

We headed down a narrow road among the wretched huts and pilings, a hidden, seamy, stinking side of the city. Detritus and fish heads floated at the water's edge. We turned toward a grain shed, went round to the back where we met up with Rancon's men. After dispatching one of them as a watch, Geoffrey headed us toward the grimy tavern where we entered the brawling world of dockside squalor.

Making sure my braids were tight under my cap, I followed Geoffrey past carousing sailors, mercenaries, and wharf women bunched around tables and stools. In the jostling, I was handled vulgarly by both sailors and whores. My nerves jangled, so frightened was I that I might be discovered. Finally, seated at a table beside Rancon, I welcomed the strong, clear liquid fire of the Greeks, which, though sticky-sweet, burned straight to my queasy stomach.

Now, no one paid me much attention. I sat silently, fearful to say a word. With my cap pulled down over my eyes, I listened closely as Geoffrey and the others plotted the next moves.

Rancon studied his drink. "It's not likely that Emperor Manuel will pursue us into Anatolia, but it is more than certain that he would detain us here, for what fate I don't wish to speculate. We need to depart swiftly and in complete secret."

I knew he was speaking to me. I downed another dollop. Geoffrey, meeting my eyes briefly, had just signaled for more when the wild-bearded figure of the boat captain loomed in the doorway. Rancon waved him over, offering him a drink. The boatman downed the liquid as if it were water, calling for a refill. That done, he huddled around the sticky table to begin the negotiations.

"We must cross immediately, within the next two hours if possible." Rancon said.

"No, Frenchman, not at that hour. You know horses, I know the sea, its ebb and flow." The captain's voice boomed over the music that rattled its seductive cadence. In the center of the crowded tavern, half-nude slatterns swayed, lasciviously slapping tambourines on their hips. Rancon signaled the captain to hold down his voice. It was clear that the Bavarian had misunderstood the secrecy of the mission.

Geoffrey pulled him aside, informing him that this was an undertaking of crucial logistic support. Rubbing his spiky red beard, the skipper took up his conversation with the same tone of conviction but with less volume.

"We must wait for the tide, good sire. Around midnight. God be willing, we can begin to carry you over then." He looked around, now fully aware of the risks. "I'll anchor just outside the harbor gate. We'll have dories there to load your men, barges for the horses." He hesitated, rubbing his big calloused hands together. "It will be costly, sire."

Rancon spilled several bezants onto the soiled tabletop. The captain's giant hands swept up the coins. He meticulously dropped them one by one into the side of his sailor boots.

"At midnight, the long wharf by the harbor jetty." Giving his mouth a swipe with the back of his hand, the captain fondled his way past the dancing women.

Just before matins, we huddled in the dark by the pungent-smelling cargo on the north wharf. Suddenly, one of Rancon's guards sprinted toward us. "The emperor's patrol is headed this way! I'll warn the others."

"Jesus, in his mercy, what are they doing here? Has the alarm gone out? Have we delayed too long?"

"I don't know. Quick, duck behind these barrels of ale."

We skittered like the rats we had disturbed and hid under a nearby canvas. The patrol, only six strong, clattered by.

"Are they making their usual rounds or looking for us?" Rancon wondered aloud.

"Will the boatman be fearful and not send his dories?" Afraid to breathe, I was terrified with that possibility. We'd be trapped.

"I think not. He's an honorable sort and not fond of the Greeks." His voice was a monotone. "The hour draws near, that I do know."

"Will they show a light and be discovered?"

"They'll have to light their way. We cannot show a torch now."

"Look!" I pointed into the gulf of darkness, "a lighted boat approaches!"

"Yes, and the patrol too." Rancon, one hand on his sword, lifted the cover for a better view. The mounted patrol wheeled about, horses clopping in step, shaking the dock beneath us.

"Saint Hubert help us, we are lost." I didn't know whether to whimper or pray.

What next occurred happened so fast, I'm not sure what took place. Suddenly the patrol was upon us at the same time the boatman's dory pulled dockside, unloading five weathered boat hands. With shouts and curses, they lunged at the soldiers, surprising them with the ferocity of their onslaught. Our knights quickly saw the danger and seized the opportunity to spring into the fray, swords drawn. Eleanor's dagger, too, was at the ready, and good it was that I had it, for after some fast stepping, I was tripped up by a fallen Greek guardsman who grabbed for my boot. He held on with a death grip.

I seized Eleanor's dagger. and plunged it into his forearm. Rancon was shouting, "To the barge, squire, to the barge!" I felt in peril, but the weapon, stuck in the guardsman's flesh, bore Eleanor's royal identification. She could not be implicated in this mess. I had to twist her dagger out of that spurting, thrashing arm.

"Help, Geoffrey, help me!" I struggled to free the dagger, all the while fending off the guard. In a flash, Geoffrey subdued him with a crack to his skull, and I finished my gruesome task. My hands shook violently as I tried to wipe the blade on my tunic.

Amid shouts and wrestling, I hurled myself into the dinghy with the others. Shortly, the clash of swords and agonized yelling eased. The emperor's patrol was wounded, some dead, the rest in disarray. A barge nudged dockside, slammed down the planks, and loaded the horses. One boatman's cheek was opened, and one of our men had his arm crushed by a fallen horse.

It was a short trip in crossing, our lighted boats gliding over the smooth, blackened waters dappled by moonlight when the clouds would allow. Though we were now out of immediate danger, I stood at the gunnels trembling, trying to ward off tears. My heart was still pounding when Geoffrey came to my side.

Moving into the shadows, we held each close. Traversing the Bosphorus with moonlight reflected in the paddles' wake, I realized how deeply I loved him. His lips caressed my neck, his arms pulling ever more tightly around me.

"We must be very careful, dear lady. When the others join us, we cannot be seen together at all. If there were any hint of dishonor for either of us, they will use it against us with the king." We sat together on a heavy round of rope. "Louis seems to be in a beatific daze." Geoffrey went on, "Galeran can sway him all too easily. You are in peril, my love; you could still be taken as hostage for Manuel." His lips were so close to my ear, the heat of his breath warmed me.

Now with the oars pulling us across the silvered blackness of a calm, moonlit sea, my heart, flooded with excitement, felt a mixture of desire, fear, and anger. An old rage returned, taking my throat, my voice. The hateful realization hit me. With the queen's entourage or not, I was chattel still! And in danger!

Blindly, I turned on Rancon demanding, "What say you, Geoffrey? Will Galeran trade me away yet?"

The rage edging my voice was not lost on him. His spirits flagged and his voice sounded flat, lifeless. "I cannot predict, lady love, but he and Cardinal Lisieux argue that you should be left as a pledge of safety for the rest of us. Many of the barons are in accord."

He drew a deep breath, his eyes held mine, then scanned the coast of Anatolia. The lumbering ship had begun to slow.

"We're approaching Turkish territory, and my watch has learned that Emperor Manuel has, in an act of military expediency, just made a traitorous pact with the various Turkish rulers. Through my negotiations, he had promised more support to us, and now backs down. It does not bode well for the expedition."

From the drawn look of his face, the tightness around his mouth, the tense lines around his eyes, I understood how heavily the charge lay upon his shoulders: to maintain order among the queen's vassals, to represent her at the councils, yet to bear the relentless yoke of disdain piled on by Galeran and some of the northern nobles had taken its toll. He had always to be the diplomat, free from taint, yet Galeran, in a position of power, was treacherous, his mind working in peculiar ways, fueling dissension rather than assuaging it.

I regretted that I'd been so unfair, confronting him for things that he was powerless to direct. I reached to touch him, taking his face in my hands, pulling him toward me. Our lips met, open, warm. I returned his searching need. When I heard boatmen approaching to hoist lines from the gunnels, I pulled away slowly, aching with desire. It wouldn't do to be observed.

"And you, dear Geoffrey," I was short of breath, hoping my voice conveyed the love and passion I felt, "as leader of the queen's forces, need to be above reproach in all things. Oh, I know." I leaned against his chest, felt his heart beating hard.

"Thank you, my love, for taking me away from Manuel." I sighed as the reality of our escape returned. "Constantinople has widened the breach between our forces, hasn't it?"

Rancon sank to a bench at the hull. "Lady, you know by now I am a quiet sort. We see more than we say. And I have been observing many things."

He examined the jeweled hilt of his sword, absently polishing the rubies that shone there. "It all began to fit together. I'd seen the machinations of the Greek nobles, their exaggerated courtesy only masks the coil of greed that drives this empire." He gestured toward the shore we were nearing. "You know they have lost ground in the Holy Land and are eager to extract the help of the Franks to regain it. Do you know that some Frankish factions are willing to negotiate for certain rewards, that their greed matches that of the Greeks?" A discouraged sigh escaped him.

"Some nobles are ready to pledge to foreign sovereigns! Others, including the avaricious Mortimer, are foolish enough to want to place Constantinople under siege; meanwhile, all the King wants to do is be at his devotions. And I," he shrugged, "I want only your well-being." He took my hand, and brought it to his lips, his voice dropping to a husky whisper, "and your love."

"And I yours."

Barely discernible in the dark, Geoffrey's face softened with his vulnerability. After hearing his concerns, I began to understand more clearly how many factions riddled our forces. Difficult days lay ahead. I pressed myself to him, meeting the intensity in his eyes, feeling the desire that coursed through both of us.

"We can't speak of this again, my heart's love." The taste of tears flooded my mouth. Blinking hard, I set my cap, wiped my sleeve across my brow with the back of my hand in the clumsy way a young knight would do. We disembarked, a noble and his knight, to set up bivouac sites for the marching Franks.

Later, away from the others, we settled in a brushy thicket at the sand's edge. A crisp moon waned in the early morning sky. Alone in my small tent, I removed my outer vest. Slowly, the tent flap moved aside. Geoffrey, trailing his armor, approached me, his eyes never leaving mine. He unbuckled his sword and began to undo my underbinding, letting his fingers brush softly across my breasts. I pressed toward him.

With dawn painting the sky in rainbows, my resolve and restraint, like Penelope's threads, unraveled. On the shores of the Orient, all barriers between us dissolved in a rapture of color and textures, lost as we were in the sounds and rhythms of lovers' harmony.

CHAPTER 17

Lake Ascania, Asia Minor

*I*n the days that followed, Geoffrey and I were forced to behave as though our night of passion had never occurred, but my heart longed to be at his side as he set up the encampment on the shores of Lake Ascania. Two contingents from the queen's provinces, as well as the forces led by the king's younger brother Robert of Dreux, had soon followed on our heels.

Keeping my identity a secret was no longer possible for the news of my abduction swept through our forces. Geoffrey and I took extreme pains to avoid each other. As it was, I feared there were suspicions. Mayhap it was my imagination, but Mortimer de Mur, arriving ahead of the others, had seemed to smirk and whisper to his followers as I walked by, sending a clammy feeling down my back.

Within two days, the billowing standards of Aquitaine advanced down the road toward us. The queen and her entourage had made the crossing without incident, and the next noontide we were all together again, enjoying the midday meal near the wind-rippled waters of Lake Ascania. On the other shore, mountain forests heavy with stands of beech and oak flamed red and gold against a backdrop of evergreen pines. Waters lapping against the copper-colored ramparts of Nicaea blurred the colorful reflections like an artisan mixing tints. The dangers of Constantinople were far behind me, or so it seemed.

Eleanor surveyed her new setting. "A fine place to gather our thoughts now that we are out of Emperor Manuel's clutches." She paused to pluck a pomegranate seed from her lower lip, motioning for Hulga to dampen a napkin.

"We have since learned that while Manuel was making demands on our nobles and wishing to hold you, cousin, for his nephew, he was secretly negotiating a treaty with the Turks! What treachery! I would not give one fig for his word. Thank Charlemagne's Staff we didn't give in to his outrageous demand." She put an arm around me.

"Sir Geoffrey stands by me. He is convinced the abduction was the only thing to do. It finally forced Louis to make a decision to move on, and good that was for many of his barons were anxious to get on the road. They had tired of Manuel's posturing promises."

My face burned with embarrassment at the conversation. It had been a daring move on Eleanor's part to defy the emperor's request and refuse to leave me as barter for safe passage. Still, my escape had become the focus of more division between Eleanor's allies and the king's conservative circle. It worried me, and I felt vulnerable. And the possibility that Geoffrey and I might have been observed began to haunt me. I hid my feelings by conducting a detached survey of the newly established camp area.

Back from the littoral, the encampment stretched for more than a mile. Colorful high-topped tents lined the perimeter, their backs to the lake. Only a few sentries had been placed at the waterfront. The rest of the lords and barons had formed their armies into a tight half-circle, establishing the watch at strategic points along the camp's edge. Thus protected, the cooks had access to fish the lake or hunt game birds near the wooded marshland to the west.

In the pavilion area where the Burgundian princes grouped, a lot of activity caught my notice. I squinted to see more accurately, but the sun blinded my vision. Puzzled, I inquired of Eleanor. "Do some of the barons meet without the king?"

"Yes, they have just begun to do that and it troubles me." Eleanor shook her head impatiently, her gold tresses shining with copper highlights. "Louis is relinquishing too much control over the expedition. Many of the lords are irked that the brave and daring Franks came all this way and did not lay siege to Constantinople. An utterly senseless scheme."

I examined the animated gathering more closely. "Do they still haggle over that? I had thought that it was agreed there would be no laying siege once I was fetched some safe distance away." My cheeks flushed again with irritation. How I hated being at the eye of the storm.

"Phillip fumes that the Germans rush ahead and plunder all the Turks' gold and silver." Sybelle's eyes widened with her anxious look, perhaps recalling yet another unpleasant encounter like the one I had witnessed between her and Phillip at the lakeshore the night before. He was in his cups again, ranting about the women and their baggage carts.

Sybelle went on, "It seems that Mortimer de Mur runs to Galeran stirring up more resentment at our wains and wardrobes. Between them, they have established a litany of complaints."

An osprey dove into the crystal waters for a sleek wriggling fish. Splendid white cranes, numbering hundreds, fed and settled at the east end of the lake. My spirits began to sink at the squabbling.

"Oh, let them have their complaints!" Eleanor spat out the words, a defensive set to her chin. "It matters little about our baggage. There are numbers of servants to care for it. That is not the trouble." She pitched a pomegranate peel at a hovering shorebird. "The problem is that we dally too long. An inertia seeps into our souls. By Saint Benedict's boots, isn't it enough to be going to Jerusalem? To the Holy Sepulcher itself? I know this is the land of the early Christians with their admirable agape, but why prostrate ourselves at every altar and grotto along the way? It is the Holy City that we seek. It is those byways that we will tread to save our souls from hell. To linger here till winter is to waste our resources and the day's light." Her voice became shrill with frustration.

The queen looked across the lake where small boats with sails of every color glided in to tie up for the evening. Sunlight cast a saffroned path along the great mountains to the east. Chill winds blew off the range to the north.

"How differently would my Uncle Raymond lead us," she speculated. "He is my father's brother, you'll remember, and my only male kin." Her face took on a look of admiration, "he would have had the same courageous ingenuity as did his father, my granpere, when he fought the first crusade." She stooped to pick up a stone, casting it into the lake. "Now, granpere's plan to seize yonder Niceae—"

A clattering of horses hooves cut Eleanor's story short. A small group of horsemen appeared, not from the main road, but from a trail leading out of the woods to the east.

"Eleanor!" My voice revealed how startled I was, "Who would approach here with no banners flying, no trumpet call?"

While Nicaea was some distance from Constantinople, I judged it was near enough for me to be in jeopardy should the emperor insist on the Franks yielding me, if not as bride, perhaps as hostage. After the rumblings I'd heard, treachery by our own forces seemed a possibility. Mortimer's shadowy figure came to mind. My legs felt mired in mud as I tried to move quickly toward the queen.

"Who have the sentries let pass into the encampment? These men are strangers, and by their garb, they look like Turks!" Eleanor's tone expressed the same concerns as mine. "Do they come from Manuel? We know he is in league with the Turks after all. The turncoat!"

Eleanor called to Hulga mending bedclothes under a stand of golden poplars. "Quickly, Hulga! Send Germer to me. It is urgent!" The girl sprang up, scattering burnished leaves in her wake.

"It is best that we return to our pavilions where the guardsmen are stationed" Eleanor spoke tersely, taking my arm.

"Whatever are Turks doing here?" Sybelle's brows creased upward as she worried, "I wonder where Phillip is?"

Hoping to outrun my feelings of panic, I scurried ahead with tunic held high. I reached the tent, wondering if I were to spend the rest of the expedition forging one step ahead of Emperor Manuel. Or were Frankish resentments so rampant that both Rancon and I might be forced to flee immediately into the Cappadocian wilderness, there to be torn apart by wild beasts? Eleanor's firm manner calmed my racing heart.

"We'll know more when Germer gets here. Meanwhile, just stay out of sight."

Minutes later, Germer's mount cantered toward our pavilions where a waiting Eleanor had posted extra sentries. The horse wheeled and Germer alighted. His breath came in gasps when he tried to speak. The queen spoke first.

"Germer, there are strangers arrived here. The men are dressed like Turks and are nearing the king's quarters by now. Find Sir Geoffrey or Lord Hugh. I must confer with them at once."

"I'll find them, Majesty. Sir Geoffrey pointed out which hunting trail they would take." Germer struck off in the direction of the wooded hillsides.

Rancon had confided to me that if the king needed to stop at every crucifix, there would be time enough to hunt and cure the venison abounding in the foothills to the north. The hunting party had been out since daybreak.

The thought of seeing Geoffrey sent warmth flooding through me. How difficult it was to act casually toward one another. Tenderly, I recalled the night of the escape when I had felt his arms about me, remembering how I had leaned into the hardness of his body, aware of the scent of him, his pulsing vigor, his passionate tenderness, our loving surrender to each other.

Thecla and I whiled away the afternoon sorting out the herbs, noting which supplies were low. Toward dusk, a rider cantered into the camp. I recognized Geoffrey's practiced horsemanship before he approached our pavilion area. How I ached to run to him, put my arms around him, pull him toward me, taste his salty kisses. Instead, I dutifully occupied myself with the poultice dressings that Thecla was muttering over.

Geoffrey dismounted, tossing three fat, dun-colored hare to the cooks working at the fire circle near Eleanor's encampment. When he looked at me, his face was calm.

"Dress these fine fellows," he ordered, never taking his eyes from mine. My heart soared as he hesitated at the tent's entrance, his strong features framed by the purple trappings at the door. "They've fed in the stemple fields just outside the governor's palace. He will be happy to hear of their disappearance."

Rancon winked at me, his lips hiding a grin. A sporting day's hunt had done him good. The lines by his eyes had relaxed. His shoulders seemed to sag less. There was a spring to his step as he climbed over the large rolled carpet which served to keep some of the debris from tracking into the tent.

In a grand gesture, he knelt before Eleanor. She bade him rise; then, smiling, he moved toward me, took my hand, holding it over-long, his lips at my fingertips, stirring me again. When he loosened his leather vest, dark sweat stains showed on his over-tunic.

"Majesty, what news calls me forth?"

"There are strangers here, Rancon. I know not who sent them. The king is still visiting the holy solitaries; he may be remaining at a monastery in Cappadocia." She shrugged in dismay. "I fear that Lady Madeleine may still be in some danger. Hasten to find these men, discover their business here. They are in the pavilions of the Burgundian barons. I know I can trust the Count of Dreux to...."

"But he is not there, your Grace." Rancon's agitated interruption unsettled me. "The Count of Dreux hunted with us. I'll see to this at once!"

Rushing from the tent, Geoffrey mounted his horse in a leap, spurring it toward the encampment where the turbaned strangers had last been reported.

Darkness had settled on the camp when Rancon returned. The plump rabbits, now a deep brown, dripped the sharp-sweet odor of wild rosemary onto the smoking coals. Two pots of stemple, nut-colored and grainy, boiled on another grate. The royal table, lighted with two thick candles, had been set up on a level glade a short distance away.

Geoffrey approached the fire circle with two strangers at his side. They bowed low, not looking up till Rancon addressed them.

"Her Majesty, Eleanor, the Queen of France."

"Ah, many praises to you, Majestic Queen." The gangly man who spoke called himself Rogano of Tarsus. He had come, he said, only to bring good tidings. "Emperor Conrad before you has brought a great victory to his noble cause. There were spoils and treasures abounding." He looked hungrily around the table at the pieces of royal silver. "Like this."

He gestured toward the table, opening his hand as though introducing the pieces to their owner. Gritty nails curled over his fingers, and his index finger shone with a sapphire ring of great price. His mouth, stretched into a crooked grin, showed two missing teeth. His worn tunic glistened with oil stains.

Rogano moved nervously from one fur-booted foot to the other. "We wait to tell the King of France the joyful tidings, too." He grinned more widely. His mean-eyed companion, apparently capable of no speech, bowed several times. Underneath a soiled, knee-length tunic hung a strange kind of pantaloon fastened by bandage-like wrappings going from knee to ankle, bearing the dust of many roads and morsels of many meals.

"What did you in the service of Emperor Conrad, if indeed that was your place?" Eleanor inquired; her voice held an edge.

"We were sent from the Emperor Manuel to act as special guides for his Highness, the Teuton, Conrad." Rogano's eyes twinkled with his reply.

"You were sent to guide Conrad? You were not sent here to this encampment by the Emperor Manuel?" Eleanor glanced at Rancon. They both relaxed visibly. I found my breath again, praying for no more alarms.

"You are sure that you are not here with a message from the Emperor Manuel?" Eleanor pressed the men.

They looked at each other and shook their turbaned heads in unison. "No, Majesty, we come to tell you of the great German victory. We will stay with you till the king returns and guide him to this rich place. But," Rogano's eyes, black as olives, swept to the circle, "we are very hungry. The day's journey was long and tiring. We did not stop at any rest-place. We carried good news only for you." He bowed again to the carpeted ground.

"Thank you for so tireless a journey, Rogano of Tarsus." Eleanor turned to Rancon, "Please see that they are fed, then show them quarters by Louis' guard station. He will want to speak with them immediately upon his return." Then, in their native Langue d'oc she queried him. "When does Louis return? He seems over-long in his devotions. We have need of him here. Is Galeran about?"

Rancon shook his head.

"As for them," Eleanor caste a sidelong glance at the interlopers, "I do not trust them a minute."

"Nor I, Your Majesty, if even for that long. I thought it best for you to meet them." Rancon studied the scruffy fellows. "They are called Turcopoles people bred by Turkish fathers with Christian mothers." He continued to speak in the language of the provinces. "They are used by our Frankish forces for many purposes, as soldiers, guides, scouts or messengers. Because of their dark appearance, they can go places where we Franks cannot."

Rancon paused for a moment as though weighing his next words. "You should know that since their arrival and their news, even more disagreement has erupted among the forces. Now, several nobles are anxious to depart to engage the enemy. They don't want the Germans to have all the glory. Mortimer threatens to lead them out at dawn."

Eleanor tried to interrupt, but Rancon held up his hand. "I reminded him that the queen's men were to be in the van. He argued that this is not the queen's expedition, it is the king's and that since Louis is not here, he will take a company and scout ahead. He is foolhardy, your Grace, and I believe he will do it."

"Well, since it is the king's expedition, it is for Louis and his other commanders to judge, or Galeran. They should be back soon. I hope they have met no harm."

"If you are concerned, your Majesty, I'll increase the guard and send out a search party to see to Louis' whereabouts."

"Good. Place these Turcopole messengers where they will do no harm, then return here to our table and some excellent roast hare."

"Thank you, Highness, but I have much to do. Goodnight, your Majesty," and with hunger in his eyes, a bow to me, "Goodnight, ladies."

Led by Raoul holding his torch aloft, Rancon stepped into the light-flecked night taking the mysterious visitors with him, Aquitainian guards close by.

By terce the next day, Raoul found us in front of the pavilions sorting herbs for the day's meals.

"His Majesty had been lost, Queen Eleanor, but thanks to Holy St. Denis, he has been found and escorted back to safety by the search party."

Eleanor and I exchanged looks of relief.

"And, your Majesty,…" Raoul hesitated.

"Go on, lad," Eleanor urged.

"The turbaned strangers escaped into the night without a trace."

"There's more, isn't there?" Eleanor walked toward him.

"Yes," he gulped. "Mortimer de Mur has departed with a large company of men. He reported to Sir Geoffrey that he was anxious to march for the glorious honor of God."

"And the more imminent reward of plunder," Eleanor finished.

Raoul, anxious to be done with his odious message, blurted, "They struck out in the direction of the Germans' great victory, on the middle road leading out of Nicaea, as advised by the Turcopole guides."

"A pox on his rebellious hide! Tell Sir Geoffrey to join me as soon as he can. This is what happens when the king goes willy-nilly about his side trips. By Saint Benedict's beads, he should attend to the matters at hand! Are we directing a marching expedition to aid the Holy Land or a pilgrimage for celibates?"

Geoffrey appeared an hour later. "I have tried to see Louis since his return, but he is not to be found." Rancon's resigned shrug signaled his frustration.

Eleanor's frown reflected her chancellor's mood. "Mortimer's departure implies a disarray among our forces that troubles me greatly. Is there no command to alert the rest of the camp to assemble for marching orders?"

"Not yet. I'll send word when it's time. I must find the king. He's reportedly at his devotions somewhere by the lakefront. I'll keep you informed. Farewell, your majesty."

Rancon rode out of sight. I sought some soothing wintergreen among the herbs, so unsettled a feeling had I.

CHAPTER 18

Lake Ascania

Through the restless night we awaited word from Rancon. At dawn, Thecla nudged me. "Come, we'll look for fennel and cedar bark." She handed me the worn herb sack and, grabbing our capes, we tip-toed over the threshold. The moon, a sliver scythe, was fading in the west, and sunrise over the mountains spread coral in the skies. Germer left the fire to the cooks and joined us.

Thecla's abundant store of cures never ceased to intrigue me. When some of the pilgrims became ill, she had created a concoction of chestnut leaves and bark that helped the bilious yellow clear from their faces, leaving only splotches around the eyes. Fussing and humming about her pots, she had also brewed an elixir of lavender blossoms and wine, which helped cure severe liver pain, but supplies were running short.

By the time we reached the marshy slope, the sun had splashed a gilded sheen upon the lake. Small white shorebirds strutted and danced in the lapping wavelets, and nearby, horses nibbled at the grassy edges.

Groaning off her gray cob, Thecla tossed the worn flaxen bag from her hefty shoulders. We spread out, she to the east toward the road, and I toward the woods. Germer hugged the marsh line. We searched for comfrey, penny royal, and fennel. Later, we'd look for cedar bark in the foothills.

It was a soothing pastime, digging for the pungent autumnal herbs. Early sun warmed my back, the earth cold to my touch.

"Lady Madeleine, you must see this!" Thecla thrashed through the underbrush toward me.

"What is it, Thecla?"

"That puff adder Mortimer has changed his course. He is returning to camp for some reason of import."

We hunched in the shelter of the high bushes. Mortimer was the last person I wanted to see. "Look, he is in the company of messengers from the Teutons! By Saint Catherine's sword, those are their emblems." I recognized the banner from the days in Paris, when Conrad's envoys had puffed their Germanic pride down the halls. They seemed less arrogant now.

"We must inform the queen at once."

"Her majesty sleeps still, I am sure." Germer had crept to us.

Thecla rearranged the folds of her worn saffron tunic. "Aye, the queen sleeps still, and I say, Germer, that the queen will not sleep when she learns that we saw Mortimer the viper returning this way with Teuton messengers."

"You're right." We stole back to the royal pavilion, Thecla all herbs and agitation. She woke Sybelle who rose up on one elbow.

"Thecla, what are you doing about so early? Is it daylight?" Eleanor sat straight up immediately. "Thecla, is Florine...?"

"No, Majesty, no, all is well there. She sleeps better these nights, but you must hear how weasel Mortimer has returned with more heralds in tow. But these men wear no turbans; they wear the Teuton emblem, and their helms are black."

"He returns with Teutons?" Eleanor grabbed her wrap, flinging it around her. "He marched off yesterday with Turk guides who steal away in the night, now he reappears with heralds who come from Conrad?" Heading for the door, she asked, "Where is Germer?"

"Right at tent's edge, Majesty. I'll fetch him here at once." Thecla gave a toss to her head, tidied a strand of whitening hair back under her cap, then swept the tent flap aside with a flourish.

Upon Germer's arrival, questions flew. "Why does Mortimer return with heralds? Is he so soon victorious? Make haste. Bring me news." Eleanor pulled a long strand off her forehead.

Thecla retrieved her bag of herbs. "It is good to be of such high spirits at daybreak," she announced, "though my bones tell me there is trouble to come by the day's end." She lofted the sack to lodge overhead in the guide ropes.

"Why would Mortimer return so soon? And for what reason are there more messengers from Conrad except to crow of their great winnings?" Eleanor hurried her hair for the morning's grooming, brushing its swirls with swift strokes; then putting a small ivory comb device to work, she went carefully through the long, thick honey-colored strands in her hand.

"Events are beginning to go awry. And where is Louis? Rancon has apparently not located him. I loathe the lassitude with which Louis is running things." Eleanor bit her lip. "He ignores the hostile activity with which we've been met. He simply must be more involved, more realistic."

"Surely someone could influence the king," I speculated, thinking how adept Rancon could be if given the chance. "Of course, they would have to get past Galeran first."

The sun was well up when Germer's news cascaded out to stun us. "Mortimer has returned, and Rancon, after some searching, seems to have found the king."

"Were those German messengers with Mortimer?" Eleanor interrupted.

"Yes, German messengers are with him. Those Turcopole guides lied, Majesty. More than that, they are guilty of treachery."

"Treachery? More than deceiving us?"

"Yes, Majesty," Germer's eyes widened as he revealed the details. "Several days ago, high in the mountains, these curs led Conrad into an ambush, pilfered what spoils they could off the fallen Germans, and, for some reason, came into our camp to tell the lie of Conrad's victory. In truth, the German leader has suffered a massacre, losing three-fourths of his troops."

"Suffered a massacre? Sacre Cor!" I jumped to my feet.

"Indeed, Lady Madeleine. Many of the wounded struggle to reach Nicaea. The Emperor Conrad is on his way to meet with King Louis." Germer's report spilled out. "It is said that he seeks counsel with our king and more than that, these vaunted Germans need money, supplies and victuals."

Germer motioned to Thecla. "The Emperor of the Germans is believed to be suffering from tertian fever, his head a rage of heat."

"Ah, those perfidious guides! I knew they had the hearts of jackals, those two leering fools. May they roast in hell!" Eleanor threw her brush aside and began to dress. "Make the area ready for proper show. I suspect we will have many visitors this day."

Eleanor's suspicions were well founded. Our first visitor was Geoffrey. He had barely time to take my hand, before revealing, "His Majesty, King Louis, has been located in a wall cave nearby. He was reluctant to leave his devotions, but he now returns to camp."

Trumpets sounded. "That's the signal," Rancon nodded. "Louis wants his forces to stand at attention to await the arrival of Emperor Conrad." In a flurry of activity, Rancon ushered us to the assembly area.

Flanked by his bishops, with a contingent of Templars and Hospitallers forming a receiving column, Louis awaited the Emperor's arrival.

I stood on tip-toe to see, as a ragged royal guard led Conrad into camp. Louis stepped forward and announced to the faltering emperor, "I welcome Emperor Conrad, my warrior brother in Christianity." Conrad, flushed with fever, lurched forth to bow before

Louis. The king bade him rise, then bursting into tears, removed the wallet at his waist and in a simple, spontaneous gesture of charity, handed it to the German sovereign.

"As King of France, I declare all our resources to be shared with our brothers who struggle to quell the enemies of Christ!"

Galeran, at the king's elbow, paled at the gesture, but once the deed was done, nodded slowly in support. I was not sure whether it was in disbelief or stunned approval. For the royal head of France to remove his wallet caused a stir among the assembled nobles. It was, in anyone's terms, an unheard of act of generosity.

Mortimer blustered forward to raise his pennant and his voice. "By God, let us all avenge these cowardly deeds. I will not rest until the last Saracen is dead! May Saint George lead us to the foe!"

Over the tumultuous cheers shaking the ground, Eleanor put her elbow into me. "Is he not most like the lizard that changes color? Quick to change as with the wind."

As I agreed, Count Phillip raised his veteran's sword high, proclaiming, "We will slice our way to Jerusalem!"

His knights rallied round his colors shouting, "It is God's will! Jesus Christ be Praised!"

The cheers abated, giving way to a milling concern among the Franks who gestured toward the trail. Through the swirling dust, the first German wounded arrived, many in hastily assembled pine-bough stretchers dragged by a few spavined mules. Their faces ashen, their wounds still etching blood onto their crude bandages, the injured and the dying were borne into the camp. Eleanor took several of the royal wives into her care.

The Hospitallers set up an infirmary, but the wounded far outnumbered them. I recruited Sybelle and arrived at the makeshift quarters searching for Charles. He welcomed our assistance, and the three of us set to work together. Thecla, quick to bring her ointments and dressings, stood at our sides.

"Here, Thecla, we must staunch the blood."

"Madeleine, help me with this splint. This man's bones are splintered; aye, we can only wrap it." Charles calling for aid, sent Linnert for more interns.

As Sybelle pressed bandages into the flesh-torn wounds, I treated the skull injuries with the heavy sleeping drug. Thecla laid compresses where she could, then left. There was little else to do for the glassy-eyed men, paralyzed, but still alive.

When supplies ran out, Sybelle and I returned to our tent where we helped each other wash the smell of blood from our hands and arms. Wordlessly, we disrobed and poured water to set our tunics to soak.

Thecla had heard us come in. Rising up, she gathered me in her arms, stroking my brow.

"It is too much to see all at once. Too cruel. You must have some herb brew that will help you to forget. Here, drink this."

I took the fragrant drink down in a few gulps, then crumpled to my pallet.

Darkness engulfed the encampment. With the jongleurs stilled, the lutes and viols silenced, grief rose from the fire circles. Neither crackling flames nor prayerful conversations could drown out the constant swinging of picks and scraping of shovels that hollowed out graves for the men who did not live through the night.

Minstrels chanted, not gay roundels but 'requiem aeternam' throughout the black hours. In spite of Thecla's brew, I slept little, and toward night's end, I lifted the tent flap for more air. Off toward the gravesites, I saw the glimmer of a lantern, heard men shoveling, softly and with care. Still digging graves? No, but where the fresh graves pushed up the earth, cravens and cut-purses slithered here and there in the half-light, pilfering what they could from a fallen knight's last resting place. A voice from the shadows seemed to direct them. I swear it was Mortimer's. Shivering, I returned to my bed, hearing the muffled, eerie night. I longed for Geoffrey's soothing embrace.

❦   ❦   ❦

Two days later, both the dispirited German complement and the well-equipped Franks gathered on the wide plain that eased toward the lake. In that crisp November dawn, Chaplain Odo's doleful voice carried beyond the sad murmuring of the assemblage. For the benefit of both the bereaved and the comforters, he read from a ragged piece of parchment the inspired words of Holy Bernard.

"Advance in confidence, you knights, and boldly drive out the enemies of the Cross of Christ; be sure that neither death nor life can separate you from the love of God which is in Christ Jesus. How famously do such victors return from battle! How blessed are such martyrs when they die in battle. For if they are blessed who die in the Lord, how much more blessed are those who die for the Lord?"

At the conclusion of Mass, Sybelle and I returned quickly to our quarters.

"Does it cause you to doubt when you know that the German duchesses, Gertrude and Ursula, turn back now, returning to Constantinople?" Sybelle searched my face, waiting for an answer.

"Yes, it does. But, Sybelle, we have always known there would be dangers. I have come to realize that there are many deaths." I hesitated, searching for words. "To have stayed in Constantinople in a brocaded jeweled cage would have been one death for me, away from Paris, from Poitiers, away from you, Eleanor and little Marie. They are my family now. A slow death, but a dying nonetheless. Eleanor taught me long ago that there are many who would cage us. So we must not cage ourselves. And, Sybelle, fear puts the lock to the cage." I would recall those words many times in the coming months.

Sybelle slowed her pace. Glancing afar, she seemed lost in the high peaks across the lake. At length she turned to ask, "You don't think to march into the point of a Seljek sword is worse than being caged?"

"Ah, but Sybelle, we choose it. We choose it. We choose to die for Our Lord and for our own redemption. We use our free will."

We walked in silence until we reached our campsite. Camp hands had struck the tents, lashing them securely onto the baggage wagons. A few small canopies remained and there the cooks stirred up the breakfast meal, a hearty fish soup with hot stemple bread.

Hurriedly, we washed down our vittles and gathered on an open field where our Frankish forces readied to march out after bidding Godspeed to what remained of Emperor Conrad's army. Eleanor exchanged a questioning look with me when we learned that the emperor, ailing as he was, had been persuaded to continue on to Jerusalem with Louis.

The rest of Conrad's entourage took their places to trek back across the straits. Tattered banners flew above the once-glorious army that now turned its back on Jerusalem. Forfeiting their vows, princes and pilgrims headed in the direction of Constantinople.

As I waved to the departing women, my throat tightened and I struggled against tears. A knot of sorrow pushed at my chest. Around its edges, diminished though it may be, fear lay coiled, waiting to reclaim me.

Like the wings of a giant bird, the two marching columns spread out from the central area. One, disarrayed, stretched to the north, its decimated numbers faltering in the direction of the Bospherus. The other column, in step to the marching drums, fell in behind the Frankish vanguard with its bright banners aloft, purple and gold. Heeding Conrad's urgent advice to avoid the mountain passes, Louis had agreed to set out toward the levant seeking the coast along the Aegean Sea.

I searched for Geoffrey. I found him, his face intense, head held high, directing his men. Our eyes locked briefly as I rode by, nothing more.

Far to the rear, pilgrims sang, "He who goes forth with Louis, what has he to fear from hell?" Their voices, like the mist, hung with the ghosts above the fields. I turned in my saddle. The last German column had moved out of sight. My conversation with Sybelle hummed in my mind. "But we choose it. We choose it."

Plaintive bird calls echoed from the water's edge, then like the haunting pilgrims' chorus, faded from the desolate shores of Lake Ascania. Shuffling feet and the insistent thump of the marching drum were the only sounds. What, I wondered, had I chosen?

CHAPTER 19

Ephesus

*E*ncouraged by the crisp November weather, our expedition marched at a better pace. The animals held up well. Though the baggage wains faltered on the stony paths, there was little grade, and the large sumpter horses were not strained excessively under their loads. Each night, when cloud-swept sunsets flamed to the west, Germer barked orders to the cook servants. Camp hands raced against the fading light. With tents hoisted and cook stations busy, we dined well on fresh fish and rice cakes. Good wine and snapping fires helped erase the memory of the German misfortune.

Rancon eased his horse to my side before heading up the vanguard. Our eyes signaled the secret between us. I kept a casual tone. "The further we progress from Constantinople, the less threatened I feel by Emperor Manuel's forces. I'll be ever thankful for your brave rescue."

"I would do it again in a minute, M' lady." Geoffrey smiled. We rode along the arid coastal terrain before he continued, his face clouded, "There is still baronial acrimony over my part in your abduction. I had hoped it would cease, but it hasn't. Nor do the planning sessions go as well as they could. Louis listens to every side, then promises a decision later. One that never comes." His knee grazed mine and he was gone.

We crossed the scrubby plain into Smyrna where, a thousand years before, the disciples of Jesus had spread the good news amid the silver olive groves and fruitful vineyards. At our evening meal, Geoffrey revealed more disturbing information.

"We've had a difficult time persuading Louis not to stray out into to the plains. He wants to meditate in the manner of Saint Anthony, paying homage to the solitaries and monks hidden away in craggy caves. He's insisted on staying in one of the high corries to be nearer God." Geoffrey paced the pavilion, a nervous gesture more like Eleanor's behavior than his. "The council has finally persuaded Galeran that he must insist the king press on. Galeran agreed to do so, deciding that we'll head straight for Ephesus. We are to spend several days there."

With a curt bow, he turned to leave. Eleanor pursued him, "What is it your keeping from me, Sir Geoffrey? It is not like you."

Geoffrey flushed in discomfort. "It's nothing, really, I probably shouldn't mention it—"

"Please, Geoffrey, you are my contact with reality. What now?"

He avoided Eleanor's inquiring look. He was struggling with something, but what?

Geoffrey, shoulders hunched, lowered his voice, "Last night, I went in search of the king on a matter of supplies when I came upon him in an isolated bramble thicket. His Majesty was—was—nude, reciting from the Psalms. 'My soul weeps for sorrow,' he repeated. Then, in the chill of the night, he uncovered a small hamper and, exercising meticulous care, began to cover himself with ashes." Geoffrey hesitated, looking to me. I signaled him to go on. She needed to know.

"It appeared that his Majesty was taking up a vigil for the remainder of the night. He whispered prayers and contritions for the sins of his soul and those in his charge, especially his beloved wife." Geoffrey seemed torn between awe and embarrassment. "Then," he spoke slowly, "I heard Galeran's voice from the shadows. 'You have prayed long enough, good Majesty.'"

"Louis seemed not to hear. I stepped into view, and the king asked me, 'Ah, Rancon, would you not watch one hour with me? Come, remain here till Prime, then will I cleanse myself and meet with the others.'"

Eleanor sighed. "Jesu!"

Rancon continued, "I felt out of place. There was Galeran, clenching his teeth, imploring Louis, 'Come, your devoted Highness. I will have your squire see to your bath. You must be ready to meet with your vassals by then.'

"Galeran ignored me and soothed Louis, 'We shall pray at every mass till we reach Ephesus, Majesty. We'll meditate on the words of Paul, once addressed to the holy men of that city. Let wives be subject to their husbands as to the Lord.'"

Rancon cast a cautious glance at Eleanor and me before continuing, "Galeran's face gleamed with pride as he shot me a knowing glance. 'That, Good King, that—could be heard by your wife and her ladies at every service from here to Jerusalem.'"

Flushing, Eleanor rose to leave. Geoffrey laid a gentle hand on her arm. "Wait, there's more. Louis, his face pinched, had shivered in his ashes. 'Has the queen transgressed in some way that I know not?'"

"Galeran sent another burning look my way. 'Well, Highness, the sad truth is that she continues to have plainsongs and dancing, even as we frequent the places where the saints have been martyred. Her servants buy wine, and,' Galeran's eyes grew cold, 'Count Rancon then joins them.'"

"Enough, Geoffrey," Eleanor clapped her hands over her ears. "When will our concerns be heard?" She joined Rancon in the pacing, organizing her thoughts. "We must move on; there is food in short supply for the wagon masters, we need to bargain for salt so that we might put down more of the fish that are so plentiful, wagons need leather for mending."

"Dear Eleanor, I raised all these questions. When the king pulled his pilgrim shawl tightly around him and moved toward the royal pavilion hopping like a playful child to avoid the sharp pebbles, I gave up."

Eleanor looked to the heavens. "How helpful it would be if there were a prayer for husbands!" She thanked Geoffrey for his report. He took my hand and kissed it tenderly, then departed, leaving us to hope the wine supply held until we reached Ephesus.

For several mornings, we had listened dutifully as Odo read the St. Paul epistle at every Mass. Echoing over our covered heads, his voice carried to the timeless fields. He hoped these words might make us more worthy for the visitation to the cathedral at Ephesus, where we heard yet another delivery of the apostle's message silencing women.

As we left, Thecla stooped to pick up a terra cotta shard. "Artemis once spoke here." The old woman's round cheeks were freckled from the sun. She winked at me, her lips slanted in a half-smile. "And now there are messages to still all that. There's the assembly horn. Let's be on our way."

The road out of Ephesus sloped upward slowing our pace. Eleanor turned in her saddle to converse with me. "We'll celebrate Christmastide soon. We shall try to make our pavilion as festive as the palace at Bordeaux, though we, ourselves, will be less so."

I forced a smile. The terrain had become more challenging and so had the maintaining of supplies. Count Phillip had demanded that Sybelle render her brocaded cape to barter for grain with the truculent Greeks at Ephesus. Eleanor and I soon parted with ours as well. The week before, Eleanor had instructed Germer to trade the silver trays that the covetous Turcopoles had so admired. He had returned with two goat kids, a scant bag of oats for the larder, dried fruits, some lentils and green ale.

Thecla complained that the foodstuffs were diminishing too rapidly. Eleanor's steward came to ask for more gold. The question of adequate provisions nagged at her far more than it did Louis, who steadfastly insisted that since God had willed them to be on the journey, He would provide.

Once beyond Ephesus, we marched past the deserted settlement of Smyrna where lofty mountains watched the seas. The coastal lands turned hostile. Townsfolk drove their flocks high into brushy canyon crevices, dreading the unbridled pillaging for which the Franks had become renowned. Quick to heed the alarms spread by Turks or Greeks, who had given up all pretense of aiding us, cities slammed shut their gates and closed their markets to our armies and the suffering pilgrim hoards.

Our nobles made desperate entreaties outside forbidding limestone walls, their squires forced to hold silver ewers aloft. Others displayed gold-bordered linen tunics to blow in the wind. Then, crafty merchants, squatting atop the walls, would lower by rope their baskets to exchange provisions for our Frankish treasures. Often, victuals returned down the walls in amounts much lower than had been agreed upon. Prices escalated as the march wore on.

Early Christmastide week, we mustered at dawn. I readied my gear for Germer to load and finished dressing. The girdle given me by Eleanor that celebratory night in Vezelay pulled easily past its usual tying place. A shadow fell across the doorway, and I looked up to see Rancon. His handsome face was taut with concern.

"Good morning, Geoffrey." My eyes fixed on his. "The queen has gone on the staging area. I am delayed this morning."

"We are all delayed, I'm afraid." Cautiously he took my hand, stepped close enough for his leathery fragrance to stir me. I ached to hold him, have him take me in his embrace. "We've been en route from Metz for almost seven months, and the expedition is several weeks behind schedule." His face creased with worry. "I had hoped to be well on the road to Antioch by now. Things are out of control."

Impulsively, he reached for me, holding me close, stroking my hair. Aching for more, I pressed against him, lifting my face to his—a dangerous act, I knew. Our lips met, rousing more desire. Trumpets echoed from the staging area. Slowly, I let him go. Geoffrey swung onto his horse and headed toward the royal guard. He turned to wave, leaving me to treasure his salty taste and a love I must deny.

After I reached the assembly area, Eleanor, Sybelle and I fell in ahead of the red litter which bore Thecla and Florine. A company of Bretons headed the van, while Rancon and the royal guard protected us on either side. With their lances flashing like a long silver cord, they rode two abreast whenever the road allowed. A troop of Templars followed, then the rest of the entourage kept pace as best it could. King Louis, accompanied by Count Phillip and his guard of seasoned Flemish knights, brought up the rear, protecting the floundering, ill-fed pilgrim hoard.

By late afternoon, we had negotiated the narrow pass opening into the wide Dercervion valley. The vigorous Meander River, a throbbing, light-green avenue broken at frothy, bouldered intervals sliced diagonally across it. Ample banks and sloping, dry meadows decked with bleached sweet grass would provide good quartering for the troops and horses.

"Halt now, in the name of the Lord!" The call echoed down the lines. Soon, our pavilions were established, colorful purple and gold standards set into the soil. A row of festive bannerettes, gay as jester's rags, danced in the breeze. We prepared to celebrate Christmas. "This," Eleanor announced with more spirit than I had seen in some time, "will be a wondrous place to celebrate the Feast of the Nativity."

I wanted to match her cheerful mood and sought out Thecla.

"Come with me to search some dried berries and bay leaf, Thecla. You will know where to look."

Florine reclined on the recently arranged pallets by the fire grate. "Will you join us, Fluorine?"

Nodding yes, she raised herself with some effort from the low cushion on the carpeted floor of the tent. Thecla walked with us past her medicine wagon. Looking toward the high Phrygian peaks surrounded by dark, round-bellied thunderheads, the old woman shook her head slowly from side to side.

"I do not like this place." Her hands worked at her elbows and back. "It will rain, M'lady. I feel my joints begin to ache." Her mouth drooped in a way that told of an impending sulk. "I could heal myself at once with a simmered quince, but they are not to be had at this season. Or," she continued with a sigh, "I could rub on wine and deer-fat salve and stand in front of the fire, but there is no elm wood here, and only that will do." Eying the clouds again, she cursed under her breathe.

"The fires are of scrub oak, Thecla. Won't that help?" I wanted to keep her soothed. Thecla never replied, or if she did, I couldn't hear her above the sudden uproar.

In the distance, howls and a frenzied sound like that of beating drums slipped through the pass. At the same time, two lookouts raced into the camp area, shouting, "Take cover! Into your pavilions!" A blast of horns summoned troops from every quarter. "We are under attack in the high meadows!"

With nimble movement, Thecla scooped up Florine, a firm grip under one arm. I took the other side. We sprinted toward the tent, lunging for cover. Hulga, Eleanor and Sybelle had begun to stack rolled carpets and cushions along the sides. Thecla positioned herself to shield a trembling Fluorine, whose face looked like clay, her eyes shut tight.

"Queen Eleanor!" Geoffrey shouted above the clamor. Fully armed, his helm close by his eyes, he burst in. "Are all the women here?"

"Yes, Geoffrey. Who attacks us?"

"Saracens! Put on armored vests if they are close at hand. Lie low behind the cushions. Stay until you get word to do otherwise. I'll send more guards at once." He looked hard at me. "Dare not venture out!"

"To arms, to arms!" Amid the uproar, the camp set itself for battle. Horses tore past, their hooves splattering the tent with soft meadow soil. Calls for warriors echoed far.

A flurry of knights churned by and headed toward the high meadow. Led by Count Phillip, the army of Flanders advanced first into the fray, followed by men-at-arms on foot. Saracen marauders, atop their fleet ponies, swept out of the pass to capture or damage the heavy Frankish horses grazing there. Beating small Oriental drums and wielding sharp, slender lances, the Turks plunged their weapons deep into several of the sumpter horses, slicing at their flanks. A wave of Infidel bowmen, protecting themselves with round shields, followed close. Blood spattered the parched meadow grass.

Count Phillip yelled, "Hah! The fools dare to charge us in an open field. They beg defeat." His experience with the Saracen enemy had taught him well. Leading his lancers into the melee, he commanded his men to advance. "Forward, for the love of God!"

My heart pounded as loud as the battle drums. From my position lying prone on the tent floor, elbows propped on the rolled carpet, I watched the battle up on the hill. There, Phillip clutched his prized lance under his arm, steadied by a sinewy hand made firm and strong since childhood. He charged into the tangle of horses and men. A veteran cavalier, he held his shield to him at the same time he directed his horse with his left hand, lance at the ready in his right.

Amid the clash of steel, the thought that our warriors might not hold sent chills through me. I dared not imagine our fate if we were to be captured—or worse—much worse. I made sure my dagger was at hand. I had fought once for my life, and though terrified, I could fight again.

But our chevaliers, led by Flanders, rode as one with their steeds. With skill they urged them forward. Phillip swiftly found his mark, and blood spurted from the neck of an oncoming Turk. Pulling free his bloodied lance, the Count of Flanders yelped in joy, regrouping with his men. He had drawn first blood.

"Onward for Christ our King!"

"Death to the unclean beast!"

"For Christ and for King Louis!"

Shouts rang out in the fading light. Men hacked and plunged, yelling encouragement to one another. Salutes of bravery echoed on the slope. Close by, Phillip swiped at another Turk, watching him tumble from his pony. Pursuing him to the death, Flanders left his opponent's dark curly beard matted with blood, his face, a mashed crimson pulp.

As quickly as they had come, the band of hooting tribesmen circled their nimble ponies, then fled eastward into the rocky passes. In a wake of blood and excrement, they left their dead on the field, cast down on the wet grass. Up the line, on a command from Mortimer, the light-armed horseman began pursuit.

Phillip wheeled, his face brimming with rage. "Sound retreat!," he commanded the trumpeter by his left flank. "For Christ Sake, sound retreat!" The command spewed from his sweat-covered lips.

At the sound of the horn, the mounted bowmen reined their horses hard and returned to the field where Phillip waited. His face livid under his helmet, he yelled, "Look you, and learn it well!"

He stood in his stirrups. "That is a tactic of the Infidel dog, to draw us after them. They are circled and wait for us in the pass to fight us on the hilly, broken ground. Pursue them not."

"Then they will call us cowards!" Mortimer's chest swelled, his puffy jowls spraying spittle.

Phillip glared at the mercenary rogue. "We are not cowards who do not follow into a trap, fool. We will fight another day, you may be sure, Mortimer."

Mortimer turned to his aid, a sullen look on his face. When Phillip's back was to him, he mumbled something, and spat.

Now, Flanders' breathing eased. "Let us give thanks for this victory on the eve of the Nativity of the Prince of Peace." Guiding his sweaty horse, speckled bright with blood, Phillip lead the victors down the grade, back to the encampment.

To my relief, I spied Rancon returning from the high meadow. His sword held high, he cantered the perimeter of the camp, checking on each company, positioning the men, alerting the royal guard to prepare for a long night's watch.

Flanders' company lost no men. Six lancers had wounds, one lad suffering a serious slash that left his shoulder bone exposed. The rest, victorious knights, had gleefully shared their booty, cutting purses and jeweled neckbands from the dead. Circling the battle scene, Phillip's whole being exuded victory. Perhaps, he had felt what he had longed to feel, the thrust of the lance, hot from his hand, and the throb of the warrior's pulse strong in his loins.

Led by Mortimer, a few bloodthirsty warriors began to decapitate their victims, searching for poles upon which to display their trophies, a perverse salute to the Prince of Peace and a sight which will always revolt me. Observing Mortimer's distorted countenance as he shed blood at so close a range had left me shaken, remembering his debased slaughter of my men.

Finally, the victory trumpet blared. Stretching, Eleanor and Sybelle got up from their crouched position. Sybelle fell to her knees. We joined her.

"Deo gratias, we are spared. Good Saint George, you blessed the brave Franks this day."

"Amen."

With Thecla's bag of salves slung over my shoulder, I hurried to find where Charles would set up his infirmary. The Hospitallers had begun to lift the wounded into carts. Above their groans, Florine's high-pitched laughter followed me across the soiled, spattered battlefield.

CHAPTER 20

The Meander River

I had done all I could helping Charles. I returned to our encampment. When I stepped into our tent, tension, heavy as sheep's wool, hung in our pavilion. Geoffrey had ordered that all meals be taken within the shelters, warning us to stay armed and on guard.

"The Saracens could return at any time. They know this terrain as we do not, and can roam at will." He looked directly at me. "Be watchful at all times."

Our supper of dried venison mixed with gruel was difficult to swallow. Thecla's soup had a strong, rancid flavor that even her mixture of spices couldn't disguise. Thecla spied my hesitation with the drink.

"What, not liking the porridge? I say drink it while you can." The old woman pushed aside the tent flap and sniffed the air. "There are no good cooking smells tonight, M'lady." She rubbed her elbows, went to the opening again, drew a long breath, heaving her large bosom, then returned still fussing at her elbows. Her eyes had a far away look. "There is the smell of rain, M'lady, too much rain, so drink your gruel while ye may."

Thecla seemed to be in one of her moods, so I downed the soup. The taste lingered at the back of my throat. Or perhaps it was fear again, pushing at my defenses. Or sadness at the bloodshed.

My utter disgust with Mortimer intensified. It was hard to be anywhere in his presence. It may have been my imagination, but he seemed to find a way to be where I was more times than I care to count. To observe him engrossed in his love of murder, frothing to have more victims, reawakened that dreadful day of flight when, under the smoky skies of San Sevier, first I saw him kill. Now, close to the smoldering thorn-bush fire, I fought back both fear and sorrow.

Sybelle inquired, "How fare the wounded, Madeleine?"

"Only five defenders suffering from serious wounds, deep ones that may fester if not properly treated with vervain poultices. But Charles is becoming more skilled with the stitches. He may become an excellent surgeon by the time we reach Antioch."

"And soon we will." Eleanor joined in cheerfully, pleased to be guiding the conversation once again. "Uncle Raymond will greet us so graciously. Antioch is a place of great riches, judging from the generous gifts that he has sent to our court. His messengers spoke of a city of beauty and ease. I'm sure many friends await our arrival."

Eleanor adjusted her tunic, assuring that the light chain vest stay in place, then she settled onto the soft pallet, pulling a heavy skin over her. Firelight flickered off the copper wisps of her hair. Her face showed fatigue, her eyes held no sparkle. Our somber silence in the close environs may have bothered her for she attempted to brighten our spirits. "Madeleine, it is the eve of the Nativity. Say the verse for us."

"And there were shepherds abiding in the fields, keeping watch over their flocks by night."

"Now let us sing the refrain," Eleanor directed. "Oh, I do wish Jacques and Eliaze were here, but Rancon would not hear of it. Very well, we will raise our own voices in response. All together now."

"Gaude, gaude, Emmanuel.
Rejoice, rejoice, Emmanuel
For Christ is born to Israel."
We chanted the sweet refrain. As Eleanor would have it, faith supplanted fear. The Gloria became a spirited roundelay in the manner of Eliaze.

"And here is a surprise even Madeleine knew nothing about!" Eleanor brought forth a satchel of sweetmeats and honey cakes that she had been hoarding for Christmas Day. "They will be the more enjoyed tonight!"

Sybelle offered half of hers to Florine, who crammed the sweets into her mouth, smacking her lips like a child. The rest of us put our fears aside, and with our palettes savoring flavors long wished for, mumbled good tidings among ourselves. After Thecla passed around a wet cloth for our washing, we bedded down. The royal tent fell silent except for the rhythm of fitful breathing, a descant to the hissing coals.

Shadows of firelight danced on the canvas walls. The measured night calls of the guard-watch and a rising wind blowing off the river were the only sounds. In my slumber I stirred, hoping one of the night voices might be Rancon's. The insistent wind nagging at the tent flap gave me hope that Geoffrey, as he had when we traveled the Danube, might creep in to lay beside me, his lips brushing my cheek.

Shortly after midnight, Thecla, unable to sleep for the pain in her shoulders, heard the first clap of thunder rumble like the voice of Jehovah across the eastern mountains. She claimed the sound throbbed in her veins, and echoed in her temples. "I smell rain, M'lady, the smell of rain floods my nostrils; aye, a dull ache to the marrow of my bones. We must wake the queen." She began to tremble, and breathing heavily, crawled from her place in the corner to shake Eleanor's shoulder.

"Queen Eleanor, you must awake!"

"Thecla?" Eleanor's hand flew to the dagger at her side. "What is the danger?"

"Rain, Majesty, such rain! I see it. I smell it. We must go for higher ground!"

"Thecla, how know you this? Are you certain?" I held a sputtering candle to the old woman's face. I had known Thecla to forecast weather in my younger days, but never with this intensity. Perspiration clung to the pained furrows in her forehead.

Suddenly, wind gusts forced the tent flap to burst its ties; the high tent poles shuddered. The others, fully awakened, leaped from their pallets. In rushed Germer, two camp hands at his side.

"Majesty," Thecla begged, "I pray you get the sumpter horses and haul the wagons first, go higher up on the plain. The medicine wagon, save the medicine wagon!" Thecla draped the bedcover over her head and rushed barefooted, to follow Germer into the ragged, black night.

I pulled on my boots, tied my tunic high, called the guards to join us. We searched the gusting winds for the horses and the wains that held the falcons. They had been supplying what little game we had. I called to Jacques and Eliaze in their small lean-to.

"There is danger, move your chattel. A grave storm approaches!"

Eleanor, with Sybelle's help, hauled Fluorine up the grade of the hillside. "Send more men here! Send for Rancon, we need help! Be quick! Dismantle the pavilion!"

All at once the skies let go. Raindrops felt like whips against my face. I dug my feet into the ground, seeking the pebbled way, but stones loosened themselves and rushed toward the river. The path became treacherous. Blinded by the surging wind, I searched for Eleanor.

"Where is Florine?" It was Hugh, his cape furling wildly. He forced a stave into the hillside to stabilize himself.

From the slope above us, we heard Eleanor. "Over here! Oh, thank God, you have come."

Eleanor, breathless from the effort of holding Florine upright upon the shifting ground, released her burden to Lord Hugh. He lifted his wife to safety.

Grabbing Sybelle's hand, Eleanor pointed upward. They disappeared into the night. I clung to a tree, overwhelmed by the sights before me. Lightning danced like the devil, highlighting the chaos, giving form to disaster. Wagon masters blindfolded the panicked horses. Men and animals moved in a midnight frenzy to hitch what wagons they could. They struggled to free the wheels of hitched and loaded carts. Horses whinnied and balked. And the river rose.

The once green-avenued Meander now raged a muddied, watery avalanche. Cries of beasts and drowning men carried beyond catastrophe. Winds that had seemed capricious now drove with a force so malicious that pavilions, their supports upended, tumbled like spinning acrobats toward the rising river. It had become a surging wall of water that battered its way down the rocky passes. Vengefully, it dragged with it all creatures, wagons, tents and pilgrims who could not escape its fury.

After a struggle, I reached Charles in the infirmary tent. It had been pitched behind a boulder, and though tilting badly, it still stood. Inside, Linnert, Charles and other Hospitallers had wrapped the wounded as best they could, and were loading them onto carts headed for higher ground. Later, I found Germer, and with his aid, rescued the falcon mews and tethered the horses on higher slopes. I crossed back to the royal site, only to discover the pavilions dashed to the ground.

"Where is everyone?" One of the serving boys pointed further up the hill where several wagons were drawn together. My soaked boots dragged heavy as stones. The long, exhausting struggle to haul the horses up the sodden hillside with the slipping wagons behind them had spent me. I yearned to find shelter. My vair cape was drenched, a wet burden to my shoulders.

A robust arm startled me, encircled me, supported me against the biting wind. I turned toward Geoffrey, his curly hair dripping under his helm-caplet.

"You have a way of disappearing, my lady. It puts a twinge to a man's heart. Let me show you where the queen is." He did not release his hold, but pressed me to him deliberately, his hand close under my breast sending a rush of excitement.

"Oh, bless you, my love." Short of breath, I let him bear my weight. "I tended the wounded, moved the falcons. We cannot lose them now, and Germer had to be everywhere at once. I helped wherever I could."

Geoffrey's rain-swept face, strong and determined, lit with a brief smile. He tightened his hold and helped me maneuver through the mud to a landing high on the hillside. Several of the wagons stood together as a shield against the wind. At their center rested the red litter, placed atop flat rocks large enough to hold ground against the flood waters.

"It is cramped, but it's the safest place for now." Geoffrey shook his head, while he looked down at the pounding river. He shouted against its roar. "We are losing too much. Several wagons into the river with supplies and arms. It does not bode well. It is said the king is praying by the river; I must leave you now."

In the darkness, our lips met, a warm brief refuge. When I kissed the rain from his cheeks, Rancon, his voice husky, spoke with haste. "God guard you, my lady love."

"And you, my dearest." Shivers swept through me. I longed for his sheltering warmth. Reluctantly, I banished such thoughts, and climbed into the litter. I would have to settle for some dry clothes.

Inside the cramped area, I answered questions from Eleanor while pulling off my soaked skins and tunic. Thanks to Thecla's forewarning, and Hulga's unexpected presence of mind, the litter contained dry clothes stacked to its ceiling. Through chattering teeth, I told

Eleanor and the others that Germer had run the falcons and the medicine wagons to higher ground.

"Thecla refuses to be anywhere but with her medicine wagon," I reported toweling my hair, "and Rancon will confer with you as soon as possible. There are many losses requiring his attention." I recalled how the rain fell in a line, tracing the top of his lip. "He reports that we are safe from attack, because even the fleet Saracen ponies stumble on this treacherous ground."

Eleanor was just as well off not to learn where Louis was or what he was doing, nor did she inquire. Gradually, the frost left my feet, and in the huddled warmth of the litter, I squeezed between Sybelle and tearful Florine, whose arms cradled her swelling belly. I tried to nap in spite of the relentless pelting atop the lacquered roof.

"What think you, Eleanor?" Though she pretended sleep, I knew she was awake.

"My mind whirls with many thoughts. How will we resupply? How numerous was the enemy? I can feel my confidence waning, not so much in my own men, but in the other expedition leaders."

I wondered how many of his worries Geoffrey had shared with her, but, given the desperation of the moment, I resisted discussion.

"Banish the frustrations from your mind, Eleanor. Things are always better by the light of day."

Now as though to torment herself further, she began to fret aloud that the torrents falling about us would loosen the slabs upon which the litter rested. The vision of us all swept into chaos frightened her, and me as well.

"Try to think of other times," I soothed, "think of our festive, shining Christmas in Bordeaux."

"I had so hoped to be in Antioch with my Uncle Raymond for this day, not confined to a dark carriage amid the acrid smells of wet furs and skins." She began to weep. I took her hand. Finally, we both dozed, disappointment shaping our dreams.

CHAPTER 21

Cadmos Pass

A wedge of bright light sliced into my troubled dreams. Sir Geoffrey, bathed in frosty sunlight, stood at the wain's open door.
Creases of fatigue framed his eyes. I reached for him, held his hand
to my lips. The thought of waking up with him at my side for the rest
of my life was much too inviting. However, his thoughts were with
the business at hand.

"Your Highness, I have been with Louis and his council for most
of the night. They've decided that we'll leave this treacherous river
path and cut through the next mountain pass. From there we'll find
our way to Sattalia."

"What about the Saracens? Do you think this is wise, Geoffrey?"

"Think it wise?" He repeated her words laced with a ring of mock-
ery not intended for her but reflecting his own exasperation. "No,
Majesty, I think it foolish. Some of our men say that it is likely to be
the same canyon where Emperor Conrad met such disaster, but
Galeran and his followers urge Louis to it, ignoring all other opinions."

He had just finished speaking when Charles, still wearing
drenched clothes, hiked slowly up the path. Dark circles sat beneath

his eyes, and Thecla, at his side, looked equally spent. She held his arm for sure footing. The men greeted each other.

"How goes it, Sir Geoffrey?"

"Is there other news, Charles?" Eleanor inquired.

"Not good. The wounded did well in the storm, but I come to warn you to stay to yourselves. There is fever among the pilgrims now. It started when we left the marshes of Ephesus, and many of the faithful are ill. Wretched souls, they have so little nourishment. The endless fogs along the river swamps hatch pestilence."

Thecla's eyes narrowed. She shook her head. "Oh, Sweet Luke the Physician, heal us, and Jesus, Healer of all, there is little we can do for pestilence. Even I, with my gifts from the wise women of yore." Her voice trailed off as she glanced around, pleased to have everyone's attention.

"Pestilence is very hard to cure in mobs like these," Thecla preached, sweeping her hand toward the flooded plain where the sodden crowds huddled in the cold. "Now, if I had just one or two people, say in the royal house, where I could minister at every opportunity, then…." She paused dramatically. "But with a mob, there is little we can do except move quickly from them. Pray for their souls that they may see God in heaven, for they surely will not last to see Him in the Holy City."

"Louis must know of this. He won't like the news." Eleanor looked at Geoffrey then dropped her eyes to the small object in her hand, rubbing its smooth lines with her fingertips. The soapstone icon of the Virgin Mary from Empress Irene became her solace. She worked it nervously when her spirits flagged.

"I'll inform the king and will send word of the hour of march." Rancon's gaze stayed locked with mine, "Or come tell you myself." As soon as the men had disappeared, we clambered out of the litter to stretch our cramped bodies in the cold bright air of Christmastide.

The clear skies continued through the next week, allowing us to dry out and take stock of our losses. The results were grim. Many of our diminishing supplies had been lost in the flash-flood, our food-stuffs as well as wagons and horses. Droves of the pilgrim hoard had met a mortal baptism in the raging Meander waters.

"Be prepared," Geoffrey warned us, "to trade every luxury you have. The king is running short on funds, and Galeran has said that your baggage is on the line."

Willingly, we offered what remained of our scarves and woolen tunics for fresh horses whenever trading was possible. Treasured gold bracelets from the Empress Irene went for grain and foodstuffs when they were available in the small, avaricious villages.

"Count Phillip has convinced Louis to employ the three swarthy Turcopole guides who have joined our forces." Geoffrey sipped his tea, an herbal brew that Thecla had scavenged from the brushy plain. His thick brows formed a crumpled line, and he shook his head as though ridding himself of gnats. "It seems they have the ear of the king's advisors informing them which passage to follow over the steep pathways. These guides say it is best to travel yonder pass through the mountains." Rancon pointed to the mountain barrier. "They say it goes through to the coast and the sea port of Sattalia, where we can resupply and finally be off for Antioch."

"Pray this time they tell the truth. When will we set out?"

"Count Phillip will be assigning marching orders for tomorrow. You will know as soon as I hear." Next day, Thecla, Germer and the servants set about packing for the early morning departure. Only the heavy skins which served as our bedding remained. All else had been rolled and packed away in the last hampers.

With a high polish to his helmet and a shine to the sword at his side, Geoffrey appeared at tent side with news. "We leave after Mass for the climb through the mountain passage. Count Robert and I have been assigned to lead the vanguard across the mountains at Cadmos Pass." His eyes danced with pride. "We'll use a company of Templars to guard the flank for we'll be hauling several of the wagons that carry the arms and equipment."

"And where will the others fall in?" Eleanor closed her purple wool hood against the cold.

"King Louis' order of march will comprise the men of Burgundy and Flanders under Count Phillip and the others will follow. His Highness will bring with him the large sumpter wagons, the foot soldiers and his light cavalry."

"And the pilgrims also, the people on foot. What of them?" I worried about the task of the Hospitallers. The Turks had continually harassed the marchers from the rear in sporadic, murderous skirmishes. Charles, with a dangerously small contingent of bowmen to protect him, often remained behind to treat the wounded.

"With his special guard, Louis will be at the extreme rear to bring along the stragglers and as many of the infirm as can still travel." Rancon was silent for a long moment. Thoughtful lines creased his brow. "The others will have to turn back or perish."

"They will perish also if they turn back, won't they?"

"Yes, they will!" he snapped. Seeing the expression of pained surprise cross my face, his manner softened, "But hasn't the pope pledged that these faithful will see God face to face in moments of their last breath?"

Geoffrey's response irritated me and I retorted sharply, "With better nursing, many would not see God quite so soon. I know the Hospitallars do their utmost, but there are not enough of them for the huge numbers along. I could have helped."

"I know Galeran has forbidden you to aid the wounded, and I'm sorry." Rancon tried to comfort me.

"Yes, he has 'forbidden' me." Why was it that women were always the ones 'forbidden' thusly? And Galeran had put to me directly his reasons for restraints. It was an ugly exchange.

"Dear lady," his voice oiled, "were you too close to battle danger, I fear the Greek mercenaries who are everywhere, might kidnap you and demand ransom."

His baleful eyes had peered out maliciously from his sallow face, "You, Lady Madeleine, have caused enough furor by your so-called heroic abduction from Constantinople." He fondled the edge of his sleeve, then pointed a long finger at me. "Your consent to marriage with the emperor's nephew could have avoided the privations which our holy caravan now suffers."

Galeran's twisted accusation had hurt and infuriated me. The memory of it still stung.

"And there are other troubles." Geoffrey's serious expression alerted me.

"What other troubles? What could be more troubling than to have the truth so distorted that now the outcome of the crusade rides on my shoulders." I wavered between fear and tearful rage.

Geoffrey hesitated. "It is your serving woman."

"Thecla? What could be...? Go on."

"There are some suspicions that she can predict the weather."

"Yes, her bones were hurting." I felt my cheeks coloring with anger. "Have aching joints become a sin?"

Geoffrey took me in his arms, brushing aside the hair that blew across my eyes, caressing the flush of indignation at my throat.

"I don't believe these things, I only tell you of the gossip. Mortimer especially complains of her, says she is of a dangerous type."

"How so?" My heart pulsed.

"I don't know, my love, he didn't say," he whispered as he guided me inside the tent, where he held me to him, kissing me tenderly. "Be on guard, my lady love."

"I will, dearest one." My breath returned as his voice soothed me. Though his tone was casual, I sensed his desire, and tried to avoid the rush of emotion flowing through me. I ached to linger in his strong embrace, but Robert of Dreux was approaching. Moving over the tent's threshold and away from him, I changed the subject. "I know you have other troubles as well."

"Aye, grain is perilously low, and the route becomes more dangerous. We'll travel in tight formation. That's the strategy to route the Seljeks. More of them have been sighted in the mountains."

Young Dreux, hearing the last of Rancon's remarks, added, "You're right, Sir Geoffrey, these treacherous bastards want to lure us away from the main column, a tactic which worked to massacre the Germans. We'll not make the same mistake, though the forward scouts have reported slain Germans along the way.

Rancon stared in disbelief. "You mean we now travel the same perilous route?" He surveyed the mustering area, his breath a low whistle, as though struggling to dismiss the unanswered question.

"Sir Geoffrey," Dreux adjusted his jewel-crested scabbard before he spoke, "my men are ready to head the vanguard with your Aquitanians."

Wagon masters warned us of the steep climb ahead. "See to your wheels for loose rims, check the brakes," they instructed the apprentices as they themselves carefully examined tack. With the last saddle cinched and the forward guard assembled, Rancon methodically dispatched heralds to all the noble pavilions under his command.

"Prepare to move out for the pass through Mount Cadmos!"

Proud was Sir Geoffrey to lead the van on that day's march. When he met my glance, he squared his shoulders and smiled. Yet, as he and Dreux took the lead, a shiver of apprehension flitted across my heart.

Pulling on my gloves, thin to the finger after so many months' use, I mounted and joined the others. After several hours travel, the amber summit of Mount Cadmos towered heavenward above the brushy foothill. The next minute it disappeared behind banks of misty clouds swirling against a cobalt sky. Rancon's news about Thecla had made my anger simmer. When I finally spoke of it to Eleanor, my feelings spilled out.

"Galeran has become more impossible with every mile. He not only forbids my Hospittaler work, blames me for our hardships, but now casts suspicions on Thecla."

"Oh? In what way?" Eleanor turned toward me, her eyes narrowed.

"Someone has told him that we were forewarned of the Meander storm by Thecla—that we were spared much of our provision because of her urgings." I glanced nervously about, to insure that no one was within hearing. "Mortimer also complains of her, though I don't know why. Geoffrey reported that Galeran suspects her powers. He and Cardinal Lisieux are questioning if she has gifts from the devil."

"By Saint Benedict's boots!" Eleanor gasped. "Madeleine, this is a danger. We must say nothing, nor should we speak any more of her cures. Should she have other wisdom for us, we must keep secret about it. The cardinal's suspicions peril us all."

Eleanor frowned, her lips pursed. After a few thoughtful moments, she commented, "Their talk of Thecla is very dangerous indeed. Galeran has completely mesmerized the king; I have lost what remaining trust I had in Louis' judgment for he seems to have resigned all power to that Templar wizard. Make no mistake, Galeran could bring Thecla harm if for one moment her arts were to become suspect." She looked about with unusual caution before she whispered, "Were to be seen as conjuring."

"Conjuring!" Conjuring, Dear Jesus, what memories that word stirred up. More than one midwife or village healer had been hauled through the town screaming her innocence to no avail. Bound and tied to the stake, the victim's charred flesh would permeate the sullen skies. I must protect Thecla at all costs. My thoughts were in a turmoil when my horse's misstep jarred me and I had to focus on the narrow trail. From my vantage point, I noticed that the rolling foothills lay far behind us. My mount negotiated a precipitous angle along the side of travertine cliffs covered with scrub oak and thorn bush.

Limbs of German corpses at the trail's edge forced my cry. Most had been picked clean by carrion feeders, but their tattered uniforms were the mark of Conrad's army. The white bones in the underbrush were fed the giant vultures. Emitting croaking sounds, they bated their wings in mock warning, inspecting our narrow, struggling column. The bird's wing-span was as wide as a baggage wagon was long. Disinterested, they bent their feathered beaks voraciously back to the shiny bones at their feet.

"Those curse 'a God creatures of hell are too full to fly." Thecla, ever the vigilant, poked her head out of the medicine wain. "Cover your mouth with your veil when you pass these bodies. They bring illness and fever to us. Never breathe the vapors of the long-lying dead." She held a cloth to her mouth.

Her eerie, muffled warning unnerved me. The rancid gruel we had consumed for several meals lay sour at the back of my throat.

Eventually, cold air blowing off the snowy crest helped clear my head. My strength returned; the riding blisters at my ankle and my nausea cleared up, improving my spirits. Morbid a path as it was, by Saint Paula's good grace, we were finally on the high road to Antioch.

CHAPTER 22

Through Cadmos Pass

*H*igh road it was, an arduous ascent. Steam puffed from the horses' nostrils. They struggled with the footing on the pebbled trail, which had grown more treacherous with each switch back. Frosted thin air seeped through my cloak. My spine shuddered with cold. None of my clothes had completely dried since the soaking at the Meander River. Suddenly, my mount collided with the rear of Eleanor's horse.

"Saint Benedict's boots! Why are we stopping here?" Eleanor looked down to her right at a sheer precipitous drop. A tumbling river gushed from its deep ravine. Scrub oak and poplar had given way to thick, stunted pines, leaning into the wind. They stood like sullen gnomes gloating at our misguided folly. The same primordial wind that had distorted their gnarled limbs whipped at our faces, stinging our eyes.

Eleanor clutched her horse's chestnut mane. I know she forced herself to glance down the rocky slope. My eyes followed hers, though I wish they hadn't. There, held by jutting boulders, and beyond, splayed upon the river banks, lay more rotting remnants of Emperor Conrad's army. Sprawled, like dead salmon on a river bank, eyes open wide, they had, in the name of Christ, spent their lives in futile spawn. The buffeting wind seemed more cutting and cruel than before.

"My head is spinning," she complained, "and I must hang onto these reins for fear of toppling." At the trail's edge she surveyed the stark surroundings. "My God! How foolish to have chosen the same pass where Conrad met disaster."

Glancing down the perilous embankment where the thorn bush had snagged a remnant of banner, I shuddered at the sight of more warrior bodies stuck in the gorge beyond. The river thundered; wind pained my ears. My mouth felt dry, lips stuck to my teeth. With fear draining strength from me, I nodded, "Yes. Yes, that is surely the way we have chosen."

Suddenly there was confusion on the trail far ahead. Horses neighed, spewing pebbles down the slope.

"Watch your mounts!" Rancon, far in the lead, barked the orders as he turned toward us.

"Bowmen on the alert!" Dreux countered.

Eleanor, hands cupped to her mouth, called up the hillside, "What's the delay, Rancon? What lies ahead?"

Weaving his way through the wagons and horses, Geoffrey came to join us. Within the friendly entourage, we dropped the stiff formality. He reached for my hand and held it fast.

"Rancon, what is amiss?"

"A sumpter horse has burst his veins and dropped to his knees. The spent creature blocks the trail. My men are trying to free him and edge him into the gorge without losing the wagon. It carries extra lances and shields, and provisions we must salvage. We'll have to find another animal. This passage is not meant for our large wagons and dray horses." He put his hand to his chest, "The air seems thin here, it takes our breath."

His eyes looked troubled. "Our underfed animals are no longer strong enough for this tough ascent. We wanted for fresh horses at the last way station, but as you know, there were none."

Long will I recall how the ancient settlement of Laodicea had come into view, surrounded by a moribund silence, more awesome than its naked walls. Beyond the rusted gate we had spied empty buildings, barren save for wild dogs sniffing at rats. Instead of the bustling city ready to trade with us, the place had lain deserted, stripped clean of all foodstuffs and equipage. The order to resume march had hung like a requiem in the air.

Thecla lumbered up the road cutting off my macabre recollections. She stepped among the mounts with remarkable surefootedness. "Majesty, they have taken us from our litter. They," she shot a look toward Rancon, "say we must go by horse or by foot, Highness. The Countess Fluorine can do neither one."

"The litter is unsafe on this trail, Thecla. I am very sorry," Geoffrey countered patiently, "but we will travel slowly to get the other wagons over the pass. I'm afraid your horses will lose footing."

He looked at Eleanor. "We have lost another wagon already. You'll see when we travel the other side of the mountain. It lies in the river. All lost, driver, squire and four horses, may God have mercy."

"Give Florine my mount," I volunteered. "This mare is surefooted and faithful, and I will lead her. I'll walk awhile." My cordovan boots had held up well over the rocky byways since Niceae. Perhaps the exercise would bring some strength back to my legs and stay my trembling knees.

Taking the horse gently by the bridle, I started back down the incline where the litter shone like a ruby against the snow-cropped ledges. Rancon fell in step with me.

"Do have care, my love and walk well within the escort." He scanned the cliffs and outcroppings. "The Seljek scouts dot the corries like white muzzled bears. We're not deceived. I'll find another horse for you when I reach the vanguard."

In the shadow of the litter, he wheeled quickly, gathering me to him. I welcomed his lips on mine, searched for his warm taste. On the high mountain escarpment, we clung together. It began to snow, and I wondered what chill realities lay ahead.

Rounding the corner, Thecla clucked lasciviously. "I'll tell Florine you are here," she said with mock propriety and a deep bow. She flung open the lacquered door and helped Fluorine to my horse.

Rancon threaded his way back up the mountain road. This high country was unsettling in every way, and I wondered if Geoffrey and I would spend our lives in sporadic embraces and quick exits.

I led the horse carrying Florine, stepping carefully up the narrow, perilous road high into the cloud level, where swirling snowflakes hampered visibility. Clouds mixed with snow and fog in a spiral dance that taunted the sharpest eye. Wagon wheels crunched, struggling upward toward the heavens.

My horse took all of my attention. Its hooves kicked and tripped on the stony path. Whimpering Florine gasped aloud with every misstep. The sharp command, "Halt, in the Name of God!" echoed down the mountain. I welcomed the stop, though the wind forced me to hang onto the reins and brace myself perilously against a boulder jutting out on the steep incline.

We had edged off the side of the mountain onto a narrow defile, where towering rocks shouldered us toward the slim ledges at the summit. Rancon and Dreux approached to speak with Eleanor. "Your Majesty, you know our original orders were to stop here at the summit and camp till we are joined by the king's company and the rest of the straggling entourage."

Winds whipped at Sir Geoffrey's short leather tunic. The mountain flaunted a punishing climate of its own that blasted through the high pass flinging sleet in our faces. It was impossible to hear.

"Let's get behind the boulders out of the wind." Dreux held the furry ear-flaps of his cloche.

Eleanor held herself tightly with both arms. Close against a boulder, she escaped the gusts. We were forced to shout above it.

Rancon surveyed the ledges and caverns that comprised the overhang above us. He sent a scout to see to their size. The youth was swift in returning.

"Sire, there is little room there, only several small caves, and a few ledges, nothing more. There is evidence of recent fires, sir."

"We cannot camp here for the night. The wagon master said the wagons won't hold the hill; our pavilions will fly off the escarpment if we raise them here. And even if we don't...." Rancon paced to the edge of the road, and looked again at the scout. "It's impossible. The enemy has camped here recently and there is no protection for us."

"You are right. It is impossible to defend, Sir Geoffrey." Dreux had to shout. "We have no clear view and far too many people. There is no battle array that could protect our party. We know how fast the enemy is. Our best chance is out in the open where we can see them coming, with a river or mountainside at our back, not hemmed in here where our horses are useless." He studied the scarred cliff-side. "We could be ambushed. The weather does us no favors, either."

"But the orders are to remain here," Rancon insisted.

"Then the orders are wrong." Dreux's voice held its husky edge and his brow contorted with frustration.

I was amazed to hear such words spoken by the king's brother.

Eleanor looked startled as well. "Dreux, then what do you think we must do?"

Robert of Dreux was a clear-headed noble, so different from his older brother, the ever-hesitant Louis. His was not the need to seek thoughts from every noble on this march. For that, Eleanor admired him; further, he made his opinions known and seemed willing to take a risk.

Eleanor had been quick with her question. In spite of the cold and snow, we were repelled by an odor that had become far too familiar. Close by on these desolate mountain heights, bodies lay a-rotting. Neither the queen nor I wanted ours to be among them.

Dreux continued in his bitter tone. "The Turcopole guides prove to be misinformed, again. There is no rest site here at all." He resurveyed the pass. "If anything, it is a trap."

"Or they lie to us as they did to Conrad." Geoffrey's tone was full of cynicism. "Why," he wondered aloud, "has the high command trusted these Turcopole guides when others had proved so nefarious? I'll send our own scouts forward to search for a site ahead. Perhaps they will have a better view on the downside of the mountain. Dreux, what say you to that?"

"I say, by the sword of Saint George, do it and be quick about it. We want grazing too. With weakened horses, we are no match for a Seljek foray."

Dreux's firm decision appeared to reassure Eleanor. That done, the elements and hostile boulders called for some respite. She sent for Germer.

Soon a fire of thorn bush flickered feebly in spite of the assaultive winds. Germer had scavenged remnants of Teuton wagon parts reminding us of Conrad's disaster. The German royal emblem hissed its curling gold-leaf paint into purple flames.

We gathered behind massive reddish outcroppings, finding slight warmth at the fire's edge. With the others in the lead party, we waited the return of the scouts whom Rancon had dispatched ahead. Sybelle hunkered close to Florine with her back against the wide rock. "How desolate a place. Never have I been in any similar clime, so frigid and so foreboding."

Knights stood guard, peering into the mists for any sight of the enemy behind the massive natural battlements. White-clad Saracens, moving as one with the foggy snow swirls, could easily advance. Sybelle confided, "I wish Phillip were with us. These young Aquitainian soldiers, not used to such treacherous disadvantage, seem apprehensive."

"So are we all." I retorted, hurt by the slur on Rancon's abilities.

He and Dreux paced to and fro. Finally, unable to bear it longer, Sybelle called out, "Let us pray for the return of the scouts before Vespers." Fumbling deep inside the reaches of our tunics, we brought out the smooth, sacred images from Empress Irene.

"Ora Pro Nobis." Our prayers, like the smoke, curled heavenward from the bouldered crevices.

The scouts returned through the mist before Vespers. They reported that below the cloud cover, the mountainside was free of snow, quite temperate and featured a meadowed tableland some miles into the valley below.

Relieved at the news, Rancon hurried to head the column out of the choked narrow summit. "Let the wagons forge ahead, by the grace of God!"

The wagon master began his chore. Pack mules, laden with shields, clattered close upon the bowmen and Templar sergeants. They picked their way down the descending road. Loose rocks and narrow sharp turns made the going hazardous.

Returning to our contingent on a dead run, Sir Geoffrey addressed the men in his own company. "I must send two runners to the king warning him to push straight over this pass and join us in the meadowland below." He paused for a moment to catch his breath. "What brave heralds, aided by the swiftest angels, will take the message?"

Five squires pushed their way to the forefront. Rancon picked the two tallest, one a raw-boned lad whose legs would carry him well. The other, a bit shorter, but an excellent bowman, would be protection at his side.

"Rub ashes on your face and hair." Rancon signaled for Germer to bring an old bag to him. "Here, lads, don these shepherd's robes and be off. Tell the king the pass is dangerous, to make haste over it. Tell him we wait for him in the valley below. Be off now; be watchful and Godspeed!"

Dreux reported to Eleanor while Rancon took the lead. "Though he does bring the bulk of the baggage trains, Louis cannot be far behind us. It may be slow going."

"And slow going Louis can make it," Eleanor interrupted, "thank Saint Perpetua we saw no solitaries along the way, or he would stop and pray with them."

Dreux ignored the queen's sarcasm. "We've dispatched swift runners to tell him to continue with haste over the pass and move quickly into the valley."

Numb with cold, we deserted our bleak site. Geoffrey shouted the marching order. Guiding our spent horses, we shambled down the steep descent, leaving Cadmos Pass to the vultures.

CHAPTER 23

Cadmos Plain

O ur forces raced the daylight, and by dusk had set up tents on the wide meadow at the base of Mount Cadmos. Beneath a cluster of scraggly tamarack trees, their irregular branches swaying in a mild wind, we supped.

"This wind comes from the south, perhaps from desert lands." So volunteered Evard of Barre, commander of the Templar garrison. While he had not traveled this route before, he claimed knowledge of the general terrain leading to the Holy Land. He, Rancon and Dreux shared the evening meal with us, a welcome stew.

Germer had snared a pair of scrubby partridges from the dry brush clumped on the valley slopes. Aside from the sedge grass, the place had offered little else other than water from a narrow river, and a level, defendable stretch. The camp faced southeast with the river snaking its left flank. Guards watched the extra horses and what arms-laden wagons had triumphed over the precipitous dangers of the pass.

A starless winter's night closed in. I pulled my red cloak tightly against the cold. We awaited the arrival of King Louis and his long, ungainly caravan. Rancon was disturbed by the losses of material and men we had suffered and he paced the rim of our encampment repeatedly asking Germer, "Has there been any sign of our messengers?"

"No, Sir Geoffrey, Raoul heads the sentries watching the far trail. He'll tell us at once."

We talked quietly, each one of us covering the anxiety we felt. I knew Rancon was very nervous, paying me little heed, forever looking to ask about any news. Hulga passed wet washing cloths after the tense meal, and still no word from the runners.

By firelight, Geoffrey's concerned expression while he talked with Evard, drew me to him more than ever; the set to his jaw, the line of his cheek, dark with a day's growth of beard. Desire stirred deep within me. Perturbed at my thoughts, I acknowledged the voice of my conscience, sensed the warnings of danger all about us.

When I glanced at him, his face flushed by the fire's heat, his cheeks burning warmth, I yearned the more. Our eyes locked for a charged moment and longing flared between us. Not now, I told myself. But danger paired with desire, intensified my need for him. And danger there was, not only from the enemy lurking on the ledges behind us, but, as always, the threat of discovery could mean a risk to our very lives.

Perhaps Geoffrey sensed the guilty need to banish the spell between us, for he rose abruptly. "I must see to the guard outposts. We should have some word from the king soon. Good night." With a formal gesture of farewell, he set off for the far end of the encampment. I hesitated for a moment, then followed him.

At the sound of my footsteps, Geoffrey spun around, "Who goes there?"

"Geoffrey!"

He wheeled around, caught me in his arms. I held him tight, my mouth seeking his. While the strength of him pressed against me, his hands searched under my vest, fanning the flames of my desire so that it astonished me.

Approaching footsteps caused us to spring apart. Geoffrey called out, thick-voiced and tense, "Guard, here! What know you of the king's company? Any runners? What word of our own scouts?"

"No, Sir Geoffrey, nothing." Pointing toward the pass, the sentry continued, "There stirs nothing there but the wind and hungry wolves howling on the mountain ledges."

"Well done, fellow. Rest now, you'll return to duty at the Matins hour, midnight."

I dodged into the shadow of the cook wagon, tried to still my thumping heart. What had come over me? How rash to have followed him.

Rancon rejoined me, wrapped me in his cape and took my face in his hands, "I must leave you now. There will be another time for our love, I promise." His lips brushed the tips of my eyelids. "Return to your pavilion, my lady love. Dream of me."

I tore myself away, urging my desire to ebb. In the distance, Rancon called to a young soldier at the fire circle, "You, Sergeant. Double the guard around the horses and pack animals. Keep a careful watch this night."

I entered our tent brazenly as though I had stepped away for a breath of fresh air, nothing more. I joined the others in preparing to bed down on the thick skins. My legs throbbed with fatigue as I stretched them out to the ends of my bed. I dozed off, wishing Sir Geoffrey lay between them.

In the darkened tent, Sybelle felt me stir fitfully beside her. "Madeleine, are you awake?"

"Yes, Sybelle. I am restless. Why do you ask?" I wondered if my disappearance with Rancon had been observed. "I can't sleep for the pains along my legs. My feet ache." I whispered the truth, not wanting to disturb Eleanor or Florine. "In spite of Thecla's ointments, I feel many painful miles on my blisters from coming over that mountain trail. And you, Sybelle?"

"I have fears for Phillip," she murmured into the confessional darkness, "I know that Louis has been lost before, causing us worry, but it is not possible to become lost on one road, and one road only. Not even for King Louis."

Sybelle was right. Nor could I shake the sense of foreboding. Rancon's call to the guard to keep a careful watch this night had heightened, rather than allayed, my concern. His voice had stayed with me like a night companion, intimate and close, warning of danger.

Sybelle continued to fret. Unable to stay still, she sat upright. "Listen to the wolves howl. Do you think they are close?"

I lifted my nightcap to listen. Sounds of a wolf pack rolled off the foothill shelves at the base of Cadmos Mountain.

"They are some distance, Sybelle. Don't worry."

Dim outlines twisted from the watchfires and glimmered through the tent side. The wind had shifted carrying its keening sounds down the canyon pass. The two of us lay still, our eyes wide open.

Something nagged at my awareness as I listened to the night. What was it? I held my ear to the sound. What I heard made me gasp. Shades of Charlemagne, those cries rising above the animal howls were wolf-like, but were not wolves, they were human—the voices of men! I sprang up, toward the heavy canvas curtain. The night watch raced in with news of the approaching marchers, and at once, the camp exploded in a shower of torches.

Drawn to the lighted path, the first bloodied figure staggered in from the howling darkness "Ambush! Ambush! The Seljek murderers have attacked the king and his army on the pass! Many have perished! Oh, help us."

A young knight crumpled to the ground. His left arm hung loosely under his haberauk. His right hand relinquished its grasp on the jasper handle of his sword. Blood spread garnet onto the torch-lit ground.

Cries resounded throughout the camp; lines of wounded men stumbled in. From my vantage point, I saw Rancon lurch from his tent; witness to the sickening sight—members of the king's guard wounded and full of horror.

"Oh, my God!" he cried, gripping a tent stake for support, "the worst has happened!"

He seemed paralyzed for a moment before he shouted orders to the lightly armed bowmen, followed by the mounted knights. At his command, one full patrol had remained in battle gear and were at the ready.

Dreux sprinted to Rancon's side. "I've roused the rest of the men to defensive positions. The Seljeks could be hiding anywhere in the foothills, ready to finish their heathens' work! Take up your positions on the south flank," he shouted, "Evard, take half your Templars and stand your posts at the east!"

Maintaining order, the remainder of the company provided the Hospitallers with tight security, protecting both flanks and heading the van. In a frenzy of action, Charles pitched rugs and coverings into carts. He and his helper lashed the long litter poles to the sides of the wagons. The rescue party set out for their fallen comrades.

The sight of the ghoulish cavalcade horrified us. Soldiers, bowmen, drivers, carters, pilgrims, stumbled in with tales of terror.

Louis' wagon master, his contorted face an ashen gray, sputtered details of the disaster. "Our sumpter wagons jammed at the pass, baggage wains slipped into the depths of hell, swept away by the river's surge. May God have mercy, then boulders loosed to tumble on the lines of cowering pilgrims huddling on crowded switchbacks below, hesitating to advance into the confusion. They met Christ this day, as did the lads from your party, whose entrails fed the buzzards overhead."

He wiped sweat from his forehead, tears from his cheeks. Someone offered him a swig from a flagon of ale. He drank, licked his cracked lips and continued, "Then the wild Seljeks fell upon us. Like grinning devils, they beat tambourines and drums while their Infidel bowmen spurred swift ponies toward us. Never a stumble! Jesus, how sure-footed they were! Many of our people were lost," he wept. "Pray God for mercy and forgiveness."

He fell to his knees. In a final agonized burst, he cried, "Me thinks the king is lost, perhaps slain by an Infidel sword. He, the holiest pilgrim of us all." His shoulders rocked with sobs.

The crowd lamented the king's fate. The camp erupted in disarray as fathers sought sons. Brothers ran to search among the wounded, who trudged in by two and threes.

Grabbing a pair of buskins, I pulled on a short tunic, and bolted from the others to join Charles. I would face Galeran's consequences later. I hurried past several of Louis' nobles huddled by the large fire circle. What I overheard made me stumble. These survivors were heaping curses on Sir Geoffrey Rancon's name! I felt as if I had been struck by a mace.

Mortimer, bleeding at his forehead, shouted bold accusations of treason. Galeran, his tunic ripped where the red cross blazed across his chest, seconded the demands for retribution. Agitation and distrust threatened more disaster. Through a softly falling cold mist, Phillip's voice rose above the rest. His inflammatory words cut through me like shattered glass.

"Our beloved king is missing in action, and the queen's deputy has not a scratch!"

The long-festering split engendered in the early days of the Paris councils had swelled like an infected sword slice. Never healing, it ruptured now, spewing hatred and vitriol onto these stony slopes. Under the pressure of a battle lost, of warrior leaders slain by the Infidel's blade, tempers erupted, raging out of control. Their grievances were heightened in the distorted light of disgrace which Christian knights had suffered at the hands of the Infidels.

Now the milk of Christian charity turned sour. The need for blood vengeance pulsed strong, and set ancient rituals of revenge in motion. Shouts clamored high above the consolations and questions. They carried past the slopes and reached to the dark trail where I had begun to seek the wounded from the battle's edges.

"Rancon left the pass, inviting this disaster! He is guilty of treason!"

Guiding a litter of wounded men to the make-shift hospital area, I slipped by the wrathful barons unnoticed. Their ranting assaulted me; a cold sweat prickled on my face and neck. Rancon? Treason? The queen's deputy, treasonous? This noble knight, a traitor? They must be crazed. My breath closed on itself and I covered my mouth to keep from sobbing out loud. For the second time that night, I stepped into our tent.

Eleanor seemed dazed. "They think Louis might have fallen in battle." Seeing my devastation, she said, "Oh, God, Madeleine, listen to this incrimination of Rancon. How can they turn on my loyal man? He did no wrong," Her eyes widened in horror. "Who shall have advocacy for us, if not Sir Geoffrey?" She put her hands to her chest, drawing a quick, shallow breath. "I feel as though a great boulder has come to rest here."

"Nothing can be done till daybreak." I was living my own terror. "Then we'll learn more of Louis' whereabouts. Even the most ignorant Saracen would want ransom, not murder!"

Eleanor's eyes welled with tears. "Surely, Louis would not be lost while on pilgrimage. How could God do that to the devout? Have I come all this way to be so rewarded by the Almighty?" She sank to her knees. "To be abandoned on these miserable steeps? And now, with Rancon implicated," a fear skipped across her face, "might the barons not turn on me?" Collecting herself, she reasoned, "Surely, God would not take Louis, so pure in his intention; surely, He would not take him now. I could never imagine such a wretched plan, never!"

CHAPTER 24

Trial on Cadmos Plain

*M*y queen sat frozen at the rear of our tent, mortified by the partisan hostility raging through the camp. The relentless winds through Cadmos Pass had chapped her skin, leaving her face reddened. White outlines traced her taut lips. Never had I seen her so distraught, nor had I felt so helpless in soothing her. At my bidding, Thecla offered her a sleeping brew.

Eleanor had just begun to relax when a wave of tumultuous praises rolled from the north end of the encampment. Voices raised in prayerful thanksgiving filled the area.

"Deo Gratias! May Christ be praised! Saint George has delivered him!" The camp erupted in one roar, shaking our very tent poles. "The king returns! Thanks be to God in all his forgiving goodness! Our King Louis is alive!"

I sank to my knees. "Thank you, Blessed Mother and good Saint George, you have saved our king." Eleanor knelt briefly; her hands trembling. She rose, steadied herself, paused to gather strength, and stepped into the night's turmoil. She waited for the sight of her husband.

Parting a wedge through the feverish clamor, the king, perched upon a skittish, head tossing Turkish pony, jogged into the crowd.

His sweat-stained pilgrim's tunic had offered little protection to his person. Thorn-ripped arms and legs oozed blood. His eyes were glassy and his lips bore a dazed smile as he wrestled his testy mount toward Eleanor.

Blood had clotted on his left brow. He met Eleanor's anxious gaze through his tears. Sobbing softly, he blurted, "God in his infinite wisdom has spared me, that I may continue my pilgrimage and deliver you to Jerusalem," his voice faltered, "to save your soul, my queen." He slumped forward in his saddle, one leg dangling to the ground.

Charles helped Louis from his horse, guiding him toward our tent where a freshened bed had been prepared. Eleanor followed. From the shadows a hand shot forward, grasped her arm, detaining her.

Galeran's cold eyes fastened on hers. "His Majesty will come to his own pavilion as soon as it is ready. The king has his own physician and chaplain. It is not God's wish that he be here with the women!"

His glance swept the corners of the tent contemptuously. "And, mind you, keep that hag of a so-called healer away from him."

Eleanor looked first at Galeran, then at the hand clamped upon her arm. "Please unhand me." He did so at once. "You may be the king's deputy, Galeran, but I am his wife, and his queen. Mark you that." Her eyes held fire, yet she spoke evenly. "I will see to his wishes." She glared at the monk, rubbing the spot where he had dared touch her.

Some northern barons pushed their way to our pavilion, clamoring for Galeran. Rush lights illumined their tortured faces. "We seek the king's word. Let Rancon be hoist on the gibbet for his outrageous treason! Galeran, you are our voice. Say but the word. Call the bishops and the other nobles to council!"

"Better yet, Galeran," Mortimer's voice rasped from the group, "let us have Rancon now! We'll avenge this betrayal!"

Mortimer's inflammatory demands struck like a blow; I clung to the canvas for support, my throat dry and tight. From the corner of my eye, I glimpsed Louis struggling to rise from his cushions. Grasping a pilgrim staff, he staggered to the pavilion arch, where his bandaged appearance caused a hush. Defying Galeran's prohibitions, Thecla had hastily administered a hot herbal potion of comfrey and poppy seed and had begun to dress the skin wounds on his legs and arms. With one arm in a sling, the king stepped beyond the arch, his mouth working nervously. His voice was hoarse but firm.

"My barons, in council after morning Mass, we will seek justice, not revenge. Meantime," he intoned, "we must tend our wounded and bury our dead. We'll gather on the morrow at first light."

He limped toward the litter which his serving men had pushed through the crowd to his side. Nodding to Eleanor, he disappeared into the swirl of lords who milled at the pavilion's edge. They followed him to his headquarters, which, at Galeran's direction, had been set up far from the queen's.

Nausea immobilized me. Mortimer's desire for blood was not to be denied. His ragged boast cut through the night. "Were I to meet Rancon at this minute, I would cut out his liver and feed it to the buzzards. Where is the traitor?"

"He leads a patrol to bring the stragglers safely into camp." It was Sir Hugh who had spoken, a tone of sanity amid a whirl of night madness.

Eleanor understood well the full range of the tragedy. "You know I have long felt the oppressive weight of hatred and jealousy that has always existed on the part of the northern nobles. If they could have, they would have dispensed with me. Since I am the king's wife, they dared not. But, Jesu, would they dare hang my deputy?" Her lips trembled. "The thought sickens me. My dear friend Rancon," her eyes met mine, "and our loyal advocate."

Though my heart ached, I was not blind to other implications. The vilifying of the queen's deputy was a blow to her prestige as well as an insult to all of the marching Aquitainian assemblage. The hissing coals held little warmth. I couldn't stop shivering. Eleanor moved to my side, put her arm around me.

"Madeleine, I will give a forceful argument at the council tomorrow. Geoffrey is my deputy. I have a right to plead for clemency. He will not be harmed."

Eleanor's profile shown in the faint light, and I took comfort in it. Distress deepened the lines of her face. She held her head high, a determined set to her jaw. Fire-flicker laid dark shadows under her eyes.

I tried to sleep, but fear tightened its vise. The sweet features of Rancon crept into my half-sleep, and I wanted to weep myself into oblivion, but couldn't. Cold dread overrode my grief, freezing my tears before they formed.

Before daylight, herald's trumpets roused the camp. Had the night's cruel drama had been a nightmare? Eleanor had not moved all night, locked in her wretched vigil. Wordlessly, we prepared ourselves for what lay ahead.

After early Mass, King Louis immediately called his council. Queen Eleanor, escorted by Lord Hugh and three other nobles led the way, while Sybelle and Florine chose to follow after me. Alone, I walked across the stubbled slope to the sunken meadow where the assemblage had gathered. I was ill-prepared for the sight that greeted me. His dark hair tousled, his eyes downcast, there stood Rancon, hands and feet bound in chains! Horrified, I gasped aloud. Geoffrey's head snapped up, and he looked at me through the burdened disgrace in his eyes. At his side, stood the Count of Dreux, head bent, though neither his feet nor his hands were shackled.

Under sullen skies, the nobles and bishops had divided themselves into two groups, each forming a half-circle on the rocky valley floor. The depth of the impending peril crystallized. How swiftly the council had transformed itself into a deadly tribunal.

Presiding as judge, a pale King Louis sat huddled on a raised litter draped in royal banners. His lips looked parched. His head still bandaged, rested on one hand. Was he competent to make sound judgments after his brush with death?

Sybelle lowered her eyes when Count Philip handed a billet of charges to be read by Galeran. His thin voice recited the poisonous litany.

"Sir Geoffrey of Rancon, you stand accused by your peers of disobeying the orders of the day. Ignoring previous marching orders and without counsel of any sort, you urged your command to march through the pass, the agreed meeting location. You endangered King Louis and all the train which accompanied him. Such disobedience is punishable by death." Several nobles chorused agreement.

The Aquitainians shouted "No! This is not just." Lord Hugh argued, "Sir Geoffrey dispatched messengers to tell of the change in plans." He could not be heard amid the shouts.

Someone called, "Death is the just punishment for treason!" That someone, of course, was Mortimer.

The words burned my heart and sent a searing pain at my ribs that sent tremors down the length of my body.

Cardinal Lisieux rose to speak, sending a wave of despair through me. Objections subsided, and the assembly became hushed. Only the buzzards, squawking as they slowly circled the new graves, violated the silence that had settled like fog upon the valley.

Would the Cardinal speak in Geoffrey's behalf? "Please, Jesu," I prayed. "let this man of God sway the barons to clemency."

"Your Majesty." He puffed up like a tumbler pigeon under his magenta robe. "We, the churchmen, prelates and bishops have met through the night, till dawn broke upon this saddened place. We agreed, after prayerful deliberation, that it is most righteous to charge Count Geoffrey Rancon with the sin of desmesure—recklessness." He licked his lips savoring the treasonous word. "Yes, my noble brothers, the sin of recklessness."

His words left me shorn of hope. I looked at Eleanor; her whitened face remained a mask of stone.

Lisieux surveyed the circle assuring that everyone received his pronouncement. "For by his actions, Rancon has spilled much blood. He is guilty of wasting the manhood of brave Christian soldiers who would not have died, had he, as leader of the vanguard, not disobeyed his commander's orders. It is for this sin that he must die as a just punishment for so great a transgression, and so grave a loss. Most intolerably, he has threatened the life of our blessed king by his rash and treasonous actions."

He bowed deeply to King Louis before joining the others. He caught Galeran's approving look and held it, like a sacrament, between them.

The Count of Dreux stepped forward, placing himself directly in front of Louis. "How is it that Rancon is accused, and I stand free? Am I not as guilty as he? We both found the pass to be a place of grave danger. You, brother, my Lord King, should have sent scouts ahead, as we had dispatched the messengers to you. Those Turkish guides had once again confounded us Franks, just as they had the Germans. They lied to you about the pass and you issued orders on those treacherous lies!"

Dreux moved closer to Louis, placing his foot on the dais. "Now, my brother and king, I must remind you, we heard of no Teuton who was tried for their disaster as we two are here. And if you try Count Geoffrey of Rancon, then you must try me also, your brother, Count Robert of Dreux."

He had raised a good point, causing the nobles to mumble to one another, looking first at Galeran, then to the king.

When the restless hubbub of dissension and disagreement faded, Eleanor approached Louis.

"Majesty, may I speak?" She approached him slowly, holding her grey tunic skirt carefully to bow the more graciously to him.

"There is no place in this council for her, Your Majesty!" Galeran slithered swiftly to Louis' side.

"This is a council of justice, Galeran." Louis replied evenly, though his voice was weak. "The accused is Her Majesty's vassal and her Deputy. The queen may speak on his behalf."

"Thank you, my husband." Eleanor faced the hostile assemblage, her shoulders square, but not arrogant, her manner respectful, not meek.

"It is with all respect and sorrow that I speak. I thank God for your royal safety, and I grieve the lost ones. I, too, want revenge, but to take it upon our own is not justice. How can we punish the king's brother and not the queen's deputy?" Her voice did not waver. "How can the queen's deputy be thus condemned and not the king's brother? It is not justice to do so. Neither man did wrong, but saw to the safety of their charges. I beg, in your mercy to us all, to our cause, be just to both men."

Moving to stand by her women, Eleanor stared at the council members who exchanged glances of scornful silence. How fierce a pride I felt in Eleanor's defending so boldly and so well.

Arguments erupted. The respected Templar, Evard, ventured to speak courageously, "It is said that the king's marching force had become disarrayed, with some knights not wearing their armor, and that defenses had not been orderly along the trail."

Mortimer, his jowls wagging, yelled, "Orderly! How could there have been order, when the queen's baggage wains had staggered us all? How can there be any military order when we march with such vanity and foolishness?"

Others raised their fists, their voices full of wrath. Amid the din I overheard the words, "...and Rancon's whore of Gascony!" My head began to spin.

Arguments escalated, voices ragged with hatred rose and fell. Soon, it became apparent that order would not be restored. A tiring King Louis was forced to declare the trial over.

"My lords and nobles, let us adjourn. Think on these things most carefully, and pray for guidance, and a decision."

On signal from Galeran, Templar guards took Geoffrey and Dreux from the scene to tents that were north of the camp, beyond hearing.

With his gaze on Eleanor, Louis intoned, "Pray that Our Lord will guide us to a most just and blessed judgment."

Eleanor rushed forward to object. When it seemed that Louis might vacillate, Galeran darted to his side. Louis hesitated, then repeated his dismissal. Stricken, Eleanor backed away.

Later, within the dim recesses of our dwelling, despair hung like a brooding cloud. Temporarily shielded from the glare of disaster, Eleanor, her face a mask, attempted to pray.

"I want to pray, but the words can't form beyond my disbelief that one of my most valued nobles and trusted deputy, a man of honor, is on trial for treason." She knelt for a while, but had to give it up. "Anger simmers too hot in my soul."

Many hours dragged by before a page summoned us to reconvene on the forlorn slope. There, Cardinal Lisieux stepped forth to read the decision of the assembled body. I forced myself to listen, standing as tall as was possible.

Dreux was stripped of his command. Geoffrey's fate was worse; he was to be banished from the expedition entirely!

Eleanor, eyes spitting fire, wheeled toward Louis. He shook his head and shrugged his thin shoulders in a gesture of powerlessness.

Banished? Rancon banished to leave us now? Banished to fend for himself in this Seljek wilderness? Moving without seeing, I staggered back toward the pavilion to bury my face on Thecla's shoulder. I drank deeply of the heavy brew which she offered. As I lay there, my head began to swirl with images; of the planning in Paris, of my thrill when I learned Geoffrey had been assigned to the queen's entourage, of the idyllic river voyage, the deepening of our bond in the dawn hours at Sophia, my daring rescue from Emperor Manuel and our passionate hours on the shores of Anatolia. Rancon, his thick dark brows coming together as he listened to me, his tenderness, his smile, his caresses, all began to spin round and round. My desires for him yesternight, which seemed like a lifetime now, haunted me.

At Nones the same day, Sir Geoffrey Rancon, accompanied by a small force of faithful knights and a handful of armed foot soldiers, assembled to journey back over the fateful Cadmos Pass toward Ephesus. Aquitainians lined the road, standing in silent and bitter farewell. Queen Eleanor, her voice quavering, commended him for his loyalty, bravery and service.

Geoffrey appeared not to hear her. Though I could not know what he was thinking, I heard him whisper aloud, "Recklessness, yes, my love, yes." I could barely hear him above the shuffling feet and clanking armor. "Recklessness. It has cursed my life."

Christ's wounds! Did he think for a minute this judgment was just?

Rancon dropped to one knee before his queen. Then, my beloved turned and looked long at me. Another brisk turn, and without a backward glance, he led his small force toward the rising road. The mists, like a tattered shroud, enveloped him.

I tried to raise my arm in farewell, but it hung dead at my side.

*   *   *

That night in the tent on the valley floor, I was visited in dreams by the holy women approaching the Holy Sepulcher.

"Quem Quaeretes?"

"Jesum ad Nazerum."

"Non est hic."

Spoken from the depths of the tomb, the words, "He is not here," brought an agonized moan from my lips. My companions soothed me as best they could, and I shook with grief till I was spent. And, yet, through the agony of my own despair, I sensed the heat of Eleanor's rage. Neither sorrow nor icy nights would soon douse that fire.

CHAPTER 25

Wandering

The next weeks passed as though in a shadowy dream, with dark figures shuffling here and there amid an unforgiving landscape of rock and thorn bush. We regularly stopped before sundown to camp in the wilderness. One night, in the icy gloam of an approaching dusk, I hunkered in the falcon wagon. My raptor pulled at its jesses, ignoring my hand. She displayed her drooping shoulders lamely, turning away from the raw horseflesh which I held out to her.

"You must eat this or you will perish soon," I urged. "See how your feathers hang." The bird reached feebly for the meat. On the other two perches, the remaining falcons, near death, turned their hoods from side to side in slow apathetic movements. Using my dagger to slice more morsels, I pleaded, "Can't I tempt you with this?" Their debilitated response made my spirits to flag even more.

For days we had wandered aimlessly in the Phrygian Mountains, a terrible retribution from God, or so Chaplain Odo had preached at morning mass. "Now will the troubadours be still? Now will worldliness cease? Will the forbidden falcons at last be banished?" His voice whined over his morose congregation. "Now may we be worthy, following the example of our blessed king." he pled, "to continue on this Christian march in the way Holy Bernard and His Holiness, Pope Eugenius, had so proscribed. Let us pray."

If it had been Chaplain Odo's intention to shame his congregation, his words found their mark in me. Recalling the night of the Cadmos disaster, I've confessed a hundred times how desirous I was to lie once again by the firelight enfolded in Geoffrey's arms, our legs entwined. The heat of my passion had glowed anew when we embraced and if intention is sin, then I sinned. If events had permitted it, I would have bedded with him, for that is where I ached to be. And now, I knew I must atone for my sins of the flesh, for my lust. Daily, I tried to do that.

The cart tilted to one side, startling me as precious water slopped from the jars. Should I be caught feeding meat to the falcons, it would not go well. When Thecla heaved herself through the opening in the canvas, my pulse stopped racing. The old woman's brow creased in a frown, made more ominous by the sand and grease lodging in the lines of her face. She crouched by my side and fumbled deep within her soiled tunic fetching forth two hunks of bread.

"They are covered with ashes and horse grease. Here, take them. I know you feed your rations to the poor and bring what you can to the birds."

"People starve because of me. I don't deserve to have the meat."

"What nonsense comes from your mouth!" Her weary eyes flashed anger while she placed her thick fingers gently on my cracked lips. "People starve because the king is ill-advised and takes the wrong trail day after day," she growled, "so that we wind our way up one gully and down another." She raised her eyes to heaven, crossing her hands over her breasts. "King Louis says that God will guide him. No, Lady," her shaggy head moved side to side, "people starve because our knights plunder and murder at every chance, so the natives drive their goats and sheep far into the mountains ahead of us, so we have no grazing for our horses, nor hunting with our birds, no meat for our fires."

Thecla circled her arms in agitation gesturing in a wide arc toward the hooded creatures. Her raised voice riled the falcons who pulled weakly at their restraints. "And people starve," she added wearily, "because it is God's way to take them to Him."

Her expression softened as she reached toward me and pushed aside the strands of unkempt hair blocking my eyes. Her gnarled hand moved to my cheek as though to brush away a tear. "But, my dear child," she soothed, "they do not starve because of you."

For a moment, her tender words lessened my suffocating guilt. I reached for the hard, ash-bitter bread and broke off a small piece to chew. It was the first food I had taken that day save for some grass broth, a bitter vetch, that Thecla had insisted we all drink, admonishing us, "Without liquids for your organs, your humors will be out of balance and your lips will dry and crack open." With her scolding finished, she half-smiled, "Then you can never sing plainsongs again."

The thought of singing anything but my last prayers seemed remote. Suddenly, a gloved hand ripped the canvas door aside, jarring us both.

"Here, now, here it is!" One of Mortimer's henchmen addressed me gruffly. "Out of the cart! We are to take the falcons for Sir Mortimer's stew and seize the cart for our wounded. Get out at once."

The small chunks of bread turned to stone in my stomach. Hastily, I stumbled out of the mews, followed hard by Thecla, her face creased with hatred, her lips line-tight.

"For the queen's falcons to be seized by these ruffians spells trouble," she whispered, hurrying to catch up with my brisk pace. Wanting to hide my humiliation, I hoped to reach our tent before anyone could see me.

"All is evil now, Lady. We have no food save the horses who drop from starvation, we wander in the mountains like the Jews in the desert, and now the queen's falcons and cart are seized, like a commoner's."

The old woman looked at the grey sky where a thin sickle of orange sun disappeared to the west. "It is a sign." The crone scanned the darkling heavens for meaning. Night descended, cold and bleak as my spirits.

Next morning, Eleanor had little time and less energy to fret over her falcons. "If it suits that whoreson, Mortimer, to seize my starving birds, let him. After losing Rancon, the falcons hardly seem worth fussing over. But on principal, I'll inform the king of his insolence after I have a good meal, which doesn't seem like anytime soon. Of course, Louis is used to fasting."

Her remarks were cut short for we were rousted out to muster for the day's trek. The journey began with a climb up a long, brushy ridge which topped the wall of a steep canyon. Using the staves cut long ago for us on the shores of the Danube, we hiked over the rocky terrain, stepping perilously over tree roots and small boulders, watching for rats and ferrets, hungry as we. Larger predators walked the ledges, snarling at us from the ridges.

Germer directed the other grooms leading the queen's horses, the last who displayed any vigor. With the animals so spent, grooms and squires were forced to assist the famished creatures. Despite Eleanor's objections, I threw myself into the strenuous task. It helped blur the memory of Geoffrey riding toward the wolf calls and corries of Cadmos Pass, easing the terrible ache clamped around my heart. My arms strained at the trying work, tugging at the halters from the front while servants pushed the carts and the few remaining wagons from the rear. A fit penance for me.

Like the relationship between a knight and his mount, I understood the strange companionship, a respectful dependency, that had developed between the travelers and the beasts of burden, for it was sure knowledge when an animal dropped in its tracks, it would soon provide some sustenance for our bellies.

Shouts from up the ridge interrupted my thoughts. There a spavined sumpter horse lay collapsed amid its load. Lord Hugh, commanding the forward group, ordered guard units along the line to stand by.

"The enemy roams the hillsides. Soldiers to your places!" Hugh's voice cut the air. Heralds trumpeted the warning. After the foot soldiers rallied, and bowmen, their shields glistening feebly in the muted winter sun, had scrambled to their positions, the vanguard leader summoned the eager butchers to approach.

They lost no time in wielding their long sharp knives, slaughtering where the creature had dropped. No part was wasted. Cooks gathered blood in buckets or goatskin bags. Squires fought for bones for their master's stew. The poor hunkered at the edges, begging for the king's portion which he gave at every slaughter. Finally, skinned, bled, and dressed, sides of horse flesh hung on the cart stakes to dry, thumping eerily in time with the marching drum as we moved toward the next rest. Grooms beat away the huge vultures circling above us.

"Prepare to move on!"

The call echoed down the hill and I, eyes fixed to the ground, urged my mare forward up the trail. I couldn't distinguish the beasts' blood from the blood of many travelers, who, noble or peasant, no longer had shoes for their cracked and bleeding feet. My own feet stung from the sharp pellets punishing my boot soles, thin as parchment now.

After traveling the ridge till the February sun arched high, weary guides returned to report that the trail came abruptly to an end. Far from leading to the river which would trace the way to Sattallia, we had trudged to the brink of a dark, barren ravine worn deep by wind-driven torrents.

Thecla approached. The old woman took my hand tightly within her callused palm, speaking hoarsely, "You see, Lady Madeleine, you do not cause this hunger. It is those who, in their stupidity, take us day after endless day on treacherous paths that lead to nowhere but hell."

Thecla's remark held little consolation. Winding back down the rocky trail, we passed a group of the poor horde whose matted hair crawled with vermin. Their feet were bloodied pulps, some with toes missing. Others, too weak to walk, were borne up by devoted comrades. Daily, emaciated corpses fed the giant vultures.

"Look," Thecla remarked, "their wingspread embraces them like Satan's cape, snatching them from the very arms of God."

Hot tears streamed down my cheeks. Hadn't we all been snatched from the arms of God?

By nightfall, we gathered in front of a feeble fire where we supped on a meal of horse-liver broth and a hunk of rice cake. We ate quickly in silence, afraid to speak of anything. Eleanor gagged, wiping quickly at the residual drops of liver broth which she could no longer endure to swallow, its pungent taste too foreign. Her face had become gaunt, giving her eyes a luminous quality.

"You would have thought that if Louis were so anxious to save my soul he might have picked a more direct route." She pulled a piece of meat from her teeth. "Let's retire. Louis' sacred journey will be early on yet another path to Sattallia. Perhaps, tomorrow our leaders will find the right one." She hummed a few notes of Louis' marching chant. "'What have we to fear from hell'—what indeed," she bristled, "these days have all been hell, every step of the way!"

Her visage bitter, her manner irritable, she made for the small crowded tent; it was all that remained of her royal, carpeted pavilions. Everything else had been sold or dumped hoping to spare the last stumbling horses.

Thorn bush embers blinked in the brazier. We lay on our pallets; Eleanor's eyes welled with tears. The expulsion of Rancon had been a devastating blow to her prestige and badly damaged the morale of her forces who wished only to be done with this disastrous pledge. The king's emboldened barons made no secret of their resentment of her. Mortimer's seizing the falcons had demonstrated that. Led by the prelates, they dared scurrilous remarks about the misfortunes that might have been avoided had the women remained where they belonged, at home. And I knew what they called me.

"Are you asleep, Madeleine?" Eleanor nudged me gently.

"Not I, Eleanor."

"Nor I." Sybelle turned toward her.

Florine, heavy with child, forced herself up on one elbow, pulling the covering off the rest of us.

"Nor I, my lady."

"Then lay you down, Florine, for the cold creeps in among us." Sybelle gently rearranged the bedding over Florine's belly, a round dome in the cinder glow.

"My ladies," Eleanor began, her voice quavering, "I must speak of this. I have wronged you by bringing you thus to cold and hunger. How mistaken I was to speak of songs and feasts and endless sights."

I began to mummer objections. Eleanor reached over to put a hand to my lips.

"Shh. Let me finish. Should we get to Antioch, and daily we find the road less sure, and you do not wish to continue the journey, I will feel no rancor. I have brought you to great hardship amid promises of grandeur. How misguided was I to think that this would be an easy venture. I had often heard it spoken so. Warriors, it seems, shape the truth of battle in the retelling. I had imagined it would be a somewhat perilous a time, but nothing like this." She paused, groping for words. Drawing a deep breath, she confessed, "I have wronged you and our Lord Jesus Christ, his Holy Mother and our own Saint Magdalene."

Sybelle's soft voice broke the silence. "My lady, I know that Phillip has been like an enemy to you, as have the Flemings who follow him, and my loyalties have been tested, that is certain, but I am Angevin, and the friend of your childhood. I am over any bitter feelings, Eleanor. Remember, I travel to Jerusalem to see my stepmother Queen Melisende." Sybelle hoped to comfort. "Oh, Eleanor, she will be proud to think that the Queen of France comes through such hardship to the Holy City which she rules."

The familiar mantle of guilt descend upon me. My heart raced. I knew I must speak my truth to the dark, to the soft breathing of my friends. I would say what had remained unspoken.

"When Sir Geoffrey left, my heart left with him. I have been only half a person here, going through the motions of my prayers and—and my penance. Working hard so I wouldn't have to think about my sorrow, nor share my guilt." I realized another truth, "And I wanted no show of solace from you, Eleanor, and in that alienation, I had none to offer to you while derision rested heavy upon us, but because you are queen, you must have felt it most of all."

Rising, I moved to kneel before her, "For this I ask your forgiveness. I am your companion and your devoted servant. I will, I must, go through the gates of Jerusalem with you, dear Majesty."

A sweep of relief quivered so deep through Eleanor, she shook in a spasm of sobs. "Then I, too, am forgiven for this ordeal?"

Remembering Thecla's words, I was quick to respond, "We are all forgiven of this ordeal, dear Eleanor, for not all of it is of our making. God's will is sometimes strange."

"Yes, and, heaven knows, made stranger by the leaders of this march!" Thecla joined in, not having missed the exchange. Her night vigils with Florine included her sincere devotion to eavesdropping.

"Shh, Thecla. I can say that, as can my vassals, but for you, it is a danger. Temper your boldness." Eleanor listened at the tent's sides. "I'm actually beginning to feel at peril, because I'm so unpopular with the king's men."

Her chin thrust upward, "And still, I would never have surrendered you to Manual. I don't believe we should be punished for that."

The mention of Manuel triggered my most treasured memory and I slid down into my bedding, remaining silent, jaws shut tight against my sobs.

Another long silence. Sybelle's soft voice relieved it.

"Good night, sweet sisters. Veni Sancti Spiritu." Offering the prayer was her way of soothing.

"Amen." Our voices hung in the cold.

Now that the air was cleared, perhaps we could join Florine, who had dozed deeply for some time, her back pressed close to the carpet Thecla had rolled against the draft.

"I smell fog in the air," Thecla whispered as she sneaked from the tent. As was her practice, she left us to place a long, narrow swatch of thick lamb's wool along the rim of the tent top. The old woman crept back into the tent to maintain her vigil, pitching more twigs onto the fire. "Tomorrow we will have some water."

By the end of the next day's grueling march, through steep, rocky terrain, all the moisture had been sucked from the lamb's wool strip that Thecla had placed on the tent top to gather the fine droplets of fog that had visited the tent folds like shifting voile. Each of us periodically pressed the pungent thick fuzz to our mouths to suck the moisture hidden there. It brought relief to our stinging throats and stiff tongues.

I had become accustomed to the thickness of my tongue, but I could never become accustomed to the taste of horse blood. I had refused it again at the evening meal where little conversation other than prayers had been uttered. Tightening the soiled girdle around my waist, I huddled under my fur cloak.

A secret fear now walked at my side almost daily, a guilty panic, constant as the cold. In the silence around the fitful fire, frost and danger at my back, I understood how swiftly folly turns to penance. No tambourines, no dances from the lackluster troubadours, no merry, snapping eyes, no nights filled with laughter.

The haggard faithful could barely raise their voices in the brave chant that once thundered through the forests at Metz. "He who goes forth with Louis, what has he to fear from hell?"

Above our listless conversations, the wind carried their pilgrim chant, weak but constant. The poor crowds further down the line watched their numbers dwindle daily. When the lurching cadavers finally gave up, they were laid to rest, pushed against some boulder or thicket and surrendered to the vultures whose heads, bright-red and grooved, bore the look of Beelzebub.

"Veni Sancti Spiritu, Veni Sancti Spiritu."

"Come, Holy Spirit", they implored, and it did.

Reddish flames bubbled the horse flesh turning on the spit above hot coals. Tortured spirits appeared to cavort to the sounds of snapping grease. How near to hell are we, I wondered. Running my tongue over the grit on my teeth, I reminded my soul, "He has made my teeth grind on gravel, and made me cower in ashes."

The following evening King Louis decreed that we should all attend an evening Mass where, he promised, the plans for the next day would be discussed. We arrived at the sputtering bonfire in time to hear Louis finish a tearful prayer. Haggard and frail, he spoke with conviction as he urged his barons to press onward, likening their wanderings to Jesus' days in the desert.

Odo, his chaplain, obviously distressed by the king's comparison, ventured to respond, "Majesty, for the glory of France and for the glory of the Holy Land, we cannot be forty days. Look about you, Highness. Knights have become foot soldiers from the death of their horses; armor and jeweled scabbards lost or traded for food have made paupers of rich men."

"The chaplain is right, dear King Louis." It was Count Phillip who spoke, his voice bristling, yet respectful. Observing the look of wan disapproval in Louis' eyes, Phillip spoke more evenly.

"Majesty, we must find our way out of these mountains on the morrow. Otherwise we face disaster. I propose that we send out three separate searching parties to find the way to Sattallia. We cannot last much longer, lost and without provision. It is not possible to remain the fighting soldiers of Christ that we ventured here to be."

There were agreements and nods of approval.

"What think you, Galeran?" Louis glanced toward his deputy, who leaned on a cane by the fire's edge.

His eyes sunken, his face a jaundiced mask, Galeran spoke with distinction. "We must send out scouts, Your Majesty. We have dissipated all our strength. Though we have dumped most of the baggage that has brought us to this disastrous plight," he shot a look in our direction, "we still cannot continue in this way, willy-nilly through the mountains. Send the scouts ahead. Have them snare us a native who will be persuaded with a knife at his neck, to guide us."

"But we are penitents here," sighed Louis, a glow of piety to his eyes. "Perhaps God wants us to purify our souls before entering the Holy City." He tipped his head to one side, his hand behind his ear. "Listen, listen to the sounds of the faithful."

In spite of the icy night, my palms started to sweat. I was afraid Eleanor, muttering under her breath next to me, would blurt out something that would bring more vitriol upon us.

Evard of Barre preempted her, speaking sharply. "Those are the last songs of the starving, Majesty. True, they save their souls, but they do nothing to keep the Infidel from desecrating the paths of Christ. That is our charge, Majesty. To make safe the way of the Lord. With God's grace, and your permission, Your Highness, I will send, in all directions, three small armed cadres of my best foot soldiers to find the way to Sattallia."

The gathering, impressed with the show of Templar candor and bravery, agreed quickly, urging Louis to take Evard's advice.

Louis finally acquiesced. Smiling sweetly, he bade the nobles take their leave.

"Brave men, be you ready for an early march." He knelt in prayer while the rest of his men hurried by torch to their camps, anxious to guard what horses and possessions remained. Sir Mortimer came close to my side, and with a menacing smile brushed up against my buttocks.

"By Saint George, Lady Madeleine, think you now we have made our beds, we best lay in them?" He took a step closer; I could smell his sour breath.

"But not the bed you had in mind, I'll wager." Snickering, he slunk off into the night. A daring insult to the queen's woman, but no more perfidious than sending her deputy to certain death.

When I joined Thecla outside our quarters, she held the rushlight to my face, "What, M'lady, has happened.

"That Mortimer—"

We were startled by a cadre of lightly armed Templars appearing out of the fog, trotting close by our pavilion toward the eastern out-post. Unaware that their orders were to dress as Kurdish shepherds and head out at first light in search of the route to Sattalia, the old crone cursed while she labored to place the lamb's wool swatch atop the tent. The breeze had shifted, urging the fog in closer to the far side, out of her reach, forcing Thecla to nudge the swatch over to the other side.

"I feel more pain at my hips and knee joints," she complained, turning her face upward to the sky, then west. The old woman licked her lips, tasting the mist. Tears streamed from her eyes, her sparse, gray lashes unable to stem them. She crumbled to her knees.

"Great Mother of the Winds, glory be! Lady dear, taste the fog!" Thecla smacked again at the salt falling on her lips from the west-borne fog.

I pressed my own chapped lips together. "Jesus be praised, it is the taste of salt water! The ocean must be near!"

Had Thecla but known the mission of the scouting cadre, she could have pointed them westward, to the gully running out of the mountains toward the sea, to the port of Sattalia! Later that day, they stumbled on to it.

CHAPTER 26

Sattalia

By Sext the next day, the sun had struggled through the fog leaving wispy vapors to trail into the canyon behind us. Strains of Te Deum, the hymn of thanksgiving, carried above the shuffling sounds of bone-weary travelers as they trudged along the sloping pathway.

"What is it we have to be thankful for," Eleanor asked, "for our aching stomachs and the foul taste of horse blood in our teeth?"

"The singing has a different quality." I turned around to be certain. "Listen, it doesn't come from the stragglers far behind the army column. The sounds come from our knights in the vanguard."

Eleanor cocked her head to one side, her cheeks were drawn and chapped. "Praise God, cousin, could we have finally found the sea?"

"It must be so! I'll ride ahead." I dared not spur my stumbling beast, so worn was she, but I did coax her up the line, where I was met by a runner.

"The sea, the sea! We are approaching Sattallia!"

Like wildfire, the word raced through the parched entourage. Thrilled, I hurried to inform the queen. "We approach the plains of Sattallia!"

"Sattallia!" Eleanor's eyes brimmed with tears. "At last, we can be resupplied, Madeleine, we will be rid of filth and fear. Now, we'll prepare ourselves for the final push to Antioch. My kinsman, Prince Raymond, will give us welcome and celebration. It can't be too soon for me."

"We have been through an ordeal, we have." My stomach wrenched at the memory of the past fourteen days.

"I am sick of the whole enterprise and my patience is near an end. Day by day, I steel myself to endure till Antioch."

Eleanor's forbearance was at an end, I knew. If Rancon's dismissal had broken my heart, it had broken her spirit as well. Since Geoffrey's disastrous expulsion, she had become obsessed with the flaws of Louis' leadership. Often, fighting to control herself, stifling her rage, she would ask, "Where are their plans and strategies? Are they so able? Under these arrogant and peevish bishops and nobles, the whole enterprise has come to naught but poverty and starvation, day by day! And I will tell you another thing. If it hadn't been for the many valuable items we had carried along, we would all be skeletons in the gullies, for there would have been little to trade, to garner the vittles we did obtain, as miserable as they were."

When Eleanor exploded like this, I became fearful that she be overheard and would tell her so, but to no avail.

"We have been led to impoverishment, cousin."

In silence, we continued out of the rocky defile onto a broad, muddy flood plain. Once carpeted with grasses and weeds to feed upon, the field lay stripped, over-grazed by enemy horses and sheep. My horse slowed, each step an effort. The crusader train had bunched up across the fen-like stretch between the mountains and the valley. This hazardous and rarely traveled route would take us to the east walls of the city.

"Let us march straight on, perhaps we can arrive by midday." Eleanor's spirits had risen at the sight of civilization when suddenly, we came to a dead stop. "What delays us now?" she asked irritably.

Cloaked in mud, Germer approached, slogging toward us to report that mud flats stretched, black and puckering, to the outskirts of the port city.

"We won't be through them till past Nones, Majesty. The horses are too spent to pull anything. We, knights and men, must push them toward the city. They are beyond flailing."

"Oh, by Saint Benedict's boots! Why do these trials persist?" Eleanor snapped, before she read Germer's drawn face and noticed his hands, blood-raw from the endless work. They held her horse's muzzle gently.

Tears pressed to her eyes. Softening her manner, she chided, "Well, my horse bears a much lighter burden that when we left Metz, eh Germer?"

A faint smile pulled at the edges of the lad's cracked lips.

"I want you to handle my horse, Germer. She falters now, I can feel it. Lead us to Satallia, lad. Christ knows you can do it as well as anyone."

We were denied entry into the city, and forced to camp outside its walls, yet the city was bustling, and the first days outside the city wall, set high above the ocean, were a pleasant improvement. An on-shore breeze blew in from the Mediterranean, bringing the fresh smells of salt laced with spicy, winter fragrances from unknown islands. It reminded me of crisp winter days on the coast of Gascony, when the air smelled sweet enough to drink. Ships bobbing in this harbor had arrived from Cyprus carrying supplies of grain for bread, kegs of olives and salted fish. In the city, the plentiful waters were healthful and clear.

Supplies proved extremely costly. Haughty city officials allowed only the king's messengers inside the city walls while we were left to squat outside the gates hunkered in the tattered remnants of our tents, their torn folds dancing in the wind like jester's rags.

Our desperate forces traded their last possessions for the price of an egg, an onion or a loaf of bread. At the market quickly set up outside the city, the better to fleece us, Thecla and I bartered the queen's jeweled bracelets to put a fat hen in the pot.

From the heights of the market place, I scanned the area where the poor pilgrim hoards had sought shelter crammed between the ancient double walls ringing the city. They huddled there like obedient dogs. Starvation stalked their ranks unchecked, for they had no bracelets. Assured by faith in God's Promised City, wasted away in their pilgrims' rags, they surrendered their weathered staves and willingly shivered up their souls to their Redeemer. I would speak to Charles about helping them the best way I could.

Germer trudged in from the nearby fields.

"How goes it, Germer?"

He shook his head. "Many of the animals have been pushed too far, starved too long, so that when they had grazed awhile, they choked with a horrible retching sound, then laid themselves down not to be stirred again. Those surviving are too few in number for our trip." Blinking back his tears, he paused to look back at the field.

"It is awful to see them founder and retch." I put my arm on his shoulder, grown more muscular from the trials of the road.

"The talk in the market is that there are no horses to be bought in the whole city, not for whatever armor or treasure remains with us."

"Have you spoken to the queen of this?"

"No," he shook his head, "but I have spoken to Sir Hugh. He said he had informed the king, who paid him little heed. His Majesty replied that all the knights must be refreshed, then the matter of the horses would be taken up." He paused, a hopeless caste to his face, "His Majesty says it is in God's hands."

"So now we delay further?" The boy nodded.

"Her Highness will be in a frenzy over the wait."

And so she was as we attended the council meeting called after the nobles' immediate hunger had been satisfied, when men had washed away the grime and mud, and treated the sores rubbed and rusted into their armpits by their armor. When, finally, the wines of Cyprus had rinsed away the taste of horse blood, we learned the appalling news. The last leg of the march would take us through miles more of barren wastes. Even the warrior Burgundians stared in silent disbelief. Many of their ranks were without horses; half of them without shoes.

Nobles prodded the king to seek immediate sea passage. He blinked at the circle of hostile faces, fidgeting with the heavy cross at his thin neck. His face bore an expression of gentle rebuke. Louis' whispered words astonished me.

"Knights," he intoned, "do not have the privilege of resting in a place where their horses die of hunger. A penitent, should, moreover, suppress his desire to rest; and a devout man, even though weary and ailing, should hasten to the goal of the undertaking, and it befits both to be crowned as martyrs whose souls God takes from such toil to Himself."

The king's remarks caught his men by surprise. Louis was blind to his army's plight.

No one stirred till Count Phillip rose to face his monarch.

"Just as a king should command what is brave, so too should a wise knight attempt what is possible." His face flushed, Phillip chose his words carefully, not letting too much wine blare forth.

"Majesty, you know that I have survived many battles," the Count grasped his emerald-studded sword hilt for emphasis, "and, indeed, I have fought for the Holy Land. I am your faithful vassal, as I was your father's, yet, my Lord King, don't you see that many of our men are without armor?" Phillip gestured toward his compatriots. "Your nobles, who have won their honor as chevaliers, as warriors on horseback, now walk at the side of their squires and among the common foot soldiers. All rank has vanished. Majesty, look you, they walk among them without boots or shoes. How can they march to Antioch?"

The barons called out, "It's true! It's true! Flanders speaks the truth." Phillip seemed as surprised with his support as did the king.

"Why should we march for endless days through wild torrents and heathen Turks when we can sail to Antioch in four or five?" It was Mortimer who spoke up. Impulsive energy glowed on his florid face, spittle at his lip's edge.

"And what of horses and victuals?" Lord Hugh questioned, his voice thick, cheeks wan beneath his rust hair. Perhaps he was thinking of Florine. "We are spent, now, Your Majesty, and can do little to subdue the enemy when we meet him." He gestured toward the queen's vassals, impoverished and without arms.

Hugh's eyes flashed bright with passion. Our men, under his leadership, had been shunned since events at Cadmos Pass, yet we had shared the hardships every step of the way. He was tormented as was I with the memory of Rancon's march back to oblivion. The sight of his pregnant wife scrabbling at horse meat scraps haunted him as well.

"My Lord Majesty," he pushed on, "consider that we might continue—for continue we must for the sake of our Lord, Jesus Christ—by ship, to the port of San Simeon, and from thence the short trip to Antioch."

Louis clasped his cross with both hands and turned to Galeran for a whispered conference. Galeran placed his hand over his eyes as though lost in thought. Louis whispered loudly, "How can we best be faithful to the Lord and live the life of our forefathers on their Holy March? It is a question of such weight." He shook his head and kissed the cross.

Beside me, Eleanor hissed a prayer, "When, Holy Father, will you send us a monarch, a leader, a man of decision?"

"Majesty," Galeran volunteered, "we can sail! I will see to the commissioning of several ships. The Greeks will gladly watch us depart our hoards from their principality. They will rejoice!"

"Your Majesty," Phillip spoke up in support, "we do not want to depreciate the deeds of our fathers, but events went more easily for them than they have for us. They captured Niceae by cleverness and gained riches. They engaged the enemy and won the battles. They laid siege to many cities and made themselves wealthy from plunder. Here, we have won neither profit nor renown." Those remaining words, Phillip spit out as though they were vetch.

"You are my trusted vassal, Count Phillip. May God be with us 'till we meet on the morrow with our brave army new-equipped." Louis clapped his hands together, bidding us farewell, and with Galeran limping by his side, made for his modest pavilion.

Eleanor was still fuming when Lord Hugh arrived at our tent. After a warm greeting with Fluorine, he, Eleanor and I stepped outside into a cooling afternoon. Wisps of smoke hovered over the vast encampment as cooks prepared meager servings of grains or soup.

Hugh's mouth quirked to one side, "In spite of intense opposition, the king still insists that we march overland, ignoring the starving conditions of his footsoldiers and the grim shortage of horses."

"Jesus have mercy! I don't know what has possessed Louis! I'll ask to see him. He must listen to his nobles. For once they are right!" Wrapped against a stiff breeze in a bright azure cloak, her last one, Eleanor glanced overhead at a sky tumbling with ugly clouds. The deep circles under her eyes reminded me of the gaunt mosaic saints on the walls at Hagia Sofia.

"Please arrange a meeting for me. Isn't it a wretched state that my husband forces his wife to press to see him?" Blinking, she added "We would run to Antioch if we could, eh, Hugh, to be in the shelter of our kin, a fellow Poitavian?" Tears flowed down her cheeks, but her lips held a determined line. "I insist on speaking with Louis, immediately. And I want the Lady Madeleine to accompany me as a witness to the conversation. I think Louis has become addled with too many prayers and not enough bread."

Rain beset the city, swelling the cascading cataracts to splash a thousand feet down the face of Sattallia's palisades into the sea.

Spumes rose high into the air and muddied the angry waters thrashing against the cliffs. The small port offered no shelter in severe weather and with seas running so high, galleys deserted Satallia to harbor elsewhere in safer berths.

The downpour railed against the stones in Hadrian's gate. It sluiced along the pebbled roads to the ditches outside the walls, where it soaked the skeletal forms of the faithful swarm, their backs hunched against the city's forbidding wall. Interspersed by sporadic choruses of coughing, the motionless cadavers droning "Veni Sancti Spiritu.," rolled like a tortured whisper along the rain-swept walls. Water bubbled over the corpses blocking the crude canal.

Charles and I had visited the ailing pilgrims less frequently. We had no medicine, and what scarce food we brought led to scuffling among the desperate. Charles was concerned about another danger.

"At first, I thought it was the result of the long march and lack of food and water. These symptoms might be the same dysentery hounding the poor since the flood near Ephesus. But now, sister, convulsions, the tottering gait, and faces swollen round as the moon make me wonder if another scourge lurks among the people. Put a scarf to your mouth and follow me."

He led me to a ditch where a stack of corpses floated. Two men from the wainwright's shop, faces upturned, lay staring heavenward. Their cheeks were raven black.

"Jesu, we must tell the queen at once!" I reeled away from the dreadful sight. "On second thought, dear brother, you must go to the king! Great peril stalks this portal of hell."

Next day at the conclusion of Mass, a sodden Louis faced us, speaking in a wistful tone. Tipping his head to one side, he arched his eyes toward the sky. "We have prayed for horses, and none have been found. We have then sought for ships that cannot berth in this port for the fury of the stormy seas. Now, God has visited the poor hordes with pestilence. He fears we delay too much in our journey. It is His wish at this time, that we hasten on our quest. When the waters calm, then I promise, my lords, we will set sail for Antioch. Now, it is God's will."

"God's will and the plague have finally moved Louis to action. God knows I didn't," Eleanor observed as we made ready for the sea journey, a task that went quite quickly, since our remaining possessions were so few. At great expense, Eleanor had garnered passage for her remaining vassals. Others, she had released from their pledge, knowing that they were no longer able to sustain themselves in any way.

On a bright March morning a week later, Louis stood at the ship's prow. The seas beyond the harbor stretched smooth, blue as lapis lazuli. The king wanted to bless the thousands of forsaken pilgrims and soldiers lining the walls and docks of the harbor. Our Frankish nobles abandoned thousands outside the squalid city for want of money for passage.

In charge of the motley footsoldiers and the remaining bowmen, a slight young knight from Anjou had volunteered to lead the vanguard through the unforgiving wilderness to Antioch. Standing at attention on the grey limestone pier, he called out to Louis, "O Lord King, wish us well, by God's Mercy." He gestured toward the others crowded around him, lacking any semblance of military order. "We will make the march without you, our leader."

The morning light played off his oval shield. "We are rushing to meet death, but if God wills us to prevail, we can avoid the death which threatens us. Bless you, our king. We will meet either in the Holy City on this earth or far above in Heaven. Fare you well."

Louis' cheeks ran wet with tears. He alternately waved his hand or formed the sign of the cross, blessing the remaining army in the same fashion as had Lisieux, before the cardinal had scurried to his quarters to assure cover near the captain's cabin.

Galeran stood with Louis at the bow, Dreux and Hugh leaned at the gunwales with heads bowed. Phillip stood stiff at attention, his jaw muscles working. He avoided looking at the faces of his footsoldiers standing on the shore, spears at their sides.

"Weigh now the anchor, for God's Sake!" The order cut the air. As a rusty chain creaked in farewell, oarsmen pulled at the long oars. The vessel sliced through the glassy, calm harbor heading for the open seas.

Through my blurred vision, I watched Charles fade from view. He had chosen to stay.

In our last conversation he had told me, words tumbling out, "I—I will stay yet awhile, then march with the last remaining company to Antioch."

He had held up the small case of instruments containing needle and thread which Thecla had given him so long ago, and reasoned, "I can still stitch a Saracen wound, even if I can do little to stem the sweep of pestilence and famine."

I could not deter him, and drying my tears nodded when he promised, "I will see you at our journey's end. At the Blessed Tomb in Jerusalem." I embraced him, the ache in my soul spreading.

Eleanor waved a bitter farewell to those nobles she had released from service. Then she took me gently by the elbow and led the way to our pallets on the fore deck where a crude shelter had been set up.

"We'll join Florine and Thecla." Her once radiant smile was flat, her eyes weary.

"At last, thank all the powers that be, we embark for Antioch where all will be as we had hoped."

CHAPTER 27

Antioch

The perilous voyage was a disaster with waters—and us—heaving violently. What had been promoted as a short trip became a three-week torture on the high seas. I spent my days hanging over the gunnels pitched by the green-blue waters and losing what salted herring and rice cakes Thecla had coaxed me to eat. When, at last, we were put ashore at San Simeon, a French-speaking Turcopole, well liveried, urged us into a decorated litter drawn by handsome horses. Perhaps the worst was over. We were bound for Antioch, just a short journey away.

"Thank Holy Mary, Star of the Sea, we're free from that stinking boat." Eleanor hunched forward, her hands on her knees. "I couldn't have lost my gruel another time. Poor Florine, I'm certain you're happy to be on terra firma again."

Florine, her knuckles gray, gripped the worn cushion. Her head hung to one side, deep circles shadowing her bleak eyes. "This lurching is not much better. I pray the Lord that I may never have to budge from solid land again."

"Nor ride a horse?" Sybelle asked listlessly. She slumped against the side of the coach, her thin face spent with fatigue. The sea air had tightened her copper hair into tight dull ringlets that dangled in disorderly heaps at her shoulders.

"Not for a while, isn't that so, Florine?" I reached over from the corner and gently placed my hand on the large, round dome pushing from her front.

"Did you feel the baby move?" Florine put her hand atop mine to guide it to the side of her belly. "Hold! There's kicking—there." Her eyes brightened slightly, a rose tinge flowing to her cheeks. "We've come here just in time, I do believe. Thank Blessed Mother Mary. I feared I might deliver this babe in the vermin pit of our ship's quarters." Fluorine continued to palm new places on the astrolabe of her abdomen.

Sinking back into my corner, I noted the serene expression on Florines face. She wanted this baby. Recalling all the hardships, I counted the times we had struggled to keep both mother and child alive, when Florine had seemed not to care, had wanted to die. Now, she nurtured the life inside her. At Thecla's bidding, we had seen to it that she had whatever food we could find—nuts, berries, whatever the morsel, Florine had first choice. Now, the baby seemed lively, stretching a leg to shape a sweeping bulge along its mother's abdomen.

In moments like these, my chest hurt and I felt an emptiness; my every attachment had been stripped away—husband, child, then gallant Geoffrey offered to the treacherous corries of Cadmos Pass, and most recently, Charles, to the diseased squalor of Satallia—vanishing from my life like figures fading into the dankest fog.

During the dismal nights as I tossed in troubled sleep, the mysterious dream would recur, and again, in the daylight, during my waking hours, leaving me confounded and puzzled. Yet, at the same time, it soothed me as though the Magdalene herself were following my soul.

"Whom do you seek?" I would wake with the words echoing in my ethereal memory. Whomever was left to seek? In a swell of despair, hot tears streamed down my cheeks.

"Don't weep now, dear Madeleine." Sybelle spoke softly, brushing my tears with her hand, fingers protruding from a tattered glove. She held up its ragged form in a gesture of surrender. I smiled feebly as the litter, drawn by the spirited horses provided by the Prince of Antioch, jogged us smartly up the wide road skirting the Orontes River. The ancient magnificence of Antioch could not be far.

Suddenly, our pace slowed. "Could it be that that Louis has found another shrine to visit. Oh, Saint Benedict's boots, please say not and let's continue on this road toward the safety and care of my Uncle Raymond." Eleanor fidgeted with the soiled tassel of her cape as we crawled to a stop. In exasperation, she flung the curtain aside and leaned far out of the door.

Through the open flap, strains of singing floated in. Far up the road, tumultuous activity burst out along the old Roman highway. A vigorous Te deum swelled from an approaching crowd. In the freshening breeze, a rainbow of banners and pennants fluttered toward our wain as tabors sounded and trumpets blared.

"My most heavenly God, it seems the whole town of Antioch has come to greet us!" Through glistening eyes, Eleanor pointed to the colors of the Aquitainian standard, flashing high above the others. "Oh, Blessed Saints, I would run to greet them, but my legs would falter. Look at us, tattered and feeble."

Ducking inside, she ordered, "Quick, hand me my crown." Sybelle fit the circlet of gold atop her head while I arranged the wisps of hair escaping her braids.

Eleanor summoned an elegance I had thought diminished beyond all recall as the Duchess of Aquitaine stepped gracefully into the daylight, savoring the incense that filled the air. She stared at the man who stood tall before her. His blue eyes held a twinkle as they looked steadily into hers. A short golden beard framed his smile.

"With great honor and deep love, I welcome my niece, Eleanor, Duchess of Aquitaine and Queen of France."

Eleanor drew in a long breath. "My uncle Raymond, my childhood friend, you have come to look much like my father, your brother. Joy floods my heart, so longing for it."

"Queen Eleanor, we have prayed for your safe arrival. In our chapels as well as in our churches, we begged God to deliver our Poitavian sister."

The warmth and acceptance Eleanor had longed for all these many months washed over her. Overwhelmed, she offered her hand, tears spilling down her cheeks.

Prince Raymond took one step, sweeping his niece into his strong and sheltering arms. He held her close against his broad chest.

At once, I liked everything I saw about Prince Raymond—his ready smile, sparkling blue eyes, his short trim beard, the color of tawny fox, and his protective, unguarded way with Eleanor. He certainly smelled better than anyone I'd been around in the last several months.

"On to Antioch! Come, we have much to talk about." Seeing Eleanor's condition, Raymond quickly lifted her onto his horse, signaling another for himself. I clambered back into the wain, wishing my lips weren't cracked and that my dress looked less like a scullery rag.

Amid fanfare, chants and tambourines, we paraded through the great iron gates of Antioch embraced by the affectionate goodwill of Prince Raymond. Prayers of thanksgiving fell from my lips without end.

For two days we spent our mornings on our knees in the decorative royal chapel, its wrought gold altar as elaborate as some we had seen in Constantinople. In the afternoons after lunching on lamprey, dried figs and bananas topped with honey, we rested. When our strength began to return, we were visited by costumers and seamstresses. Chattering foreign words, they draped us in the finest silks and the brightest brocades the Orient had to offer. After measuring here, tsk-tsking there, they scurried off to their sewing rooms.

An early spring had burst upon us, and Eleanor, like the countryside, underwent a miraculous transformation. She blossomed, exhibiting an abandon I had not observed since our girlhood days in Bordeaux. She gloried in the jasmine's scent; the dove's sweet call. As she moved through the garden terraces where fountains splashed in pristine grandeur, her face relaxed its tense lines. Gone was the look of troubled vigilance. All Antioch's embellishments imbued her with a sense of happiness. And they brought her to a deeper understanding as well.

"I had not known how much I have longed for the ways of my homeland, my Aquitaine," she confessed while we were dressing for the evening festivities. "Raymond showers us with such hospitality. There's much here to be enjoyed, Madeleine. Beauty, works of art, food, dance, music. It is a place of luxury, is it not?" Not waiting for an answer, she continued, "Until now, I hadn't fully realized how tired I am of Louis' austerity and his fetid, dark palace on the Isle. I've had my fill of his tattling monks and bishops, trailing him like a covey of quail, their ermine-trimmed robes, scattering dust whilst they whisper to him some extravagance of mine."

Eleanor tied the sapphire girdle at her waist. "And I will never forgive the banishment of Rancon, an utterly despicable act. Louis could have intervened. How it weighs on me."

The mention of Geoffrey's expulsion stung me, and I struggled to maintain my composure. "Aye, cousin, it has all been very hard, but we are here now, and should thank God for our safe arrival." When Eleanor spoke of Louis in that biting tone, I tread cautiously, wanting to be reasonable. "Until this woeful journey you have gotten on well, really."

"Perhaps we did, since we never had any choice in the matter, but I feel caged in some terrible way I can't explain." Her voice drifted off. She gazed out the window toward Mount Silphius, where baro-

nial mansions quilted the verdant hillsides with their colorful gar-
dened terraces.

"Observe," she pointed to the rich estates, "that Uncle Raymond is
only a prince, yet he lives more handsomely than does Louis, a king.
Indeed, in Aquitaine we had a certain grandeur, too. I had quite forgotten. Our hardships these past months could make us forget even
the most exquisite of pleasures. Come, we'll see to regaining some of
them this evening at the banquet."

I scrutinized my cousin's appearance closely. The exotic ointments
Thecla had found in the local bazaars had, as though by mystical
absolution, removed from Eleanor's face most of the damage done
by the windswept cold and lack of adequate rations. She looked radiant; her hair, vibrant and honey-colored, shone in the amber shaft of
afternoon light.

Noting its use by Raymond's young wife Constance, Eleanor had
applied blue eye shadow just below and along the line of her brow,
lending a deep lavender cast to her eyes. Her cheeks bore the pink
color of a full rose.

"Come, dear Madeleine," she urged, "don this silk shawl with the
golden threads. Its rose shades bring out the color returning to your
cheeks."

I twirled the shawl above my shoulders where it floated, light as
air and as richly patterned as the flower-filled meadows blossoming
around Lake Antioch. Pulling it softly round me, I secretly hoped it
would bring warmth to my heart, chilled as it was by the sorrows of
Cadmos and Satallia. Oh, that I were more like Eleanor, more able to
caste off misfortune. Forcing a smile, I followed her into the fragrant
eventide where a splash of stars had begun to ripple the wide sky.

In Raymond's palace, the great hall glowed from the huge rush
lights placed in every corner, reflecting off the colored glass and myr-
iad gems worn by the assembled guests. For the most part, the barons of Burgundy, newly outfitted at Raymond's expense, seemed to
be in good spirits. Yet, there were moments when some conversa-

tions, especially among the churchmen, wagged behind the backs of their hands.

Within my hearing, Galeran, his head nodding in its priggish way, spoke to Cardinal Lisieux. "Look at the Christian knights taking part in this." He pointed to the sprinkling of rosewater, poured from delicate pink quartz pitchers. Each noble guest received the perfumed water to put to his beard and lips before drying his hands on white linen cloths offered by a serving boy.

Lisieux frowned disapprovingly, all the while sipping the finest Lebanese wine, chilled with ice chunks run in by Saracen slaves from northern mountain slopes. His attention was drawn to loud activity among the queen's people. The men of Aquitaine, Gascony and Brittany had assembled at the eastern side of the hall where boisterous greetings rang out among the men and women of Raymond's lavish court.

"Come, sit here with us, my cousin! Long years have passed since I have had news of you and your kin." And so it went for Eleanor's vassals. No longer shunned as interlopers, her nobles received hardy welcomes in the easy ways of Poitavian manners. Many of Raymond's men, like the Prince himself, were second or third sons of high birth who had sought their fortunes in Outremer. Tonight, faces flushed with excitement, they called out remembrances of their homeland, where many of them had been fostered out together in the southern noble households. Now, they clustered in raucous groups to renew the friendships and kinship bonds begun in childhood.

Seated on a dais above the crowd, Eleanor radiated joy at the sight of so much good cheer. "Through all those terrible days and tortured nights, Madeleine, I had dreamed of Antioch. Didn't I predict the glories awaiting our arrival? Now, nothing disappoints. It pleases me to see my nobles so well received and royally treated."

While the festivities overjoyed her, she reveled in the attentions that Raymond showered upon her. I had realized that as queen, she had deserved such attention, but now, as I observed the two of them, I understood how much she had needed it.

In a minor violation of protocol, Eleanor had been seated at Prince Raymond's right, but King Louis, seated on Raymond's immediate left, seemed not to mind. However, it was to Eleanor that the prince addressed most of his remarks. Resting his arm casually at the back of her chair, a gesture which caused her to flush and one that did not go unmarked by the Pilgrim King, Raymond leaned close to her, locked in intimate conversation. Eleanor gazed up at him, enchanted by his adventures in England and elsewhere before settling in Outremer. He told her of negotiating with the Byzantine powers over his rule in Antioch. She responded brilliantly when he asked her opinion of Emperor Manuel.

Raymond listened intently to her answers, nodding his head in concentration. He asked further questions about logistics, the condition of the Frank forces, their dedication to the freeing of the Holy Land.

"They are the most accurate facts that I can give, to the best of my knowledge," she explained, "since my attendance has been barred from all councils and decisions."

Raymond drew back in disbelief. "But you are queen, Eleanor. You must have a say. In Jerusalem, Queen Melisende acts in the stead of the young Baldwin till he comes of age. There are factions who challenge that and it causes dissension, but she has just as many defenders who say she must take part in the domain. And, as Duchess of Aquitaine, you have committed so many of your own vassals to this campaign."

He gestured toward the group whose boisterous laughter filled their section of the hall. Several of them, noticing their host's attention, rose to their feet, resplendent in the new attire received from the Prince.

"We salute the Prince of Antioch, our countryman and our gracious provider."

Raymond rose and stood tall behind his gold-embossed chair. Handsome in a bejeweled caftan of costly green and turquoise silk, he received the toast with a courtly bow.

At the west side of the hall, the Franks appeared to be enjoying the repast. Mortimer de Mur looked particularly jovial, his lips smacking at his wine goblet. I had the unseemly feeling his smiles were directed at me, for whenever I glanced that way, his eyes, bright with wine, were looking at me—or so it seemed.

Robert of Dreux rose, lifting his goblet high, "To the noble Prince of Antioch, our blessings and our gratitude!" The Frank response followed, quite proper, yet lacked the enthusiasm of the Aquitainian kinsmen. Dreux, concealing his embarrassment, sat down quickly, yet Mortimer's looks remained overlong in my direction, giving rise to eerie feelings.

Raymond, still standing, turned to King Louis. "The Prince of Antioch salutes the King of the Franks and praises his courageous march to free the Holy Land."

Celebrants rose to their feet to drink the toasts. Raymond turned to Eleanor. His voice carried to the corners of the crowded room.

"And with great love and in the spirit of kinship, I toast my beautiful niece, our charming Eleanor, Duchess of Aquitaine," he paused just slightly, and looked toward the Burgundians at the west side of the hall, "and Queen of the Franks."

Cheers rippled through the great room, yet if Raymond noted how restrained the king's faction was in their responses, he didn't show it. His eyes remained pleasant in their blue depths, but he couldn't have missed the fact that Galeran and some of the northern nobles had not risen.

Unperturbed, the prince called out, "Now let us celebrate with sweets, dances, games and songs of every land."

Upon his steward's signal, young slaves the color of hazelnuts raced to the tables bearing trays of food. Roast lamb stuffed with dried apricots and bulgur wheat was glazed with pomegranate wine in which ginger and cinnamon sticks had simmered for two days; chicken, sauteed with onion and parsley and sprinkled with almonds, spilled from platters ringed with magenta flower blossoms.

A turbaned eunuch struck a thick Oriental brass gong as tall as he, and in moments, Saracen slave women, bare to the waist, bells at their heels, rushed into the festive crowds. They hoisted trays larger than shields filled with sweetmeats, candies of sugar and honey, and oranges stuffed with cinnamon figs that tantalized my nose.

Amid the fragrance of sandlewood smoldering at the braziers on the mosaic columns, Eleanor, sipping ruby-colored wine, watched the undulating, sensual movements of saffron-veiled dancers. Tabor and lute, so long stilled from her ears, sounded forth in unfamiliar harmonies that seemed to mesmerize her.

"There are places in the mind," Eleanor confessed later, as we pre-pared to retire, "which wine unfetters to spawn thoughts searching for words to speak them. Tonight, the headiness of drink and too much gaiety crowded me. I longed to join those dancers and their swaying rhythms. What has come over me I don't know, but I felt the heat rush to my cheeks when—when words formed and tumbled from my lips. I turned to Raymond and whispered that—that—I could stay here forever!"

Eleanor's revelations I found puzzling, and in trying to recon-struct the evening, I did remember that Louis, averting his eyes from the dancers, had been fast at his Book of Hours, mumbling a Lati-nate thanksgiving seemingly unaware of what transpired between uncle and niece. Raymond had pressed Eleanor's hand affectionately, I supposed to let her know he understood. It had seemed harmless enough to me at the time, and I fell asleep with Eleanor prattling on about the grandeurs of Antioch and tomorrow's outing to the coun-tryside.

❀   ❀   ❀

Under clear, warm skies, we set off on a sightseeing trip to the enchanted waters of Daphne. We visited the famed cleft of Saint Thecla, a place in the wide face of marbled stone mountain where, the legend told, the hillside opened up to engulf Saint Paul's convert Thecla, saving her from a bloody death.

Legends which abounded among the orthodox guides, enraptured us as they told of Saint Thecla's bravery in the face of attack by wild animals. We cheered when we learned of God's intervention, saving her from the soldiers who had been ordered to slay her. This entombment, added Princess Constance, was by the saint's choice, earning her the reputation as the first Christian woman to be martyred.

Here, Thecla, whose face had taken on a self-conscious, beatific expression unfamiliar to me, prostrated herself before her namesake's shrine for a long hour. The rest of us prayed for a much shorter time.

"I have few prayers left in me," Eleanor declared.

A sumptuous picnic was set out for us, while others sported with falcons. The long sloping meadow bustled with young vixen, rabbit, and pheasant. I remarked at how well-trained the birds were, suppressing the bitter memory of how ours had been seized for Mortimer's soup.

When the hawks had had their fill, we put aside our gear and feasted on fruits, cold quail, and wine the color of pink roses. We spoke about life in Jerusalem. Sybelle wished to know of the stepmother she had never met and her half-brother, the young King Baldwin.

As we began a leisurely ride back to the castle, I wondered if Queen Melisende had the dark arched brows or blue-black hair that I admired in the women of Constance's' court. Surrounding us, they spoke a variety of thick-accented French which enabled our conversations. These resilient women had been traded as child brides to the ruling Antiochean Franks by leaders of the Christian Armenian provinces in exchange for treaties of protection. They were handsome, straight-backed, excellent horsewomen, holding the reins of their ponies expertly between their long, dark fingers.

"I hope my stepmother will have a head of hair as dark as the mountainside," said Sybelle, reading my thoughts. "Look, it is blue-black in the dusky shadows."

We had cleared the meadow following the wide road to the palace, when a turbaned figure on horseback galloped at reckless speed toward us. My heart skipped. Who, clothed as a Saracen, would dare to approach a royal party with such careless haste?

"Who is that madman?" Eleanor asked Constance. The Princess laughed.

"It is my Raymond. He often rides alone, wildly and fast."

The frothing steed pulled close by Eleanor's side.

"Hallo!" Raymond held out his hand. "Come, ride with me as you did in the summers at Bordeaux." He signaled for Constance to take Eleanor's reigns and reaching over, gracefully lifted her to his horse. "Now, my duchess, let's see how well your knees hold for the ride." Raymond spurred the horse slightly and placed his arm around Eleanor's waist holding her to him.

With one hand, Eleanor grasped the mane, with the other she cast off her headgear. That done, she bought it to rest on the firm, sure arm that held her fast beneath her breasts. The animal's vigorous rhythm cantered beneath her. Encircled by the thick strength of Raymond's grasp, Eleanor, hair flying, seemed the free spirit I had known in our childhood. She looked ecstatic, as though she were momentarily liberated from all that bound her. Astride her fabled winged horse, she and Raymond sped toward the royal palace. Its tall stone tower loomed high over the river, now flowing with amber and peach waters in the setting sun. Catching the spirit of daring, the

Lady Knights, Sybelle and I, spurred our horses and raced with them.

Sounds of our giddiness and laughter filled the courtyard. It was unfortunate that King Louis, walking with Galeran, each with his psalter open, had just turned the corner to discover the queen, astride Raymond's exquisite stallion, enclosed in his bronze arms. Louis stared at the woman who bounced to the ground. Her tunic hung in disarray, her hair, a tawny, wind-blown tangle, fell wildly to her shoulders. Cheeks flushing red, her glowing face turned upward, Eleanor offered Raymond her hand and her most radiant smile.

King Louis' pale eyes blurred in pained confusion. He fled from the courtyard wordlessly with Galeran limping close by his side, his cane rapping an ominous tattoo upon the stone walk.

CHAPTER 28

Antioch

$\mathcal{P}$rince Raymond could not have been more lavish. He feasted the nobles until their energies were more than replenished. He replaced their armor with expertly crafted Oriental chain mail, and when hunts and feasts and brothel visits had sated the noble appetite, Raymond summoned them to convene for matters of greatest importance. His business, the heralds had stressed, was urgent. Queen Eleanor, with all her ladies, was to be present. Eleanor was ecstatic as we hurried to our places inside the great hall.

So recently the scene of festivity, the great hall, now stripped of that frivolity, took on a military look, transformed as it was by the regalia and banners from King Louis' forces hanging side by side with the bold standards of the Outremer Provinces. The colors of Aquitaine graced the far wall. A cross of burnished gold stood at the center.

The gathering was one of grandeur, and I was amused at Louis' nobles, clad in their handsome new clothes—doublets and tunics of brilliant silk trimmed with fox. How gallantly the men struggled with the deadly sin, vanity. Lisieux unable to restrain his preening, tossed a red cape over his shoulders casually, stroking it covertly. Mortimer stretched his thick leg in admiration of his glistening new grey boot, turning his foot this way and that. Count Phillip, in conversation with Dreux, ran his fingers over the jeweled pattern in his scabbard as though counting every ruby. They had not looked so prosperous since the court at Constantinople, nor had we. Our gowns, rainbow silks and golden embroidery, were far more fitting for a party than a pilgrimage. The one exception, solemn Louis, wore a new grey pilgrim's garb, as drab as the expression on his face.

Suddenly, buzzing conversations halted when trumpets blared the arrival of the Prince of Antioch. Raymond, with his wife at his side, approached a raised platform where a couch draped in fawn-colored lion skins awaited the royal pair. Bidding those present to be seated, Raymond signaled his agile eunuchs to bring in a large map to be pegged on the wall with silver nails. Upon the calf-hide, laid out with thick, pigmented lines was the Saracen-held city of Aleppo.

Raymond rose and began to speak, his voice booming across the crowd. "Your most Royal Majesty, Louis, King of the Franks and leader of the valiant expedition sent to purge the Saracen from our midst; sweet Queen Eleanor, my niece, who gives joy to our city; you most noble barons, and my Aquitainian brothers, I call you together at this critical time. You see before you on this map, the city of Aleppo, so recently fallen to the Infidel."

The Prince shifted his position so the assembly might view the drawing. "This great city," he continued, "now in the hands of the perfidious emir, stands as a source of danger and terror not only to the pilgrims who would make their way to the Holy City, but also as a menace to all forces of Frankish occupation battling to keep the lands safe for those who love and honor our Lord, Jesus Christ."

Bowing his head in respect at the mention of the Lord's name, Raymond paused. He used the opportunity to glance from under his jeweled turban, his eyes darting about the room. His audience seemed to be receptive, no more.

With a staff of polished olive wood, he pointed to the right-hand edge of the extensive drawing. His eyes sparked excitement.

"As you can see, the city of Aleppo flourishes on both sides of the Kuwek River. It is a comely establishment, well fortified. You'll notice these curves denoting the hills surrounding it. Here stands the citadel, in the northwestern part, situated on a hill and circled by a deep moat. This dark line surrounding the city marks the wall, a heavy one and thick, except here to the south, where, my spies report, damage from last spring's earthquake has been slow and shoddy in repair."

He turned to face his listeners amid a stillness which lay thick upon the hall. "Your royal Majesty and all you brave knights, you loyal Templars, ever true to Christ, I believe we can, with your amply re-equipped army, lay siege to Aleppo and return it to the provinces of Christian sovereignty." He glanced expectantly at Louis.

The king looked from the map to the cloth of his pilgrim's garment. He appeared lost in the contemplation of its weave, fingering it as a merchant might, counting its threads.

I began to squirm inwardly. If Prince Raymond was offended by the king's reticence, his expression remained bland. He continued, his voice showing no strain.

"You, Count Philip of Flanders, a man of proven valor and experience, you would lay siege to this south wall. We have siege engines at the ready. My battalion, two hundred strong, would march to positions in the western hills, there to charge on signal after the citadel is set afire. I will dispatch my knights and a number of Turcopole archers and footsoldiers, tested warriors and swift in battle.

"The nobles from Aquitaine," he nodded toward Eleanor. Her eyes had left his only long enough to peruse the etched hide more closely. She seemed captivated by her uncles' strapping presence, his assured manner.

"How well he has laid out his plan, to every detail," she whispered aside.

"Yes," I nodded, yet, my palms felt clammy and I had an eery pull in the pit of my stomach. Tension thick as ermine persisted in the hall.

"Your knights, Queen Eleanor," Raymond continued, "would lie in wait at this defile to ambush the emir's troops as they seek to engage the Flemings from the rear flank." Eleanor lifted her chin slightly, looking deeply pleased with the acknowledgement.

Commandant's exuberance ran high in Raymond. He spoke faster, his enthusiasm unbridled. He spun around from his map, facing Louis. "You, your Majesty, on the given signal, would mass your troops in lines of two, here, five miles outside the gates, flying your royal banners high with your armor flashing, men and horses fresh. With his city thus besieged, I believe the emir would surrender at the sight of your mighty Frankish warriors!"

Raymond stepped back from the map and held the pointer out to the side, with his hand relaxed atop it. Puffed with pride, he bounded from the platform toward Louis.

"What think you, Majesty? Let Saint George be with you while you speak of joining in these brave deeds."

All eyes rested on Louis. Now, surely was the opportunity for the armies of France to show their glory, to recoup the losses in the mountains of Phrygia, the desertion humiliation outside the walls of Satallia. This day, they could begin to fulfill their pledge to Pope Eugenius. Head on, their armies could challenge the power of the hated Saracen!

Rather than a quick response of allegiance, Louis appeared muddled, lost in thought, regarding Raymond with what appeared as an expression of disdain. There was something to the unfamiliar set of his mouth I didn't understand. Eleanor and I exchanged astonished glances.

Time dragged, slow as ants through honey, yet the King of the Franks made no effort to address his barons, who waited for their monarch to speak first. A clammy reticence ruled the silent hall, the stillness broken only by the rustle of new silks and swords as his men shifted fitfully waiting for Louis.

At length, the king stood. He looked first at Eleanor, then at Prince Raymond. His voice carried an aggrieved tone to it that I could not fathom.

"It is a grand plan, that you, Prince Raymond, my queen's uncle,"—he bit the word uncle—"have put forth. Yet, is does bear careful consideration, and I would ask to think and pray on it, and then to have a privy council with my own barons to render our judicious reply. Pray, in your goodness and hospitality," again he bit at the words in a manner uncharacteristic, "you will excuse us now that we may attend to this most important matter." At his side, Galeran nudged him, nodding approval.

Eleanor gasped. Could Louis dare to equivocate at this critical moment, withdrawing from this meeting? On what grounds?

"And what thinks the queen?" Raymond, his profile rigid, inclined his head toward her. "Pray speak, Queen Eleanor."

Galeran rose to object. Raymond raised his hand, staying him in his place at the king's side.

"I will speak for my own vassals, Count Raymond." Eleanor's voice cut through the great hall. She took a deep breath, then gestured toward her followers.

"Looking at these nobles, I can see that they are ready to be at your side in this daring and well-studied strategy. Your plans are carefully drawn; you give us excellent review here, and in all the ways of Bernard of Clairvaux, you attempt what he has exhorted us to do," she burned a look at Galeran, "to make the way safe to the Holy Land, to preserve the roadways for the faithful. I do believe that was our charge."

She turned to the assemblage, ignoring the expressions of disapproval which the northern barons, save the Count of Dreux, held for her. Their stiff carriage, their steely looks, signaled customary resentment at her boldness, but she argued on.

"It is to the benefit of all of Christendom to use our forces thus, and certainly with the valiant knights of Antioch, the siege cannot fail. Need I remind you, my husband, that it is also a serious matter of honoring blood ties to give aid to our nearest kin, my uncle, when..."

"I would wish to continue these arguments in private." Louis, in an unusual show of rudeness, cut her short. "I will confer with my men." His face pallid, his voice trembling, Louis stood. "If it please your Lordship, we will leave your presence and be convened elsewhere. On the morrow after prime we will come together, if that is agreeable with you, Prince Raymond."

Raymond accepted Louis' terms. His guests filed out, leaving the hall empty save for his attendants, Eleanor and I.

"Please stay, Madeleine, I feel a rush of shame, as profound as the humiliation I felt at Rancon's expulsion. I thought I should never relive that."

I agreed to remain if for no other reason than to protect my queen from the gossip Sybelle had reported to me last night. There was concern that she was too much in the company, often unattended, of her uncle. It was true, I must admit, that brows raised over the hours Eleanor and Raymond had spent together, of their hunts, hard-racing rides, and long conversations, head to head, but it was innocent, I would swear. While the others left, I faded quietly into the background, watching as a servant dutifully rolled up the map.

"Raymond," Eleanor stammered, "I feel you have been betrayed. You have seen Louis at his most vacillating, stupid self. I—I can't explain it."

"You didn't tell me you were married to a fool."

"No." Eleanor replied bitterly, "because I dared not acknowledge it even to myself."

"Has he a monk always at his side?"

"Aye, a monk at his side and monkish ways inside. I am so miserable. I am so little treated as queen," she hesitated for a moment, tears filling her eyes. "or wife." Eleanor began to sob.

"Here, dear niece, no tears. A glass of wine for your sorrows. Server! Bring us some wine."

"That Louis should dare to hesitate to join forces with you is an outrage! You are my uncle, my nearest male relative. It is a violation of all the laws of the land for Louis to refuse the kinship request for aid. By Christ's Blood, why are we here if not for that?" Eleanor wiped away her tears. "A rank and heinous violation."

Drinking deeply from a goblet of rich raisin and date wine, she moved neared Raymond. He radiated with vigor as energy seemed to radiate between them. It appeared to inspire her further and Eleanor spoke rapidly in their native tongue, the Langue d'oc.

"Louis' vacillations have become an unbearable burden. I am a woman of decision."

"Perhaps he will come forth after council with his nobles," Raymond replied while he poured more liqueur into her empty goblet. To my surprise, she accepted it.

"Augh, the barons!" Eleanor fanned herself with a silk scarf. "So stodgy and gross. I'm sick to death of their cold, obstructing ways. They have been at odds with me from the beginning. They treat their wives brutally and would so treat me if they could. And the churchmen! They hawk my every venial sin! It doesn't matter how generous I am in lands or monies to their monasteries and churches; they insult my women, and like Bernard, disapprove of our dress and manners, troubadours and songs."

She paused long enough to offer her cup for more wine, which Raymond filled. After a gulp, she went on. "Bernard himself has judged me too harshly. It is through his relentless preachings that I am made to bear all the slights and aspersions thrust at me by the fatuous Galeran, with his sidles, whispers and womanish ways. I expect him to curtsy to the king one day soon." Eleanor gave way to a fit of giggles before she went on.

"Galeran appeared on the scene after a terrible run-in with the old Cistercian. Bernard forbade me to have part in the councils when I had supplied at least half the nobles. When he wasn't sermonizing me to mend my ways, he displayed such extremity of judgment as to bully me with threats of consanguinity." Eleanor, breathless from her diatribe, took another sip. Slowly, her eyes widened, dry now of any tears.

She said nothing, and wishing I were anywhere but here, I sought escape by gazing through the open door into the garden where a fountain splashed into a marble pond, rose-colored and round. A rash of lavender clouds quivered in its reflection. Orange blossoms loosed their evening fragrance while overhead, a thrush warbled its spring evensong, full and flourishing.

When Eleanor spoke, it was with a tone I had never before heard, a throaty sound from deep within her.

"Consanguinity, Raymond." Her breath released slowly.

Surely the drink had suffused her mind with the wildest of thoughts. Raymond listened closely.

"Consanguinity," she repeated, "Of course!" She jumped to her feet. "Yes, yes, that's it!"

I stared into the fountain, letting my thoughts splash about, caught in the ripples of conspiracy which seemed to be surfacing. What was Eleanor thinking? Here was a side of my cousin I had never seen.

"Raymond, do I keep my patrimony always, even," she chose her words thoughtfully with a caution that liqueur could not blunt, "even in divorce?"

My head began to spin with the dizziness of these remarks. Eleanor moved to the couch, sitting nearer to Raymond, so near, his beard brushed her cheek. I looked around anxiously, my eyes sweeping the landscape for spies. There were always spies, and Eleanor's words and now her behavior edged toward a whirlpool of disaster. Were they to be observed by any of the Louis' factious nobles, or, Jesus forfend, Galeran's, it could be extremely dangerous for us.

At first, Raymond seemed uncertain of his niece's intent. He stared at her, his profile handsome in the dusk. After some hesitation, he answered carefully, a measured response spoken in barely audible tones. "Yes, your holdings and revenues go with you. Till the first male heir, then it is his when he reaches his majority."

"And would I retain the title Duchess of Aquitaine, with all its wealth, prestige and privileges?"

"You know you would, dear niece." His eyes held hers.

"And could you, dearest Raymond, as my uncle, help me rule? As my protector?"

"I think...we could come upon some solution." He held her hand fast.

My ears rang. I tried to read Raymond's expression. Was he as aware as I of the treasonous aspects of this conversation? Regretting that I had heard any of it, I prayed for its end.

"And," Eleanor's voice trembled, "might I remain here till we do?"

"Dear Eleanor," his lips grazed her ear, "you may share whatever is mine."

"Good" Her hand found his. She brought it to her lips. "Thank you, dearest Raymond. I must leave now." Eleanor rose, a little unsteady on her feet. An evening zephyr blowing from the desert skirted the courtyard. It pressed the supple silk of her bodice to ripple at her breasts like a soft caress.

"I am tipsy," Eleanor laughed. "Drink undoes propriety." She took Raymond's face in her hands. "And you are much too handsome in the evening glow." I looked away from their embrace.

"We must return to our quarters, Madeleine."

With a fond smile, she addressed Raymond, "There will be more to discuss tomorrow. We'll learn of Louis' decision, and—he will learn of mine."

Scurrying across the courtyard, Eleanor displayed a dangerous sense of freedom. I needed time to gather the courage to question her as to what was in store for us. There was no doubt that she had made a decision, but what it was I couldn't be sure. Her discussion with Raymond had been daring beyond all measure.

I prayed that there been no spies lurking in the shadows. Treason had been in the air, and I was fearful of this carelessness. It was not like Eleanor. How would she approach Louis? I was certain he had no idea of the degree of her anger. And what had led to his sullen behavior toward her? Had Louis come out of his saintly stupor long enough to give credence to the palace gossips?

After the terrible months that we had endured, the despicable treatment we had received from the factious nobles, the imposed separation from her husband, and her humiliation in Rancon's banishment, it was no mystery that Eleanor would flourish under the lavish attentions of Raymond.

Mayhap, the conversation I had just heard was no surprise to Raymond. Was it this madness that they had discussed those many hours? Thoughts of the properties in Aquitaine must have been tempting ones to a second son like Raymond. After the recent fall of Aleppo, the Prince may have become more acutely aware that his opulent Syrian domains would always teeter on the brink of murderous disaster.

But what was Eleanor thinking? We were in a foreign land, far from the source of her wealth. Antioch, the opulent gem, was dependent on Frankish military support for its survival. This was no place for the queen to take rebellious action against the king and his supporters, and when we reached the privacy of our rooms, I would strongly advise against any rash moves.

Eleanor began undulating and twirling, imitating the dance movements we had seen at last night's party. She danced toward our quarters, singing to herself,

"Saint Benedict's boots won't dance with me,

For this queen shall monkless be!"

I thought better of any advice. Such erratic behavior didn't bode well for my counsel or the vows I had made to reach Jerusalem by Easter.

As we readied for bed, Eleanor removed her regal golden circlet. She held it fondly, tracing its pure beauty.

"You belong to me no longer. You ask too great a price. To wear you is to suffocate and die. It is to let my youth wither and fade under its Capetian curse. I'll be prisoner to Paris and the Papacy no longer."

"Eleanor, be most thoughtful, dear cousin."

"There has been too much; it would take more parchment than any chronicler would have. Rancon's banishment followed by this latest insult, the refusal to join my kinsman on the march to Aleppo…it is beyond enduring."

Placing the crown carefully on the marble table near her bed, she signaled me to extinguish the lamplight.

"It is over tonight."

CHAPTER 29

Antioch

*T*he words, it is over tonight, drummed in my ears all the next day. When Sybelle asked, "Why was Eleanor not at the vesper service?" I winced, and the more when she added, "It is not like her to miss a feast of such importance as the Annunciation." In truth, I didn't know what Eleanor was like at this point.

I dodged past peacocks strutting their spring blue-green brilliance in the courtyard gardens. "She had a meeting with Louis which was of highest importance and couldn't be delayed." I hoped my voice did not betray how my palms felt clammy at the thought of last night's events. Sybelle mustn't know of the scene between Raymond and Eleanor, nor of the queen's determination to act.

"She's very distressed about Louis' response to the Aleppo plans." I forced a casual tone, my mouth dry with the half truths. "She's is very moody, of late, laughing one minute with Raymond and her lords, poking fun at Galeran and the stuffy men around Louis, then next minute, she becomes angry. I know she is furious at the king for hesitating to join Raymond."

"It doesn't go unnoticed when she ridicules the king's followers, since Phillip is one of them." Sybelle's response held an unusual edge to it.

"I know; she's too thoughtless with her remarks at times." Sybelle would be amazed at how thoughtless the queen had become. "Then, after some flippancy, the next moment she is secreted with Prince Raymond, coming from those interludes either merry or pensive." I paused, starting to perspire with the deceit I was engaging in.

"Eleanor suffered rebuke by the king's lords for something that was not entirely her fault. While Geoffrey was banished, Eleanor still bore the brunt of the blame. Here she seems not maligned but rather adored." Sybelle's brow raised in a gesture of disapproval. "And furthermore, her carefree manner is viewed as improper by most of the barons. They resent how she seems to have forgotten our fallen ones."

"Her gravest concern, at the moment, seems to be the lack of Frankish allegiance for Raymond." I tried to explain Eleanor's position, "Surely you can understand that; he is, after all, her closest blood kin. Beyond that she seems, for the most part, happy enough." I didn't feel free with Sybelle this morning. The sown seeds of conspiracy had led to sprouts of distrust.

The pace of events had begun to overwhelm me, for I still had a heavy heart. I found myself searching among the men, hoping to see Rancon or Charles enjoying themselves like the others at the jests and feasts. "Eleanor can put grief behind her, it is true. She says that we did expiation for our sins by starving in the cruel mountains and vomiting the rotten meals on the seas. Yet, we survived, and now that we are in Antioch, she believes it is time to rejoice. In some ways, I envy her ability to do it." Cautious lest I reveal too much, I added, "She told me that she could stay forever in Antioch, and that, one day, if she could have a court all to her own liking, it would be as grand and as worldly as this one."

Sybelle stared at me in wonder, her lips pursed. She remained silent, as though needing time to study the complexities of Eleanor's dispositions. "Surely she could have attended the devotions with us if for no other reason than to give thanks to that Good Shepherd and his Holy Mother for guiding us from adversity to the benevolence of Prince Raymond and his opulent hospitality."

Before I could come to Eleanor's defense, two youths sprang up from the carved stone benches outside our suite of rooms. One was squire to Florine, the other, Count Phillip's.

Florine's squire spoke rapidly saying that he was to deliver the message to Lady Madeleine exactly as it had been spoken to him by the old woman, Thecla. Hands at his sides, he announced self-consciously in a sing-song voice, "It is Florine's time and I am in the very hands of the devil. Come to Sir Hugh's lodgings at once."

The other, a letter given to Sybelle, was on parchment written in the delicate hand of Phillip's chaplain.

"The Count of Flanders would be honored to have you join him for supper at his apartment tonight. He will send for you shortly after vespers."

The invitation seemed to perplex Sybelle. "Phillip has spent much time carousing in Antioch's taverns. He and Mortimer have visited the baths which, I've been told, also house a brothel. He's had little time for me and less consideration for the vows of abstinence which Louis has so assiduously kept to these nine months." Sybelle's reddish lashes blinked as she remained thoughtful.

With Easter-tide almost upon us," she said gently, "I had planned to speak to Phillip of confession so that we might receive the sacrament of Holy Eucharist together on Easter Sunday in Jerusalem. This may be my chance."

When we entered our quarters, Sybelle called for a serving maid to select a proper gown from the many Princess Constance had given her. She chose the emerald green gown trimmed with stitches of golden thread. Her eyes took on the shades of sparkling deep oceans and I knew she was happy.

The words from Thecla made no sense. Still, I methodically gathered together a night bag and called for Germer to bring a horse. The two of us left for the baronial palace settled against the mountains.

There, Florine and Hugh had been housed with Hugh's cousin, a deputy to Raymond.

Germer, quick to find his way about, led me across the city. Bells called Christians to prayer while, at the same time, echoing male voices sang from sky-high minarets and signaled the Saracen to prostrate himself toward Mecca. The sky deepened purple toward the sharp, black outlines of the mountains. The scent of night-blooming jasmine filled the air. A crescent moon filled with silver was flanked by a few bright stars.

A good night to be born, I decided, putting aside the blight of Florine's child. What the devils were that Thecla had spoken of, I could only guess. There seemed to be an oversupply of them these days. However, Princess Constance had promised Florine that her own court physician would be available to her when the time arrived for her childbirth. Perhaps that offer had troubled Thecla. How like the old woman to be nettled by the fact that the princess thought she might need any assistance. But, in the hands of a devil? This sounded very serious.

"How much farther, Germer?"

"Just up the hill past those tall trees."

After we rounded a stand of fragrant cedars, the house came into view. The gatekeeper admitted us behind the high walls. Wedges of amber lamp-light gleamed from the tall windows in an upper room facing onto the stone courtyard.

A servant, dressed in yards of light voile, ushered me to the stairway. Taking them two at a time, I entered a long, ample room covered with thick, richly colored carpets. Along the creamy walls, delicate mosaics outlined fragile lilies and flecks of burnt orange shaped a poppy field. In the center of the room, a raised platform held a thick pallet, covered with white sheets. A light coverlet lay upon Florine's sweating figure, her sunken eyes appearing darker against the stark, white pillows surrounding her. At her side, Thecla, her body crouched and tensed, stood poised for combat.

A brazier placed a few feet away from the bed held a deep copper cauldron steaming vigorously. Its vapors floated toward the open window. Seated in the shadows next to the window, I noticed a figure swathed in white.

"There!" Thecla eyes blazed. She pointed her long forefinger. "There sits the Infidel devil."

The figure seemed to straighten, rather than quail, at the identification.

"Who is it?" I whispered, uncertain what Thecla wanted me to do.

"Go and see. It is the court physician." The old woman's lips pulled tight as lute strings.

"Why does he not approach here?"

"I have sworn on the bed of Saint Elizabeth that I would throw hot coals. Go, look you."

I walked slowly to the window. The figure rose to meet me. From under the head covering, a cascade of black, curly hair tumbled shoulder length. A long face, proud and beautiful, turned toward me. Under dark curved brows, eyes, almond-shaped and the color of dark summer plums, met mine. An elegant woman of impressive height acknowledged me with a deep bow.

"I am Kashari, physician to Princess Constance." Her French was fluent, with only the slightest accent. "I have delivered all her babies, strong and healthy. You have seen them." She studied me carefully, perhaps observing that I was not so volatile as the other one. She motioned toward Thecla.

"The old woman will not let me near the bed to see what needs to be done. The labor goes too slow, I think. I have birthwort and other herbs and medicines as I know the old midwife does also, but she will not speak with me. My princess had ordered me here, so here I must stay."

In a gesture of defeat, she shrugged her shoulders and threw up her hands. They were most unusual—long graceful fingers, topping a wide palm, with the thumb far from the fingers. Strength and competence I thought, and breathed a sigh of relief.

I glanced toward Thecla, busy wiping the sweat from Florine's brow. The old woman's face held a scowl that warned me not to broach her. But cross her I must, for Florine had begun to cry out in pain, deep guttural cries that heralded momentum in the birthing.

Approaching Florine's able protectress, I removed the small ivory icon, Empress Irene's gift, from around my neck, and plotted with Thecla.

"Thecla, I will bless this Saracen woman with the image of Our Lady, the Mother of God, whose Annunciation we have just celebrated on this day. Then will she be free of taint for this moment. Look how Florine pales, yet there is no progress. This physician has brought forth many babes. What say you?" Sweat began to drip between my own breasts, for the water on the brazier steamed at full boil.

Thecla's leathery face showed relief as she wiped at her gray brow. She had not let the heathen touch her charge, yet I hoped Thecla believed that, were Kashari to be purified, she could allow her to come to the bedside. Then, her tired soul would not be in jeopardy, nor would Florine suffer any more of God's punishment for the sins of Eve than the usual childbirth pain. I prayed hard the ploy would work. Florine emitted another agonized cry.

"Thecla," I snapped, "trust in Our Holy Mother." I brandished the figure before her.

"Yes, Lady, you are right." Thecla nodded. "Cast out the devils, for my Florine has death written on her face."

I moved swiftly across the room toward the court physician.

"Madame Kashari, you know that we have different ways. I must bless you now with the power of the Mother of all women, and the Mother of God."

The woman called Kashari gave a short, impatient sigh. "Do what you will. It is the woman on the bed who is important. She will be the mother of the dead if we do not begin to force the labor. I know, I see it often in your women." Her face drawn in concern, the physician hesitated for a moment before ordering, "Quick! Warm these oils, and bring more sheets. Tie one for her to bite on. Let her cry out. It will help her push while I massage and stretch her birth gate."

The Saracen midwife moved with assurance toward Florine. Over her shoulder she asked, "Where are the other women of your entourage? They should be here to chant and dance. To encourage this mother to bring a new life into the world."

"Look, she bleeds so!" Shaking her head, Thecla wiped blood from Florine's thighs, at the same time daubing away the sweat from her own brow with the back of her arm.

The labor was not going well. Florine lay exhausted, and still no babe.

Kashari looked up at the old woman, concern etching her face, her dark curly hair, damp with perspiration, clung to her forehead. "The head breeches not. It is buttocks. Bring the lamp closer. What think you?"

Thecla shuddered at the cries coming from Florine; her eyes, glazed with the pain of hard labor, sought no one but rolled upward in agony. I crouched behind her on the great bed, grasping under her arms, propping her to ease her struggle for breathe, but she continued to gasp.

"There is only one hope, a procedure of danger, requiring much skill," Thecla whispered to me. "It would be treacherous now, with the womb losing so much blood before delivery."

For the first time since she had been forced to the stranger's side, the old woman looked directly at the interloper. Compassion glowed from the Saracen woman's dark eyes. Thecla relinquished her charge to the Infidel woman.

"You must turn the baby or we will loose them both." Thecla's voice was hoarse, muscles in her face quivering with strain. "May the blessed Saints be at this birthing now. Help me trust. I cannot lose my beloved charge after all these dreadful months."

Thecla studied the agile skill in Kashari's hands. "Bless, oh Mother, those hands," she prayed aloud while edging out of the way, "which will bring life to us here."

Instantly, Kashari moved in, positioning herself for the procedure, requesting a hot cloth soaked in vinegar and camphor to rewash her hands. After the cloth had been steeped again in boiling water, the physician swabbed gently at the birth canal, then motioned for a jewelled jar of unguent, sharp smelling and slippery. Summoning the serving women to help Thecla restrain Florine's legs, she instructed, "Hold her legs. She cannot thrash about. The womb is too spent, and may easily rupture."

While she guided her hands adroitly around the fetus, Kashari spoke softly to Florine, now semi-conscious.

"The baby wants to help."

Florine fought her restraints, emitted a hoarse scream, and fell back in a faint, a dull blue line edging her twisted lips. I cradled her against my breast enduring the short, dreadful wait till the violent rush of fluids spilled upon the sheets.

In another minute, Kashari handed a baby girl to Thecla who blessed her and placed her gently across her mother's stomach. I rested Florine's pale hand atop the squirming babe. She stirred, the blue slowly receding from her lips.

We formed a circle round the bed. Our damp faces, illuminated by lamplight, glistened like amber carvings. Gazing at one another, we dared to smile while tears of thanksgiving flowed down our cheeks. The room smelled dense with birthing fluids and the sweet, nutmeg breath of the newborn.

The infant began to squall while Thecla, tenderness in her gnarled hands, sponged the blood from her head and face.

"Madame, by the Great Mother's goodness, I do believe this babe has her father's red hair!"

Through the open window the bells pealed the hour of Matins. and pleased I was to lead devotions.

"My soul doth magnify the Lord
And my spirit hath rejoiced in God my Savior."

The others responded in chorus, as Kashari stole silently to the window and turned her haggard eyes to gaze across the blackened night toward Mecca.

CHAPTER 30

Antioch

Sunrise had brightened the room by the time I left Florine snuggling her babe. Weary but exhilarated, I was anxious to bring Eleanor and Sybelle the good news. The awakening streets of Antioch bustled with vendors, hawkers, and tentmakers setting up shop. Guards pushed open the great, creaking gates to admit a large, restless caravan. Dusty traders led ill-tempered camels toward the caravanseri, there to refresh themselves before selling their wares under a rainbow of billowing awnings set in the shade of the city's far wall. Perhaps Eleanor and I would pick a gift from there later this afternoon.

Before long, I sensed something was amiss. "Our appearance this morning attracts the townspeople's attention, Germer. They look and point to us. What do you think is the matter?"

"You're right, Lady. I can't tell what it is."

"Well, bless us, Germer, I thought it was that I was without sleep, and felt so disheveled."

We reached the fountain square where gossiping native women drew water for their clay amphora.

"I see no Frankish soldiers about." Puzzled, Germer scanned the streets carefully. "I see no one from…" His remarks were cut off by a young Poulanc woman who approached him, her hips swinging, her deep-set green eyes fast upon him.

"Are you not the queen's man? Why do you tarry here when she has left in the night with her cowardly king?"

I stared in disbelief.

"What, woman? Take care when you speak of the Frankish King and her Grace, Queen Eleanor. What is this rumor?"

"It is not rumor, lady. They stole out by St. Paul's gate in the darkest hour before Prime. Sadara's young soldier," she pointed toward the smirking woman, "was pulled from her bed when a comrade plucked him away from between her thighs. A good thing too, for her father would have beaten her badly had she been found out."

Laughing, the women continued their water-gathering, dipping clear liquid into their jars. Full of recent events, they departed, refusing any more conversation.

Like one struck from behind, I was reeling from the blow. Lightheaded, I clutched the reins. Words caught in my throat. "Quick, Germer, to the palace. We must see to the queen at once!"

Weaving through carts and caravans, we picked our way to the royal quarters. Once arrived, I rushed to the suite of rooms we had shared. The bed chamber was in disarray. Some of Eleanor's wardrobes, filled with new purchases and gifts, had vanished; others lay tipped on their sides with the contents strewn here and there. Sybelle's things were undisturbed. Her bed had not been slept in.

A covey of terror-stricken eunuches and servant girls cowered in the corner, gagged and bound together by our long, silk scarves newly purchased at the bazaar.

"Germer, help me free them at once!"

As though expecting harm, the servants, once untied, bolted from the room, their utterances a jumble neither of us could comprehend.

My knees gave out and I sank to the side of Eleanor's bed. "Germaine! Germaine!" She should be here. How had Germaine escaped being bound and gagged? I felt lost, hovering between confusion and alarm. My head drummed with pain. Lacking food and sleep, I reached a shaking hand for the water at Eleanor's bedside. My eyes fell upon a cordial glass. I sniffed at its remains. A faint odor stayed at my nostrils—of what? Something familiar? Yes, recently familiar. I tried to push past my mind's numbness. Poppies, of course! The potion that Kashari had given Florine to help her sleep.

What had happened here? Who would dare drug the queen? Surely it was treachery! After all the months of hardship, how could there be dangers here in the court of Eleanor's uncle? I would go to him at once. The prince would know of Eleanor's whereabouts.

"Come with me, Germer, I must find Prince Raymond!"

The prince was not seeing to business today, I was informed, but had stayed the morning in his private rooms. With Germer's encouragement, I insisted that I must see him immediately. The urgency in my voice sent the Turcopole squire scurrying to the family quarters.

After a wait that seemed unduly long, he ushered me up a wide flight of marble stairs to the lush second-level garden where Raymond and Princess Constance were at table surrounded by a bevy of silken-haired toddlers, their fat legs bare to the spring sun.

Raymond glanced up in surprise. His face wore an expression of chagrin, yet his eyes had the dull look of one deeply disappointed.

"What is my niece's woman doing here? Are you left as hostage?" I'm certain Raymond had no intention of insulting me, but the remark was not without its cut. He regarded me listlessly as he remained seated, nor did he bid me to sit on the low cushions near his chair.

"Your Excellence, know you not the queen has been abducted? She is not in her rooms! Things have been tossed about. I am sure there is treachery."

"A fine story, my lady." Raymond concentrated on the date he was pitting for the child at his knee. "Were you able to read you would see in this letter that Queen Eleanor had chosen to leave."

"I am well able to read, Prince Raymond," My eyes did not leave his. "Let me see my queen's hand."

Raymond reluctantly passed the note. His jaw bore the hostile set that I recognized as a family trait, a device to hold anger clamped between the teeth.

"My dear Uncle, It is my duty and my will to accompany his Majesty, my husband Louis, to the Holy Land as was our sacred intention from the moment of our pledge. We see to it now, without further delay. Your grateful niece, Eleanor, Queen of the Franks."

"This is an awkward forgery, your excellency. It is neither her hand nor her rhetoric. Nor," I lowered my voice, "as you well know, was it her desire to leave at this time." Here was dangerous territory.

Raymond looked away quickly, but I persisted, "She always signs first with the title of her inheritance, the Duchess of Aquitaine, then her queen's title. I know she is in danger. The servants were bound in her quarters! Did your guards hear nothing?"

"She is not in danger. She is in the company of the king." Raymond gave me an acerbic look, thrusting an object toward me. "Look, she sent me this ring as proof. Is this not Eleanor's ring?"

Examined the emerald closely, then met Raymond's half-hearted gaze, "It is, Prince Raymond, but, it must have been taken from her coffers. Bring your servants in. Question them." Anger strengthened my tone. "Do it soon, for God's sake! My queen is gone, taken, as Saint Magdalene is my witness, against her will!"

Raymond stared at me. His handsome face weary, vulnerable. "Yes, and so is all the Frankish army. The lords and dukes. Some Poitavian barons too, have followed their queen, albeit, now it appears, perhaps, under duress. Still, I know of only one who will remain here to be in allegiance with me, and then for only a while. Hugh will stay while his wife recovers from childbirth. Then he plans to return to France. He is confounded that Eleanor deserted half the Aquitainian forces here."

"I swear to you, she would not do that."

Raymond gave his attention to rolling up the sleeve of his caftan before he continued. "Some of the nobles followed to join her, but Hugh insists he must return to France. He fears the queen's interests may need protection there. He, like you, feels that there may be foul play." He spoke deliberately, lifting one of the babes to his lap.

His manner became distant, head tilted to one side, as though listening to voices from the past. "This turn of events does not bode well for me. Here in Outremer, we live on the edge. I have both Byzantine and Saracen thirsty for my blood. And the clever Nur a Din arises to provide strong leadership to the warring Saracen factions. He unites them and our enemy grows stronger every season. It would have been so opportune to take Aleppo. Now, I have lost that strategic advantage and," his eyes misted, his voice trailed off, "the company of my niece, Eleanor." He put the child down absently.

I started to reply but he continued. "It is hard for me to believe that Louis would do anything so rash, but perhaps his Templar eunuch might so advise him. After all, it is no secret that the king has led a disastrous expedition, winning nothing, cringing from battles, bringing no booty to his followers, abondoning his forces in Sattallia, they've yet to show up. He has lost much stature here. To lose his wife and queen as well, with her rich patrimony, would have been a calamity for him," Raymond whispered, "while a great advantage for others."

I was growing impatient with so long a discussion. I tried once again to speak, but Raymond interrupted, "Louis Capet has rendered most of France into poverty from his mismanagement as we have seen and heard from Anjou and elsewhere." He ran his hands through his hair and faced me. With his blond lashes half obscuring his eyes, he whispered, "She was going to divorce him and remain here, did you know that?"

His question startled me, and I answered with care, my voice matching his whisper. "I knew that was something she had wanted to do. Oh, by Veronica's veil, Prince Raymond, all the more reason to suspect that she is kidnapped and taken against her will! She wouldn't have deserted me here." I tried to stifle the pleading tone.

Raymond turned away and began peeling an orange for one of the children bobbing at the table. Without words, he had dismissed me.

Tears rushed to wash the hundred thoughts spinning around in my head. In my desperation, I thought wildly that had Rancon been with us, this never could have happened. Bolting from the garden and blind with agony, I raced toward the slick marble stairs.

❧   ❧   ❧

Through a throbbing consciousness, I felt an even deeper pain. At my elbow, yes, that's where it was.

"Yes," I said aloud. "That's it." My lips felt thick as sandal cords.

"Ah, that is good that you can speak to us."

I forced my lids open to meet intelligent eyes which I recognized; intent and bright, they were a dark plum shade. Kashari continued to observe me while she probed with fingers supple and strong along the edge of pain that pounded at my elbow.

I turned my face to the wall with a moan, so overwhelmed with despair was I. My attention was forced to my injury and the ministrations Kashari now performed. With a deft motion, the court physician put a poultice at the swollen elbow joint. It pulsed with such an ache that I was forced to ask about the injury.

"What has happened to me and where am I? These are not my rooms."

Kashari smiled, her teeth white against the dark of her skin. "You ask two questions. You shall have two answers. You have injured your elbow in the fall you had this morning, and you are in the royal infirmary which I oversee. Imagine how surprised I was to see my assistant in midwifery here, suffering a nasty head wound and a swelling arm joint. You seem very distraught, Lady, and I know you do not want to talk. Please have some broth now, then sleep. I shall be here when you wake. Sleep."

The broth slid down my throat, a comfort. Under heavy lids, I watched Kashari's strong profile, silhouetted against the dusk, fade from view.

Once lost in a labyrinth of dreams, I found myself wandering in the desert wilderness. Far in the distance I could see Eleanor appear on a mountain path, then disappear. Discovering the Holy Sepulcher hidden under a ledge guarded by a lioness, I could hear against the background of the animals an angel, asking "Quem Quaeretis?" Trying to open my mouth to answer, I find no words, no utterance forms, only sobs sounding in the desert air.

Sitting upright with such haste that Kashari rushed to my side, I struggled through my tears, "Kashari, I must leave here. I must follow Eleanor! I must go to Jerusalem at once. I can't stay abed. I pledged to go to the Holy Sepulcher with my queen, and there must I be. Whether she went under protest or not, we pledged to do this together. We have endured so much." Sobbing and spent, my head spinning, I fell back upon the pillow.

I spoke in a voice not sounding like mine. "And daily, I know that I have my own quest at the Tomb, though I know not what that is." I drifted off again into semi-slumber.

Kashari leaned close to my ear. "Perhaps I can help you. I go often on that road to Tripoli. Sleep now, we will make plans at daybreak."

"How?" I murmured.

"Caravan." whispered Kashari.

"Caravan? How utterly impossible." Giving the physician a scornful look, I dozed off to a more restful sleep. Kashari spoke of caravans no more.

After many weeks of drinking the curatives of steamed eel broth and tolerating the odoriferous mustard poultices, my injuries gradually healed. Visits from Florine, Thecla and the baby sped my convalescence. The old woman gloried in her role as nanny, and only with the sourest of looks would surrender the infant to the wet nurse for feeding, a task far beyond the talents of Thecla. On those afternoons, there was gossip and endless speculations as to the truth of Eleanor's departure.

"What does her Majesty mean, to desert you thus?" Thecla's brows closed. "It is not like her. I believe you are right, Lady Madeleine. The queen would never depart without you. Thank God the way is well marked to the Holy City," Thecla carped. "Perhaps the king's fools will arrive in good time."

"I remember the preparations in Paris. Eleanor does nothing without thought. On every move she thinks ahead." I struggled to blink back tears. "She would never have deserted me, Thecla. She risked so much to rescue me in Constantinople. I pray that she is not in danger."

"Her Majesty is well protected you maybe sure. Remember that Louis' army is rested and well equipped, thanks to Raymond's generosity."

"The Prince has asked that we stay a short while in Antioch before returning home." Florine had garnered the baby from Thecla and held her close.

"Stay here, Lady Madeleine, and then travel home with us." Hugh offered.

"Oh, I fear not, Sir Hugh. I must go to the Holy City to join Eleanor as soon as I am able. I am a member of her household. I hold a royal charge. Surely, Count Raymond will furnish an escort." Trying not to wince, I gingerly worked my elbow back and forth.

A week later, tired of delay and ready to travel, I felt quite strong when I approached Prince Raymond to petition for an escort to Jerusalem.

"Lady Madeleine, that is impossible. I have received news that the Byzantine vassal in Phrygia has thrown off the yoke of Emperor Manuel and plans to gather an army to march on the outer reaches of our principality. I need every man I have." Raymond stroked his wiry mustache, gazing toward the hillside. "Sir Hugh remains here with us for a time. Perhaps he will provide you some men. I can give you shelter while you stay and provision for your leave, but I can spare no protection on the road. I need every man I can muster." He paused for a moment while he frowned at the bell sounds rolling through the window. "Or it is possible for you to go with one of the caravans."

"Caravans?"

"Yes, if you travel like a native, your chances are fairly good. Our physician does it regularly. She has come back to us safely many times over the years. Speak to her. She leaves on the morrow, I believe."

Watching my step on the polished marble, I sped for the wing of the palace that housed the sunny infirmary. The words of another time echoed in my ears, a time that seemed so long past.

"We must move about or die. In any case we die, don't we? One is quick, the other slow."

Eleanor's face appeared, and the words of my own pledge echoed, "I will join you, even to the ends of the earth!"

"Oh, dear Mother of God," I prayed, "let me not stumble, let me be there in time!" I darted up the last steps and, breathless, stood at the door of the wide, airy room.

Kashari knelt on the floor packing a large canvas bag full of supplies. She raised up in welcome. "Ah, dear friend, just in time to say goodbye. Let's look at the elbow once again."

"Let me come with you, physician." The words tumbled forth.

Kashari glanced up from her inspection. Under arched black brows, her eyes widened in surprise. "On caravan? You seemed so distrustful that I have never mentioned it again. Are you certain, Lady Madeleine?"

"Yes, by all the Saints, I am certain. Time runs out, and the moon begins to wax full." My determined urgency surprised me. I was making no sense at all; perhaps my humors were running hot, as Thecla had said they did near the time of a full moon.

"Very well, Lady, I am honored. Let us see to some proper traveling clothes." Kashari went to the wall and from the carved hooks, pulled down two multi-colored shawls, then began ruffling through a massive striped carpetbag at the foot of her bed.

"Here, step into these pantaloons. Then get your provisions together. You will be my assistant on the healing tour I take to celebrate Persephone's return. We'll depart tomorrow at first light."

CHAPTER 31

On Route to Hammim

*M*y spirits began to lift the first day out in spite of the rocking camel ride. At least I was doing something. However, I welcomed our first evening stop. Kashari's skilled guide, her cousin Yusuf, had coaxed my camel to its knees, and there I leaned. Its broad, smelly back offered a resting place to my tired back. I had already become skilled in judging the artful distances which avoided the testy animal's habit of spitting.

Quickly learning the knack of native travel, I tightened my pantaloons' voluminous folds around one leg and stuffed them into my soft black kid boot. Perspiring at my hairline made my scalp itch from the binding material around my head, and I resisted an urge to fling off the turban, so much heavier than the wimples I had worn. Removing the veil hooked by a silver pin to the side of my head covering, I complained, "I am afire under all this clothing. Kashari, must I wear all this? I can't breathe."

"Better keep it on, dear Lady. We want to hold our good fortune and continue on to Shayzer. We will reach there midday, then we turn off to the settlement near Hammim. There you will be safer. For now, it must stay on."

The caravan had come to rest on an arid plain overlooking the wide Orontes river, with its green waters sliding south along the barren gullies toward Hammah. The leave-taking from Florine, Thecla and Germer had been a wrenching one. I was to tell Eleanor of Lord Hugh's decision to return to the provinces and that he would try to make contact by letter with her in Jerusalem. The hopeful expedition begun in Paris had dissipated forever in that tearful farewell. Now, alone and unsure, I was back on the road to Jerusalem.

From my vantage, I could view the endless line of the caravan, stretching its coiled way along the ledges. It was a grand caravan that had formed at the crossroads outside St. Paul's Gate in Antioch. There, it had met up with merchants, pilgrims, drovers, and monks from the deserts, as far distant as Bagdad and Anbar. Gathering traders and travelers as it went, its ranks had swelled in numbers to make the spring trek to Alexandria by way of Jerusalem and Mecca.

Bearded officers in the service of the Emir in Shayzar, exotic in their embroidered tunics and soft fur boots, rode directly behind the caravan master. Their spirited, finely bred horses were outfitted with bridles of emeralds and rubies, made the more brilliant in the sun.

Behind them a string of camels swayed under tapestries, flowered carpets and multicolored thick pillows. Following them, a score of camels, owned by a wealthy merchant from Bagdad, kicked up the dust. Slung over their humped backs, kid skin bags filled with oils and wines quivered and sloshed with each step.

Merchants from Anbar nudged their stubborn beasts, balking asses, to drink, their cargo no secret for its pungent aromas rose above the stink of animal sweat and urine. I drew in my breath to savor the cloves, cinnamon, nutmegs, turmeric and cardamom brought from mysterious lands.

Oxen, black as the charcoal they carried, required little feed and much beating, a job done by hungry urchins happy for the food they would get at the end of the journey.

Kashari explained that the family of Samaritan Jews who walked beside their mules, speaking Hebrew to one another, were being allowed to return to Jerusalem after many years in exile.

"See," she pointed out, "the indigo stains on their hands show that their trade is that of rare and skilled dyers. They will be visiting their relatives in Tyre where those Jews who survived the first crusade are now allowed to live."

Moslems, Jews, Christian Syrians and Armenians, Byzantine, Arab and Egyptian merchants had banded together in caravan for safety. On these long journeys, commerce, not crusade, held sway. Those who couldn't keep up would be abandoned, left to the mercy of the assassins and rampaging brigands waiting in the barren hills to prey upon the unprotected. The rest of us would forge ahead with the silver-driven merchants.

A column of eastern pilgrims had made their camp along the roadside. My breath caught when I recognized the unmistakable cross of the Hospitaller order on the shields of three of them, young lads tending to the others. I searched their young faces, and ran to question them, a fruitless endeavor for they had come from Anbar. No news of anyone from Sattalia, except that plague was believed to have decimated the city. When I inquired after Sir Geoffrey and the small Aquitainian company that had headed back through Cadmos Pass for Ephesus, there were no answers at all.

Returning to my campsite in a somber mood, I spoke little while supping on almonds, dates, pine nuts and a thick, sour milk which I would never come to like. Kashari left me to my thoughts, going about the business of settling in for the night. Yusuf spread out a thick carpet, then stacked the rolled baggage around the side of the camel.

"We must sleep now." Kashari spoke gently, her hand on my shoulder. She gestured toward the ground covering.

Without a tent?" I scanned the long caravan lines. No tent to be seen anywhere, just a few canvases propped high enough off the sandy ground for a body to squirm into.

"It doesn't rain now. It is not too cold. And it is a delay. Caravans move as fast as possible. Come, take this pillow. You will be comfortable."

"Next to the camel?"

"Yes." Kashari smiled, realizing I had much to learn. "She keeps us warm, and she will not move unless Yusuf prods her. See how happy she is to rest there on her knees. Look." Kashari moved to the camel's side. "I put my pillow right at her ribs."

Observing Kashari's comfort, I placed my own pillow at the camel's side. The animal turned its head, regarding me with a sullen gaze. Under a light canvas covering, with Yusuf at guard, I tried to sleep. My elbow, still not completely healed, throbbed under me. I lay watching the sky.

Splashed in siver under a waxing moon, the promontory lay quiet in the mild night. Kashari breathed rhythmically at my side. I thought of Florine and the baby and the wise, caring ways of Thecla. And what of Eleanor and Sybelle? I missed them and prayed as I had every day that they would come to no harm.

I tried to picture Rancon's image by firelight that last night on the plains; the curve of his mouth, the desire in his eyes; his image appeared for an instant, then disappeared leaving a black night grazed by moonlight. Filled with longing, I struggled to ward off despair. On the cliffs in the distance a lioness growled to the night and paced before her lair. It was spring and the time of cubbing.

"Easter is near," I sighed, "and I am miles from the Holy Sepulcher." Finally, my elbow ceased its painful twinges and, drifting off, I welcomed the visitation of the biblical women of my dreams.

In the days that followed, we traveled the rocky pass from Shayzar to Tripoli, threading our way beyond Mt. Lebanon on the south and the Nusayriyyah mountains to the north. Branching off the old

Roman caravan route was the dusty link with Hammim, weaving its pebbled way toward Kashari's first destination. An anxious curiosity gripped me as Kashari directed us to break away from the caravan to join four well-armed grain merchants. They were hardy Syrian Christians ready to accompany us into the winding canyon as far as the Maronite mill, known for its fine grain and active trade.

"How can grain be grown in these mountains?" I inquired, remembering the stretch of Bulgarian wheat fields fanning softly toward the Danube.

"The grain is cultivated on a wide, sheltered plain above the mill. I believe it is so fruitful because the fields are fed by springs bubbling from the rocky base in those foothills near Mt. Lebanon." Kashari pointed off toward the mountain in the distance.

"But who dares to run a mill this far away from the protection of a fortification?"

"A convent of nuns runs the granary and the mill. They are guarded by a cadre of Marionite monks. The establishment has thrived there many years, perhaps since the time of Constantine, who, it is said, endowed the land and built the convent for his sister." Kashari paused to get her breath.

"Go on." Kashari was a wonderful teller of stories. "Well, this youngest sister was mute, and therefore her bride price could not bring a rich acquisition to the lands of the emperor. Because she was a favorite of his, he built her this place instead, and I tell you, it is a fortification in itself and has lasted through many attacks."

Kashari scanned the ledges overhead. Satisfied, she continued, "The monastery supports itself with the proceeds and offers shelter to those who come their way. It is nearing the time of harvest and the sisters will allow the poor villagers, both Christian and Moslem, to come glean the fields when they themselves have finished with the harvest. That is also when the dispensary is most busy and where our work will begin."

We left the chalky road and began to traverse the gray, rocky slopes of the foothills. With the relentless sun high overhead, I begrudgingly appreciated my thick headgear. Atop an outcropping high above us, granite outlines of the massive convent walls rose skyward shimmering in the heat.

After a last treacherous turn, we arrived at the gate. Isa, one of the merchants, was brother to one of the convent nuns. He alighted from his mule and pounded a stone upon the thick, dark gate. Not a random knock, I noted, but one in measured movements. Three loud taps with the rock, then two softer. Grateful for the cool shadow tracing its base. we leaned in close to the thick wall.

What awaited me here, I wondered, so far from my plans and hopes? Kashari offered me a drink from the waterskin. I had learned to let the water trickle slowly down my hot throat. Rinsing fine powdered dust from my mouth, I glanced along the top of the wall to a place where a small lookout tower perched, closed on all sides except for loopholes the size of a face. None appeared there.

The high mountainside offered an excellent view of the arid plain. Far to the west, dust swirled on the horizon. Large flocks of livestock kicked up the sandy terrain, followed by numbers of people, like dotted specks, on horses and donkeys. Close on their heels, a swarm of camels rode behind them.

"Bedouins," Kashari pointed to the southeast, "going high into the mountains for their summer feeding. They will go up that pass over there to the other side of Mt. Lebanon." Squinting more closely, the physician commented, "But, they are not all Bedouins. There appear to be warriors with them. That's strange."

Responding to my frightened look, Kashari added, "But we are in no danger, for they are traveling in another direction entirely."

Relieved, I turned my attention to the dry plain. Where grain could be grown or harvested, I could not imagine. My speculations were interrupted by a call from the tower, "May God bless the travelers who come to our door!"

At length, the iron ring turned in the massive carved door. A nun, her mirthful face as round as a tambourine, ushered us into the courtyard.

Through an open gate at the other end of the enclosure, I caught sight of sloping hillsides, billowing with golden grain stalks, while across a vigorous riverlet, a silhouetted waterwheel hoisted cups of liquid power to the granary downstream. I had not seen anything like it in all my travels, nor in Eleanor's domains.

"Welcome sister physician, we have missed you." A tall woman, oval-faced with flecked, hazel eyes, greeted us. The black Benedictine habit framed her face.

Eying me with curiosity, she unleashed a barrage of inquiries. "You are a Frankish woman, are you not? How is it that you travel here? Do you come to join us? I am Mother Superior, Mother Hildegarde," she smiled, showing large crowded teeth.

I separated the questions, not sure which to answer first. "Yes, Mother Hildegarde," I began, "I am Frankish, from Gascony. I'm afraid that I don't come to join you, only to stop for a while. I am on my way to Jerusalem to rejoin the Queen of France and the Countess Sybelle. Sybelle is stepdaughter to Queen Melisende." I hesitated, unsure how to reveal the rest. "They have gone ahead by some day's travel. I hope to join them as soon as I am able to arrange it. I will be grateful for any help."

"We will speak of that later. It is Lent and we observe the rule of silence during these hours. But we will not forget." Mother Hildegarde nodded, never taking her curious eyes from me.

After a silent meal of dried fish and flat bread followed by Lenten devotions in the refectory, Kashari and I were shown to our room, a small cell whose slit window overlooked foothills waving with grain before they sloped to meet a thick border of olive trees. Across another stretch of hills, vineyards reached to the top of the rise where a small, spired monastery perched. Its south wall supported a tower similar to the one from which we had been welcomed at midday. A formidable stone wall surrounded the vast settlement.

"Are there more sisters over there, Kashari?"

"Oh no, those are the brothers. Maronite monks dwell there and it is from their fierce protection that the sisters' granary has had so long a time of prosperity. Those brave men of the bow and arrow from Armenian and Syrian tribes are well known for their marksmanship. They are greatly respected among my people."

Kashari faced me. "And they are known also for their kindness and for their charity. On the morrow, when people come to us from the outlying villages for the first wheat gleaning, they will receive not only treatment for their ills, but they will receive as well, a measure of flour for their firesides. And so it is. In midsummer, when the grapes are gathered, they receive a measure of vinegar and raisins. When the olives are pressed in the winter, they receive oil, and when it is time for the spring harvest and healing, they receive grain and health."

"But, how is that you come this long way?"

"I am sent here at Prince Raymond's request. It his way to show goodwill to the outlying villages. He sends gifts to the strong Maronite monks as well, for they do a service for the Franks by keeping peace in this remote territory."

Kashari unrolled her mat on the floor. "And, so, my friend, let us rest, for a little after daybreak, there will be many people waiting at the gate."

Eerie sounds startled me awake. Perhaps they came came from the screeching, round-faced owls harbored in the towers. Still heavy with fatigue, I sank back to sleep.

Through my deep dreams, I heard voices pleading, others giving commands. Awakened by a sense of urgency, I shook Kashari who, sitting upright, now heard the terrifying sounds. My skin crawled. They were human screams.

Sister Catherine, the night sister, looking harried, appeared at our cell door. "Please come, physician, and you, too, visitor. We must pray for the casting out of evil demons in Sister Inviolata She is possessed sure."

Kashari pulled on her tunic and started to reach for her bag of herbs and instruments.

"She is not sick, physician, she is possessed. Come, we must move quickly. It happens frequently."

Kashari seized her medicine bag, telling me to follow her and Sister Catherine down the narrow, dimly lit corridor. We reached the last cell, where a wiry Sister Inviolata was springing up and down on her cot.

"I will rise up to the Lord!" she announced in a scream, bounding upward from the straw-filled mat beneath her.

"She is very out of balance." Kashari whispered to Mother Superior. "Her color is bad. Her humors are not in balance. Look at how sallow her skin is. Has she been fasting for long?"

"Yes, she is one of our most devoted sisters, and fasts often. This is holy week, and she has had only the oldest moldy bread which she snatches from the chickens and soaks in water."

Sister Inviolata let out another scream and began to run in circles.

"Have you a chess board?" Kashari asked above the racket.

"Yes, physician, but it is put away for Lent."

"Please get it for me. And then bring me a pot of hot water so that I may make some tea." When Kashari opened her bag, I recognized the smell of mugwort. Familiar, too, the sweet smell of the poppy which I remembered from Florine's delivery, that curative which calmed her pain and gave her peaceful sleep. Kashari pushed lobelia and mint into my hands.

"Crush these to a very fine powder."

"I will, but we must pray, and soon."

"Yes, you can pray, but we must do other things as well, and in haste."

Mother Hildegarde raised a brow in interest, but Sister Catherine's face pinched with anxiety. "But it is Belial we must caste out." Hildegarde persisted. "We must fetch Father Emmanuel. I'll start the torch signal in the tower."

"That may not be necessary." Kashari was very cautious with her remarks. She once told me that it was well known among her fellow Moslem physicians that the Christians were only too willing to give power to the devil when people acted in this crazy manner; however, in Islamic hospitals, physicians knew it was a question of unbalanced humors which contributed to the unbalanced mind, and for Kashari, there was no doubt that Sister Inviolata displayed all the symptoms of the latter.

"You may signal from the tower if you wish, but leave me with her for the length of time that it takes you to recite the Litany of the Saints, which you will be saying in the chapel. But first, I urge you, bring me the brewing pot and the chess board and figures."

Kashari spoke deliberately over the yelled posturings and antics of Sister Inviolata, who was now engaged in a loud dialogue with Saint Jerome.

The women hurried to comply with the physician's wishes. The sisters rushed back with the requested supplies, then scurried to the chapel, looking over their shoulders to catch a glimpse of Kashari's mysterious ways. Mother Hildegarde lingered as though to measure her own judgment in allowing this treatment for Inviolata.

We went about our work with such a calm that Sister, seeming more assured, left us to join the others for the "casting out" prayers.

Kashari set up the chess board on a small stool near the wall. I mixed the potion according to her exact directions, which she called out above the soothing invitation she offered to Inviolata to stop her jumping and join in the game. Eyes blazing, the nun ignored her.

Undaunted, Kashari addressed me, "Perhaps the Lady Madeleine will join me, then?"

I had finished mixing the potion and carried it over to the chess board. Seating myself at the board, I moved my pawn with an exaggerated flourish, forward one square.

"Move two squares at the first! Two squares!" Inviolata coached, darting to our sides. While she pensively pondered the chess board, Kashari invited the distraught nun to share a warm drink with us. Inviolata gulped the mixture, spat, and returning to the other side of the room, called out to the mice, warning them that Saint Jerome had declared it was their last day on earth.

By the time the sleep-hungry congregation had completed the litany, Inviolata had been coaxed to down a good measure of the potion. She had become somewhat calmed, now pacing back and forth. Kashari suggested that they both walk the long, dark hall. The physician signaled me and I took my place beside our patient, walking back and forth along the passageway.

When we returned to the cell, Kashari, waiting for the right moment, pointed to the game board. I guided Inviolata in that direction. Finally, the nun sat on the floor to engage in a game of chess. The women were well into the game, when Hildegarde peeked into the room. She threw her hands together in a prayer of thanksgiving.

"Our prayers have been answered. Oh, thank our Lord, Jesus Christ and his Gracious Mother."

"Yes," replied Kashari smiling patiently, "but see that she drinks this tonic at intervals throughout the night, and take her for several walks down the hall before daybreak."

"We will be up all night."

"Yes, and so will she. But if we do this for two days, using the tonic and boiled grain broth, she will recover, I am certain. I would continue the prayers every sacred interval for the rest of the season. Should these symptoms occur again, give her the same treatment and walk and sing with her. Do not let her go to sleep, but walk her in the courtyard all day or take her to the fields to work. Do not let her sleep for two days, keep someone with her at all times, to talk to her, dance with her, sing to her, get her to join with you in the songs of praise."

Sister Inviolata seemed much more herself. Though she talked rapidly, her words were rational. With a vigorous wave of her hand, she demanded Kashari's attention back to the chess board.

"Look to your knight, physician!"

CHAPTER 32

Hammim

Next day, after two hours sleep, we rose at dawn, left our small cell, and descended the outside stairway leading to the courtyard. I attended Mass while Kashari went into the fields to bow toward Mecca. Afterward we met outside the kitchen, where the smell of fresh bread beckoned us.

"We will have to break fast very quickly," Kashari advised. "Soon the villagers will arrive at the gate, bringing their ills to be treated."

"Good! I see that I have much to learn from you." A surge of excitement swept through me, and in spite of our adventurous night, I felt little fatigue. As I stretched languidly upward toward clouds reddened by the sunrise, I traced the outline of the limestone wall past the convent wing. It was there I noticed a figure slip away from the high window, seemingly no longer interested in observing us.

Throughout the next day, an endless stream of patients passed through the infirmary. Amidst a cacophony of different dialects and the strong smell of camphor, I worked side by side with Kashari as we set splints, lanced tumors, balanced diets (to restore wet humors), and diagnosed leprosy in a young lad from the mountain village close by. He would have to go to a leprosarium run by the Hospitallers in Sidon.

Just before Vespers, Sister Ambrose, in charge of the dispensary, asked that Kashari look with special care at Sister Ireanus, a new arrival from the Maronite convent in Damascus. Kashari examined her patient, observed how her hands bore the shiny lesions identifying her disease, Ambrose's suspicions were confirmed, Ireanus, too, must make the sad journey to Sidon. Kashari arranged for the boy and the nun to accompany her when she took her leave. Her next stop was to be the hospital on the outskirts of Sidon.

"So you will go next to Sidon?" Mother Hildegarde inquired of Kashari, "and you, Lady Madeleine, will journey on to Jerusalem? Is that certain?"

"Yes," I answered anxiously, surprised at how much I wanted to be on my way. "I will need help to get to Acre where I can join one of the pilgrim caravans that brave the desert roads to the Holy City. My only wish is to reach Jerusalem as I vowed—and to join the Queen." I had felt I was under deep scrutiny by Mother Hildegarde, and a self-conscious blush made my face feel hot, I changed the subject. "For now, however, there are still many people who will need help. And how is Sister Inviolata?"

"Sister Inviolata has stayed by her chess board through the night, playing with different convent members in shifts assigned by the hours."

"Good!" Kashari was pleased for she had stipulated again that Inviolata was not, under any condition, to sleep. She could enjoy periods of recreation, although such pastime was frowned on by some members. Kashari's unique treatment directed that the ailing sister was to skip and sing from midday till Lauds without cessation. Sister Ambrose of the merry tambourine face most enjoyed this duty, and when she headed Inviolata back to her chess board, I saw that both of them were breathless and ruddy-cheeked.

Inviolata's laughter, raucous and crazed that first day, had become quite controlled, almost normal by Nones the second day. On the morning of the third day, as I was playing chess with her, she startled me as I was ready to move my knight.

Marching to the window, surveying I know not what, she addressed me brusquely, "What am I doing here, when there is work to be done at the mill?"

Leaving the window, she went to the washbasin and began rinsing her face. She asked me to take her to the chapel, and thereafter she wished to see Mother Superior to ask for her work duty. It was there I left her.

Mid-morning, I spied Inviolata through the makeshift voile curtain in the dispensary. She waved to me as she passed on the way to the loft above the mill chute. There, beyond the curve of silver-tipped olive trees, she would return to her task, cleaning amphorae for transporting grain to market.

At the close of our work-filled days, Kashari and I enjoyed a simple supper in the small guest dining area. Afterwards, I left my teacher to join the sisters at chapel for vespers. I remembered the souls of those departed and prayed to be reunited soon with Eleanor and Sybelle.

For me, the nightly services were a solace, yet there was an unnerving aspect which had begun to creep into them. While I tried to slip into the chapel as unobtrusively as possible, wherever I knelt for the services, I sensed I was being watched. One eventide, turning quickly after the last ave, I caught Mother Hildegarde's flecked eyes sharp upon me. She pretended to be looking at the altar, but I knew differently, and was not as discomforted as I was perplexed. What about me could interest her so? I was not to have that answer for several days.

Finally, the last of the villagers had been treated and our work high in these mountains was coming to a close. We packed away the medicinal ointments and their warming spoons. The speculum, the scalpel of finest Indian steel, and splints of olive wood were wrapped with meticulous care and put back into Kashari's canvas bag.

Outside the infirmary, we watched the last patient gather her flour and few belongings to start homeward. Wrapped tightly about her head were several bands of cotton holding chunks of strong-smelling camphor close to her scalp. We knew her severe head cold would be cleared by morning.

Removing the thin cloth that had served as a screen for our makeshift clinic, I slowly folded it into Kashari's bag. The great gate, scraping on its ancient hinges, closed behind our last patient. Stillness hung over the yard.

The veins of newly unfolded leaves stretched their patterns against the setting sun, translucent, fragile, trusting in the softness of spring. Fragrant rosemary and sage blossomed in the convent garden. Four nuns entered through the west gate and shook off the mantle of dust covering their habits, and placing their bows and quivers at the wall, made for the well, where they washed up before Vespers. Four other sisters, appearing from nowhere, took up the standing bows in silence, donned the quivers over their black robes, and departed toward the far wall with its towers rusted by ochre shadows in the gentle, vernal dusk.

The days in the high mountains had seemed like a dream. I had been at peace; some of my sadness had diminished. I regarded Kashari fondly. I realized we would soon be departing on our separate journeys. From the chapel, immediately above us, sounds of lyrical chanting broke the quiet.

"Alleluia, alleluia
Panis Angelicus, Jesu Domini."

"Ah, it is the feast of the Lord's Supper," I remembered, "I must go to chapel. Will you join me?" Though I knew Kashari would refuse, I invited her anyway. Her company was a comfort; I wanted to include her in the ceremony of bread-breaking. I was beginning to realize how much I would miss her.

"No, Lady Madeleine, I must praise Allah. You have noticed how shortly I have prayed these last days. Allah, may He be praised, is forgiving, but He has an end to his patience, though Allah is magnificent."

"I understand." I reached to embrace her. "Bless you, Kashari. I have learned so much from your wise teaching these past days."

"And, you, lady, have brought a great skill to our work." A twinkle danced behind the fatigue in her dark eyes. "I think you will be a physician one day."

Kashari walked toward our cell where she, in solitary devotion, would kneel on her prayer rug, her face toward Mecca. I turned toward the hewn stone steps that led to the chapel where the community had gathered, raising jubilant voices to praise the Eucharistic gift of the Last Supper.

"Alelluhia, Alelluhia!" I sang aloud to the swallows dipping for gnats. I took the stairs two at a time to reach the small chapel.

Incense curled around sunbeams and smoked its way toward the chapel's horseshoe arch. Candlelight played on the round cheeks of Sister Ambrose's face as she read from a book with stiff parchment pages, their sides glittering with gold and cobalt illuminations.

"Pacem relinquo vobis, pacem meam do vobis.

Peace I leave with you, my peace I give to you.

Do not let your heart be troubled or be afraid."

The words nourished my spirit. "Do not let your heart be troubled or be afraid." My heart was troubled. Away from my Queen, bereft of Geoffrey and Charles, away from the strength of wise Thecla, I trusted blindly in whatever forces would guide me to Jerusalem.

"Be not afraid," whispered my soul. "Be not afraid." Praying desperately for faith, I prepared myself for the sacrament of Holy Communion.

Mother Superior distributed the blessed bread, the Eucharist, to all the congregation with choir's plainsong echoing against the walls, "A new commandment I give you, that you love one another, that as I have loved you, you also love one another."

I drew a deep breath, and with it, experienced a profound release. A knowing came to me and I allowed myself to be enveloped by it. With glowing trust that escaped my understanding, I realized that I need not be fearful.

"Why?" I asked myself. What had changed?

There was no time for an answer; my meditations were suddenly interrupted. I found myself surrounded by the community of sisters who had gathered about me, holding each other around the waist to form a circle. They seemed to be singing directly to me,

"Let your heart not be troubled, let your heart not be troubled.

Arise, let us go from here. It is the return of spring and of greening."

Filing from the chapel, the women escorted me down the stairs to the refectory where each place setting held a small loaf of bread, dried herring and a cup of wine. A circlet of green leaves and wild flowers on the plates was meant for each woman's wrist. Full of wonder, and following the others, I put mine on.

"Now comes a greening of the spirit, Lady Madeleine. May you flourish in love," they chanted.

A spark within me kindled and grew. An intense love filled my soul; My heart pushed away its binding sorrow. Only love remained, a greening, freshened joy. I began to speak.

"I feel new in the world, like the fresh,
sweet grain on the slopes.
My spirit is as deeply hued as the wild flowers
sprung up along the river bank.
I am free and pure as the snowy egret
skimming above its flowing waters."

Where had I learned the verse I had just recited?

"Enjoy our repast, for after this supper celebration, we will veil ourselves, eat nothing nor speak a word, till we meet in the inner sacred place on Easter dawn." Mother Hildegarde's eyes held mine,

"Please do not leave us before then. Someone will come for you at the appointed time."

Deepening lines in Mother Hildegarde's face showed her tension, and there was an urgency to her request, as though it were almost ordained that I must stay.

The experience in the chapel haunted and mystified me, Why I should not depart till Easter, I didn't know, but I responded to Hildegarde's request by lighting numerous candles and offering anxious prayers that Kashari's escort not arrive till after Easter. Not free to reveal my experience to Kashari, and at the same time not daring to ask her to delay, I ate little and slept less, listening distractedly when Kashari instructed me on diet rules for balancing the humours. To my relief, no escort came through the huge gates in the next days.

At dawn on Easter morning, I awoke to a tap on my door. "It is time." A unfamiliar voice spoke through the wall.

Dressing quickly, I stepped past Kashari, already face down on her rug in prayer. Following my guide, I joined the solemn procession of holy women. Still veiled in black, the congregation entered the chapel, their sandals scuffing the hard stone aisle.

The chapel lay in darkness. Where were the torches? Certainly our celebrations at Vézeley had seen a profusion of light and flowers on Easter morn.

When all the sisters had gathered into the chapel, Mother Hildegarde came slowly to the front, a massive key in her hand. Proceeding her, two women held the dimmest of tapers. Hildegarde moved to a door to the right of the small altar. Inserting the key, which turned hard in the lock, she tugged the door open.

"Remove your veils, Oh holy women, that you may see the truth."

The chapel whooshed with a mysterious whisper of veils rustling to the shoulders of their wearers. Hildegarde's voice broke the stillness. "Oh, enter now this sacred place," she sang.

The group moved on with me following close, jostled toward an ancient doorway that seemed to swallow the faithful. I stooped to fit through its small entry. Once inside, I found myself in another chapel, larger than the one I'd just left. This structure was unknown to me. My eyes became more accustomed to the dark, and glancing about, I discerned a rugged slab of raw mountain. This chapel had been hollowed from the core of the rough, rock sides! Yet, on every wall, life-like figures seemed to guard me. Sister Ambrose lit a torch and held it to the side where a small outlet drew the smoke upwards. From a vast stillness, voices chanted the question,

"Quem Quaeritis, O Cristicolae?"

The assembled community responded,

"Jesum ad Nazarenum."

"Non est Hoc."

The sounds seem to come from the very walls.

"Where, then?" asked the congregation, looking at what appeared to be a tomb in the shaft of wall.

My spine shuddered in recognition of the haunting words of my dream, and as I stood trembling, I saw my surroundings more clearly. One side of the chapel radiated with colors emanating from rich mosaic figures hovering like sentries on either side of the of the cave-like opening. On one side, the figure of a woman stood, holding a sheaf of grain, in one hand, in the other a cruet of oil for anointing. On the opposite wall, more mosaic work depicted a woman with an alabaster jar in one hand and a scroll in the other. Her cape shone a deep blue. I let out a cry, for the figure resembled the apparition of my dreams.

The fragrance of spikenard permeated the place. To my left, the congregation passed a jewelled alabaster jar of ointment from hand to hand. Each woman dipped her thumb into the mixture and placed a dab on her own forehead, then turned to anoint the woman on her left. In the crowded room, people moved slowly as in a dream, but the oil warmed my forehead, helping me to know that this was not a dream. Suddenly, there was quiet; the congregation faced the opening in the wall.

My skin began to tingle, for someone was emerging from the tomb dressed in the same manner as the Magdalene figure on the wall! In her hand, she held a leather packet the size of a book.

As the figure approached closer to our circle, I recognized Mother Hildegarde. She slowly opened the leather case to reveal several scrolls. With delicate care, she held one parchment toward the flickering light. Hildegarde began to read.

"Sister, we know that Jesus loved you more than other women. Tell us the words of the Savior which you have in mind since you know them and we do not, nor have we heard them."

"The Savior said to me, 'Blessed are you, Magdalene, since you did not waiver at the sight of me.'"

"Oh, Magdalene, Mariham, the happy, whom I shall complete in all the mysteries the things of creation, speak in boldness because thou art she whose heart straineth toward the riches of heaven more than all your brothers. Speak, oh happy one."

"My lord, my mind intelligent is at every time for me to come forward at every moment and utter the explanation of the words which she said. But I am fearing Peter who hateth our sex."

"Know, sister, that no one can keep anyone filled with the spirit from answering. I know you seek in a manner in which it is worthy to seek."

Mother Hildegarde rewound the scroll, returning it to the packet. She kissed the cover, stepped away from the altar, and turning, walked toward us. Stopping in front of me, Hildegarde handed me the disintegrating leather case!

"We have waited and prayed for you, Lady Madeleine, to do this work for us." Her eyes, smoky dark, held mine in rapt gaze "You will take these scrolls to Jerusalem. Queen Melisende will have them transcribed in Bethany. There, at the convent of Saint Mary Magdalene, the Queen's sister is Abbess, the Princess Abbess Jovetta." She waited for the words to sink in.

"She will be expecting you. We will send her word. Now is the time to speak in boldness."

Too overcome to respond, I stood, frightened at the pounding in my ears. What was this charge from a holy woman of bare acquaintance? The packet felt so light, I wondered why its contents were of such importance.

With the thick fragrances of ointment and incense overwhelming me, I dropped to my knees, suffused by bell sounds and the choir chanting the melodious sequence for Easter Morning.

"Say, happy Magdalene! Oh, say, what did'st thou see?"

CHAPTER 33

Heading for Acre

$\mathcal{M}$other Hildegarde's prayers were answered. Kashari's escort didn't arrive till two days after Easter, giving us time to see to our traveling gear. Kashari had spent the interval teaching the infirmary sister and three novices her vast knowledge of things medicinal—how to cleanse the liver and to balance the humors; which ointments to mix for midwifery; how to use the poppy and henbane for pain, and how to set broken bones. I was both assistant and student, each role delighting me.

When I wasn't with Kashari, I was left to wonder at the task that Hildegarde had assigned me. She refused to discuss it further, her dark eyes turning cold as they fixed on mine.

"You will learn more upon your safe arrival in Bethany. Dear Lady Madeleine, your energies would be better spent praying for that prospect than drilling me with questions for which I have no answers."

Her response left me puzzled, and it was with some concern that I wondered just what it was I had agreed to deliver.

On the morning of our departure, Kashari and I stood in the shadow of the great wall of the mountain abbey. As I embraced her affectionately in farewell, impulsive words spilled out, "Come with me to Jerusalem!"

The physician looked at me with half a smile, yet there was no laughter in her eyes. "Lady Madeleine, I am forbidden to enter Jerusalem. My father's brothers were slaughtered there." Staring into the hazy distance, Kashari seemed lost in some remembrance, her face hardening in an unsettling way.

"Your Christian conquerors boasted that Infidels' and Jews' blood ran higher than their horses' bellies. Even now, were I to go there, it would mean my death or enslavement. I am, in the words of the people who control the Holy City, known as a 'hateful Infidel.'" Kashari's lips tightened as she looked off to the west.

"So," she let out the breath she had been holding, "I will go now to Damascus; we are admitted to that city. I will be allowed to heal many people, both Christian and Muslim, Allah be praised." She struggled to mask her own disappointment. "It is hard to leave you, my helping companion, the Christian from across the sea."

She tilted her head to hide the tears welling in her dark eyes, black lashes holding them back, "The chances of our ever meeting again seem slim in Allah's plan, of that I am certain, but may Allah guard every moment of your path. I do pray, dear sister-healer, that we may see each other again one day."

With a quick flick of her wrist, Kashari pulled her veil across her face and moved toward the small wheat-bearing caravan. She, Sister Iraneus and the young boy were now in the protection of her fierce, well-armed brothers who had come to fetch her. After turning around only once, Kashari coaxed her mule cautiously down the precipitous trail toward the main road.

I watched her go, feeling the lump in my throat would surely choke me. How hard it was to say another good-bye. I had come to dread them. I'd not linger on this departure. It was a miracle that it had happened at all. I treasured Kashari for her kindness to me and for what she had lovingly taught me—I would have those teachings and her mild, generous soul with me always.

After my farewells, Hildegarde led me to the gate where the sisters had gathered to chant a farewell prayer. She blessed me, stressing again the importance of my mission.

"The scrolls must arrive in good order, and soon. I am sending you with my most trustworthy guards. They will see to your safety with their lives, I can promise you."

Leading a string of pack animals loaded with grain, five black-turbaned Maronites plodded toward me. After a laconic round of introductions, Brother Nicodemas, the towering man in charge, helped me to my donkey. Sister Hildegarde primed him with last-minute instructions before he hurried me through the olive groves and down the steep trail crisscrossing the mountain's face. I paused to take a last look at the high-walled, mysterious refuge. Overhead, the face of Sister Inviolata beamed from the ancient tower as she waved wildly in farewell.

"Come, Lady Madeleine, we must not miss the large caravan traveling the main road to Acre," Brother Nicodemas said. His eyes scanned the wide desert below. "To travel with them is a guarantee of our cargo's safety and our lives."

Hours later, we waited in the shimmering heat for the caravan. The jangling camel bells and lowing oxen announced its arrival shortly after high noon, a long caravan, easily as large as the one I had joined outside Antioch's gate. Its members were as diverse as the others had been, and though I scanned it hurriedly for a familiar face, I discovered none. Brother Nicodemas said all were strangers to him, including a small band of monks traveling with pilgrims from Malta.

On the second day out, the desert sirocco kicked up. Vicious winds forced the caravan master to order a halt. "Lead your pack animals and horses into the caves along the hillside. Over there—amid the rocks! We must wait out the windstorm. It is the cursed sirocco," he shouted in disgust.

"May Allah give us patience, there can be no travel now. We must stop, find shelter in those caverns yonder, and take leave of the road, or we shall become lost. Stay by your cargo, and keep on guard." Peering over his shoulder, he warned, "There are brigands who live in these caverns. Their only delight, may Allah curse them, is to set upon unsuspecting merchants such as I." He rubbed his hands together anxiously, causing his sizable ruby rings to click as he did so.

"Just roll up in your travel carpet," Brother Nicodemas advised me after we had found a place along the limestone wall of the cavern. His was a reassuring presence as I struggled to maintain balance amid a noisy tangle of confused pushing. Travelers and pack animals scrambled for some kind of order, shoving each other for room. Animals balked, while their handlers, spitting sand and wrathful curses through their teeth, prodded them. The space reeked of fresh dung.

"How I hate these delays!" A long-toothed merchant clenched his fist to heaven, wailing to all who would listen, "Each hour lost can mean missed connections or vanished profits in a busy port city like Acre."

"Aye," agreed the leader, "In the summer months, the rush of galley traffic from Constantinople and Venice comes and goes as regularly as the sparkling tides. Great fortunes sweep in and out with the tide's surge." His ruby-ringed hands clicked again.

Cursing, the merchant led his camel to the back of the cavern, followed by the pilgrims and the monks from Malta. Strange it was that they didn't bother to speak to Nicodemas or his comrades but averted their faces as they passed by. Perhaps they had taken a vow of silence, so said Brother Nicodemas. "It is not unusual for monks to take the road, begging and praying, never saying a word for months on end."

Too hot to roll up in my carpet, I had propped it up in a triangular shape fending off the fits of wind pushing sand into the hollows of the caverns. From my shelter, I could study the loquacious Brother Nicodemas at my leisure. The black turban he wore accentuated the thick brows that rose and fell as he spoke. His mustache and beard were white against a swarthy face, which held an expression of good-natured optimism. His teeth, though uneven and gapped, whitened his ready smile.

"I was quite startled when Mother Hildegarde summoned me to be the escort for you," Nicodemas confided. "I am more often called upon to guard the precious cargo of oil or wheat that helps to support the abbey and all its charitable works. Still, Mother Hildegarde insisted that you must get to Jerusalem without delay. Her instructions were for me to arrange further travel for you from Acre to Jerusalem with one of the many pilgrim caravans that set out from there. Hildegarde's command was all the message I needed," he laughed, and I was impressed at how quickly he took to his task.

"Travelers are always heavily guarded by the Hospitallers or Templars once they set out from port towns like Acre on their way to the Holy City," Nicodemas replied to my questioning. "While there is always danger from brigands, the roads from the port cities have become more secure under the Frankish occupation of Palestine. The Templars are brave men and fine. You will travel in safety."

Feeling safe, I hunched up against the pocked cave wall with my hands around my knees. The precious scrolls pressed against my breasts. I had placed them, wrapped in a long piece of fine linen, close to my heart. I wondered if Brother Nicodemas knew of my cargo. Hildegarde had requested me to deliver it into the hands of the Abbess Jovetta at Bethany, warning me, "To avoid grave danger, speak of this to no one."

"Look you not so uneasy, Lady Madeleine. I see you glancing this way and that. There are no robbers to worry of here. There are too many of us." When Brother Nicodemas grinned, his wiry brows almost met his turban. He gestured toward his compatriots, as well as several other armed guards huddled about their cargos, their backs to the wind-swept opening. "Merchants, too, are a tough lot. Look at their long swords and sharp daggers. Experienced fighters, they, and have left many a brigand's corpse to feed the lions."

He must have been observing me as much as I had him. I was frightened. What if I were robbed and the scrolls discovered and destroyed? Or more of a fright, and one that I had begun to ponder quite regularly, what if the scrolls fell into the wrong hands, like those of Cardinal Lisieux? Or once arrived in Jerusalem, what if I were to arouse the suspicions of Galeran? I shivered at the thought. What would Galeran say of these smuggled scrolls and their secret words? Would I be called heretic? Heretic! The word sparked like crackling fire in my mind. How could I go forth in boldness? I imagined the face of Galeran and his reaction to the content of the scrolls, a disturbing thought, and I decided my mental wanderings might be better spent at my devotions, so I recited the soothing prayer Kashari had taught me in the peach-colored burst of a spring dawn.

"O my God, the best of thy gifts within my heart is hope of Thee and the sweetest word upon my tongue is Thy praise, and the hours that I love best are those in which I meet with Thee. Oh Lord, my plaint to thee is that I am a stranger in Thy country, and lonely among Thy worshipers."

An ache of loneliness for Kashari came over me. How patiently she had taught me the prayer, translating the rolled sounds of Arabic into a language I could understand. I ended the devotion with a petition of my own. "Please, dear Holy Magdalene, set a watch o'er my lips, and get us soon to Bethany. I am not the bold courier for this charge."

The rounded dark of the cave enveloped me. Oblivious to the constant sounds brushing my awareness, I drifted off to sleep.

❧   ❧   ❧

The rustle of someone shaking my arm awakened me. I froze with fear. When I discerned the dark monk's robe, I relaxed some. I didn't have time to question what Brother Nicodemas could want, for a finger was put to my lips, and, a good thing it was, for I would have cried out in astonishment. I thought I had gone daft, that I had searched too many faces, but there was no mistaking the intense blue eyes, the dark brows, barely distinguishable in the womb of the cave.

"Geoffrey? Dear Jesus Savior, is that you?" I rubbed my eyes; surely this was a dream, a ghostly apparition.

In a stealthy move, the phantom was at my side, his breath on my cheek, a smile forming at his lips. His face, wind-burned and tanned, was thin, his expression wary.

"Have no fear, my love. I have come for you. We will hide a time in Malta, then back to our homeland. It is risky, but we can do it."

I felt his trembling and took him in my arms. "My love, what—how?" The questions didn't matter. Hot tears streamed down my cheeks. Geoffrey leaned to kiss them away.

"I thank the God above that you are alive, and not slain on some mountain pass, stowed in some rocky cave." My heart beat erratically as I held him to me.

In the pitch black, camels stirred and men coughed. My pulses raced with fear at his discovery, then remembered, no Franks here to hoist him on the gibbet, but still there were always spies.

"When we reach Acre," he whispered, gently stroking my cheek, "we will sail for Malta."

He reached to hold me closer, and the scrolls pressed into my breasts, reminding me I was not my own woman…yet.

"Alas, dear Geoffrey, I—I cannot do that, not yet. no matter how thrilled my heart is at the sight of you, my love." I pulled back the monk's cowl, running my hands over his hair, his brow, tracing his lips with my fingertips, touching the features I loved so well, had so yearned for, had so mourned. "You must be careful. I must go to Bethany—I mean—Jerusalem. Eleanor has been abducted. There is much confusion, but, I—I must reach Jerusalem."

Nicodemas's snoring burst forth in irregular snorts and he turned in his sleep.

"We will meet in Acre, make other plans," Geoffrey whispered. "I will send for you. If Providence has seen us this far, it will see us further. I dare not kiss you more, my dearest, but I will find you in Acre."

He took my hand; warmth flooded through me, as well as hope and courage. Slowly, his hand slipped from mine as commotion broke out on the other side of Nicodemas, bringing the cave inhabitants to wakefulness. Wordlessly, the monk from Malta slipped away toward the cave's entrance.

Within the dark recesses of a desert cave, my life had changed inexorably. In my most desperate fantasies, I had never imagined this. My love was alive and at my side! With sacred scrolls pressing at my breast, I tried to sleep, but so stirred up was I, I gave it up. With my hand pressed to my cheek where Geoffrey had kissed it, I watched the sky through the cave portal. The night's last indigo gave way to purple streaks and then to golden daylight.

Soon we were on our way again. With a thousand thoughts assailing me, already daft from the night before and made worse from the hot sun, I spent much of my time twisting around in my saddle, searching for the monks of the desert. If I continued to ride backwards, I chided myself, I would be completely addled by the time we reached Acre.

CHAPTER 34

Acre

*A*fter three days' travel, thanks to Brother Nicodemas' vigilance, I arrived safely in Acre at midday under a blazing sun that had turned the sky a bright, baked blue. At the outskirts of the city, the formal caravan broke ranks and sought shade beside the high, caravansari wall.

The deep cistern in the courtyard held cool water, which I drizzled down my parched throat. From my pack, I took a rag and poured more liquid from a nearby jug, dripping moisture onto my wind-burned cheeks, taking care not to rub them too hard for fear of tearing my dry skin, flecked as it was with grit.

My detested, itchy, black headdress I tightened at its edges, for this caravansari with its tents and bazaars, its exotic Arabian perfumes and cooking smells reeking of garlic and cloves, was a hotbed of activity, swirling with every kind of person, but...no monks—no monks of Geoffrey's garb caught my eye. I scanned the sea of faces but found only Genoese sailors, Teuton mercenaries, Greek merchants, assorted beggars, and sly miscreants, thieving wherever they could as they wove in and out of the crowds.

In the few moments I had been there, two heated arguments had erupted, one ending in bloodied lips, the other with a nasty arm wound where dagger point had opened the flesh. My immediate thought was to give aid. Instead, I cowered near the cistern, becoming very involved with my washing. It was not my desire to appear anything but a dusty traveler.

With calloused hands, I finished cleaning away the sands of the road and felt the scrolls tight against my body. They had taken on a life of their own, like an unborn child within, carried close to my heart. I felt stronger having weathered the long journey and thought that I might have the stamina to be courier for this mission after all. I thought wildly how Geoffrey's miraculous appearance might fit into the next few days.

When I straightened up, I was startled to be facing a youth bearing the bold, white Hospitaller cross on his tunic. I wrenched at the sight of him, so like Charles he seemed—the same stature and the same deep grey eyes.

"I beg your pardon, my Lady," he spoke hesitantly, appraising my trail-worn Saracen cloak, "but are you not the Lady Madeleine, the sister of Charles of Gascony?"

"Why, yes, I am." My hand flew to my heart to feel for the scrolls' safety, and there it lingered as if to soothe the pain I felt at the mention of Charles. "Do you know of my brother's whereabouts or welfare?"

The young knight's face clouded. "He was last at Sattallia. A great plague broke out there, taking most of the remaining pilgrims. Charles stayed with them, and there is some hope for we have brothers who survive plague and live to tell the tales." He paused to bless himself.

My knees stopped their shaking for I felt an ember of hope, and I vowed to cling to the possibility of Charles' safety.

The raw-boned boy approached me respectfully, putting a hand on my shoulder. "My name is Amaurey, and I am sorry, Lady, that I couldn't bring better news, but I pray for his safety every day," he spoke softly. "But now I must ask you to gather your baggage, for you are expected at the traveler's inn near the caravansari."

"Expected by whom?" Speaking was difficult. "Brother Nicodemas was to meet me here, after he had arranged my safe travel to Jerusalem." Distraught and puzzled, I kept my eyes peeled for sight of Geoffrey. He was nowhere in the roiling, crowded marketplace.

"Please come with me, Lady. There you can give alms, for God loves the poor." Amaurey's grey eyes, never wavering from mine, had turned a deep smoky shade. "The monk from Malta would bless you for it."

My spine began to prickle, and without further delay, I followed the lad across the hectic square, dodging our way down a crooked lane toward a squalid-looking two-story inn situated at the far end of the worn, limestone lane.

The inn keeper, a sleek-skinned Turcopole, regarded us without curiosity as we climbed the stairs to the room. Amaurey set my bag inside the door and said that he would return within the hour.

Left alone, the sound of my own pulse drummed at my temples and rose above the tinkling chimes that hung at the open window. Street calls and church bells seemed miles away. Suddenly, there was a soft knock at the door. I moved to open it, but before I could raise my hand to the latch, so paralyzed was I, Geoffrey pushed open the door and swept me into his arms.

I gloried in the strength of him, thinner now but more taut under the coarse monk's robes. His lips were kissing the tears from my lashes, tracing them down my cheeks to my mouth, where I met him with a passion of my own. We clung to each other, enraptured.

His hands, so tanned, reached to remove my head covering.

"How is it I must always loose bindings from you, my lady love?"

My hair tumbled free, and I smiled with embarrassment at the sand flicking from it. Holding my chapped face with gentle hands, Geoffrey whispered, "At last. I have dreamed of this moment, ached for the sight of you." He held me closer, his lips on my hair.

"You, my dear, are—are—beyond words." I could say no more except, "How I love you, Geoffrey." I kissed him long and hard, and the smoldering hunger of all our days burst into flame. When at last we pulled apart, I put words to one of the questions whirling in my head. "But, my love, how did you escape the treacheries of Cadmos Pass?"

He put his hands to my lips. "We haven't much time, my dearest one," he whispered, "Acre is a danger for me. Louis' men are coming in for a grand council meeting, and there is a bounty on my head. I know little of Eleanor's abduction, but it is said that she can do nothing for herself and even less for us. That makes our lives the more imperiled. But have no fear, love, for I have booked passage for us at dawn tomorrow. First to Malta, from there to France. Come back with me to France where we will be safe in my own domains, with my own forces to command."

Breath left me as though I'd been struck in the chest. "P—passage at dawn?" I stammered. "Oh, dear Saints, Geoffrey, but I cannot! I have been entrusted with a charge of deep meaning." I stopped for a moment, torn in half. I had to be careful—speak of this to no one—were my orders. I trusted Geoffrey above all others, yet, I wasn't sure what to tell him. Summoning my courage, I drew him back into my embrace.

"Come, dearest, I must tell you of my awesome choices."

I bade him lie by my side on the thick sleeping carpet and revealed to him all that had transpired since Cadmos Pass. Geoffrey told of his rescue by a solitary in the mountains who helped him to Ephesus, from there by sea back to Antioch, where, hiding in monk's garb, he had learned of all that had transpired. Finally, he had traced me to Hammim and had foraged as a mendicant in the mountains till I came out of the pass with Brother Nicodemas.

"Must you sail on the morrow, Geoffrey? Come you with me as we had hoped, come with me through the gates of the Holy City!" My very soul soared at the thought.

He was silent a long time, holding my hand to his lips. "I dare not stay," he shook his head. "It means my life. With Eleanor so discredited, the Burgundians would be pleased to hoist me high, then draw and quarter me. Remember, those be serious charges at Cadmos."

I began to tremble, tried to think of some solution, gained some time by stroking his cheek, tracing his profile with my fingers, and realizing that to be in his arms for the rest of my life was what I longed for. But the pressure at my breast reminded me of my solemn charge. I was no freer than he, and I felt doubly bound. Not only had I to deliver the scrolls, I had to join Eleanor, my Queen. I had promised her that. How could I sail forth to France while she remained, by all appearances against her will, in Jerusalem?

"God in his goodness has brought us together this time, Geoffrey. I pray his sweet grace, He'll do it again." I tasted salt from my tears. "And, my dear one, I fear that my errand be such that if I be found out, it could mean my life as well."

"God forbid!" Geoffrey ran his hands to my breasts and as I met his waiting lips, a discrete knock on the door preceded Amaurey's hissed warning, "Sir, your grace, two cadres of Frankish forces march through the north gate with Cardinal Lisieux's banners at the vanguard. "Tis said the king arrives tomorrow, with Count Phillip of Flanders and the Palestinian Princes."

"Holy Savior!" Geoffrey whispered. "Neither one of us can be discovered without terrible consequences, and were we to be caught together it could be certain death. I must be off." He took my hand and pulled me to my feet.

Hastening to the sideboard, I poured from a flagon of wine to ease the choking pain in my throat. "I would that I could go with you, but...."

The packet at my breast seemed to pulse with my heart. "I must finish my journey to Jerusalem—and to Bethany. I have pledged." The sobs would not be curbed. "I have promised." Hot tears streamed down my cheeks. The knocking at the door grew impatient.

"Here, Lady, my love, what time is this for tears?" Geoffrey kissed them away. "Go now with this escort. Tell the others I am alive. And remember me at the Holy Sepulcher. God be with you, my heart, I'll send word when I am safely home."

Embracing me with wistful tenderness, he turned, and with a whirl of his robe, was gone.

I gathered up my belongings and followed my escort into the square. There was no sign of Geoffrey. He had been swallowed up by the swirling crowds and gleeful merchants readying for the arrival of the visiting Frankish dignitaries to their markets.

"Have you no woman companion?" My young guardian looked about.

"I did have, but she is an Infidel and so could not accompany me to Jerusalem." The heaviness of my heart kept me silent and I wondered, without Geoffrey at my side, if I had chosen the right way to move about—or die.

The next morning we were on the road but a short time when the sounds of a trumpet signaled heralds riding fast upon us.

"The royal party approaches en route to Acre!" We hastened to the side of the road.

"Make way! Make way! Clear the way!" Snorting animals drove us further off the road.

Amaurey cantered toward me, calling, "It is the Queen of Jerusalem! She's traveling to Acre for the grand council."

"It is the queen? Queen Melisende?" My hopes were raised. "Oh, Amaurey, I must speak to her, I really must. Can we hail the entourage?"

"It is somewhat irregular, Lady Madeleine, but since you are one of Queen Eleanor's court, I suppose it is not too unseemly. I'll speak with the Templar Captain."

Spurring his chestnut horse, Amaurey disappeared into the dust. How I yearned for some word of Eleanor and Sybelle. Perhaps they were in the party! Spring weeks had melted into early summer since their abrupt departure from Antioch. Perhaps they were with Queen Melisende en route to attend the council. If there were to be a council of any sort, surely Eleanor would be there! My spirits soared.

Amaurey returned in good time. "The royal party travels without the Queen of France, but you are in luck, Lady. Queen Melisende will see you. She waits in her wain up the road. Follow me."

I adjusted my wimple and tunic as best I could. Eleanor would have wanted me to appear composed.

Melisende had alighted from her carriage. She wore a jeweled crown worked with amethysts. Her hair, a deep auburn shade, reached just below her shoulders. Over a wide-sleeved tunic of purple silk, a soft brocaded mantle reflected bits of diamond to the sun.

Queen Melisende smiled broadly, her crown glimmering in the bright sunlight. Even from a distance, her deep-set dark eyes were commanding. At closer view, I noticed they were almost black, yet soft, beneath thick lashes. Her flushed cheeks pushed up close to her eyes when she smiled, which she did when she reached for my hand to raise me from my knees.

"At last, Queen Eleanor's lady does arrive, and safely so! It is the Lady Madeleine. Welcome to the Holy Land. I greet you with joy and offer all that I can for your needs. Countess Sybelle is in good health and Queen Eleanor becoming so. They have been praying daily, as have we all, for your blessed arrival. They are in Bethany now and await you there."

Melisende stopped for a moment, then continued deliberately, "As does my sister, the Princess Abbess Jovetta."

I bowed deeply to this friendly ruler, struck by her command and her cordiality. The news of Eleanor perplexed me. Had she been ill? With no Thecla, I wanted to inquire more, but Melisende's studied look forced a reply. "Your Majesty, I thank Our Lord Jesus Christ and his Blessed Mother that I am safely here that I may meet and honor you."

"Thank you, my dear Lady." The Queen held her deliberate gaze. "Happy is Magdalene too, that you are here and will soon be in Bethany. May you speak in boldness there."

My heart skipped. Was I imagining that the queen's remarks had some veiled acknowledgment of my errand? How could it be? Yet 'Happy Magdalene, speak in boldness,' were the exact words of the anthem from the secret scrolls. There could be no coincidence. I chose my reply carefully.

"Yes, your Majesty, I thank Our Lord's companion, the holy Magdalene, as well, and I long to fulfill my vows at the Holy Sepulcher." Through dry lips, I forced the words. "And to do any other holy works that I may have to complete."

Melisende seemed at peace with my answer. "That is the way of the Lord." Her tone was measured, revealing little. "I will dispatch some of my own guard to take you at once to Bethany."

The scorching heat of the day oppressed me. Spiraled vapors skipped along the road's dusty width, ready to encase me. My throat tightened. I had to speak quickly, words spilled out hoarsely, "Majesty, I must first go to Jerusalem, there to complete my pilgrimage. It has been too long delayed."

Melisende regarded my remarks and looking about her, surveyed those within hearing. Responding slowly, she lowered her voice. "Yes, I know. Your stay at Hildegarde's abbey was a lengthy one."

My knees almost gave way. How could she possibly know I had been at the monastery high in the hills outside Hims? Were there spies at the abbey as there had been in Eleanor's court? My queen had been easily abducted. That perfidious fact suddenly pricked my mind like a needle. Was I now in grave danger? Heresy. The word cut through me like a dagger. I was struggling to reply when a voice, hissing like a recurring night terror, intruded.

"Where were you, Lady Madeleine? I didn't hear—at an abbey, was it? We had thought you had chosen to remain in Antioch as you would not in Constantinople. How misguided were we to suppose you would do that."

From beyond the shadow of the litter, riding over to my side, the gaunt figure of Galeran approached, his steamy face sallow underneath his helm. Beside him, mounted on an ebony mare, Mortimer de Mur stared at me, his lips forming a sardonic smile. Dismounting, he approached me, bending in an exaggerated bow.

"Ah, the good Lady Madeleine. How do you fare, my dear." He actually reached for my hand, daring to place a damp kiss there.

"Yes, dear lady," his eyebrows raised, a smirk on his thick lips, "we thought you had stayed in Raymond's care." His innuendo was clear.

I fought for composure. Was this a trick? A trap? I knew Mortimer's villainous bent. I replied as casually as my fear would allow. "Galeran—And Sir Mortimer. I am journeying to Jerusalem to finish my pilgrimage." Surprised at the confidence in my voice, I said deliberately, "and to join Queen Eleanor." Sensing danger, I searched Queen Melisende's face for some signal of reassurance.

She smiled briefly, and leaning toward the thin monk whose mount had edged me further off the road, spoke tersely, as though to dispel any more discussion.

"Well, no matter where the Lady was, she is with us now, thank Our Lord, Jesus Christ. Galeran and Sir Mortimer, I would be much pleased if you would hurry ahead to Acre. Please inform his Majesty, Louis, of the Lady's safe arrival, and tell the Templar commander, Duke Melmar, that I will need a contingent sent out to meet me. My sister Hodierna's manor estate is not far from here. We will quarter there till the guard arrives." Melisende looked fondly at me, "Meanwhile, I am sending this weary traveler to Jerusalem by special dispatch with my own royal escort. From the Holy City, they will take her to join Queen Eleanor in Bethany. She is awaited there."

Galeran appeared to wince at the thought of a fast ride, strenuous and punishing as it was. Slapping his reins upon the shoulders of a nearby young squire, he shouted, "Get us some vittles for travel, fool!"

The lad scurried to his task.

Galeran snapped at Melisende, "Your Majesty, I will see to it."

Mortimer, his lips slack, stared at me with a smile that made my skin crawl. I overheard Galeran say to him, "More bitter that death is a woman. When will we be rid of them?"

"Some have their uses, Galeran, some have their uses, but I doubt you would know what they were." His guffaw was lost in his dusty retreat; his over-the-shoulder glance troubling.

I took comfort in the small escort the queen had furnished for me, but the encounter with evil Mortimer troubled me. It left me with a feeling of foreboding. I had observed Mortimer upon a road long ago. The memory of that brutal sight shook me. I felt vulnerable and wished that I were still traveling incognito with the fierce turbaned Maronites at my side or the valiant Sir Geoffrey.

At dusk, we made camp along a sheltered ledge not far from a stand of stunted willows drooping over a bare trickle of a stream. Amaurey busied himself with the animals as the guard set about preparing a shelter. It had become overcast and sultry, with thunder echoing in the distance.

I went to the stream to wash away the day's dust. A stirring in the underbrush caught my attention, but I thought nothing of it. A thirsty animal, no more. I removed my sandals and bent to gather some water into a wooden dish. Suddenly, an arm wrapped around my waist, pinning me in a vise-like gripe. A hand clapped over my mouth. Stunned, I craned my neck to look into the craven eyes of Mortimer!

"Will the whore of Gascony not lift her tunic for me as she did for the queen's man, Rancon?" His question rasped with his spit against my ear. "The whore of Gascony;" How loathsome he was.

I snapped my head away; my head covering fell to the ground. Mortimer's wet lips found my neck. While he began fumbling with himself, his other hand clamped over my mouth, I kicked out in all directions, but bare feet are no weapons. I struggled, my arms flailing, trying to find his groin with one elbow, at the same time trying to reach for my dagger with my free hand.

In his excitement, Mortimer took his hand from mouth, tearing my tunic, exposing my breasts, casting the precious scrolls upon the sandy bank!

"Amaurey! Amaurey!" my last words before he struck me a heavy blow. I remember nothing else except my body twisting toward the ground in a way that would cover the scrolls. My dagger lay next to me. The sight of Amaurey crashing down off the ledge spun round and round.

Mortimer's body rolled off me. I must have been unconscious only a short time but long enough to allow one of Melisende's guards to send an arrow swiftly through the chest of my assailant. His weight sagged atop me, then fell convulsively to one side. Feelings of terror and remorse enveloped me. Still naked to the waist, and shivering uncontrollably, I gathered the scrolls, clutching them to me.

"Please bring me a cloak, Amaurey." My mouth tasted blood.

"Yes, Lady, at once."

He paused, looking at Mortimer's limp body, "There dies a dishonorable man." Amaurey addressed the stern-faced guardsmen. "We'll cover him as best we can, and travel by the last light away from here."

Under indigo skies, we settled in new, well-guarded surroundings. Yet I trembled, glassy-eyed and frightened. Sleep came not to me that night.

CHAPTER 35

Jerusalem

$\mathcal{F}$or two days we trekked the wide, sandy road toward Jerusalem. By late afternoon, our pack animals, spent from pulling up the last switchback along the Judean Mountains, needed the sparse shade at the cliff side. The chalky dust coating stole what little moisture remained in their nostrils. My beast needed a rest. I dismounted and Amaurey offered the water bag. I downed the final dregs from the sagging container.

"Will you have a hardboiled egg and some dates?" he inquired.

"No, Amaurey, I have little need for food. The weight of a dead man so recently upon me has taken what appetite I had. I'll keep my fast these last miles."

After our near-starvation in the mountains, and my stay in the monastery, I had found it increasingly easy to go without food. It gave me a strength I had not known before.

Amaurey munched on dried fruit. Before he had finished, he beckoned me to follow him around the twisting trail past a high, rugged outcropping. From there, he promised, I would look east across the fruitful Kedron Valley to behold the shining walls and towers of Jerusalem! When I rounded the curve, the city rose like a vision, shimmering above the heat waves, vibrating skyward from the valley floor.

A happy rush of tears streamed from my eyes as joy flooded my soul. "I am here! Oh, Amaurey, I am truly here! Oh, Jerusalem of my heart! Rejoice ye with Jerusalem!" The verse escaped my lips, "and be glad with her. Rejoice for joy all ye that mourn for her. I will extend peace to her like a river."

"It is the city of God." Amaurey bowed his head.

"Hurry! It's almost dusk and the shadows lengthen. I must reach the alter of the Holy Sepulcher this day."

Ecstatic with anticipation, I began the rocky descent leading through the striated boulders to the wider road stretching toward the Damascus Gate. In the Kedron Valley, sheep lowed while ancient notes from a shepherd's horn carried to the timeless, pale stars just visible above the Eternal City.

Alone went I through the Damascus Gate. A moment later, Amaurey reached me and we wound our way through the streets, some of them steep, others twisted and narrow. I felt oddly acquainted with the route, like a timeworn traveler who had wandered the city years before. The noises, the smells, the sights gave me a familiar comfort.

I just slipped in among the last pilgrims to be admitted to the shrine. Shortly afterward, the huge gates scraped against the marbled threshold and shut down for the night. I dropped with a soft thud to the marble floor at the tomb's altar. In that cool darkness, waves of devotion swept through me. My hands were folded at my breast, tight against the secret packet. All the hardships and bereavements washed away. Charles appeared to me, his expression one of such peace, relief touching deep within me.

My head throbbed, my heart pounded. Suddenly, I was bathed in light. From near the sepulcher, a voice, soft as that of a woman's, asked me:

"Quem quaeretis, o christicola?"

Through dried lips I whispered, "Jesum ad Nazarenum."

"Non est hic."

"Then where?" I sobbed, searching wildly about.

"Learn to speak with boldness, Magdalene, for we are within. WE are within...within."

The ethereal voice, mingling with an aroma of myrrh and spikenard, faded into the the tomb's dim recesses. Brilliant tapers surrounding the sepulcher held me fast. Looming large as stars, they filled the room, then shrank, small as pinpoints, then shone not at all. Darkness thickened about me. The alabaster jar slipped from my grasp.

I opened my eyes to a strange room, small, adorned only by a simple crucifix. More refreshed than I had been for months, I was suffused by a profound feeling of inner peace. I couldn't recall what had happened at the Holy Sepulcher. The experience of last evening blurred in my mind, yet I felt so changed. A soft knock at the door interrupted my musings.

"Come in."

"Praise to our Lord, good morning and welcome to you, Lady Madeleine."

"Thank you, good sister, but where I am this morrow?"

"At the Convent of Saint Catherine's, where Amaurey, the Hospittaler, has safely delivered you."

My greeter's gray brows fell into a frown as she examined me more closely. "He said he found you in a dazed state at the Tomb of Our Lord. It is not uncommon." Her concern changed to a smile as she bid me dress and break my fast.

After expressing my gratitude for the convent's generosity, Amaurey and I had one more stop before Bethany. The Hospital of Saint John, founded by the Knights of Saint John, the order that claimed both Amaurey and Charles. As we rode through the streets of old

Jerusalem, again I wondered how it was that they seemed so familiar to me. I recognized the street names as well.

"Lady Madeleine, why do you wish to visit the hospital?" Amaurey inquired. "Why don't we go directly to Bethany if that is your blessed destination?"

"Perhaps it is because the famous Hospittaler headquarters had been Charles' destination."

Amaurey seemed pleased with the answer and, nodding his head in approval, took my bridle.

Once beyond the convent enclosure, the imposing building in the distance caught my eye, for high above it, the Hospitaller's banner with its white five-pointed star hung limp in the breezeless morning. Though it was still early in the day, heat vapors played from the parapet and swirled into the cobalt-blue sky.

On our way, we were besieged by vendors pushing toward us, hawking their wares in many languages. Their babble echoed off the vaulted overhangs that closed out the sun. In the shadowed cobblestones along the curving avenue, pilgrims from many countries lined the narrow stone alley in front of the money exchange.

Near the front of the hospital, we came upon a stand of dozing camels, oblivious to the maladies of the sick and dying who lay piled in the oversized wicker baskets strapped to their sides. Cramped together, covered with flies, the sick suffered in the heat, waiting for admission to a place set aside for newly arrived pilgrims.

Leaving my horse in Amaurey's charge, I entered through the hospital's wide vestibule. Inside, many young people, men and women, walked among the ailing, seeing to their needs. Charles's presence hovered near me.

"Did you find whom you were seeking?" Amaurey asked of my visit.

Bells tolled noontide from the Holy City's burnished spires. "Yes, yes. I saw him everywhere. His spirit is everywhere that there is love."

Melisende's royal guard rejoined us for the journey out of Jerusalem's protective walls. We turned down crowded St. Cosmos Street where we dodged camels, dogs, goat carts, and sheep. Going right on Josephat street, we passed the house of Pontius Pilate and trotted past the Sheeps' Pool, its waters shimmering like green jasper in the sun. With bells echoing behind me, I left Jerusalem through the Josephat Gate, over the Brook of Kedron and around the Mount of Olives to the chalky descent that sloped toward Bethany.

The trip went quickly and soon yammering Bedouin and Pulani children ran from their hovels crowding the roadside in Bethany Village to wave at us. I returned their greetings half attentively for my gaze had fastened upon the tower and church dome just beyond the eastern slope of the Mount of Olives. A rush of excitement rippled through me. Shielding my eyes from the afternoon sun, I could not quell a cry of joy.

The abbey in Bethany rising above the village greeted me like a beneficent guardian. There, on the edge of the wilderness, stood a magnificent structure splendorous in the midday sun. Its dominant feature, a massive tower-like fortification, rose to the south along the ancient road leading from Jerusalem to Jericho. Constructed with stones of hewn ashlar and polished rock, impenetrable protective walls stretched out from either side to embrace the church and the abbey within its towered strength. Along the south wall, a spiked iron gate denied intruders the inviting shade of a long portico.

"Few abbeys in France can be more grand than this," I remarked to Amaurey. My gaze paused on a high marble capital carved in Romanesque scrolls not unlike those in the Cathedral at Vézeley.

"What a place of beauty! And I can smell a garden!"

A welcome thought, for the arid grit of the ride, though a short one, stuck like powder to the perspiration on my face. When I licked my lips, I tasted salt and sand. The fragrance from the garden, shaded by a high stone wall, promised a yearned-for solace. It seemed a place of refreshment and shelter set against a musical background of high, sweet voices floating from the adjoining church.

A trumpet rang from the tower announcing our arrival. Within minutes, a pair of young boys, Benedictine novitiates, were shoving each other in their hurry to remove the long bars. The gates screeched their welcome and we entered the courtyard.

Bursting from a huddle of confusion, stable boys, the color of fresh dates, whisked away the horses to be stabled downwind at the settlement's edge. Small children bounded about the yard, excited by the new arrivals, running circles around the guardsmen. Novitiates assigned to the garden set their hoes aside the better to observe us.

The cacophony bemused me, for I had expected an unworldly serenity from the abbey at the desert's rim, more like Hildegarde's convent. Barely had I dismounted when Eleanor rushed to my side, hugging me close. Sybelle encircled me tightly on the other side, tears falling carelessly down her cheeks.

"Thank all the Saints you are safe and well."

"Yes, and you are with us at last. Let me look at you." Eleanor surveyed my every inch. "You are not harmed in any way then, cousin?" Eleanor patted my cheek while holding my hand. "Oh, cousin, it has all been so hard." She lowered her voice. "There is so much to tell." She paused, then added, "And you, traveling the wilderness without us, you too, must have many stories to weave."

Eleanor's appearance was a terrible shock, and I struggled not to betray my concern. How thin and pale she looked, and what a flatness to her eyes, those eyes that had always held a sparkle in their blue depths. I reached to hold her closer. Whatever had befallen her, it had wrought a devastating effect. This was not the same woman who had charmed Antioch. I was bursting to tell of my meeting with Sir Geoffrey. Surely that would perk her up.

I began to speak when Sybelle interrupted, "We prayed for you every mass and at eventide." Dressed in a simple pale blue tunic,

Sybelle's color was high with the heat, and the hardships seemed not to have distressed her in the same ways that they had Eleanor.

In the shadowed arch, a handsome woman waited under the portico, hands clasped together, enjoying the jubilation of reunion. Sybelle took my arm and we approached her together. "I am now certain that your messengers are heavenly, dear Abbess. Lady Madeleine, meet the Princess, Abbess Jovetta, my newly met sister-kin."

The abbess grasped my hands in both of hers. "We have waited long for your honored arrival, Lady Madeleine. You have had the blessed prayers of many for your safe journey here." She nodded in approval. "Sister Hildegarde chose wisely, I see that now. Is all well with our sisters there?"

"Yes, Abbess Jovetta, well indeed. You are always in their prayers."

"That is good," she laughed. "We need many remembrances here on the edge of the desert." Jovetta waved toward the tower. "Those fine soldiers, our brothers in Christ, like to think that they defend us, but we would not last long cowering in that tower. We all know it. It is the prayers of our sisterhood that allow our work here, though those brave men help to make it possible." She gestured again toward the tower and Melisende's royal guard.

"Young Amaurey, take your comrades to the kitchen. We have fresh bananas and honey. They arrived yesterday from the valley as part of our summer tithes. A feast indeed. And you, Lady Madeleine, after you are refreshed, and when you are full of news from your country women, I will hope to see you in my study." She pressed my hand as she drew me aside, leaning so near that I could mark the rim of brown that circled her hazel pupils.

"I trust that you have something for me," she murmured.

"I have Abbess Jovetta, I have," I felt ill at ease under the deep surveillance of Jovetta's gaze. I was also discomforted because I didn't know what knowledge Eleanor and Sybelle had of my mission. What, if anything, was I free to reveal?

CHAPTER 36

Bethany Abbey

*A*s soon as I was able, I pulled Eleanor aside. "Dearest cousin, a miracle has happened. Rancon, our dear Rancon is alive—and by now, safely on his way to his own provinces."

Eleanor's hand went to her throat, "My God, in truth? How has such a wonder occurred?" Tears flooded her eyes as I recounted our meeting in the caves on the road to Acre.

"He is on his way home, Eleanor."

"Ah, by St. Denis, the Holy Helper, I would that we were."

Sybelle found us under the giant sycamore in the court yard. "Come, dear Madeleine, you have time to bathe before supping."

Chattering the whole way, we followed her to the bath house. Water drawn from deep within the courtyard's reddish clay cistern splashed over me while I reclined in the high wooden tub. The bathing room was tiled elegantly in white marble, lined with blue tiles. Sybelle and Eleanor sat on benches at the side, recounting the tales of kidnap and treachery. Now, they added, that the harsh treatment earlier afforded Eleanor had given way to a kind of grudging tolerance from Louis' bishops and nobles.

"And why not, since I am virtually a prisoner in a foreign land, removed from my suzerains and funds. While Louis' pathetic advisors meet in Acre to plan some further battles, I am quite content to stay here." She looked around to be sure no one was listening. "It is a form of captivity, albeit a very cordial one."

A twitch ticked at Eleanor's left eye. Without Thecla's ointments, her face had become freckled and dry. She carried on with her complaints. "Let Louis play at his warring wherever it is. I care not. I will always believe our forces should have marched on Aleppo. Nothing will ever change that. I won't forget Louis' refusal to rally his nobles to Raymond's side. It was a rank violation of the kinship alliance. So he best not try to make peace with me, for I find his actions unforgivable."

Eleanor dipped a cloth into the tub water and damped her face, which had become heated during the conversation. "And word has it that there is further disagreement and squabbling among the barons here in the Holy Land. Our French nobles have learned little and continue their divisiveness. And I, the source of all the blame, am far removed from it. Jealousy and avarice drive them far more than piety, you can be certain of that."

"Oh, I am certain you are right," Sybelle agreed, her brow wrinkling. "I have a feeling that Phillip conspires in some way. Since our arrival, he has been off to other provinces or engaged in whispered conferences, which stop when I enter the room. It troubles me, for Queen Melisende is my kin and needs help, not dissension."

Both women were a study. Sybelle seemed only vaguely concerned about Phillip. Her health appeared to be exceptional, and there was a serenity about her, a kind of harmony that I had not observed in her for years.

The same could not be said of Eleanor, who, in spite of the wonderful news about Geoffrey, obsessed about her calamities. "What troubles me is that I feel so powerless," she said, "forced to stay put in this so-called Holy Land; you know how I love to venture out on any excuse. Ah, how I yearn for the sweet fragrances of Poitiers. There I could be happy once again."

How flushed Eleanor was, full of anger. Her humors were out of balance and rancor dwelt in her soul. The red receded from her cheeks as she applied more water to them. Suddenly, she become excessively pale, and I noticed a slight yellowish undertone to her once glowing skin.

"It has been very difficult for you both, I know." I sorted out the many thoughts flitting through my mind, while a serving girl poured another bucket of water into the tub and began to scrub me. Her vigorous motions made me flinch and by way of distraction, I began to spin the series of adventures that had brought me to Bethany. "You will be surprised to learn of my travels with Kashari."

After revealing the wonders I had seen and the marvels Kashari had taught me, I paused, looking around at the massive jeweled walls that glowed under an evening sky. "Isn't it strange that we have ended here in this beautiful convent in Bethany, when we thought we were to be in Jerusalem's palaces all along?"

"Yes, it has all become strange." Eleanor seemed momentarily contemplative. "Still it was a frightening thing to be drugged and bound, Madeleine, tied at the wrist with my own scarf! When I awoke I was being jarred about on the road to Damascus, held hostage and forced to come to the Holy City. Were I not so wealthy with land and vassals, I believe I might have been murdered. How naive I was to think I could demand a divorce from Louis and not have that wretched Galeran take some vindictive action."

"How awful this has been for you, dear Eleanor." I reached out for her, realizing that such treatment had been a hateful ordeal and an insult to her royal pride.

Her lips quivered and tears welled in her eyes. She went on. "Those first weeks out of Antioch, I agonized, yearning for Raymond to reclaim me, to fetch me back to his lavish realm. Restless nights beyond count I tossed, listening into the blackness, hearing only wild creatures who called to the dark. Finally, the chills and fever would claim me, and I would sleep. But I can't count how many hours I lay wakeful, waiting, straining for the sound of hoof beats racing from Antioch."

Eleanor began to sob and Sybelle went to her side. "Finally, I had resigned myself to the painful reality that indeed, no one would come. No valiant rush from the prince in the castle on the Orontes River. The stay in Antioch haunted me like a dream, the aftermath of a magic potion bringing past visions and present fantasies, with their intense feelings. I realized that as Louis' wife, I was dying, that I was feeling nothing."

"And for Raymond?" I dared to ask.

"Raymond?" Eleanor shook her head, "No, my ladies, not for Raymond. I would harbor no incestuous wish. But I knew I desired someone. A man whose vitality I could feel, and who would permit and match the feelings that once raced through me. A man of vigor who would stand on his own and who would respect my ability and understand my need to stand on my own feet as well. Raymond did that. I discovered it was possible. And I've been soundly punished for any thought of my own personal happiness."

Drying her eyes on my towel, Eleanor shrugged her shoulders. "I will never forget the humiliation. And," she added, "still, here with Jovetta, it is a kind of detention, and Louis is as self-deceived as ever if he thinks I don't know it, but I do feel out of harm's way. Since my drugged abduction, I have come to watch every cup and corner. I could have just as easily been poisoned. But here in Bethany I feel safe, protected. It is almost worth the ennui."

A bitter look crossed her face. She raised her chin in the proud way so familiar to me. "Know this, my friends, that I shall never again be held any place against my will."

"I should hope not, dear Eleanor. Nor I. Yet I do not consider this stay anything but a holy privilege—to be the guest of Jovetta in this sacred place. Perhaps this is where we should have been all along, near the home of Martha and the Magdalene." Sybelle uttered the words slowly, her voice almost a prayer.

My heart ached for Eleanor as I took leave of my companions. A novitiate led me to a small upstairs room where I changed into a light woven tunic that had been laid out for me. It was the garb of newly professed novices at the convent. I removed the scrolls from inside my worn carpetbag where I had stored them carefully after the dreadful incident with Mortimer. It was the first time they had been away from my person since I had received them that joyous Easter morning on the mountain. I held them and, kneeling, closed my eyes in prayer. "One day, dear Saint Magdalene, let me know the full import of these contents. Reveal their meaning to me."

A firm hand pressed upon my shoulder. I gasped, clutching the scrolls to my breast. I turned to meet Jovetta's probing eyes.

"You have nothing to fear for them now, Lady Madeleine," the Abbess whispered, "they are where they belong, and so are you."

Evening shadows had dimmed the small room to a pale lavender, purpling the corners. Swallows called their last songs while they swooped over the bell tower, tolling the day's end. Women's voices, raised in an evensong, chorused like a sursurus through the sycamores.

Gently, Jovetta took the packet from my grasp. She kissed me lightly on the forehead. "You have done your work well."

My throat closed, making it difficult to find my voice. "When will I know what they mean? Ever? Why do I feel they mean something to me?" The question hung in the shadowed room. Jovetta's imposing form stood facing me. She placed her hand on my shoulder again.

"Join me in the chapel now, and you will come to learn what they mean to you. Follow me."

When Jovetta led me up rather than down the stone stairs, my curiosity was whetted. It was from the abbey's domed church that I had heard the singing of vespers. Why were we climbing instead of descending? I followed closely behind Jovetta who paused to light a taper from a lamp, adding its sputter to the silence. We proceeded along a narrow windowless corridor. At its end, a small door led into another hall. By now my heart was thumping.

Pressing a stone in the east wall, Jovetta triggered it to rotate enough to allow a body to pass through. She signaled me to go ahead. The Abbess followed at once and twisted a double-spiralled iron ring to close the small passage. I found myself stepping into a miniature chapel. Plainsongs floated to vaulted walls hung with brass and glass lamps. From their light, exquisite mosaics of semi-precious stones glistened in colors blue, green, purple, red and pink. Four scenes showed Jesus surrounded by his apostles, many of whom were women. Martha and Mary were depicted in several; the Magdalene recognizable by her alabaster jar. A setting of what appeared to be the Last Supper pictured Mary Magdalene seated at the right hand of Jesus. In another work, Magdalene stood beside Jesus, her hand raised. She appeared to be preaching to a group of followers as Jesus listened.

Gold-leaf letters spanned the work of the last two scenes with an inscription which read, "They will be on my right and my left, and I am they and they are I."

Spellbound, I shifted my gaze from the walls to the semi-gloom of the chapel proper, where I could see seven women present in the upper room. They stood in a circle chanting an antiphon.

"He fed them with the fat of wheat, alleluia;
And filled them with honey from the rock.
Alleluia, alleluia, alleluia. Rejoice, oh daughters.

Jovetta stood near them, waiting until the chorus ended. Then she stepped forward, her face luminous, her voice lyrical.

"Indeed, rejoice, daughters and sisters, rejoice for this worthy daughter has carried to us from afar what we have awaited."

"Alleluia!" The women chorused.

My knees began trembling. What other mysteries was I to witness? I had not long to wait for Jovetta revealed them almost immediately. She raised the scrolls high toward the light for all to glimpse.

"Here we have the lost scrolls of Magdalene, which we have been trying to acquire for many years since we heard of their rediscovery. There have been other writings," her voice took on a bitter tone, "but we made the mistake of relinquishing them to the Patriarch whose monks copied them with distortions and deletions. We asked for the originals back, but he claimed the original scrolls had been lost when the Saracens sacked Tyre. We now copy the holy writings we acquire here in our own scriptorium. My sister, the Queen Melisende, is sworn to our secret. She is considered a prodigal spendthrift by the fathers. They are ignorant of the fact that she supplies many bezants in the support our work. So be it."

Jovetta motioned to the women on her left. "These four sisters, Lady Madeleine, are the truest copyists in all the Holy Land. The other three, our translators, are fluent in all languages, but most proficient in Syriac, Hebrew, Arabic, Greek, French and Latin. They will transcribe these words and we will dispatch them to many far places, to the convents of France and Ireland, to the Sybils of the Rhine."

She approached placing her hands, one on each shoulder. Looking first to the heavens then to the others watching, she fixed her gaze on me. Nothing, not even the threat of death itself, could have compelled me to move from that moment.

Jovetta spoke in a whisper. "Quem Quaeretis, Madeleine? You ask what is your calling? I tell you, sister, it is to speak in boldness. Take copies of these truths back to the mainland. Inspire and teach other holy women to spread the truths of Magdalene, of her mission as the leader of the women disciples who met often, here, on this site. Their spirits linger here to guide us. In the stillness we can feel them."

Luminescence emanated from her as she recited, "We gather in this upper room to speak the truth of the gospels. Women, the women of Jerusalem, were also among the disciples of our Lord; women, too, can study and have universities as they did before the time of Justinian; women can teach others to know and love the ways of the Christos. We refuse to live with the heresy, 'the Sons of God and the daughters of men.' We are all the children of the Sophia spirit. We are all made in her image."

My head roiled with a spectrum of questions, spinning around like the hues of the rainbow flooding together. The colors swam round and round. Martha, at my side, could not hold me up. I felt her presence and reached for her hand. Dizzy, I began to fall, falling deeper, deeper, into the web of black-draped arms which stretched to save me.

CHAPTER 37

Bethany

*T*he July sun rose early over the Mount of Olives and stayed long in the sky, searing the thick convent walls. In the scriptorium, women worked feverishly; pages translated into French, German or Latin passed from one scribe to the next when paint dried, gold lettering set. Back and forth went I between the small rooms where scholars labored to translate the sacred writings, to a larger study housing high, slanted tables. There, tints and quills helped to complete the work.

After Nones, I often joined the students, listening to their exegesis of the scriptures or their discussions of the Acts of Paul and his coworker, the venerable Thecla, building, as they had, on the mission of Magdalene. Learning flooded my brain, stimulating and exciting me. On occasion, my own thoughts formed into arguments and I wanted to jump in. But an inner voice cautioned me: not yet, you need more study. I vowed to someday join the discussions. Too long have I been silent, frightened to recite anything but the hours or antiphons. But to dispute! A world of delight to hear these arguments!

My mood was one of constant exhilaration. In the cloister, at the sharing of the evening meal, I wondered how I could lead a so simple a life and find that it brought such contentment. I had learned to savor my life with Eleanor at the court, and before that, I had loved the bright days of my marriage. Still, the long pilgrimage had taught me much: that I could suffer personal loss and survive; that my spirit ran deep with longing; that the teachings of Thecla and Kashari had imbued me with a love of the healing arts. And more, I learned that I enjoyed physical work as much as the intellectual vistas I now encountered.

One of my dearest friends, I discovered, was solitude, a companion who asked nothing in return. And in the early hours of dawn, when the image of Geoffrey would come to me, as it always did, I knew that someday we would be reunited. I felt him to be so near.

But it was the vision of Magdalene that called most to me. Not Magdalene, the mythical contemplative penitent, bare of bone and wasted from carnal sin, in the way the patristic fathers had portrayed her, but the true Magdalene, a saint revisited, honored in the scrolls as the apostle to the apostles. She was revealed to me now as the valiant leader who had remained, unwavering, in Jerusalem when the other disciples had scattered. The woman of Bethany had elected to brave the dangers, to meet in the houses of other women, to walk among women and men to speak with boldness. She led, taught and advised others in those early, disconsolate days after our Lord's death.

These remembrances would come to me in the moonlight when stillness blanketed the abbey with the fragrance of sandalwood and sycamore, when none stirred but the owl and the night guard. Then would visions and pictures come into my mind. Tossing about one night, I decided to speak of these things to Abbess Jovetta.

I wanted to tell Eleanor, but I was afraid it would not go well. She fretted daily, and though she tried to maintain some tact, I knew how badly she desired to return home, her true home.

"I must leave Paris and return to my Aquitaine; it is dangerous to leave one's provinces for so long." Eleanor, her face drawn, walked with me toward the dining room on our way to supper.

"I long for little Marie. I'll take her with me." The tic had reappeared, but Eleanor was unmindful of it. "I do not intend to be Louis' Queen forever, no matter what he says. There are ways to acquire a divorce." She lowered her voice, beckoned me nearer to hear.

"One buys one's way to a divorce. I have seen many a lord or count put his wife away on the merest charge. The convents are full of them. Look about you. They are here, just as we are, for safe keeping, never to go elsewhere, never to lay claim to their daughters or have a say in their futures, and restrained from claiming the property they should inherit by the right of their very blood."

Eleanor's color and a curl to her lip revealed how distraught she was. I wanted to comfort her in some way, but she was quick to speak on.

"So I must leave and leave soon or my inheritance may be lost to me. We must be away from here, dear Madeleine. Jesu, how tired I am of waiting for Louis! Why can't we be homeward bound, and soon?"

We entered the cool of the long dining hall, its gold beakers and table settings glowing in the shaft of late afternoon sun. "You are right to be concerned about your claim and to want to return home, but there is work to be done here." I replied.

Eleanor's brows arched. "I have sensed a change in you, cousin, but I had thought it was from the strange and tragic events on your journey, the cruel expulsion of Rancon, Charles' fate, and the beastly attack by the whoreson, Mortimer."

We seated ourselves and began the quiet period which was the rule before the evening meal. After silence had been appropriately observed, Eleanor drummed her fingers nervously on the table during the reading. She was anxious to pursue her discussion.

"You seem so taken with these nuns, I don't understand it. I, myself, have had quite enough of convent life. I've read all that was of interest to me and know all the daily offices by heart. I have tried my hand at painting, a slight talent and even slighter pleasure. Of course, though I could offer good advice, it's not fitting that I be included in the governance of the monastery, so there is little for me here. And in spite of the thick walls, it is always so beastly hot." She poured some water on her napkin and daubed at her brow. "The shadows on the sundial in the garden have begun to shorten daily. Have you noticed?"

"Yes, I have." I worried that the transcribing be done by the time we left. Surely, we could not winter here.

Eleanor fanned herself with her napkin. "You may be assured that roasting in the desert outskirts of the Holy Land will take time off my purgatory. No matter that we have gained a Plenary Indulgence."

I was pleased to see a bit of her sarcastic wit reappear. "Now I suppose I'll have to wheedle more information from Sybelle." She leaned over to get Sybelle's attention.

"What a way for Galeran to spite me, to see that any news comes to Sybelle through Phillip but none from Louis for me."

It took her some time to distract Sybelle, whose rapt eyes were on her sister-kin, Abbess Jovetta. They seemed to have formed a close friendship sitting side by side nightly, Jovetta full of questions about life in Flanders, and Sybelle ever probing the ways of life in Jerusalem or asking about events that transpired under her father's reign as King of Jerusalem before his untimely death. Sybelle had barely known her father, and she was enraptured with the tales Jovetta spun.

Eleanor raised her voice. "Did the courier bring any news of the Franks? Have you any word from Phillip?"

"The letter came not from Phillip or Louis, Eleanor, but from Queen Melisende to her sister." Though Sybelle replied with kindness, Eleanor barely masked a glare.

Sybelle pressed her lips together slightly—her frown had all but disappeared—hesitating before she revealed the letter's contents. "It appears that the armies of Conrad and Louis plan to join with the Palestinian barons within the fortnight to march on Damascus."

"Was that the decision at Acre?" Eleanor's voice rang shrill with disbelief.

"Yes," Jovetta joined in, "a decision that distressed Queen Melisende—so she wrote."

"Por Dieu!" The expletive ripped from Eleanor's lips, ringing out above the muted conversations in the hall. "More money, more time dribbled away in Louis' miserable military enterprises!" Turning to me, she asked desperately, "Will I never again see Aquitaine and the sweet Loire? I am so sick of this heat." Her voice trembled and the yellow undertone of jaundice crept into the hollows under her eyes.

Jovetta and Sybelle regarded her patiently. I put my hand on hers, and Eleanor regained her composure.

"Why was Queen Melisende distressed? I remember she had agreed with me that the best attack would have been, as my Uncle Raymond had wanted, upon Aleppo."

"Because," Jovetta replied, "this decision is one of folly." Her expression grew serious. "You see, Damascus is the only remaining city we have an alliance with. As my sister has explained it to me, the Emir of Damascus fears the power of a new rising Saracen leader, Nur ed-Din, who comes from the east threatening to seize Damascus. Therefore, Unur, the Damascus Emir of whom I speak, has for some time aligned himself with my sister's Frankish forces in the Holy City. Of course Melisende also fears Nur ed-Din and knows that he will not rest until the other cities of Palestine are his to conquer and plunder."

Jovetta shivered at the words but went on. "Melisende has always believed that the alliance with Damascus was an important one and should not be violated." Finished, the Abbess began folding her napkin.

"Then you are in jeopardy too, are you not?" Sybelle questioned Jovetta, resting her hand on her companion's arm.

"Oh yes, my dear sister, but in truth we all are, at any moment. The watchman in that tower scans the plains of Jericho at every hour. But, as long as there is peace along the Jordan, we are safe." She ran her fingers along the folds of her napkin.

"However," she continued thoughtfully, "if Jerusalem should come under siege, we would be most vulnerable, as close as we are and as wealthy." She motioned toward the rich tapestries adorning the refectory walls. "There is much to plunder here as you have noticed. And Saracens love nothing better than to seize our holy objects, our jeweled crucifixes and our golden chalices, all part of the holy mass. They melt them down and order them made into trinkets for their harem favorites. They take our silk vestments for draperies in the harem."

Letting Jovetta's remarks sink in, we finished supper with another reading, all the more devout. Taking Sybelle's arm, the Abbess beckoned me to join them.

"Let us spend our evening recreation strolling on the high parapet stretching from the tower to the church. The glow of a blood-red sunset announces the day's end. Its beauty won't keep."

Eleanor excused herself, saying she would retire to her quarters.

We had walked half the distance to the high wall by the bell tower when I spied a Templar guard galloping toward the convent, called to the sentry to open the gate.

"Alarm, to arms!" he shouted rearing his horse to a halt in the middle of the courtyard. "Saracens to the east, riding hard out of Jericho! It looks, as God so strengthens my eyes, that they come straight this way!"

Jovetta hesitated a moment, her face blanching.

"Are you all right, my sister?" Sybelle moved closer to her.

"Yes, yes. Sound the great bell, guardsman; tell all to get to the tower!"

"Are we in the danger?" I wanted to know.

"We are always in danger, Lady Madeleine."

"The scrolls," I whispered to Jovetta, "the scrolls!"

Jovetta seized my arm. "Say nothing. They are hidden well. We can only pray. Remember where we are, the home of Mary Magdalene. Go, stay with the queen!"

I rebuked myself for my impetuous outbreak. The scrolls had survived all these years without me. I must never forget, I am only the messenger, not the source.

Soldiers fixed their positions, and I raced through the courtyard dodging the wagons and carts that were being lined up to jam against the gates once they were closed.

Parents scurried about looking for children as the great bell tolled out warning to the surrounding countryside. Villagers grabbed what they could, scampering for shelter within the fortified walls. Guards held the gates open while sheep, goats, children and elders streamed in. The village men had swept up their bows, arrows and staves. So armed, they scrambled to the high walls.

Soon every nun, novice, child and small animal had been herded into the tower, Eleanor and I among them. The nuns and village women pressed together against the granite walls in the small confines of the upper landing.

"I want to scream at the closeness and the heat which is suffocating me," Eleanor gasped, her upper lip pale and dotted with sweat.

"Here," I took her cool hand, moist with fear, and guided her to a chink in the tower that she could put her nose to. From an opening just above her, if I stood on tiptoe, I could see the Templar guards and bowmen rushing to their places. They mounted the parapets and slit windows that allowed room for bows and arrows to spray down upon the intruders.

"Madeleine, what's the threat? How much danger?"

"A great deal. I haven't felt so frightened since Mortimer accosted me on the road to Jerusalem when I was concealing the scrolls."

"The what? What are you talking about? What scrolls?"

"I'll tell you more about it later." I was furious with myself. In my moment of panic I had broken the news to Eleanor. Now I must reveal the whole story. But I would have to wait. Swirling dust skittered along the road. Tower guards yelled, warning of the imminent attack.

Jovetta stood in the center of the courtyard assigning guards to their posts. She walked calmly among the people, urging them, "Pray well and stay back from the openings." From somewhere she had obtained a short sword in a jeweled, black scabbard, which she wore at her side.

From the parapet, the Templar commander called out, "It's a band of wild brigands. They don't fly the banner of Nur ed-Din. Hold to it, you brave Knights of the Temple! Lads of the village, steady at your bows. Hold until the order is given!"

One hundred keening Saracens thundered toward the convent walls. They hurled fire torches and spears. They flogged their wiry horses to encircle the settlement. From our wall, a shower of arrows and stones dared them to try. Scores of staves, dipped in oil and set afire, flamed toward the marauders.

Surprised at the vehemence of the convent resistance, the Saracen bandits fell back, then made one more run. After meeting with our vicious resistance, they did not regroup a battle position. The enemy held their menacing spears aloft, and yelling sharp curses from their white-muffled throats, disappeared as quickly as they had come.

When it became obvious that the rambling band of bandits wanted only to terrorize, the Abbess urged the fearful people to leave the stuffy tower. We overflowed into the courtyard where a few small fires licked at the straw by the stables. Under the willow by the cistern where the sugar canes had been set to dry, more embers smoked and were quickly stomped out.

Jovetta stood on a step. "Villagers, stay the night within the walls. You are safer here. And welcome." As families foraged for spots to settle, she beckoned us to join her in her rooms.

"You must know what invectives they yelled. They said that they go to Damascus to join the armies of Nur ed-Din. There, they'll enjoy the slaughter of the Frankish pigs. They promised they will visit us another time." Jovetta drew herself up tall. "Let them. I believe we are safe for now. Our knights and our prayers do guard us well. Let us give thanks to God."

We knelt while she led prayers. Presently, she rose from her knees speaking soberly to Eleanor. "And, Your Majesty, if this is any indication, if, indeed, Saracen tribesmen stop their squabbling with each other, and are called as eagerly as these attackers to Nur ed-Din's side, it does not bode well for Christian forces at Damascus—or for that matter, anywhere in Outremer."

The Abbess stood by Sybelle, as though to study her in the candle-light. "Our sunset didn't wait, but our journey to meet Blessed Mother did. Come, let's be certain that the people have mats and food for tonight."

Wordlessly, Eleanor and I retired to our quarters.

CHAPTER 38

Bethany

N ow must I hasten to finish, for I left my chronicle briefly to join in the Magdalene celebration. It was a day etched in my memory forever.

Chorus after chorus rang through the Church of Martha and Mary this last Sunday in July, the Feast Day of Saint Mary Magdalene. Sister orders from Saint Anne's and Saint Mary Magdalene in Jerusalem and St. Mary's in Gethsemane traveled to join the observance. Our voices swelled, rolling back and forth across the aisles as each side responded one to the other in the chanting of the anthems. The church flared with the light of hundreds of torches. The celebrating holy women were clothed not in their usual black habits, but wore instead, flowing robes of sparkling white.

Joining the congregation as they chanted in unison, "I will go unto the altar of God, unto God who gives joy to my youth," I could not continue; I was too shocked to do so. I strained forward to be sure my eyes had not deceived me. There was no mistake. That was not the same bishop who had come to celebrate mass last month. The figure acting as celebrant was Abbess Jovetta! Jovetta, sleeves pinned up, was vested in the consecrated robes of the bishop!

After the prayers of the faithful, she turned to face the congregation, clasping the scroll packet! She unfolded it, her hands graceful in their precision. The Abbess raised her head and read in her clear voice,

"My Lord," sayeth Magdalene, "my mind intelligent is at every time, for me to come forward at every moment and utter the explanation of the words which have been spoken by the great Sophia, but I fear Peter, because he threatens me and hates our sex."

Sybelle, new to the ritual, remained mute, eyes bulging, while the sister congregation spoke as one voice,

"Fear not, oh spiritual Magdalene, for you excel, you who first saw the beloved face of the risen Christ, you blessed leader of the disciples; fear not, O Spiritual One of Pure Light."

Jovetta returned to the altar and raised her outspread hands.

"Oh, Saint Magdalene, let us, as one with you, speak with boldness that we may bring forth the Holy Word. Oh Happy Magdalene, happy beyond all women."

We sang the response in unison.

"Praise her who is beautiful in her speaking, Oh, praise the happy Magdalene."

Forming a serpentine line, we joined hands to process around the great pillars of the church, our bare feet scuffing softly over miniature black and red tiles stretching the polished length of the center aisle.

"I will rise now and go about the city
In the streets and in the squares;
I will seek Him whom my soul loves."

Swept up by the ritual jubilation, I sang joyfully. Sybelle tried to match my singing but was at a loss for the words. In rapturous motion, we paraded out through the carved door and skipped along the side of the church through the long portico. Our white-clad figures shone light, dark, light, spinning past vaulted arches sliced by the ochre morning light. We crossed through the courtyard on the way to the refectory for a festive breaking of our fast. Rounding the corner behind the others, I stopped short. "What miracle is this?"

There before me in sparkling red resplendence stood the royal litter of the Queen of France. Sybelle, skipping round the corner, collided with me.

"Look, Sybelle, it's our wain, our lovely red wain. It looks like new!"

"By God's holy grace, so it is! When did it arrive?"

"While we were in the church. Look, it's been repainted, and the miniature on the side panel redone. It looks wonderful. Eleanor will be pleased. Where is she? She wasn't in church. She will be beside herself when she hears of this."

"Eleanor told me she didn't care whose feast it was, she was weary of church and wanted only to sleep." Sybelle sounded her usual concern. "In fact, she said she didn't even want to arise from her cot but that she didn't want to be guilty of sloth either, so she said that she would just stay abed and think."

"Think, she better." I peered into the shadows by the far wall under the tower where a group of Templars played a game of Morelles upon a diagram etched into the pavement. Young men laughed and jostled one another while they coached the players. They did not look like villagers.

"Sybelle, who are those strangers with the knights?"

"I can't see for the shadows and looking into the sun." Sybelle strained to peer across the yard.

"Nor can I, and I have looked so often for someone I might recognize that I no longer trust myself. But, by Our Blessed Lady, his shoulders are broader and the figure taller; yet I swear I know that laugh!" I ventured a few hesitant steps from beyond the shadow of the stone pier, shading my eyes for a better view. I began to run, turning to call to Sybelle, "It is! Oh, it is! Germer! Germer!"

We met in the center of the courtyard. Germer hesitated to embrace his mistress, but I threw my arms about him first.

"Oh, Germer, what grace of God has brought you here before my eyes?" I held his hands. "How you have grown, and how happy am I and thankful to see you, here, well and safe."

"And I, Lady, to see you. I had given up though I prayed every day. When we learned that you had gone with the physician Kashari, we feared for your life." His lips formed a sneer. "Of course, to have my queen seized and carried off like plunder by her own king has set all of Antioch against the Franks. Raymond would not send one knight in the battle for Damascus. And a good thing, too." Germer lowered his voice. "The king has no victory to speak of when he returns to France, for the Saracens outwitted Louis and the Palestinian barons, and our casualties were high. Then the Palestinian barons refused to fight at all for they suspected treason on the part of Count Phillip."

His voice became a whisper for he saw Sybelle coming toward us. Continuing quickly, he added, "He is said to have bribed the Prince of Galilee not to fight so that he, as Count of Flanders and kin to Queen Melisende, might have more for his own spoils. The plan failed utterly. I can say no more."

"Germer, thank Holy Mother who brought you to us!" Sybelle looked about. "Who came else? Thecla and the Lady Florine? How fares the babe?" Questions spilled from her as fast as Germer could answer them.

"Aye, the babe fares well. Count Hugh was outraged at Louis' deceit in leaving Antioch and deserting some of his forces. He waited till the Lady Fluorine was able to travel, and they set out from Antioch as soon as possible. So anxious were they to leave that they booked passage on a merchant ship bound for Genoa."

"And Thecla with them?"

"Aye, and cursing more lively than I've ever heard. She would have Louis' soul fried and fed to the newts. Fluorine told her she must be still, or they would all win God's disfavor."

"What a disappointment for them not to see the Holy City. Perhaps they will another time," I said.

"But whose fine horses are those tethered outside the stables? Does one belong to Count Phillip?" Sybelle frowned.

"Oh, forgive me, my Ladies, I've left out some news. The King has sent the Count of Drew and Queen Eleanor's new chancellor. They, and I," he bowed with mock self-importance, "will escort the royal ladies to Jerusalem where his Majesty awaits. Then we journey to Acre where it is said passage on a fine ship has been arranged for our return."

"I will inform the Abbess Jovetta that we will leave soon," Sybelle volunteered. "When must we go, Germer?"

"Countess, I believe on the morrow."

"In such haste?" Sybelle asked sharply, her forehead puckering. "This has happened so—so suddenly after all our languid days of ordered existence. Laudes and Nones and Matins, tempered meals and companionable walks into the village or a stroll through the orchards sweet with ripe fruit." She spoke softly, a strange expression on her face. "I'll go now to find Abbess Jovetta.

"Oh, Germer, God bless you! I am so grateful for this news. Let me go and tell her Majesty. She will greet these tidings with thanksgiving and happiness. She has been in very low spirits of late and longs for her palace at Bordeaux."

My last hours at the Convent of Martha and Mary have been filled with intensive study. Jovetta has given me the names of convents in France dedicated to Saint Magdalene. "They'll watch for you. In places reaching across many borders, the women wait, looking for the scrolls so that they might instruct other faithful. They believe that Mary Magdalene of Bethany was not only the apostle of the Franks but the apostle to the apostles. She preached from here, her home, returning to Bethany frequently to fan the flames of the new faith."

Jovetta revealed truths that astonished me. Women, she claimed, performed the rituals that now only men ruled. Women preached, and performed the sacraments. Such revelations found me speechless.

"We know that this is true. You will see." Jovetta guided me to a large portfolio of pictures. "These are very ancient. They come from Egypt, but look. Those are women. Look how they are pictured with the chalices in their hands. Observe the communion bread on the tables before them. So we must instruct others to do." Jovetta carefully replaced the paintings in the leather cover.

"Let the bishops think that we are without learning or theology. Let them assume that we do without the sacraments between their official visits." Her voice took on a determined tone. "We will have them and we will perform these rites sacredly, ourselves, as it should be, as it once was, from the ministry of the Magdalene."

This was heresy, surely it was. I gathered the courage to whisper, "But Abbess Jovetta, were I to preach these things, would I not be spreading heresy?" The question formed itself and seemed to hang in the dry, hot air.

"Are you willing to speak in boldness now? To deliver the scrolls?"

This was the test; to move about or die. Perhaps it was to move about and die. No matter. Without hesitation, I whispered, "Yes! Oh, yes."

The Princess Abbess went to the altar and removed something wrapped in gold cloth.

"Please take this in your hands." Touching the smooth contours of the object, I knew at once what it was. Its shape and fragrance told me. Grasping it to my breast, I was haunted by its perfume. The alabaster jar pressed close to my heart!

Jovetta gently removed it from my grasp placing the crisp, new parchment rolls in its stead. My hands trembled as I took them, but I neither wavered nor grew faint. I whispered, "So might it be."

Leaving the chapel I had come to know so well, I walked slowly down the stairs, past the shadowed portico to the queen's quarters.

Surrounded by a few scrappy hampers, (all that remained of our seventeen wains), Eleanor reached for her ivory comb and swept a few errant strands from her forehead. "While others may have thought me at prayer, I will admit to you, dear cousin, that I habitually disregarded the scenes of holy saints in my psalter to ruminate on how it was that an undertaking that I had imagined to be such high adventure had become a shambles as though cursed in some way by God, who was, as Bernard had pointed out so often, the very power who had willed the entire enterprise."

She made a helpless little gesture, shrugging her shoulders. I wanted to comfort her, for she seemed so hurt by it all. When she faced me, in spite of my many herbal treatments, a trace of the yellowish pallor still lingered in her cheeks.

Eleanor held up the soapstone icon that Empress Irene had given us. "How long ago that seems, eh, cousin. How ready I am to return home." She tossed the small figure into the open basket.

Slowly, she rose from her cot, and as we had faced Abbot Bernard that winter long ago, we each held the other and in step together went down the narrow stairs. The glowing litter awaited in the courtyard. A tearful Sybelle, arm in arm with Jovetta, stood by its side.

"There is sadness in this farewell. May you travel with God." Jovetta's voice broke. She embraced Sybelle fondly. She appeared to be sobbing. She stood with her back to us. Moments later, when she faced us, she was composed, standing spear-straight.

Quickly, Germer, handsome in the purple livery of the queen, assisted us to board. Flanked by lines of black-robed sisters waving white handkerchiefs, we moved through the great iron gate and slowly took our dusty leave of Bethany.

Epilogue

Feast of the Assumption
(On Shipboard)

*N*ow may I put down these last observations. If I had hoped that things were any better between Eleanor and Louis, that was soon dispelled when we learned that we would be sailing home on separate vessels. In a way, I was as relieved as Eleanor. The memory of the wretched event with Mortimer would only be exacerbated by Galeran's presence. I hoped to put all that rancor and hatred behind me. Sailing on separate ships from Acre was a good start.

"Think of it, Madeleine, I will not have to suffer their presence. I am genuinely grateful. Thank heavens and the patroness of sailors, Mary Magdalene. We'll sail with a small protective force of Templars and what remains of my men."

At last the day arrived, a day of billowing clouds and stiff southerly winds whipping at my tunic as I stood at the prow of a two-masted Genoese merchant ship. In the crowded quarters below, galley slaves stayed in their places ready for orders to pull toward the open sea. The king, together with his ever-present Galeran, his remaining contingent of nobles, his prelates and priests, was on board a companion vessel anchored closeby.

The ripple of Eleanor's laugh sounded above the din of the bustling ship. "What entertains you so?" I was curious.

"I keep mapping and remapping the strategy for my divorce. Upon my return to Poitiers, I will reclaim my vast lands as the Duchess of Aquitaine. I've been listing the likely prelates who will advocate for my divorce. It might be the doty Bernard himself. May God preserve his old bones till I am at his door!"

Eleanor laughed again. "Think of our old adversary being my advocate in my claim of consanguinity!" The queen doubled over at the prospect.

It was good to see Eleanor in such high spirits. While the news of the voyage home exhilarated her, I knew that to be rid of her marriage was her most pressing desire. Skimming gulls and frisking dolphins reflected that sense of freedom. When I leaned against the rail to look more closely at the creatures, my copy of the scrolls pressed against my heart reminding me of my new charge, the treasure I carried from the Holy Land.

Jovetta had given me the name of an abbess in Gascony who would direct my mission from there. I knew nothing more. My new work might not take me to the courts of France. If Geoffrey could find me in the desert, mayhap I would find him in France. Once we reached home, and Eleanor was back in her domains, I would speak to her about founding a convent for women who would not be cloistered nor beg, but would be in the world, teaching others the truth, speaking in boldness.

On the docks, the sound of drums and trumpets faded in the distance as the members of Queen Melisende's court, young Baldwin, the Templars and the high echelon of the Hospitallers, began their journey back through the vineyards and lush orchards, past the sea of Galilee, past Nazareth, back to Jerusalem. I joined Sybelle, watching them for as long as they were in sight, not taking my eyes from the shoreline with its domes and towers. One tower reminded me of the tower in Bethany. The silhouette of Mt. Carmel rose in the distance.

Sybelle asked, "What do you think Jovetta…and the others…what might they be doing now at Bethany? Are they at prayers do you think, or perhaps at reading? It was such an ordered life, wasn't it Madeleine, with walks in the orchard and…." She started to weep and, as though in a trance, began waving shoreward with her long white kerchief.

From King Louis' vessel rocking nearby on the swells, the captain's order rang out, "Unfurl the sails for God's Sake!" Our crew sprang to action. The topmast mate shouted, "And may Saint Magdalene bless our voyage. Haul up the anchor!"

The painted sail unfurled, its magenta stripes swelling with gusts of wind. Bright pennants of Aquitaine, Flanders and Burgundy snapped above as white foam spewed from the rippling oars.

Amid the calls of gulls, we left the domes of the Holy Land glittering behind us. Climbing to the forward rail, we gazed far beyond the jade-colored sea, looking homeward. Our pilgrimage to the Holy City lay behind us.

So ends my chronicle.

0-595-21648-X